The Fields of Home

By RALPH MOODY

Illustrated by Edward Shenton

University of Nebraska Press • Lincoln and London

First Bison Book printing: 1993

Library of Congress Cataloging-in-Publication Data
Moody, Ralph, 1898–
The fields of home / by Ralph Moody; illustrated by Edward Shenton.
p.   cm.
Originally published: New York: Norton, 1953.
ISBN 0-8032-8194-3 (pbk.)
I. Title.
PS3563.05535F53   1993
813'.54—dc20
92-37788   CIP

Reprinted by arrangement with Edna Moody Morales and Jean S. Moody

1

From Colorado to Maine

WHEN we moved from Colorado to Massachusetts, at the beginning of 1912, the other children slid into city life as a flock of ducklings into a new pool. I tried as hard as I could to be a city boy, but I didn't have very good luck. Just little things that would have been all right in Colorado were always getting me into trouble. Out there, after Father died, the sheriff was about the best friend I had. He helped me get jobs with the cattle drovers that went through town, and he always told them I was as dependable as any man. In Medford, the police chief seemed to think just the opposite. Before I'd finished the eighth grade, our house was the first place he came to when anything went wrong in town.

My worst trouble came on graduation day. The night before, one of the boys in my class, who was crazy about cowboys, was waiting when I finished my after-school job in the grocery store. He'd sent away to a mail-order house for a forty-five caliber revolver and a hundred cartridges. He had them with him, and wanted me to go up to the woods and teach him how to shoot. That would have been too dangerous, so I told him he'd have to wait till morning, then we'd go down to the river, and shoot into the water where no one could be hurt.

11

I knew quite a little about revolvers, and had learned to handle one when I was ten. What I didn't know was that there was a law against shooting one in Medford, and that bullets skip on water the way stones do. We had skipped nearly fifty of them over into Somerville when the policemen came and arrested us. They kept us at the police station all morning, and the chief said that the only safe place for me was the reform school. Before he let me go, Mother had to promise to send me right away to her father's farm in Maine.

I took the night boat from Boston to Bath, and rode the twenty miles over to Lisbon Falls on the Lewiston trolley car. Mother had told me that the easiest way to find Grandfather's farm would be to go up the main street, follow straight ahead for three miles, then turn up the hill road when I came to a big, three-story, brick house.

The few people I passed on the sidewalk seemed to look me over from head to foot, but nobody spoke. I was sure they all knew I'd been sent down there so I wouldn't have to go to the reform school. I bit my teeth together hard, kept looking at the ground, and walked as fast as I could till I was out of the village. Then I stopped, set my suitcase down, and tried to make up my mind if it wouldn't be better for me just to run away and go back to Colorado. I'd grown a lot since we'd moved east, would be fifteen in the fall, and knew I could earn a man's wages on a ranch. If I went back west, I'd be able to send money to Mother every month, people wouldn't be looking at me as if I were a criminal, and everybody would be a lot better off.

I'd just about made up my mind to go when I heard a rumbling and pounding on the road behind me. A big, skinny, gray horse, hitched to a blue dumpcart, was clumping toward me. At every lumbering step, the box of the dumpcart tipped up a little and bumped down against the shafts. Above the horse's rump, I could see a battered old straw hat that jounced in time to the bumping of the cart. I didn't want to be standing there when they went by, so I picked up my suitcase and walked on.

The thumping trot slowed to a walk as the horse came abreast of me, and the man hollered, "Whoa, Etta!" in a sort of gurgly roar. I didn't want to see or talk to anybody right then but, of course, I had to stop and look up at the man. He was big and round-shouldered. Sitting there on a board across the low sides of the dumpcart, his knees were nearly up to his chin. His overalls were dirty and had a hole in one knee that gray underdrawers showed through. He had squinty blue eyes, a reddish-brown, walrus mustache, and hadn't shaved for at least a week. As I looked 'round, he spit a mouthful of tobacco juice that just missed my suitcase and plopped into the road dust. "Hot, hain't it?" he said. "Goin' to the fourcorners?"

It wasn't very hot for June, and I didn't know where the fourcorners might be, so I said, "No, sir."

"Where be you going?" And he spit again.

From the way he blurted the question, I thought he might be the sheriff, and I didn't want to get into any more trouble, so I said, "To Mr. Gould's farm."

"Tom Gould's?"

"Yes, sir."

"Get in! I'll fetch you a piece."

The horse didn't move till the man slapped her with the reins and fished on them a few times. For several minutes, he didn't say a word; just sat there with the reins loose, looking at Etta's rump, his hands resting across his knees. Then, without looking toward me, he asked, "Who be you?"

"Ralph Moody," was all I said.

In two or three minutes more, he asked, "Where from?"

"Boston."

That seemed to interest him. He only waited for Etta to take three or four steps before he said, "Big place, hain't it?"

"Yes, sir," I told him.

The farther we went, the less I liked to ride with the man. By the time he'd asked me about Boston, I was sure he wasn't the sheriff, but I couldn't just climb down and start walking again, so I sat and planned how I'd go to Colorado. I only had eighty cents, but that didn't worry me any. It was the beginning of summer, haying time, and I knew I could get plenty of work on farms. There was no hurry. It wouldn't make any difference if it took me till fall. I wouldn't really be running away; I'd just be going back where everybody liked me, and where the sheriff was my friend. Mother would know where I was all the time, because I'd work as I went, and would send her money as I earned it. I was just wondering how I'd get across the wide rivers, like the Mississippi, when the man beside me asked, "What you going to Tom's for? Kin of his'n?"

I didn't want to answer any more questions than I had to, so I just said, "To work," and went on thinking about getting across the Mississippi.

For the first time since I'd climbed onto the cart, the man turned his head and looked at me. "What's Tom paying you?" he asked.

"I don't know," was all I said.

"Don't know! Heavens to Betsy! D'you know Tom Gould?"

"No, sir," I told him. I really didn't know Grandfather. Mother said I'd seen him when I was three, but all I knew about him was from stories I'd heard her tell. Besides, it didn't seem to me that it would be a good idea to say I was his grandson when I intended to go right on west without seeing him.

The man swung his head away and spit hard, as though he'd just tasted something bitter. Then he turned back to me, and said, "Well, you will afore the day's out. Hain't a meaner man a-living. Skin a louse for hide and tallow!"

I was glad I'd made up my mind to go back to Colorado. Since I'd probably never see Grandfather anyway, it wouldn't make any difference to me how mean he was, and I wanted to hear what else the man might say about him, so I just said, "Yes?"

"Dang tootin'! So consarn cantankerous there can't nobody get on with him 'cepting that woman of his'n!" Then he stopped talking, and just sat looking at Etta's rump for a minute or two.

"I didn't know there was a woman," I said.

"Mill Durkin. Housekeeper. Cussed contrary as old Tom his-self. Fight like two stray cats in a rain barrel. Has to stay there. Won't nobody else put up with her. Gitap, Etta!"

Ahead of us, a three-story brick house came into sight beyond a pine woodlot, and I knew that would be where Grandfather's road turned off. What I was going to do seemed easy enough from there. I'd say good-bye to this man at the corner, then walk up the side road till he was out of sight, turn into the woods, and go back to the trolley line. But first, I wanted to find out what else he might say about Grandfather, so I asked, "How long has Mrs. Durkin been there?"

"Hain't Miz Durkin! Mill's a spinster, 'bout thirty. Been there five, six, seven years, I cal'late. Only help Tom ever had that stayed over two, three days. You won't, neither. Can't do noth-ing to suit him. Work the hide off'n you. Feed you on sowbelly and boiled potatoes. Run his own boys off afore they was growed."

I thought I'd heard about as much as I wanted to, so I kept still, and went back to planning about going west. We were nearly to the fourcorners when I noticed that the man was look-ing me over from head to foot. When I looked up at his face, he said, "Might look me up when you get fed up at Tom's. Name's Swale. T'other side the brook. Might use a likely looking boy." He jerked his head to the right, the opposite direction from Grandfather's, and added, "Don't need mention it to Tom."

I didn't want to hear him talk about Grandfather any more. I knew Mother loved her father and, from stories she'd told us about her girlhood on the old farm, I was sure he couldn't be half as bad as Mr. Swale said he was. I knew his younger brother, Uncle Levi, too. He was an old bachelor who lived in Boston and he had been out to see us half a dozen times since we'd moved east. Every time he came he'd been loaded down with fruit, nuts, and candy. And I didn't know a man I liked any better. I reached back for my suitcase, and said, "I'm going to walk."

Mr. Swale put one dirty hand over on my leg, and said, "Set right still! Set right still! 'Tain't no load at all on Etta. These hills is powerful steep for lugging a heavy valise. Hot this morning, hain't it?"

That time I just said, "Yes," without any "sir" on it, and moved my leg away a little. Then I tried to think some more about how I'd go to Colorado, but I couldn't seem to get Grandfather out of my head. The next thing I knew, I was remembering things Mother had told us about him; that he was born when his father was seventy-three, had gone to the Civil War before he was twenty-one; had contracted malaria in a Confederate prison and had never got over it. Before I thought, I'd said, "Mr. Gould isn't very well, is he?"

"That's depending," Mr. Swale snickered. "Tom Gould can histe a bull out of a well if he's hard put or showing off, but he's too puny to fetch a pail of water if there's somebody else about that he can shrink it off onto." Then he bellowed, "Mornin', Miz Littlehale."

I'd been so busy thinking that I hadn't paid much attention to the road or the scenery. I did know that we'd passed a couple of houses since we'd turned off from the main road but, if anyone had asked me, I couldn't have told them what either of them looked like. It wasn't until Mr. Swale hollered that I noticed a woman putting a letter into the mailbox at the house fifty yards ahead of us. Except that she was short and sort of fat, I couldn't tell what she looked like, because she had on a sunbonnet that came way out beyond her face. She didn't look up until she'd taken a newspaper out of the box and held it up in front of the bonnet for a minute. Then she turned, and called, "Morning, 'Bijah. What brings you up this way?" Her face and voice seemed to go exactly with her body. They were both round, and sort of mellow, but hearty. I liked her from the moment she spoke.

We were getting pretty close, but Mr. Swale's voice was still loud enough to have been heard for half a mile. "The old woman's been a-hankering for a setting of them Rhode Island

Red eggs of your'n," he shouted. "Fetched this hired hand up to Tom Gould, and cal'lated I'd just stop and dicker with you for a setting of them eggs. This late of the season I don't allow you're holding 'em too dear. Whoa, Etta!"

Instead of answering Mr. Swale about the price of eggs, Mrs. Littlehale looked at me, and said, "Why, he's just a young boy." If it hadn't been for the sound of her voice, I wouldn't have liked it, but she didn't even give me time to think about that. She looked right into my eyes and said, "I do hope you'll stay with Mr. Gould till he gets his hay in. Poor old man; him and Millie up there trying to do it all alone." Then she turned to Mr. Swale, and said, "Three men he's had up there in the last week, and not one of 'em worth shucks. Ain't one of 'em stayed more'n a single day."

Mr. Swale's elbow poked me in the ribs as I reached back for my suitcase. He half snickered, and said, "So I was just a-telling the boy here. Dang shame, hain't it?"

I jumped from the dumpcart, swung my suitcase down, and started to walk up the road. For some reason, a lump had come up in my throat and I didn't want to talk to anyone. I'd only gone a dozen steps when Mrs. Littlehale called, "Son," so I had to stop. She walked up beside me, and her voice barely came out of her sunbonnet as she said, "Don't let Mr. Gould rile you. He's good hearted, and his bark's a sight worse than his bite. I do hope you'll stay with him through haying."

I just tipped my cap, and said, "I will." Then I went on up the road.

After a dozen more steps, Mr. Swale shouted, "Mind what I was a-saying to you. Name's Swale; t'other side the fourcorners," but I didn't look back.

2

Grandfather's House

I KNEW the buildings on the old place the moment I saw them. Just as Mother had told us, they were set on the brow of the last rise of ground before the hill swept up to form Lisbon Ridge. She'd always said the valley lay like a great salad bowl, and that Lisbon Ridge was the west rim of the bowl. From where I walked, I could understand why she said it just that way. Pine, birch, and maple woods covered the crest of the ridge, and the buildings seemed to be nestled in below them. The square, weather-blackened, two-story house, with its low-pitched roof rising from four sides to meet the great brick chimney, stood near the roadway. Two elms, so tall their branches reached out above the roof, stood before it. And running back, almost to join with the great white barn, there was a line of smaller buildings. I knew every one of them from the stories I'd heard Mother tell. First would be the summer kitchen, then the bee shop and the woodshed. The taller one would be the carriage house and forge, with the privy and henhouses beyond. Before I realized it, I was climbing the hill so fast I was panting.

I was halfway up when I heard a dog bark. The sound came

from the direction of the barn, but it was muffled. Then there was the shrill squeal of a pig, and a man yelled in a high-pitched voice. In a moment, a woman's voice came sharp and clear, "Get out, you fool!" And the pig shrieked again, as if it were being tortured. I dropped my suitcase, and ran through a field of standing hay toward the sounds.

The barn was built on a shoulder of the hill, so that the main floor was on a level with the dooryard. On the downhill side, the foundation of huge boulders rose fifteen feet above the sloping meadow, and ran forward toward the house in a wedge-shaped wall. In the barn foundation, there were two doorways large enough for a wagon to pass through, and the noise sounded as though it was coming from inside of them. The squealing and shouting grew, and I ran up through the hayfield as fast as I could make my legs go. When I reached the big doors, I was all out of breath, and the sun was so bright I couldn't see into the darkness under the barn. While I was peering in, a man yelled, "Head him off! Head him off, boy!" And then I went heels over head into a puddle of barn slops.

In the split second before I fell, I saw a big black hog, with a shepherd dog dragging at his ear, come shooting out of the darkness. I bumped my head when the hog knocked me over and was dizzy when I tried to get onto my feet. For a few seconds, I just balanced myself there on my hands and knees while things seemed to go floating around me. The hog, shrieking like a fire whistle, went racing away, and the doorways of the barn seemed to be teetering. Framed in one of them was a woman in a pink dress, holding a broom like a baseball bat, and yelling. In the other was a little man, with a big reddish beard, that I knew must be Grandfather. He was waving a long-handled shovel and shouting, "Tarnal idjit! Why didn't you head him off? Who be you? Who sent you here?"

With my good suit ruined and his shouting at me, I couldn't help being peeved. I climbed to my feet and I snapped right back, "Ralph Moody! My mother sent me!"

We were standing facing each other through the doorway.

Grandfather weighed about a hundred pounds, and the top of his head came about level with my chin. When I spoke, both arms dropped to his sides, he looked up into my face—almost the way a dog looks up at you when he wants to be patted—and said, "Why . . . why . . . why, you're Mary's boy. You're Ralphie."

Grandfather and I just stood there for a full minute. Then he took both my arms in his hands, and said, "Stand around here, Ralphie! Stand around so's your old grampa can get a look at you. By fire, you're going to make a tall one, just like your father." He gave his head a couple of quick nods and looked up at my face again. "Favor him, too," he said. Then he squeezed the muscles in my arms, and nodded once more. "Got the same kind of hard, stringy build. Your father was a powerful stout man for a slim build. Millie, come here, see my daughter Mary's boy!"

Millie had already come. She looked at my dripping suit, and said, "Well, he ain't a sight for sore eyes! Better fetch him up to the house while I get some water het. Them clothes'll stink like a polecat if I don't get 'em washed out pretty devilish quick." Then she snapped at me, "Didn't you fetch no clean clothes?"

She only waited long enough for me to tell her there were clean clothes in my suitcase, and that I'd left it beside the road. "Well, fetch it!" she said, and started climbing up over the boulder wall to the dooryard. She was nearly as tall as I, and was neither fat nor thin. I thought she must be about thirty, just as Mr. Swale had said. From the easy way she went up the side of the high wall, I could see that she was as strong as a man, and though she spoke and acted rough, her face didn't look that way. It wasn't wrinkled, and was white instead of tanned. Her eyes were blue, and her hair was dark brown. It was drawn tight back from a white parting place in the middle, braided, and wound into a big knot at the back of her head. From the top of the wall, she looked back, and said, "Well, go fetch it! Don't stand there gawking like a ninny!" Then she turned and walked away.

Grandfather squeezed my arm again, and almost shouted, "Gorry sakes alive, Ralphie, your old grampa's powerful glad to see you, boy! How's Mary? How's all the rest the children? Six of you, ain't there? Seen Levi of late?"

"Yes, sir," I said. "Everybody's fine, and Mother said she'd write you a letter." Then I started back along the track I'd made through the hayfield. I'd only taken a couple of steps when Grandfather caught my sleeve, and said, "No, Ralphie, we'll go roundabouts, so's we don't tromp down the hay and make it hard mowing. Want to show you my new swarm of bees. Blackbelts. Fetched on from up to Canada. Powerful good honey-makers and a thundering great colony of 'em. Cal'late they'll be swarming afore long."

As he talked, he led me along the foot of the boulder wall toward a dozen or so white beehives. They were set, helter-skelter, under two great apple trees, just a few yards down the hill from the side of the house. All I knew about bees was that they had stingers and made honey, and that I'd a lot rather go without the honey than to have the stings. Grandfather didn't seem to feel that way. He kept tight hold of my arm, ducked low, and led me in under the nearest tree. Bees were as thick in the air as flies around a molasses barrel. Two of them lit on his whiskers, and I was sure I could feel one crawling on the back of my neck. I made a quick move to brush it off, but Grandfather caught my arm, and said, "Take care! Take care! You got to be gentle with bees. Might sting you."

Grandfather reached out and took the cover off the newest looking hive. Inside, it was alive with crawling bees. Down in the cracks between the dividers, I could see them squirming over each other, and it made the nerves under my skin squirm the same way. I wanted to get out of there as fast as I could, but Grandfather whispered, "Gorry sakes alive, Ralphie, mark how they're a-fetching in the honey. By thunder, won't some of that on hot biscuits hit the right spot come next winter? Your old grampa'll learn you all about bees. Curious critters, bees. Let's cover 'em over and leave 'em to their work." Then he eased the top onto the hive carefully, and I was awfully glad when we ducked out from under the tree.

The thing I wanted most was to get my suitcase and a bath, but Grandfather wouldn't hurry. He kept hold of my arm as though I were a horse and it a halter rope, and he'd stop me every time he wanted to say something. We'd just ducked out from under the apple tree, when he stopped and said, "Don't cal'late you recollect the old place very good, Ralphie. You was just a sniveling, wet-nosed young one whenst Mary last fetched you down. Long wood-shaving curls. Same color as new pine. Never liked curls on a boy. Gorry sakes, how time does fly! Must have been the summer of '98; year afore I bought the Bowdoin woodlot."

"It couldn't have been," I told him. "I wasn't born until December of that year."

"'Twas t . . . ," Grandfather flared up for just a second. Then he seemed to catch himself, and said, "Well, what's the odds? 'Twas afore Mary took Charlie and you children gallivanting off out west. Now what was it I was about to show you?"

Grandfather pushed his battered old hat back and scratched the little bald spot on his head. "Now that's curious, ain't it? 'Twas right on the tip of my tongue. Great thunderation! Don't cal'late your grampa's getting old enough to be forgetful, do you? 'Course not! 'Course not! I ain't but seventy-two. Gorry sakes! Father was older'n I be afore ever I was born. House is thirty-odd years older'n I be. There! There, Ralphie! That done it! Mark that hump of ground yonder . . . 'twixt the Pearmain and the Black Oxford apple trees? There's where Father build his first house . . . year of 1794 . . . the one where the owls come down the chimney and stole the cat. Gorry sakes alive! The old kettle's 'round here somewhere; like as not it's up in the open chamber. Used to put it over the cat, come night, so's the owls couldn't steal her away."

"Some day I'd like to see it," I said, "but don't you think I'd better get my suitcase now?"

"Gorry sakes, yes!" Grandfather said, and started leading me toward the roadway. "Better get it afore the woodchucks does. Tarnal pesky critters! Old Bess ain't keeping 'em down of late the way she used to. Eyes is getting bad. Tarnal shame the way a man and a dog starts a-falling to pieces afore their time. Old Bess ain't more'n fourteen, be you, girl?"

I'd been looking out for bees so hard that I hadn't noticed Bess was with us. As though she understood every word Grandfather said, she put her muzzle against his knee, and closed her eyes as he stroked her head. Before she closed them, I noticed they were both milky blue, and that the sides of her face were grizzled like an old man's beard. "Poor Old Bess. Poor Old Bess," Grandfather half whispered as he stroked her, "I and her kept house together nigh onto ten years afore Millie come. By fire, I must have miscal'lated somewheres. Let me see . . . Let me see . . . Wa'n't Bess here whenst Mary fetched you children down home afore she went off out west?"

"I don't know," I said, "She didn't bring me that time, but don't you think I'd better get my . . ."

That's as far as I got. Grandfather didn't seem to have heard me. He slapped his leg so hard that Bess jumped, and he almost shouted, "Gorry sakes alive! Now I recollect! Frankie fetched her home afore he went off to Portland to learn a trade. Come out of a litter old Sid Purrinton's bitch had. Must have been the early spring of '97. Great thunderation! Don't seem like 'twas more'n a fortnight agone. Yessiree, I recollect Bess being along whenst I dickered with Sid for the Bowdoin woodlot. Got in a ruction with a tarnal great skunk. Stunk to high heaven, and I had to wash her belly off with vinegar afore her puppies would nurse."

Grandfather kept hold of my arm until we were nearly halfway to my suitcase. Then he stopped suddenly and pointed up across the fields, toward the woods that covered the hilltop half a mile to the south. "Mark that all-fired great white oak yonder?" he asked me. I didn't know much about trees and, at that distance, I couldn't tell one from another.

The hill sloped away eastward toward the valley. At the highest point, there was a low growth of dark green that looked to me like pine. A little farther down, the color was lighter, and the treetops had rounded domes, so I thought they'd be hardwood. Near the bottom of the slope, the color was so dark it looked almost black. The growth was heavy enough that it seemed to be a solid bank with, here and there, a steeple-shaped top rising above the bank. Near the center, two great trees rose high above the others. They stood, shoulder to shoulder against the skyline, like twin brothers in waist-high clover. "You mean one of those big ones in the dark patch?" I asked him.

"Oak! Oak, I told you! Them's virgin pine! What ails you? Thought Levi said you was a farmer! Don't you know oak from pine? Yonder! Yonder! In a line 'twixt Niah's field and the orchard wall."

I could see a straggly old orchard on the near side of the hill, and a stonewall around it, but I had no idea which might be Niah's field, and Grandfather's big-jointed finger shook enough that he could have been pointing at a thousand trees. "Yonder! Yonder!" he said again. " 'Twixt them seedling pines and beech woods."

I didn't like his shouting at me, or his acting as if I was a complete idiot. And I didn't care which tree he was talking about, just so long as he'd hurry up and get it over with. I didn't shout back at him, but my voice was a little louder than it should have been when I said, "I can see it."

Grandfather's voice dropped down until it was as gentle as it had been when he was petting Old Bess. "Thundering great tree, ain't it? You wouldn't hardly believe it, Ralphie, but Father's sheep et off the top of it whenst he first took up the land. Had to fence it roundabouts with poles to save it. Et it back so far it growed three trunks from a single stump. You mark that Norway pine to westward; the one on a line 'twixt the two Gravenstein trees atop the orchard?"

I'd never even heard of a Norway pine, but I nodded my head, and my voice was quiet when I said, "Yes, sir."

"That's where the parent tree stood, Ralphie; tallest white oak in all the country roundabouts; the one Father clim whenst he blazed his way inland from the Androscoggin and the Almighty marked him this piece of ground. Lightning blasted it whilst I was off to war. Strong as iron. Only one little log of it left; I'm a-saving that for wagon tongues. Did ever I tell you, Ralphie, 'bout . . ."

Millie's voice broke in as though she were shouting through a megaphone, "Victuals is getting cold!"

"Victuals! Victuals! Victuals!" Grandfather snapped. "Tarnal, pesky woman! Can't think of nothing but victuals and scrubbing! Worse'n Levi!" Then his voice dropped right down, and he said, "Wish Levi'd come home. Ain't been down since the snow went off. Better fetch your valise, Ralphie. Millie won't be fit to live with if her victuals gets cold." Then he and Bess started slowly back toward the house.

When I brought my suitcase into the dooryard, Millie was waiting on the back doorstone. Her voice was sharp when she frowned at me and said, "There's soap and a tub of water in the woodshed. Better use 'em good and plenty. I ain't going to have no dirty, stinking boys around here." Then she turned and went into the house.

I scrubbed until I was redder than fire, dried myself, pulled on my clean clothes, emptied the tub, and hurried to the kitchen door. From what I'd already heard, I expected to find Grandfather and Millie at each other's throats, but they were both at the table and seemed as happy as a couple of birds in the spring.

"Come right in, Ralphie! Come right in!" Grandfather called. "Millie baked us a nice good sugar cake for dinner. Never see ary woman could bake a better sugar cake than Millie."

Anyone could have seen that Millie liked to have him say it, but she stuck her nose up a little, and said, " 'Taint up to my usual. Devilish Getchell birch I been getting for firewood ain't fit for fence rails. Got to stand and blow on it to get spark enough to melt grease."

The dinner was boiled potatoes and fried salt pork, just as Mr. Swale had said it would be, but there was plenty of it and it was good. Grandfather talked more than he ate, and he kept his knife waving as he talked—sort of like a band leader. Two or three times, he dropped the piece of pork he had balanced on it, and then put the empty knife into his mouth. "Gorry sakes alive, Millie," he said, "with Ralphie here to help us, I cal'late we'll have the hay a-flying like goose feathers. Wouldn't be a mite surprised if we had it all fetched home to the mows afore company reunion time. Ain't been to a reunion since . . . Gorry sakes . . . Ain't been since the first year you come; the summer Levi was to home. Wisht Levi'd come down this summer."

He sat looking at his plate for a minute, then his head jerked up, and he said, "Eat your victuals! Eat your victuals, Ralphie! Cal'late to get a start on the orchard hay this afternoon. I'll go provender the hosses."

3

The Yella Colt

I HADN'T half finished eating my dinner when Grandfather
left the table. From what he'd said about his going to feed the
horses, it didn't seem to me I'd have to hurry. I knew it would
take them half an hour to eat, and I was still as empty as a last
year's gourd. I'd just reached for another potato when Millie
said, "Better get them victuals into you as fast as the Lord'll allow; your grandfather won't put up with no dawdling 'round
the house." I ate so fast I got a lump under my wishbone and
hurried after Grandfather.

I'd worked plenty in the hayfields in Colorado. When I was
only eleven years old and weighed seventy pounds, I'd been
paid a man's wages for running a horserake or mowing machine.
Father could always pitch more hay in a day than any other
man in the neighborhood, and he'd taught me the tricks when I
was little. Out there, we'd put up stacks of hay that had more
than a hundred tons in each one of them, and I wanted to show
Grandfather that I knew just how every part of it was done.

He wasn't anywhere in the barn. There were box stalls just
inside the big doors. As I passed the first one, a buckskin horse
poked his head out and snapped at me. His ears were pinned

back tight against his head, white showed around his eyes, the way it does on a fighting stallion's, and his whole muzzle was peppered with gray hairs. There was a fat sleepy-looking bay mare in the next stall. She didn't bother to raise her head from the feedbox when I stopped at the doorway of her stall, and I only stopped long enough to notice that she was just fat instead of with foal.

There was a sow, nursing a litter of new pigs, in the next stall, and the rest of the main floor was empty. Pigeons were cooing somewhere in the high loft and, as I looked up, a barn swallow swooped from its mud nest on the ridgepole and glided out through the open doorway. There was the smell of new hay in the barn, but I could only see a fringe of it hanging over the edge of a low mow. On the other side, over the box stalls, the mows were filled to the rafters with bleached hay that looked to be two or three years old.

I thought Grandfather might have gone to the barn cellar, so I jumped down over the wall and went to see. He wasn't there, but the hog was. I could hear him grunting, back in the darkness. I went in, and kept my eyes closed till I could see in the dimness. In the center of the cellar, there was a pit about thirty feet square. It held a brownish pond, with a mountain of manure in the middle. There was a two-foot path around it, and, back against the walls on the three sides, there were rows of pigpens. On one of them the gate was broken and lying, half buried, at the edge of the pond. I fished it out and propped it across the path beside the open pen. Then I shaded my eyes, went out, and came in on the side of the pit where the hog was. He didn't give me a bit of trouble. As I went toward him slowly, he looked up from his rooting, grunted a couple of times, then turned and walked along the path. When he came to the open gateway, he went in.

I hadn't seen or heard anything of Grandfather since he'd left the dinner table. After I'd wired the gate into place, I decided to go and look at the horses again. As I was going through the big front barn doors, I heard Grandfather holler from behind me. He had on a wide-brimmed straw hat with a big white veil, and was down at the beehives under the apple trees. "Take care, Ralphie! Take care the yella colt!" he called as he came scrambling up over the dooryard wall.

I hadn't seen any colt when I'd been in the barn before, but I was glad to hear there was one. While I was waiting for Grandfather, I was thinking how much fun it would be to harness-break a colt. I hoped he might be old enough to ride. Grandfather pulled the bee hat off as he came, and dropped it by the pile of cordwood at the top of the wall. "Afore we start to haying, we got to get that tarnal pig in," he called as he came toward me. "Can't find hide nor hair of the pesky critter no-wheres."

"He's back in his pen," I told him. "The gate's broken, but I wired it up so it will hold till we can make a new one."

Grandfather stopped in front of me and looked up with a scowl, as though he thought I were lying to him. "Who put him in?" he asked.

"I did."

"Who helped you?"

"Nobody."

"How'd you do it? I and Old Bess has been trying to catch him for a week."

"By not yelling at him," I said.

Grandfather's face flared red. He jerked his head back so that his whiskers stuck out at me, and shouted, "Don't you . . ." Then he stopped, and just stood staring right into my eyes for a full minute. I didn't stare back, but I didn't look away from his eyes. When I was beginning to wonder if we were going to stand there looking at each other all afternoon, he said, gruffly, "Now stand back out the way! The colt ain't been used of late and he's high-strung. Most likely he'd bite you or tromp on you."

I didn't wonder the colt was high-strung. Grandfather took a bridle down from the wall, and began shouting, "Whoa! Whoa, boy! Whoa! Whoa!" The thing that did surprise me was that he started for the first box stall. That was the one where the buck-skin was. I hadn't looked at his teeth but there hadn't seemed any sense in doing it. From the way his eyes were sunk back into their sockets, and from the white hairs on his neck and cheeks, I'd known he was as old for a horse as Grandfather was for a man.

The old buckskin didn't wait for Grandfather to go into the stall. His head shot out above the half-door. It was straight out from his neck, his ears were pinned back, his teeth bared, and he struck both ways like a coiled rattlesnake. Grandfather held the bridle up in front of his own face, and shouted, "WHOA! WHOA, BOY! Whoa, whoa!" On the next swing of his head, the old horse grabbed one of the bridle blinders in his teeth and shook it. Then he let go, jerked his head out of the doorway, whirled, and clattered to the far corner of the stall. I could see it was nothing new with him, because the bridle blinders were frayed, and ridged with toothmarks.

Before I stopped to think, I said, "Let me have it; I'll harness him."

Grandfather's head swung at me the way the buckskin's had swung at him. "Stand back! Stand back, I tell you! Ain't you got brains enough to see he's a dangerous hoss?"

I did step back to where I had been, but as I stepped, I said, "Give him something hard to bite on and he'll quit that snapping."

Grandfather jerked his head toward me again, and his face was fire red. "Mind your manners!" he snapped, and then reached for the hasp of the half-door.

I was really afraid to have Grandfather go in there. The old horse swung his hind end to whichever side Grandfather tried to get past, and he was kicking like a cow with a sore teat. Each time he kicked, Grandfather would jump back and holler, "Whoa! Whoa, you tarnal fool colt!" For the first minute or two, my heart was pounding as hard as the buckskin's hoofs. I grabbed up a pitchfork and got ready to make a rush if there was any real danger. Then I had trouble to keep from laughing. It was all a show with the old horse, and Grandfather should have known it. Hard as he was kicking, the buckskin was careful to miss Grandfather by at least a foot with each hoof and, with all his slatting his rump around, he never came close to squeezing Grandfather against the sides of the stall. I don't know how long it might have gone on if Grandfather hadn't lost his temper. He swung the bridle up over his head and whanged it down across the buckskin's rump. The old horse crowded over against the far wall, and stood shaking all over, as if he were frightened to death.

Grandfather didn't shout after he'd hit the horse, and his voice was almost petting as he inched slowly forward. "Tarnal fool! Tarnal fool hoss! Must always I have to hurt you afore you'll behave yourself? Poor colty! Poor colty! Whooooa, boy!"

As soon as I saw that everything was going to be all right, I stood the pitchfork down and stepped back to where I'd been in the first place. I was hardly there before Grandfather shouted,

"Whoa! Whoa, boy!" again, and led the buckskin out of the stall. With the sound of his voice, the old horse's hoofs began to beat again, and he came out like a prize stallion into a show ring. "Stand back! Stand back, Ralphie!" Grandfather shouted. "Don't get next nor nigh his heels! He's dangerous, I tell you!"

Grandfather

4

The Mowing Machine

I'D HANDLED some pretty mean horses on ranches where I'd worked in Colorado, and was itching to get my hands on the yella colt, but Grandfather wouldn't let me go near him. The old horse would jig in the same spot till Grandfather had the harness chest high, then he'd shy away, and Grandfather would chase after him, shouting, "Whoa! Whoa, you tarnal fool colt!" I'd given the bay mare a good combing and brushing, and had her harnessed before Grandfather cornered the yella colt. "There, by gorry! There you be, Ralphie!" he sang out as soon as he'd buckled the crouper. "Colt's awful high-strung. Got to handle him gentle, elseways you'd never get a harness on him. Been spoilt by them cussed worthless hired hands. Don't none of 'em understand a high-strung hoss critter. Now you run fetch the snath and scythe out the carriage house whilst I'm hitching the hosses to the mowing machine."

I'd never even heard of a snath, let alone knowing what it was, and I didn't think I'd heard right that time. "What is it you want me to get?" I asked.

"Snath and scythe! Snath and scythe!" Grandfather shouted. "Why don't you listen when I speak to you?"

"I did listen," I said, "but I don't know what a snath is."

"Great thunderation!" Grandfather hollered. "Don't know what a snath is! Don't know much of nothing, do you? Didn't your father learn you nothing about farming?"

"Father taught me plenty about farming, and about handling horses, too," I said, "but we never had anything called a snath."

Grandfather dropped both hands to his sides, and just stood looking at me for a minute. When he spoke, his voice was as gentle as a woman's. "Gorry sakes alive, Ralphie! Your old grampa'll learn you how to farm. Poor boy! Tarnal shame Charlie died afore he had you half fetched up. Awful good man, Charlie. Shame Mary had to lose him when there's so cussed many worthless men in the world. Now you run along and fetch the snath and scythe."

I knew what a scythe was all right. Father used to have one when we lived on the ranch. When I got to the carriage house, there was a scythe about like Father's hanging on the far wall. I took it down and looked all around to see if I could find anything that might be a snath. I was still trying when Grandfather called, "Ralphie, what's keeping you? We ain't got all day!" I grabbed up a broken whetstone, took the scythe, and hurried down behind the barn where he was shouting, "Whoa! Whoa, back!" at the horses.

From the corner of the barn, I could see Grandfather down on his hands and knees behind the yella colt. The colt was the off horse—the one on the right-hand side of the pair—the cutter bar of the mowing machine was down, and, if the team had started up, Grandfather would have been right in the path of the knives. I began to run, but the crooked scythe handle kept bouncing around on my shoulder, and I was afraid I might startle the horses, so I had to slow down. Grandfather looked up just when I was back to a walk, and shouted, "What in time and tarnation ails you? Dawdling away the whole day when there's work to be done! What kept you?"

"I couldn't find the snath," I called back.

I was getting close enough that Grandfather didn't have to

shout, but he snapped, good and loud, "Couldn't find it!
Couldn't find it! What in thunder you got over your shoulder?"

Of course, by that time I knew it had to be something to do
with the scythe, so I asked, "Is it a part of the scythe?"

Grandfather stood up on his knees, with his hands drooped in
front of his chest—just the way a prairie dog stands by his hole
—and he looked up at me as if I were some kind of a strange
animal. "Gorry sakes alive!" he said at last. "How did ever a boy
grow up to your age and know so little? Poor boy! It's a good
thing Mary sent you. Your old grampa'll learn you to be a man.
Snath is the handle; scythe is the blade that goes on it."

Grandfather had the buckskin's tug wired to the singletree
with a piece of rusty old barbed wire. It was so brittle that one
strand had cracked where the sharp bend came, and an end
three feet long was trailing on the ground. He grabbed the trailing piece in both fists, and bent it back and forth till it broke,
leaving an eight-inch spike sticking out with a barb at the end.

"That won't work very well, will it?" I asked. "One strand is
already broken, and the dragging end will ball hay up in front
of the cutter bar."

"Don't you tell me!" Grandfather blurted, but I knew he
could see I was right. As he got up off his knees, the toe of his
boot caught the spike of wire and turned it up so it wouldn't
drag. "Ain't nothing the matter with that," he said as he climbed
up onto the mowing-machine seat. "Now pass me them lines,
and stand back so's you don't get hurt. Whoa! Whoa, colty!"

I knew quite a little about mowing machines. Father had
fixed the machinery for most of the neighbors we had in Colorado, and, if I wasn't in school, he'd always let me help him.
He'd traded a colt for an old secondhand mowing machine one
winter, and we'd taken it all to pieces, made some new parts,
and put it all together again. When Father got done fixing any
piece of machinery it had always worked just as well as a new
one. I hadn't had much time to look over Grandfather's machine, but in one glance I could see that it was in worse shape
than the one Father got for the colt. The cutter bar was lying in

a tangle of matted clover, two of the knife sections were broken in half, and one was missing altogether. The gears were out of mesh, and there was new red rust on all of them and along the sickle blades. If the team was started with the cutter bar dragging, I knew it might tear things all to pieces.

The yella colt had begun prancing the minute Grandfather shouted, "Whoa, colty!" I snatched up the reins, but before I passed them to Grandfather, I said, "Hadn't I better put the cutter bar up before it drags and breaks something?"

"Leave be! Leave be!" Grandfather shouted. "Pass me them reins and stand back out the way!"

I should have kept quiet but, as I passed him the lines, I asked, "Hadn't I better get an oil can?"

"Stand back! Stand back, I tell you!" Grandfather snapped. Then he spanked the reins up and down, and shouted, "Gitap! Gitap!"

The bay mare didn't move an inch when Grandfather shouted, but the yella colt went off like a skyrocket—and in the same direction: straight up. He danced a jig on his hind feet, and kept his front ones pawing up and down like a swimming dog's. When he came down, he rammed into the collar and, of course, broke the rotten old piece of barbed wire on the whiffle-tree. It held just long enough to lurch the mowing machine forward a few inches and make the slipping gears scream. With his outside tug loose, and the screech of the gears behind him, the old buckskin swung around like a slammed gate. He nearly pulled Grandfather off the seat, broke one of the reins, and tore most of his harness off.

Instead of being mad at the yella colt, Grandfather began yelling at me, "Tarnal fool boy! You scairt him! You scairt him! Why didn't you stand back like I told you? Whoa, colty! Whoa!"

Grandfather was still pulling on the unbroken line. With the yella colt turned around facing him, and with the line through the ring on the harness, it only made the horse pull back harder. "Let go of the line!" I shouted, as I ran toward the buckskin.

"Shut up! Shut up! Get out of the way!" Grandfather yelled

back, and kept right on pulling. The collar was hauled tight up around the old horse's jaws, and he had his feet braced the way a bulldog does when he's trying to pull a stick out of your hands. I still had the scythe stone in my hand, had got back of the yella colt, and was just ready to hit him and make him jump forward, when the second rein broke and the buckskin sat down with a thud. His rump missed my feet by less than two inches, and Grandfather hollered, "Now see what you done! Why didn't you keep out the way?"

Grandfather came up and began patting the old horse on the neck. "Poor colty! Poor colty!" he said soothingly. "Tarnal nigh busted the harness all to smithereens, didn't you? Ralphie, I and you'd better fetch it up to the carriage house and fix it. Awful high-strung hoss, the yella colt. Did you mark any harness rivets laying 'round the bench? Plenty of 'em in Levi's drawers, but he gets so all-fired het up if I pry one of 'em open. Wisht Levi'd come home."

"What does Uncle Levi do in Boston?" I asked him.

"Brick mason, but he ought to be a tinker or a blacksmith, and he ought to be right down here to home where he belongs. Levi ain't no more of a farmer than you be, but he can mend anything he puts his hand to and, by gorry, there's plenty stuff around here that needs mending."

Grandfather turned away from the yella colt and pointed toward a jumble of wrecked carts, buggies, and farm machines that lay half buried in a weed patch beyond a shed built back into the hillside. "Made some powerful good trades enduring the last two-three years. Yonder, past the sheep barn, there's stuff enough to keep Levi out of mischief four-five months. Fetch a pretty penny whenst it's all mended up nice. Now you lug the busted harness up to the carriage house, Ralphie. I'll stand the yella colt back in his stall so's he don't stave Nell's harness whilst we're gone. Tarnal high-strung hoss! Can't never tell what he's likely to do."

All the time Grandfather had been telling me about Uncle Levi and the machinery, the old buckskin had been sitting on his haunches. His collar was pulled up behind his ears, so that his head was stretched out almost straight, and the broken harness was hanging from it. I stepped up to unbuckle the hame strap and let him loose, but Grandfather hollered for me to stand back before I got hurt. Instead of unbuckling the strap himself, he began spanking the old horse on the rump with his hand, and saying, "Get up, colty! Get up, get up!"

"He can't get up without raising his head," I said. "You'll have to unbuckle the hame strap."

"Stand back! Stand back! Don't you tell me! Get up, colty! Get up, get up!" With the last, "Get up," Grandfather whacked the old horse a good one, and he thrashed around until he'd thrown himself flat. All four legs were going as if he were trying to run a two-minute mile right there on his side, and Grandfather was dancing in and out between the flying hoofs and shouting, "Whoa, colty! Whoa! Whoa, I tell you!"

The yella colt's back was toward me. I stepped in quick, yanked the end of the top hame strap, and let it slip out through the buckle. The hames flew off the collar as though they'd been pulled by a spring, and the horse flopped his head down and lay as if he were dead. "Now see what you done!" Grandfather yelled at me so loud his voice went squeaky. "You killed him! You killed him!"

I'd taken all the blame I could stand. Anybody who knew anything about horses could see that the buckskin was only sulking, and that he wasn't hurt a bit. I was so mad about Grandfather's yelling at me that I wanted to throw something at him, and I still had the broken piece of whetstone in my hand. Before I even stopped to think, I smacked it down hard on the old horse's rump. He came to life quicker than a scared jackrabbit, and scrambled to his feet. Then he stood there trembling all over, while Grandfather scolded me. "Don't you durst! Don't you *never* durst hit a dumb critter!" he shouted. "Poor colty! Poor colty! Now fetch that harness up to the carriage house whilst I take him to the barn."

I gathered up the harness, and watched Grandfather take the

old buckskin to the barn, or rather, the buckskin take Grandfather. The yella colt was all of sixteen hands high, and carried his head like a giraffe. Black spots were all he needed to make him look like one. Grandfather had the bit ring clutched in his fist, and was being jerked to his tiptoes as the old horse pranced

The Yella Colt

and flung his head. All the way up through the barnyard, he was dancing around, trying to keep his feet out from under the horse's hoofs, and shouting, "Whoa, colty! Whoa, you tarnal fool hoss!"

We didn't get along much better mending harness than we had in breaking it. Father had taught me how to set a rivet tight by driving the washer down with a small nut, then cutting the tail close and tapping it evenly with a hammer. The only rivets we could find on the bench were three-quarters of an inch long, and the washers were too big to fit them. I tried to show Grandfather how to split a rivet end, spread it both ways and tap it flat, but he snatched the hammer out of my hands. "Great thunderation!" he snapped. "You're worse than Levi! Fiddle-faddle 'round half a day putting in a harness rivet! Stand back whilst I fetch it a clip!" He swung the hammer higher than his head, pounded it down like a sledge, and mashed the long rivet into a flat figure S. "There, by thunder!" he said, as he looked at it. "Ain't no reason that won't hold tight as a button. Now find me three, four, half a dozen more of 'em. Your old grampa'll learn you how to be a farmer yet, Ralphie."

5

Snath and Scythe

I COULD hardly wait to get into the field so I could show Grandfather that I really knew something about haying. It worked just exactly backwards. Instead of letting me run the mowing machine, he told me to take the snath and scythe and cut hay out from under the apple trees. I might just as well have been trying to cut it with a broom as with a scythe. On the first swing, I ran the edge of the blade along a hidden rock, and then it wouldn't cut worth a cent.

To see Father swinging a scythe, it had looked to be the easiest thing in the world to do. The scythe went back and forth like a clock pendulum, and left stubble two or three inches high. For me, it was like trying to swing a dog by his tail. The crooked handle wobbled around in my hands, and the blade either stuck in the ground or just tore the heads off the hay. The stubble looked the same way my brother Philip's hair did the first time I tried to cut it.

We started in the corner of the orchard, near the gap in the stonewall. As soon as Grandfather had told me what to do, he let the cutter bar on the mowing machine down and hollered, "Gitap! Gitap!" to the horses. The yella colt started off on his

41

hind legs, the gears screeched, and the sickle pounded back and forth in the cutter bar like a broken piston on a steam engine. I watched them make the first fifty yards before I tried the scythe. The three broken knife sections on the machine didn't cut at all; just tore the grass and left it lying in snaky lines on the ground. The yella colt was still jumping like a rabbit when they went out of sight behind a tree, and every time he jumped they left a patch of dragged-down hay. Above the racket of the machine, Grandfather was shouting, "Tarnal fool colt! Settle down! Settle down, I tell you!"

The orchard wasn't more than ten acres, but it was half an hour before Grandfather got around it the first time. He stopped the mowing machine just beyond the tree I was trying to mow under, and hollered, "What in the name of creation be you trying to do?"

"I never tried to use one of these things before," I told him, "and I haven't got the hang of it yet."

"Gorry sakes alive!" he said, as he came toward me. "You might have et it off evener with your teeth. Why, you ain't got the amount of sense the Almighty give to hens."

I was mad enough at myself for not being able to make the scythe do what I wanted it to, and when Grandfather said that, I couldn't help boiling over. "It looks just about as bad as the swath you've cut, doesn't it?" I shouted back. "Only you had a machine to do it for you." Then I hooked the scythe on a limb and started to walk away.

Grandfather's voice dropped right down. "Gorry sakes alive, Ralphie," he said. " 'Tain't no fault of your'n, I don't cal'late, that you ain't been learned nothing. Here, let your old grampa show you how to swing a snath and scythe. Pass me the whetstone."

You'd have thought Grandfather's wrist and elbow were on ball bearings. There wasn't more than two inches of the whetstone sticking up out of his fist, but he swiped it forward and back along both sides of the scythe edge so fast my eye couldn't follow his hand, and at every stroke he stoned the blade from heel to point. After about a minute, he ran his thumbnail the length of the blade, and said, "There! There, by gorry, Ralphie! Now we'll see what kind of logs makes wide shingles!"

Grandfather slipped the broken stone into his pocket, grasped the hand grips on the snath, and had the scythe swinging as he brought it down. Little as he was, he kept in perfect balance as he swung the long blade, and he made it whistle each time it swept forward through the grass. Closely as I watched him, I never saw a jerk or pull anywhere. The ground was littered with stones—some of them as big as my head—and the scythe rode over every one without touching it. When he'd gone eight or ten feet, he stopped and held the scythe out toward me. "There you be, Ralphie," he said. "Ain't nothing to it 'cepting to watch out for rocks. Tarnal hard to see some of 'em where the grass is rank. Now let your old grampa see you swing it."

I did a little better after that, but not very well. For the next half hour, Grandfather alternated between scolding me for being awkward and telling me I was beginning to get the hang of it. Then he went back to the mowing machine. It was out of my sight when I heard Grandfather shouting, and thought he must be in bad trouble. I went running over there as fast as I could and, when I got to where I could see them, he was pulling at the buckskin's bridle and shouting into his face, "Gitap! Gitap, you fool colt! What ails you? Gitap, I tell you!"

Grandfather dropped the bridle rein when I came running up, and said, "Might just as leave unhitch him. Tarnal stubborn critter! Ain't ary man this side the Androscoggin River can make him pull once he gets his head sot on balking."

One of the men I'd worked for in Colorado was an expert with balky horses. I didn't know all the tricks, but I'd learned enough of them that I never had much trouble with his horses, and I was sure I wouldn't have any with the yella colt. "Let me try him," I said to Grandfather, and reached for a piece of thin wire that was twisted around one of the old horse's traces.

"Stand back! Stand back!" Grandfather snapped at me. "For aught I know he'll commence having one of his cat fits any minute now."

As if the yella colt had understood him, he began shaking his head and slatting around. "Whoa, colty! Whoa! Whoa!" Grandfather shouted as if the horse had been a mile away. "Unhitch Old Nell quick, Ralphie, whilst I loose the colt. Look lively afore he staves the whole shootingmatch to smithereens! Ain't nothing to do now but fetch him back to the barn."

That was the end of our haying for the day. As soon as the horses were unharnessed and in their stalls, Grandfather set me to sawing firewood with a bucksaw, and went down to do something around the beehives.

I didn't see a thing of Millie all afternoon, but my dirty clothes had been washed and were hanging on the clothesline. It was nearly sunset, and I was as hungry as a coyote when Grandfather called, "Leave be, Ralphie! I and you'll go fetch the cows." He came climbing up over the yard wall, looked at the pile of wood I'd sawed, and said, "Gorry sake! Ain't half bad for a boy that don't know no more'n you do about farming, Ralphie. Cal'late your old grampa can make a man out of you yet. Did Charlie learn you to handle a bucksaw?"

"Yes, sir," I said. "Father taught me to do quite a few things, and I've learned a little bit from other men, too."

"Poor boy! Poor boy! Shame they didn't learn you nothing worth while, 'cepting to saw wood. Oh, well, what's the odds? You're still young enough, and your old grampa'll learn you."

Most of the way out through the fields, he kept pointing this or that spot out to me, and telling me long stories about what happened there when his father first took the land up from the wilderness, but I didn't pay any attention to it. I'd been told enough that day—mostly about what a fool boy I was and what my old grampa was going to learn me—and I didn't want to hear any more. I told myself that I'd stay there till the hay was in if it killed me, but I'd let him do his learning to somebody else. I'd worked for plenty of ranchers, and for market gardeners, too. Any one of them would hire me again, and none of them had ever yelled at me or called me a fool boy. The minute the last forkful of hay was in the barn, I'd start for Colorado.

All the way up the long hill beside the orchard, I kept thinking about the people I'd go to see as soon as I got back to Colorado, and Grandfather kept on talking. Old Bess was walking along beside him, and he might just as well have been doing his talking to her. To me, it was just sound: like brook water makes in running over stones. At the top of the orchard, he took hold of my arm and pointed toward a field of spindly hay that stretched across the crown of the hill. "Curious," he said, "that high field yonder. Father and my half-brothers cleared it afore ever I was born. Take heed the wall here! Nary stone bigger'n a sweet punkin. Mark them little cobbles 'mongst the hay! Millions of 'em no bigger'n a goose egg. I cal'late they draw heat from the sun. First field in twenty miles roundabouts to thaw in the spring, and last to freeze up in the fall. Late and early frosts never touches it."

I'd heard what he said, but I was still thinking about Colorado, and said, "Too bad it isn't richer ground."

Grandfather jerked his hand off my arm, and snapped, "Ain't nothing wrong with the soil! Who said there was? Plenty good cow dressing and that little field'll grow two ton of good timothy hay."

"I didn't mean that I thought there was anything wrong with it," I said, "and I don't know very much about dressing. . . ."

"Hmfff! Don't know much about nothing worth while!"

"Well, I know about strawberries and tomatoes," I said.

"What you know about 'em; how to eat 'em?"

"Yes," I said, "I know how to eat them. And I worked for a man in Colorado who knew how to raise them. He had a high, warm field for them, and he always got the highest prices because his strawberries and tomatoes were the first ones to ripen in the . . ."

"Hmfff! Hmfff! Strawb'ries!" Grandfather exploded. "Time and tarnation! Tomatoes and strawb'ries! Garden sass! Garden sass! Why in thunderation didn't somebody learn you something worth while?"

"They did!" I snapped back before I could catch myself.

"Mind your manners!" Grandfather shouted. Then he reached out and took hold of my arm again, but didn't take hold hard. "Poor boy! Poor Ralphie!" he said. "Tarnal shame to let a boy grow up so know-nothing. Your old grampa'll learn you. No, Ralphie, no. This here is hay soil. 'Tain't good for nothing else. Gorry sakes, we better fetch the cows in afore Millie's supper gets cold. Ain't no living with her whenst her victuals gets cold."

We'd been walking along the brow of the hill, where it dipped away eastward toward Lisbon Valley. The crown of the hill was to the westward and, as we passed it, I noticed a few cows and calves standing at a pasture gate beyond. Grandfather slipped one arm inside mine. "Ralphie," he said, "your old grampa's powerful glad to have you here. The land's been a-crying for young hands. I done the best I could after Frankie went off to Portland to learn a trade, but I and Old Bess was all alone . . . Levi off a-homesteading in Dakota, the big barn burning flat to the ground, the malaria keeping me abed half the time. I catched it whilst I was off to the war . . . seems like it bothers me a sight worse since I lost your gramma. Kind of had hopes when Mary wed, maybe her and Charlie'd come home to the old place to rear their family. I and your father could have cleared a power of land. I and you'll clear a power of it yet, Ralphie, soon's ever I learn you to be a farmer. Father was older'n I be afore ever I was born, but he learnt me all there is to know about the land. Poor boy! Poor Ralphie! Your old grampa'll yet learn you to be a worth-while man."

When he'd first started talking, I'd wanted to squeeze his arm against me a little, but before he was through I'd taken mine off his and moved far enough away that he couldn't put it back. We were nearly to the pasture gate, and four cows were waiting there. It was easy to see that they were all milch cows, and not very good ones. Three of them had pretty good sized calves running with them, and the fourth had her head over the bars, bellowing. So I wouldn't act as peeved at Grandfather as I felt, I said, "Do you just take the Holstein in for milking?"

"No! Take 'em all in!" Grandfather said, grumpily.

Then, as I let the bars down, he and Old Bess stood beside the gatepost. As each cow passed him, he put a hand on her or

patted her and called her by name. Even Clara Belle, the Holstein without a calf, stopped long enough for him to scratch the tuft of hair between her horns before she hurried off down the lane. Next was Jessie, a thin old Jersey with a fat heifer calf. Spotty, a Durham with a steer calf three or four months old; and Marthy, just a nice old brown cow with a heifer calf that looked like a Jersey.

As we started to follow them down the lane, I said, "The nights don't get very cold here at this time of year, do they?"

Grandfather seemed to have forgotten all about the cows. The thumb of one hand was hooked around the finger of the other behind him, his head was down, and he leaned a little forward from the hips as he stumped along. "No," he said after a little while. Then, after a few more steps, "Why?"

"Well," I said, "I wondered why you didn't leave the cows with calves in the pasture at night. There aren't any coyotes or wolves to bother them, are there?"

Grandfather stopped and looked up at me as though he didn't believe anybody could ask such a foolish question. "Gorry sakes alive, boy!" he said at last. "Don't you know nothing? How'd you raise crops without cow manure? You got to take 'em in to save the dressing."

"They raise pretty good crops in Colorado—if they have enough irrigation water—and they don't put cow manure on the fields," I told him. "We put horse manure under our first potatoes on the ranch and they all went to tops."

"Hmfff! Tarnal fools! Hoss manure's for hay!" Then he put his head back down, and didn't say another word till we were at the barn.

Millie had made a johnnycake to go with the fried pork and boiled potatoes for supper, and we had some of the cake that I hadn't had a chance to try at noon, but the tea was terrible. It tasted as if it had been made by boiling musty alfalfa, and it was so strong you couldn't see the spoon handle under the surface. She and Grandfather put milk and sugar in theirs. I tried it, but it was still as bitter as quinine. Though I didn't mean to, I must have made a face when I tasted it, because the only thing Millie said to me all through supper was, "Don't be so devilish finicky about your victuals! There's worse where there's none!"

Grandfather didn't eat anything but a piece of cake and a cup of tea, and he dozed off to sleep at the table a couple of times before I'd finished. He was still asleep, with his head resting on the table, when Millie got up and took a faded old calico wrapper from a nail behind the kitchen door. She put it on over the fresh one she was wearing, tied a cloth over her head, and took a milk bucket down from the pantry shelf. I could see she was going out to do the barn chores, and said, "I'll take care of the chores; I've done a lot of milking."

All she said was, "Hmfff! I pity the poor critters!" and went out through the summer kitchen.

I couldn't just sit in the house and let a woman do the barn work, so I took my cap and followed her. When I got there, she was standing at the tie-up doorway, pulling a pair of old rubbers on over her shoes. I tried again to get her to let me do the milking, but she said Clara Belle had a sore teat and would kick the daylights out of me. She did let me slop the hogs and do the rest of the chores, though.

When we went back to the house, Grandfather had gone to bed. Millie told me she had put my things in the front room at the head of the stairs, and she made me take my work shoes off before I went up. She came to the foot of the stairs while I was climbing them, and whispered, "That's Levi's room. If you go and get it all messed up, I'll skin you alive." Then, without saying goodnight, she went back into the kitchen and closed the hallway door.

There was just enough light left in the sky that I could see where the bed was and that a corner of the covers was turned back. I didn't bother to look for my suitcase or a lamp, but took off everything except my BVDs and crawled in. I must have gone to sleep awfully quick, because the next thing I knew Millie was calling up the stairway, "Get up! What be you; cal'lating on sleeping the whole blessed day?" It was just about as light as it had been when I went to bed.

6

I Currycomb the Yella Colt

M ILLIE had a lamp lighted and was building a fire in the cook stove when I came down to the kitchen. I said good morning to her when I came in from the front stairway, but she only grumbled something about hoping she'd find the fires of hell built with Getchell birch when she got there. I didn't know what Getchell birch was but, as I washed my face and hands at the pump sink in the back pantry, I could see she was having a bad time getting the fire started. Twice, she jerked a stove lid off, threw in kerosene from a tin dipper, and slammed the lid back as the flames shot up. Both times, red glowed from the front of the stove for half a minute, then died down, and billows of smoke poured out from every crack.

The wood I'd sawed the afternoon before had been hard maple, but it had been dry and I knew it would make a good fire. I didn't say anything to Millie, but went out and split an armful of it into kindling, picked up a couple of pine knots, and took it into the kitchen. Smoke was still pouring from the stove, and Millie was jawing away to herself about it. She didn't pay any attention to me until I'd put the wood in the wood box and was taking the milk bucket down from the pantry shelf. Then she said, "Leave be! Thomas don't want the milking done afore six o'clock. I'll take care of that; you fetch the swill to the sow with the new litter. And take heed you don't tromp on none of them little pigs."

I took the swill bucket from under the sink. It was full almost to the brim with dishwater, and I was careful not to slop a drop of it until I was outside the summer kitchen. When I opened the barn doors, the bay mare whinnied for her breakfast, but the old buckskin snaked his head out over the half-door and snapped at me as I passed his stall. His teeth didn't miss my shoulder by more than half an inch. I had trouble not to dodge away from him, but I didn't, and by the time I got to the sow's pen I had my mind made up about the way I was going to handle him.

It was only quarter of five, and if Grandfather didn't want the milking done before six I'd have plenty of time. I worked just as fast as I could while I lugged water to the hogs in the barn cellar, measured them out a quart of corn apiece, cleaned the tie-up, and climbed the mow to pitch down hay for the horses. Then I cleaned the mare's stall, bedded it with loose chaff from the barn floor, and fed her, but I didn't go near the buckskin. The night before, Millie had told me to give the horses bran, but that morning I gave the bay mare whole corn. I wanted to be sure the buckskin would hear her chewing it. I currycombed and brushed her while she ate, and listened to him stamping, snorting, and raking his teeth across the timbers of his stall.

When the mare was almost finished with her corn, and when the old buckskin was nearly frantic, I slipped out of her stall with the currycomb in my hand, took his bridle down from its spike, and went toward his stall door. As his head came shooting out over the half-door, it looked like the pictures of a Chinese dragon. I swung the bridle in front of my face, just the way Grandfather had but, with the other hand, I slipped the currycomb up in front of the blinder. The buckskin bit it so hard that he turned down a whole row of the sharp teeth, then snorted, and snapped three times more in quick succession. I didn't swing the currycomb at him, but each time I was careful to see that it was where he'd bump his lips or teeth against it. After the third bump, he whirled, crowded his head into the far corner of the stall, and stood dancing.

I'd expected him to act just the way he had with Grandfather, and was inside the stall door by the time he had his head in the corner. Then I was lucky. With Grandfather, he'd gone into the corner with his head high and his back straight. With me, he went with his head low and his back humped. When I was only eight years old Father had taught me to look out for flying heels when a horse got into that position. And he'd taught me that the closer I was to them when they flew, the less I'd get hurt. Without ever stopping to figure it out, I jumped to the side of the buckskin's rump, and swung the currycomb up hard from my knee. It caught him on the near hock as his leg flew past my hip, and it caught him hard. He snorted, swung his rump toward me, and kicked again. That time I didn't try to hide the currycomb, but smashed it hard against his hock as the legs came up.

If I'd misguessed him, and he was really a bad horse, I could be in plenty of trouble, and I knew it. I had to keep telling myself so, as I crowded in against him with the currycomb ready to swing. If he ever found out he could scare me I'd never be able to handle him, and I knew he had his mind made up to find out. His head swung toward me, with his nostrils opened to the size of coffee cups, his ears back, and white showing around his eyes. Then he began to crowd. The solid wall was only two feet from my back. If I tried to dodge out, his heels would certainly catch me before I could get to the door, and I could only use the currycomb if I was in close. If I went toward his head, no currycomb could stop him from tearing me to pieces with his teeth. There was only one thing I could do: I had to scare him before he knew he'd scared me.

If it had taken me a tenth as long to think it as to tell it, I might have been killed, but it didn't. I stayed tight against his rump and, the second he began crowding me toward the wall, I started beating a tattoo on his belly with the sharp teeth of the

currycomb. His back hunched against the bite of the comb, every muscle in his body was pulled as tight as a fiddlestring, and he kept crowding until I could see the wall just behind my shoulder. Then, with a half snort, half groan, the wind went out of him—just as it does with a toy balloon that has had a hole poked in it. He didn't dance, but moved over against the far wall and stood, sulking and watching me out of the corner of his eye.

I felt a little trembly all over as I moved up to the buckskin's head. He flung it high, with his nose poked nearly to the ceiling. I could have jumped and made a grab for his under lip but, if I had, he might have bitten my hand. Instead, I swung the currycomb up where he could get a good look at it, and his muzzle came part way down. As soon as I'd slipped a thumb in behind his front teeth, he brought his head the rest of the way down and let me put the bridle on. After I'd buckled the cheek strap, I scratched his forehead with my fingers, and looked back along his body. A nerve twitched once or twice in his shoulder, but he wasn't shivering the way he had after Grandfather hit him with the bridle. I soft-talked him a little, and kept on scratching his forehead until his ears came up. Then I went for the rest of the harness and put it on. The old horse never moved an inch until the last buckle was fastened.

After I'd led him around the stall a few times, I unharnessed him and fed him. Though I knew a horse got more good from his grain if he'd eaten his hay first, I brought the bran as soon as I had the harness hung up, then curried and brushed him as he ate. He winced a little when I brushed over the spot on his belly where I'd tattooed him with the currycomb, but his ears stayed up and he didn't lift a foot. I thought it might be getting close to six o'clock, so I took the currycomb to the carriage house, straightened the bent teeth, put it back in the barn, and went to the house.

Grandfather was nowhere in sight, but Millie was slicing boiled potatoes into an iron frying pan on the stove. The kitchen was clear of smoke, and a red glow was coming from the open front of the stove. I took the milk bucket down from the pantry shelf, and asked, "Is it time to milk yet?"

Instead of answering, Millie turned toward me and looked straight into my eyes with her mouth clamped together tight. "What was you up to with the yella colt?" she asked.

"He doesn't like currycombing," was all I said.

She didn't look away from my eyes, and she didn't change the expression on her face. "Better stay away from him," she said. "He devilish near killed a couple of hired hands that tried to get smart with him. Thomas is the only one can handle him."

I kept looking right at her, and said, "I'm not going to get smart with him, and he's not going to get smart with me. How much milk do you want me to bring to the house?"

"A quart's enough. That maple you fetched in burns pretty good. Breakfast'll be ready when you're done milking." Her voice wasn't soft, but there wasn't any crabbiness in it.

When I went back into the barn, the yella colt shot his head out over the half-door. His ears were pinned back, he snorted when he saw who it was, and he snapped, but it was just to let off steam. His teeth whacked together like trap springs, but his muzzle only jerked a few inches in my direction. So he would know I wasn't afraid of him, I went right up close, but I had the milk bucket all ready to swing if I needed it. I didn't. He drew his head back in, and picked up a mouthful of hay as if there had been no one within a mile.

With all Millie's having told me the night before that the Holstein heifer would kick the daylights out of me, she didn't raise a foot when I milked her. And if she had a sore teat I didn't find it. As soon as the milk began singing in the bottom of the bucket, three cats showed up from somewhere, and Old Bess came into the tie-up and sat watching me. I aimed a stream of milk at her head, the way I used to do with our dog in Colorado, but she didn't know about opening her mouth to catch it. She just sat there, wagging her tail and licking the milk off her lips with her tongue. When I'd stripped the last drops, I found an old pan and filled it with warm milk for her and the cats.

Though I hadn't seen it, I knew the Holstein had a calf in the sheep barn. I'd heard it bawl, and she had stood at the doorway bellowing when we'd brought the cows in the night before. Millie had taken the calf's supper down to it while I had been watering the hogs in the barn cellar. As soon as I'd fed Bess and the cats, I took the rest of the milk and started to the sheep barn. I was just to the doorway when Grandfather hollered from behind me, "Stay out of there! Mind what you're doing!" When I looked around, he was coming across the barnyard toward me as fast as he could walk. "Who told you to feed that calf?" he asked me as he got closer.

"Nobody," I said, "but I heard Millie come down and feed it last night, and this morning she told me she only wanted a quart of milk at the house."

"Didn't she tell you to mind the spider web?" he asked.

"No, sir."

"Rattle-brained girl!" he snapped out, and pushed between me and the doorway. Its frame was made of heavy oak logs, and the open door sagged on thick rawhide hinges. Grandfather put a hand against each of the upright logs, peeked into the darkness of the old barn, and his voice was only a whisper when he said, "Mark it, Ralphie; the all-fired great spider web acrost the top half the inside doorway. Been there nigh onto three weeks. The old spider'll be hatching out her brood pretty quick now. You have to scooch down low a-going in. I was scairt you was going to blunder into it and smash it all to smithereens."

The sheep barn was dug back into the hillside. The roof was of poles with hay and earth over them, and the floor was solid packed clay that was as hard as stone. As we ducked under the spider web and my eyes became used to the dimness, I could see a spotted calf, three or four weeks old, penned in one corner of the old barn. A chipped white porcelain bucket was nailed inside the fencing of the pen, and the calf was butting it with his head. So he wouldn't slop the milk, I climbed the fence, straddled his neck, and poured all but a quart of it into the chipped bucket. Then I slipped two fingers into his mouth, for teats, and poked his nose into the warm milk. I'd almost forgotten about Grandfather's being there till he asked, "Who learned you how to do that?"

"Father, I guess. It seems as if I've always known it."

"Well, it's more'n I thought you knowed, Ralphie. You done it like a real farmer."

"I am a real farmer," I told him. "I just don't know much about mowing with a hand scythe."

"Hmfff! Don't know nothing about bees or dressing or hay land neither! Strawb'ries and tomatoes! Who ever heard of a farmer that couldn't swing a snath and scythe? Only fit way to mow a field; 'cepting a man can't find hired hands with gumption enough to do an honest day's work for a dollar. You seen how that tarnal mowing machine hogs down the grass and leaves half of it laying flat in the field."

"It wouldn't if it was fixed up in good shape."

"Don't tell me!" Grandfather shouted so loud that the calf let go of my fingers. "Ain't a machine made that will do ary job as good as a man can do it by hand if he's got a spark of gumption in him. Wastin'! Wastin'! Lazy, shiftless, good-for-nothing farmers nowadays; run into debt for a parcel of fancy machines that ain't worth a tinker, and go broke afore ever they get 'em paid for."

"Father always said that good machinery would pay for itself ten times over."

"Father said! Father said! What in time and tarnation did Charlie know 'bout farming anyways? Mill hand, wa'n't he, whenst Mary wed him? *My* father took this farm up from the wilderness, cut the timber, pulled the stumps, sot up the stonewalls and cleared the fields, and he didn't have nothing 'cepting his own two hands, a homemade plow, and a yoke of oxen. Hosses! Hosses! Ain't a hoss a-living can hold a candle to a Durham ox. Why I recollect . . ."

Just at that moment Millie called to us, "Victuals is ready!"

After breakfast, I harnessed the horses while Grandfather was doing something down at the beehives. I hoped he'd stay there till I had time to tighten the nuts on the mowing machine and give it a good oiling, but he didn't. He came to the carriage house doorway when I was hunting through the litter on the workbench. "What in thunderation you dawdling 'round there for whenst there's haying to be done?" he shouted.

"I was just looking for some wrenches and an oil can," I told him. "That mowing machine sounds as if it's in pretty bad shape."

"Ain't nothing the matter with it that ain't the matter with all the pesky things," Grandfather snapped. "Now come take care of Old Nell whilst I hitch up the yella colt!"

As we led the horses over to the machine, I told myself I'd keep my mouth shut even if I could see that the whole shebang was going to explode with the first turn of the wheel. I didn't do it, though. The bolt on the keeper at the end of the pitman rod was so loose that the sickle head had a half-inch play. I'd heard it hammering the day before, and knew that if it wasn't tightened it would break the ball joint off. The yella colt was prancing, bobbing his head, and kicking as Grandfather dodged in and out trying to fasten his traces. As soon as I had Old Nell hitched, I picked up a sharp stone and began tapping the keeper nut tighter. "What in time be you playing with now?" Grandfather shouted at me.

"I'm not playing," I said. "I'm just trying to tighten this bolt enough that the sickle head won't break."

"Leave be! Leave be, I tell you! First thing you know you'll have it all busted to smithereens. Hold the yella colt whilst I gather up the reins and get along. Time flies!"

Time wasn't all that flew. Grandfather had just yelled, "Gitap! Gitap!" and the yella colt had taken two jackrabbit jumps when wet grass clogged the cutter bar and the loose pitman keeper jerked the head off the sickle.

"Worthless, useless, meddlesome, big-headed boy!" Grandfather howled. "Now look what you done! Busted it all to smithereens! What in time and tarnation ails you?"

I opened my mouth to yell back, but bit my teeth together

and started for the tree where I'd been mowing. "Gorry sakes alive, Ralphie," Grandfather called after me. "Didn't cal'late to scold you. Tarnal thing keeps a-busting all the time and likes to drive me to distraction. Guess I and you'd better fetch it in to the carriage house and tinker it up a mite."

The tinkering took us all the rest of the forenoon. Grandfather blew off at me a dozen times for wanting to be too fussy, but he let me put in new knife sections to replace the broken ones, turn the grindstone while he half sharpened the rest of them, put a new head on the sickle, and tighten most of the bearings. As soon as we'd eaten dinner, he went down to the beehives and seemed to have forgotten all about haying. I sawed wood ten or fifteen minutes while I was waiting for him, then bridled the horses, hitched them to the mowing machine, and drove to the orchard.

It was the middle of the afternoon before I saw Grandfather again. By that time, I'd made a dozen rounds of the orchard, and the old machine had worked pretty well. I'd had a little trouble with the yella colt at first, but it hadn't amounted to much. He'd danced and pranced until he found that I wasn't paying any attention to him, and then he balked. It only lasted a minute or two. After I'd wired his ears together good and tight with a piece of soft wire, he'd stood, slatting around and bobbing his head. I gave him just time enough to forget he was balking, then picked up the lines, clucked to him, and he walked on, bobbing his head and snorting a little.

Grandfather didn't come near us when he came into the field. He took the scythe I'd been using from a limb of the apple tree, looked at the blade, and went to the carriage house. It was nearly an hour before he came back. Then he went to mowing under the trees as though he were all alone in the orchard. The sun was dipping down behind the tops of the pines on the ridge when he called to me, "Take the hosses in and fetch your cows. Victuals'll be ready afore long."

Grandfather went to sleep at the supper table again that night, and Millie let me do the chores by myself.

7

Uncle Levi

IT TOOK me a day and a half to finish mowing the orchard, and I had a good time doing it. The mowing machine didn't give me much trouble, and the yella colt only balked twice. Both times, Grandfather was away from the field, and the old horse hated having his ears wired so much that neither of his balky spells lasted more than a few minutes. Grandfather didn't come near the machine once while I was mowing. He spent about half his time away from the orchard, but every time I saw him he was swinging a scythe as fast as he could go.

My second afternoon was bad. Grandfather gave me a right-handed snath and scythe, and made me mow under the apple trees with him. I'd always been left-handed, the same as he was, and couldn't make the right-handed scythe come within a foot of going where I wanted it to. I tried hard enough that I got water blisters on both hands, but I couldn't keep the blade from bumping into rocks. Grandfather scolded at me all afternoon, and the more he scolded the worse I did. When the sun was nearly down to the top of the pines, he shouted, "Hang up that snath and scythe and go fetch the cows! Never seen such an awkward, useless boy in all the days of my life."

I was so mad when I brought the cows in that I made up my mind to go back to Colorado just as soon as I could get my suitcase packed. I banged the stanchion bars around the last cow's neck, stuck the hold-peg in place, and was turning toward the tie-up door when, from just outside, Millie called, "Hurry up, Ralphie! Supper's on the fire and Levi's here. I done all the rest of the chores a'ready." Then she turned and ran back to the house like a little girl.

When I went into the back pantry I'd have known Uncle Levi was there, even if no one had told me and I couldn't hear his voice. The table was stacked with big paper bags and bundles. Oranges were spilling out of one bag that was lying on its side. From the shape of another, I knew it was crammed full of bananas and, beside half a dozen smaller bags, there were two big bundles in slick brown paper that I knew would be meat.

"Hi there, Ralphie!" he called to me from the kitchen as soon as I had my cap off. "How's Thomas using you?"

I couldn't say anything except, "All right. I didn't know you were coming down."

"Didn't know it myself," he called back, "till I got Thomas's letter making out like he was on the point of death. Thomas, it's a God's wonder you ain't scared ten years off my life! How many times, right in the midst of haying, have you wrote and let on like you was dying?"

"Ain't feeling well! Ain't feeling well! Ain't been feeling up to scratch for more'n a month," Grandfather snapped at him.

"Looking pert as a peacock to me," Uncle Levi told him. "Don't calc'late there's nothing wrong with you that a little good meat to eat and a little help in haying won't fix. Didn't know Ralphie was down here. Ain't he considerable help to you?"

"Hmfff! Ain't no more of a farmer than you be! Swings a snath and scythe like it was a flail swingle! Wants to fritter away all his time 'round the carriage house tinkering up machinery! By fire! I never seen a boy that thought he knowed so tarnal much and could do so little. Telling me to plant strawb'ries and tomatoes! Hmfff! Take a man a year to learn him you can't cut stone with a scythe!"

With Grandfather talking that way about me, I didn't want to go into the kitchen, so I pumped a panful of water and was all ready to wash my hands when Uncle Levi came out into the back pantry. The first thing he did was to reach out to shake hands, and said, "Thomas don't think nobody's a farmer lest he can swing a scythe."

The blisters on my hand hurt when Uncle Levi squeezed it, and I guess I winced just a little. He turned my hand over and looked at it. Then he reached for the other one and looked at it too. "Thomas, what in God's world you been doing with this boy?" he asked sharply.

"Ain't been doing nothing 'cepting to try to learn him how to swing a snath and scythe," Grandfather snapped back.

"Why ain't you put gloves on him? His hands looks like two hunks of half et dog meat."

"Ain't going to have no lily fingered fiddler 'round here! Ain't nothing the matter with them hands that time and work won't cure. Did ever you see a decent dirt farmer wearing gloves?"

I didn't want to hear them wrangling the very first night Uncle Levi was there, so I said, "They'll be all right just as soon as . . ." but Uncle Levi cut me off.

"Thomas, it's a God's wonder . . ." He stopped right there, dropped my hands, and went back into the kitchen. Millie had just put a big slab of steak into the red-hot iron frying pan, and it spluttered and hissed so loud that I didn't hear what Uncle Levi was saying to Grandfather.

They kept wrangling all the time I was washing my face and hands and combing my hair, but they didn't shout as much as they had been. Once I heard Grandfather holler, "Mary sent him down here to be made a man out of and, by thunder, I cal'-late on making him one."

"Just like you done with Frankie," Uncle Levi shouted back. "First thing you know he'll be gone off somewheres to learn a trade."

For a minute, I thought I'd go in and tell them they didn't need to worry, because I was going away right then, but Millie called, "Victuals is ready!" And the steak did smell awfully good.

Millie didn't act at all as she had for the past three days. She had on a pink calico dress that was starched so stiff it could have stood alone, and was as happy as if she were at her own birthday party. As soon as the steak was on the platter, she whisked half a dozen big baked potatoes and a pan of hot biscuits out of the oven, brought a jar of wild strawberry jam from the cellarway, and said, "Sit right down here by the window, Levi. It's a sight for sore eyes to see you down here again. Thomas, he's been feeling poorly since spring. It'll do him a sight of good to have you here for a spell. Don't know when ever I seen a piece of yard goods as pretty as that you fetched me."

"Ain't nothing! Ain't nothing," Uncle Levi grumbled as he pulled his chair up to the table. "Scared something terrible might be the matter with Thomas, and didn't have time to do much shopping. Ralphie, didn't know you was here or I'd have fetched you something."

Grandfather didn't seem a bit hungry when we first sat down at the table. He only took a little corner of steak onto his plate and then kept pushing it around with his knife and fork. Millie scolded at him a bit for not eating, then got a cushion and put it behind his back. She scooped out half a baked potato onto his plate, put gravy from the steak platter on it, and spooned him out some of the strawberry jam, but he still only ate a mouthful or two. After a few minutes, she looked up at Uncle Levi, and said, "Levi, you got any medicine upstairs in your valise?"

She hardly had the words out of her mouth when Grandfather shouted, "Ain't nothing the matter with me! Don't need it! Don't need the tarnal stuff, I tell you! I ain't sick and I ain't tired! I just ain't hungry, that's all."

Neither of them paid a bit of attention to Grandfather. Uncle Levi was in his stockinged feet, and had them up on the little shelf under the table. He let them drop to the floor, pushed his chair back, and said, "Wouldn't surprise me none if there might be a drop or two up there." Then, while Millie unlaced Grandfather's boots and pulled them off, Uncle Levi went padding up the front stairs. I heard a board or two squeak in the chamber where I'd been sleeping and, in a couple of minutes, he came back with a half-empty quart bottle in his hand. There was a broken green sticker over the cork, and a picture of a crow on the label.

Grandfather watched, but he didn't say anything while Millie measured a teaspoon of the whiskey into the glass, put in a heaping spoonful of sugar, and filled the glass with hot water. It smelled good when she set it beside Grandfather's plate. He wrinkled up his nose a little, and grumbled, "Don't need the tarnal stuff! Ain't sick!" But he picked the glass up, and lifted his eyebrows high as he slooped a little sip from the glass.

Millie hadn't given the bottle back to Uncle Levi, but he walked around the table and picked it up. Before he put the cork back in, he turned the bottle up and took a big, long swallow. A couple of dozen little air bubbles went dancing up through the red liquor. He didn't raise his eyebrows the way Grandfather had, but when he took the bottle down he shut his eyes tight and shook his head like a horse with a fly in its ear. Then he took the bottle back upstairs.

While he was gone, Grandfather kept telling me what wicked stuff whiskey was, that the Almighty never planned it for anything but medicine, and where people went who drank it just for fun the way Uncle Levi did. But he kept sipping, too, and smacked his lips after every sip. When it was all gone, he cut himself a piece of steak bigger than the one I had, and he ate it all.

I did the milking and fed the calf while Millie was washing the supper dishes. When I came back into the house Grandfather was dozing at the kitchen table, Old Bess was sitting with her head in his lap, and Uncle Levi was asleep in the high-backed rocking chair. He had his feet up on the hot-water tank at the back of the stove, and the magazine he'd been reading had fallen on his chest. Millie strained the milk and put it away while I was blowing out the lantern and washing my hands. Then she scrubbed her hands until I thought she'd peel the skin off them. She didn't say a word to me until she'd gone to her room, brought out a long flat bolt of checkered gingham, and stood, with the pantry windowpane for a mirror, shaping the end of the cloth over her shoulders and around her neck. "Pretty, ain't it?" she asked at last in a low whisper. "Levi don't never come down, he don't fetch me something pretty."

"Does he come very often?" I whispered back.

"No telling when he'll come or when he'll go. Comes when Thomas is down sick—or when he makes him think so. Goes when they get to squabbling so devilish hard they can't abide one another no longer. Sometimes Levi has to go off back to Boston when he's got a job of work to do. Brick mason. Devilish good one I hear tell. Only man roundabouts can put the linings in glass furnaces."

As she whispered, she wound the checkered gingham back on the flat spool, folded the paper around it, tucked it under her arm, and held both hands out toward me. "Let's see them hands," she said. She took both my hands in hers and turned the palms up toward the lamp. "Devilish sore, ain't they?" she asked. "Why didn't you let on sooner?"

"I didn't let on at all," I told her. "Uncle Levi just happened to notice them when we shook hands."

"Levi notices lots of things a body wouldn't count on."

"They're all right," I said. "They'll toughen up when I soak them in salt water."

"And saleratus. Helps to keep the salt from burning so devilish bad. Sit down at the table while I fix you some."

Grandfather woke up when I sat down at the table. It was a warm night and, though the wood had burned out, the stove had quite a little heat left in it. I'd have wanted to sit near an open window, but Grandfather opened the oven door, drew the other rocking chair up close, and put both feet into the oven.

Then, as he rocked the chair back and forth, he began to tell me about the time the lightning had struck the big barn in the middle of the night and burned it flat to the ground. Uncle Levi was still asleep in the high-backed rocker and, for a few sentences, Grandfather talked above the drone of his snoring. Then his head nodded forward and he was asleep too.

Millie brought the washbasin, half filled with warm water, salt, and soda. As she set it in front of me, she whispered, "Soak 'em good now. I'm going off to bed. You take the corner chamber, next beyond Levi's. It's all ready, and ain't been slept in since I filled the tick anew last husking time. Lamps is filled and ready there on the mantel. Take care Thomas is awake enough so's he don't drop his lamp on the way to bed."

Millie slept downstairs in the parlor, and Grandfather had his room in the other front corner of the house, just off the dining room and next to the parlor. When I'd put my hands to soak, she took the lamp from the pantry, went first to Grandfather's room, and then I heard her moving quietly in the parlor.

After a few minutes, Grandfather's head came up a little way, and he began talking about the fire again. He was still more asleep than awake. His voice was soft, and the words came in little gusts, like the sound of a summer breeze blowing through dry grass. 'Twa'n't long after Frankie . . . Portland . . . learn a trade. Not a critter saved . . . Old Hannibal . . . bellered something awful. Twenty-odd feet shorter'n the big barn." His head jerked right up straight for a minute. He looked over at me, and said, "One day I and you'll build the piece back onto it, Ralphie." He spoke loud enough that he woke Uncle Levi but in another minute they were both snoring again.

The salt water made my hands sting to beat the band for a little while, and every muscle in my body ached, but I was awfully tired. The next thing I knew, Grandfather was shouting, "Levi! Ralphie!"

I must have been sleeping there for a couple of hours, with my hands soaking in the pan and my head resting on the edge of the table. When I opened my eyes, the moon had moved around so it was coming in the south window. Grandfather was yawning and rubbing his bald spot. "Gorry sakes alive," he yawned, "I must have nodded off a minute or two. Come, Levi! It's time all honest folks was abed."

Grandfather was more awake than any of us, so I didn't worry about his carrying his lamp, but lighted two from the mantel and went upstairs with Uncle Levi. His eyes were still only half open when I picked up my suitcase from beside his bed and went on to the next room.

I had just crawled into bed when Uncle Levi pushed open the door between our rooms. He had undressed down to his long underwear, and had a little round nightcap on his head. He had his lamp in his hand, and peered at me from under his eyebrows as though he were looking over the top of glasses. "Sleep tight, boy," he whispered. "Watch out Thomas don't work the tail off you." Then he went back into his own room.

Uncle
Levi

8

New Tricks

THE next morning I did the chores just the way I'd done them every morning since I'd been at Grandfather's. First, I slopped the sow that had the little pigs, fed and watered the hogs in the barn cellar, and curried the bay mare while she ate her corn. Then I tackled the yella colt.

While I'd been dressing I'd decided that I wouldn't start to Colorado for another day or, maybe, two. Before I went, I wanted to let Uncle Levi see that I wasn't quite as useless as Grandfather had told him I was. I couldn't show him very well with a scythe but, if I could keep the yella colt under control, I could show him with the horses.

Maybe I was thinking too much about keeping the yella colt under control when I went into his stall that morning, and maybe I was a little too rough with him. He fought me harder than he ever had, and there were times when I was really frightened before he stopped kicking and put his head down for the bridle. I'd just slipped the bit into his mouth when, from the stall door, Uncle Levi said, "Sort of early to be harnessing up, ain't it?"

I tried to act as if I'd known he was there all the time, but my voice sounded a little shaky when I said, "I wasn't harnessing him for work, but I've got to teach him to stand for harnessing without an hour's fight every morning. As soon as he understands that he won't get any breakfast till it's all over, he'll learn quick enough."

"Kind of hard to learn an old dog new tricks, ain't it?"

"Yes, but he'll learn," I said. "How old is he, anyway? His mouth looks as smooth as a range bull's."

"Been smooth more years than you be old. Let me see. I was sixty-four last spring, and I fetched Old Nancy home the day I turned thirty. Seems to me she didn't have a colt that next year, and foaled the yella colt the following spring. Might be a year later. I ain't real sure. By that time I was off to Dakota, homesteading. How old would that make him?"

"Thirty-one or -two," I said.

"Great day of judgment! Cussed contrary old critter! Born ugly, and never got over it. Calc'late we better get at the rest of the chores afore we have Thomas out here to boss the job. Thomas, he's a little long on the bossing sometimes. Like as not he learnt it when he was a sergeant in the rebellion."

"They're all done, except milking one cow and feeding the calf," I told him, "and Grandfather doesn't want the milking done till six o'clock. I wonder why he doesn't milk the other three cows instead of letting those big calves run with them."

"Thomas?" he said. "If 'twas left for Thomas to do, there wouldn't be no milking. Never heard tell of him milking a cow. Womenfolks always done it. Millie gets her back up at more than one cow to milk. Cussed good girl, Millie. Don't know how Thomas would get on without her." As he spoke, Uncle Levi took his big gold watch out of the bib pocket of his overalls, untied the little leather pouch he kept it in, and said, "Right on the button. Six o'clock, straight up." Then he followed me into the tie-up.

The milk was still ringing off the bottom of the bucket when Uncle Levi brought a little wooden firkin and sat down behind Clara Belle. In a couple of minutes, Old Bess came in and sat down beside him. Then, from one direction and another, the three cats came and sat beside Bess. For two or three minutes, the only sounds were the occasional mewing of a cat and the whisper of the milk streams as they plunged into the foam. The bucket was a third full when I remembered that I hadn't shot the usual squirt of milk at Bess. I reached high on the milk-bag, brought down a big teatful, and turned my fist up toward Bess's head. As the white stream came toward her, she opened her mouth wide and caught it. "There's an old dog that's been taught a new trick," I told Uncle Levi. "She didn't know how to do that when I came down here."

"Clever, ain't she?" was all he said for a minute. Then, "How you and Thomas getting on, Ralphie?"

"Not very well, I guess. Mostly, I've only had hand mowing to do, and I'm not very good at it. Especially, right-handed. I never tried to use a scythe before I came down here, and I can't always make it go right where I want it to. He says I'm more hindrance than help to him, but I worked for a good many different men in Colorado, and they'd all hire me back again. I could always get jobs when most of the other kids in Littleton couldn't."

"Mmmm Hmmm. What's this business about the strawberries and tomatoes?"

"Oh, that? I don't know why he got mad about that. I just told him that I worked for a man in Colorado who raised strawberries and tomatoes."

"Did you?"

"Yes, sir."

"How'd you get along with him?"

"You mean the man that raised the strawberries and tomatoes?"

"Mmmm Hmmm."

"Fine, but I only worked for him when there weren't any cattle jobs. We had a horse, and I could make more driving cattle."

"What did you do for the man?"

"Oh, quite a few different jobs: like picking fruit, and setting out tomato plants in the spring, and setting the new runners on the strawberry plants over for the next year's rows. You know, you don't have to set out new strawberry plants every year. Little new leaves come at the ends of the runners, and you just move them over like wires to where you want the next year's row. Then you put a handful of dirt on the runner—right near the little leaves, but so you don't bury them—and, after the field is irrigated, roots grow down from the new leaves, and then you've got a new plant, and when fall comes you can plow up the old row.

"The man I worked for had a high warm field: just like the one up beyond the orchard that has all the stones on it. It never got late frosts in the spring, and we could set his tomato plants out two weeks earlier than anybody else could set theirs out. So his tomatoes were always the first ones to ripen anywhere around Denver, and he used to get as much as ten cents a pound for them."

I was going to tell him why we always had the earliest strawberries too, but he said, "You done pretty good with the yella colt this morning. Who learned you to handle hosses?"

"Oh, Father and quite a few other men; Hi Beckman, and Mr. Batchlett. Hi taught me how to break and train a cow horse, but Mr. Batchlett was more of a trader. He taught me some of the tricks about balky horses, and I've been using one of them on the yella colt. It works all right. I just tie his ears together good and tight with a piece of soft wire. Then, after I've let him stand and shake his head till he's only thinking about his ears, and has forgotten he's balking, I cluck to him and he walks right along. I think I'll have him cured of balking altogether pretty soon."

"Shame the Almighty stood a man's ears on his head the way he did, ain't it? Makes 'em so cussed hard to wire together. Here's the pan for your cat's milk; you been dry-stripping there for the past five minutes."

By the time I had the calf fed and had gone to the house, breakfast was all on the table. The spicy smell of frying sausage

met me at the door of the summer kitchen. Millie was whisking
a pan of hot biscuits out of the oven, and called to me to get my
face and hands washed as fast as the Lord would let me. Grandfather and Uncle Levi were already in their places at the table
when I'd finished washing, and Uncle Levi was curling the ends
of his big mustache, and smacking his lips the way Mother did
when she was tasting her new batch of mincemeat.

The breakfast was really something to smack your lips over.
Instead of the oatmeal and fried salt pork we'd had every other
morning, there was a platter loaded with fried eggs and good
big sausage cakes, a nappy of fried potatoes, a plate of hot biscuits, and a jar of wild strawberry jam. Most of the talk during
breakfast was about people Uncle Levi knew but hadn't seen
for a long time. I'd never heard of any of them, so I paid most of
my attention to biscuits, sausage, and eggs. Just as I was finishing my fourth egg and sixth biscuit, Millie got up and opened
the oven door. As she gathered up the corners of her apron for
holders, and brought out a high crusted pie, she snapped,
"There's your devilish old apple pie, Levi! Never seen a man
that sot such store on pie for breakfast. It don't look to be up to
my usual."

Millie sounded as cranky as she did sometimes when she was
scolding at me, but it didn't worry Uncle Levi. He bounced out
of his chair as if there had been a spring in it, threw both arms
around Millie's neck, and danced her around in a circle. "Levi!
Levi!" she kept squawking. "Good Lord sakes alive, what ails
you? You ain't been nipping at that bottle a'ready this morning,
have you? Leave me be, Levi, afore you get my hair a-looking
like a rat's nest."

Uncle Levi took one arm loose, pulled Millie up tight against
his hip, and spanked her a good sharp one. "That'll learn you
not to sass your elders," he told her as he swung her around
again, but they were both laughing when they came back to the
table.

If there was anything the matter with the apple pie, I didn't
find it, and nobody else seemed to either. Grandfather was only

half finished with his sausage and eggs, but he pushed his plate right back, and dished a big slab of hot pie onto his tea saucer. He seemed to have caught some of Uncle Levi's excitement and, as he waved his knife with a mouthful of pie on it, sang out, "By gorry, Levi, we'll make the hay fly now! With three stout hands of us, we'll have it all fetched into the mows come Sunday fortnight. I and Ralphie'll grind the scythes whilst you're putting new teeth in the handsweeps."

I'd never seen handsweeps, and I didn't think much of them when I did see them. They were hay rakes about four feet wide, with eight-inch wooden teeth, and a handle that looked like a short, slim wagon tongue. The ones Grandfather had must have been a hundred years old. The handles had been worn thin, they were weathered almost black, a quarter of the teeth were broken, and, where bolts were missing, they were hitched together with rusty wire. When Grandfather got them down from the carriage house attic, Uncle Levi's mouth went the way it did when he was looking at the breakfast, then he almost hollered, "By hub, Thomas, why in tarnation don't you take a little care with your tools? It's a God's wonder they hold together 'twixt one time and another when I come down here."

Grandfather yelled back from the attic, "They held together all right whilst you was off homesteading in Dakota. By fire, if you don't want to fix 'em, go off and do something else. I and . . ."

I didn't want to be there if they were going to fight, so I wandered off toward the barn. The blisters on my hands were pretty sore, and I didn't feel as if it would be a bit of fun to drag one of those handsweeps all around the orchard. I'd noticed a couple of broken-down old horserakes lying with the other junk machinery out behind the sheep barn, and I went down there to look them over.

One of them was a complete wreck. It looked as if it had been run over by a freight train, but the other wasn't too bad. One of the wheels was smashed, the tongue was broken, five or six teeth were missing, and it had been robbed of nuts and bolts. I looked it all over carefully, and there didn't seem to be much the matter with it that couldn't be fixed in a few hours. One of the wheels on the wrecked one was in pretty good shape; just bent a little, but it could be heated and hammered straight. The funny thing was that the lift handle was missing from both machines, and somebody had taken the trip gears off the better one and put them back onto the wrong ends of the axle.

When I went back to the carriage house, Uncle Levi had split a maple block into little sticks that looked like kindling. He'd pushed the junk on the bench back a way from the vise, had one of the little sticks in it, and was shaping it carefully with a spoke shave. Grandfather had driven the broken-off teeth out of the sweeps and, just as I came into the carriage house, he snapped, "Let be! Let be, Levi! Time flies! Just whittle the shanks down a dite and drive 'em home tight!"

I only let Uncle Levi get as far as, "Thomas, it's a God's wonder . . ." before I said, "Couldn't we fix up one of those old horserakes down by the sheep barn about as easy as to make new teeth for the handsweeps? There's one of them down there that doesn't look too bad, and . . ."

"Worthless! Worthless!" Grandfather hollered at me. "Ain't nothing but junk!" Then he let his voice down, almost to a whisper, and his whiskers moved up so I knew he was smiling. "Got 'em to boot in a couple of heifer trades. Cal'late they'll fetch five-six dollars from a junk peddler."

Uncle Levi laid the spoke shave down so that the cutting edge was against the board wall. He'd put his glasses on, and he peered up over them when he asked me, "Did you look 'em over careful, Ralphie?"

I just nodded, and Uncle Levi started out the doorway. I went with him as far as the corner of the barn, while Grandfather shouted after us, "They ain't no good, I tell you, Levi! Ain't nary one of 'em worth a tinker! I tried mending one of 'em myself, but it won't work. Worthless! Worthless, I tell you! Ralphie! Ralphie!"

Uncle Levi didn't pay any attention until Grandfather called my name. Then he stopped, and said to me, "Ain't no God's wonder it don't work if Thomas tried to fix it. You better go back there afore he blows a gasket."

Grandfather scolded me plenty for mentioning the horse-rakes to Uncle Levi, and told me to keep my long nose out of things that were none of my business. Then he had me turn the grindstone while he sharpened the scythes, and he bore down on them so hard that the stone turned like a windlass.

Uncle Levi was gone quite a while, but when he came back he didn't say a word about the horserakes. He just began raising the dickens about all the junk on the top of the workbench. Just as we were finishing the second scythe, he slammed things around on the bench, and shouted, "By hub, Thomas, I ain't go-ing to fix your cussed sweeps nor another tarnation thing around here till I got a decent place to work! And I don't lay out to clean the junk off this bench myself neither! It's a God's wonder you ain't fetched home every dump 'twixt here and Bangor! Where in tunket did you get it all? Auctions?"

"It's all good stuff! It's all good stuff, I tell you!" Grandfather shouted back.

"Ain't worth a tinker; none of it! Can't find a usable nut or bolt no place amongst it! If you want them sweeps mended I'll have to go to the Falls and get some stove bolts for 'em."

"Wastin'! Wastin'!" Grandfather exploded. "There's plenty good nuts and bolts right there at your hand. Throwed 'em there myself just t'other day. If you can't find 'em, Ralphie'll find 'em for you." Then he slammed the sharpened scythe blade onto the floor and stamped out of the carriage house.

As soon as Grandfather had gone, Uncle Levi winked at me. "Kind of balky on us fixing up that cussed hossrake, wa'n't he? And we ain't going to be able to tie his ears together neither. Calc'late we got to cook up some other way around it. Let's see now. Tomorrow is the Sabbath, ain't it? Thomas, he has his troubles with the Sabbath. It's agin his scruples to work on it, and he won't set you a job of work to do on it—that is, excepting chores. And sometimes he's a mite careless 'bout the line where chores leaves off and a job of work begins. Never heard tell of him raising much ruction if somebody done him a job of work on the Sabbath without him knowing of it. Might happen we could get Thomas out of the way tomorrow, and run a little hossrake mending in on the chores."

"It's going to take a lot of nuts and bolts and things to fix it," I said. "Do you think I'll find enough of the right kind among the stuff here on the bench?"

"What you think I'm going to the village for? I got plenty stove bolts for the sweeps right down there in that locked drawer." As he spoke, Uncle Levi unbuttoned the cuff on one of his shirt sleeves. When he turned it back, the inside was all marked over with figures. "There they be," he told me. "Don't allow I missed so much as cotter pin or washer. Keep your nose clean while I'm gone, and don't rare into this mess of junk too hard. It'll take a month of Sundays to get it all sorted out. I was scared Thomas would set you to mowing, and your hands ain't fit for it right now."

It was more than two hours before Uncle Levi came back from Lisbon Falls. By that time, I'd made a pretty good hole in the stuff on the workbench, and Grandfather hadn't once come up from whatever he was doing down at the beehives. He did come up when Uncle Levi drove back into the yard, and was standing by the front wheel of the spring wagon when I went to unhitch Old Nell. "There you be, Thomas," Uncle Levi said, as he passed the reins to me and a flat package to Grandfather. "Them ought to hold smoke enough to make every bee in Lisbon township peaceable. Seen 'em when I was looking for carriage bolts, and calc'lated you might have some good use to put 'em to."

"Gorry sakes! Gorry sakes alive, Levi!" Grandfather sang out, as he fumbled a little bellows out of the package. It was made of brown leather, with bright tips and handles. "Shouldn't ought to have spent so much money on a tarnal pair of bellows. Little court plaster would have mended up the old ones so's they'd do me all right. Gorry sakes alive! Ain't them beauties! Ralphie, you unhitch the hoss whilst I go set my smoke pot a-burning. I got a . . ." By that time he was so far toward the bee shop that I couldn't hear what he was saying.

Uncle Levi winked at me again. "Calc'lated he might have a few bees that would need some smoking about now. No sense starting into the fields afore noon, and this'll give us time to do a decent job on them handsweeps." I'd noticed a good-sized box under the seat, with a Lewiston Sunday paper laid in over the top. There was a roll of something wrapped in brown paper. It was about three feet long and as big around as my head. Uncle Levi climbed down, rolled the round package out from under the seat, and pulled the box to the edge of the wagon. "Found about everything we'll need, 'cepting histe handle and shafts, and I allow we're smart enough betwixt us to make them out of hardwood. I'll fetch this stuff to the carriage house while you unharness Old Nell."

I was just leading her away toward the barn when he called, "Hold up a minute, Ralphie! By hub, I come nigh forgetting it. I fetched you something for them sore hands. Catch!" He tossed a package, and as it wobbled toward me, end over end, a pair of brown gloves spilled out right at my feet. They were as soft as a woman's kid gloves, and as smooth as satin, both inside and out. When I tried to tell him how much I liked them, he grumbled, "No thank you's; no thank you's! Got 'em for you; not for thank you's," and went off to the carriage house.

9

Uncle Levi Teaches Me to Swing a Scythe

As I unharnessed Old Nell, I told myself that, after my promise to Mrs. Littlehale, it wouldn't be honest of me to leave Grandfather until he had all his hay in. But, all the time I knew I was going to stay because I liked to work with Uncle Levi. The box he'd brought from the village was nowhere in sight when I hurried back to the carriage house, but he was down on his hands and knees, rolling the other package way back under the workbench. "Screen wire for Millie," he said when he looked up and saw me. "Flies in the house like to drive her crazy. Been yammering at me for going on five-six years but, with one thing and another when I been down, I never got around to making 'em."

"If the horserake doesn't take any longer than I think it will, maybe we can start on them tomorrow," I said.

"Mayhaps! Mayhaps! But, first, we got to see what we can do with Thomas. He ain't going to sit around here peaceable while we're fixing up that hossrake. Thomas, he don't cotton to machinery. Wouldn't have that cussed old rattletrap of a mowing machine around here if he could hire hand mowers. Good scythe men is getting hard to find."

"He has quite a little trouble keeping any kind of men, doesn't he?" I asked.

For the first time, Uncle Levi looked at me as if he was peeved. Before he answered, he shoved the roll of screen wire to the farthest corner under the bench, and climbed to his feet. By the time he was up, he seemed more sad than mad. He reached one hand out and laid it on my shoulder but, instead of looking at me, he looked out across the fields. "Thomas never learnt to get along with other folks," he said at last. " 'Tain't that he don't like 'em, Ralphie. He does. There ain't a man living with more love in him than what Thomas has. Worshipped Father to the longest day he lived. No man ever loved the land more'n Thomas loves this old farm—every stone and stump of it. You seen him with critters; tender as ary woman. But he has a devilish hard time showing it to people. A crossgrain in the timber someplace. Treats worst them he likes best. Ain't you heard him jaw and row at Millie?"

"She jaws and rows at him just about as bad," I said.

"Being around Thomas, it gets to be a habit. There's times it's tarnation hard not to row back at him."

I knew that, but I didn't want to say it, so I said, "I don't think Millie likes anybody but you very well."

"Millie?" he said. "Why do you calc'late she's put up with Thomas all these years? Millie don't like strangers. Fetched up that way. Her mother lived like a hermit—way up on Rocky Dundy, t'other side Lisbon Village."

"Was her father a hermit too?" I asked.

"Don't nobody know. Her mother married a man off to Portland when Millie come to work for Thomas."

Uncle Levi jerked his hand down off my shoulder. "Great day of judgment!" he said. "Here we stand gossiping like a pair of widow women. This ain't mending handsweeps, is it? Mark them pieces of clear pine racked up beneath the ceiling? Them's for Millie's screen frames; had 'em all ripped out and ready to put together four-five-six years now." He chuckled a few notes behind his mustache. "Have to devil her a little 'bout the flies, come dinner time."

Before we started on the handsweeps, Uncle Levi fished a ring of keys out of his overalls' pocket and unlocked the drawers on the right-hand side of the workbench. The top two were filled with tools. There was a place made for each one, and they were all in their places. Every metal part was covered with a film of oil, and there wasn't a rust spot anywhere. The two lower drawers were divided into sections, with sliding trays, and each section held a different size of nut, bolt, screw, or washer. "Have to keep 'em locked up," he told me, "else Thomas would have 'em scattered from Dan to Beersheba. It's a God's wonder when he can lay his hand on a wrench. Drops 'em whereever he uses 'em; got four-five-half-a-dozen planted in every cussed field on the place. Now you can go to cutting shanks on these teeth, if you've a mind to, while I turn 'em down with the spoke shave. Set your calipers a dite bigger'n the hole so's they'll fit good and snug."

I felt terrible when I had to say, "I'm sorry, but I don't know what calipers are."

"Little fellow there in the top drawer," he told me. "Looks like a bowlegged cowboy. That's the one. Open and close the spraddle with that little burr nut on the side. That's the ticket. Set it just a dite bigger'n the holes in the sweep rail."

As soon as I saw it, I remembered that Father used to have one like it in his tool chest. I could remember having seen him use it before I ever started school. He'd made an old sewing machine over into a wood lathe, with a big flywheel and spindles. When he turned things on it, he used to measure them with the caliper. As I set the width of the hole, I could see that old lathe of Father's as plainly as if I'd been looking back ten days instead of ten years. The flywheel was big—almost like a grindstone—and he got it going fast with the foot treadles before he began to cut with the chisels. I could remember his making Mother a whatnot with it. I'd stepped back from the handsweep, and was looking at Grandfather's grindstone, when Uncle Levi asked, "What's biting you, Ralphie? What you trying to figure out?"

"Nothing," I said, "I was just remembering about a wood lathe Father once built out of an old sewing machine. It had a flywheel that looked like a grindstone. He'd get it turning real fast with the foot treadles, and then he'd turn out any shape he wanted with a chisel."

"Hmff!" Uncle Levi said, came over, and gave the grindstone handle a twist. Then he shut one eye and watched it as it twirled around. "Hmff!" he said again. " 'Pears to run pretty even. There's treadles for it someplace; Thomas never uses 'em. Never grinds nothing less'n there's some poor devil to turn the crank." He looked along the wall over the top of his glasses. "There they be! S'posing we set it to spinning and see how true the center runs."

We put the treadles on, and I got the stone whirling as fast as I could make my feet go. "True as gospel," Uncle Levi said, as he squinted at it, "so long as you don't push it too hard and make it gallop. Let me see now. 'Bout all we're going to need is a dead center and a spring to hold it close up agin. I'll file that bolt end into a hold-chuck while you hunt a spring. Get a good stout one; 'bout six or eight inches long."

Within an hour, we'd rigged a little makeshift lathe onto the grindstone. It worked fine for the handsweep teeth, and Uncle Levi was careful to make every one of them just alike. After he'd calipered one of the shanks, he looked up at me, and said, "Charlie must have been a pretty good mechanic."

"He was," I said. "Father could make anything he wanted to out of anything he had."

"Calc'late you take after him," he said, and ran the chisel smoothly along the piece of kindling as he shaped the tooth. If he'd asked me right then to jump off the peak of the barn, I'd have been glad to do it for him.

We had the handsweeps fixed just as good as new, when Millie called dinner. And it was a good dinner, too, with a big piece of corned beef, boiled potatoes, cabbage, johnnycake, and another apple pie. It was a hot day, the windows were open, and there were quite a few flies in the kitchen. We weren't any more than down at the table before Uncle Levi began swatting at them and shooing them off the corned beef. "Great day of judgment!" he snapped, as if they were worrying him to death. "Flies so tarnation thick around here a man has to blow his victuals afore the flies does! Millie, it's a God's wonder you wouldn't spread a little molasses on a piece of brown paper and catch these pesky things. How's a man going to enjoy his victuals when he daresn't open his mouth for fear of getting a fly in it?" Then he turned his head so he could wink at me without her seeing him.

"Molasses, hmff!" Millie snapped right back at him. "How many hogsheads of molasses you cal'late it would take to catch all the devilish flies in Lisbon township? Ain't nothing to stop 'em coming in here, is there? It's your own cussed fault if you don't like flies. Where's them screens you been promising me ever since I come to this infernal flytrap?"

"Flytrap! Flytrap!" Grandfather exploded. "Who says it's a flytrap? This house ain't never had a screen on it, and for more'n a hundred years it's been good enough for all the other women-folks that's lived in it. Screens, hmff! Tarnal nuisances! Won't have 'em! Won't have 'em, I tell you! If this house ain't good enough for you just like it is, go somewheres else! Screens, hmff!"

Grandfather's rowing must have made the old red rooster curious. He flew up onto the window sill behind Uncle Levi, and twisted his head from side to side as he looked around the kitchen. I didn't want the wrangle about screens to go any further, so I said, "We've got a visitor."

"Great day of judgment!" Uncle Levi sang out, as he turned toward the rooster. "By hub, there's one smart critter on the place! First day I been here, and a'ready he knows there's something more than salt pork on the table."

"Ain't nothing the matter with salt pork!" Grandfather

snapped, but I noticed that he'd taken a good big slice of corned beef.

"Ain't nothing the matter with bread and water," Uncle Levi said, as he cut a little piece of corned beef and spread hot mus-

tard on it, "but it's devilish poor belly stuffing for a man in a hayfield. There you be, Beelzebub! That'll put a curl in your tail feathers."

The old rooster leaned forward and grabbed the piece of corned beef off the end of Uncle Levi's fork. It was a small mouthful for a man, but a big one for a rooster. He had to make two tries before he could swallow it and, each time, he ran his neck out like a goose reaching through a fence. Then he cocked his head to one side, clicked his bill—so that it sounded almost exactly the way Uncle Levi's lips had when he looked at the breakfast—and shook his head like a dog with water in its ears. For a minute, he stood blinking his eyes, as if he were trying to make up his mind whether the corned beef was worth the mustard. Then he turned toward the hens in the dooryard, and called, "Tuck-tuck-tuck-tuck-tuck." Before Millie brought the pie, Uncle Levi had fed the rooster a dozen pieces or more of corned beef, and he put a good dollup of hot mustard on every one of them, but nobody mentioned screens again.

We had a pretty good afternoon, working in the orchard. Grandfather scolded me two or three times for being awkward or slow, but most of the time Uncle Levi kept me working with him. We took both scythes and the three handsweeps with us, but Grandfather didn't use the sweeps very much. When we climbed over the stonewall from the pasture lane, he was as excited as a race horse at the starting post. "By gorry, Ralphie," he called out, "I and you'll show 'em what kind of logs makes wide shingles! Come on, Levi! We'll get her all in the windrow afore supper time." He dropped his scythe in the long grass by the wall, grabbed one of the sweeps I had over my shoulder, and began flinging hay like a hen scratching for corn.

Uncle Levi didn't say anything, but picked up Grandfather's scythe and kept walking slowly toward the nearest tree. I didn't know just what I ought to do, but I wanted to be with Uncle Levi, so I started to follow him. I'd only gone a few yards when Grandfather called, "Ralphie! Ralphie! Time flies! Pitch in here alongside of me!"

I should have watched to see how Grandfather was handling the sweep, but I didn't. They looked to me like little horserakes, and I had supposed that you'd drag them the same way, so I set mine down at the edge of the field and began pulling it along. "What in time and tarnation you trying to do now," Grandfather yelled after me; "play hoss? Get your backsides behind you and go at it man fashion!"

It made me madder to have him scold me when Uncle Levi was there than when we were alone. My whole head felt as if it were catching afire, and I had just snapped out, "I'm not . . ." when Uncle Levi called, "Thomas, the grass under these trees is still greener'n a gourd. Tomorrow is the Sabbath, and if it ain't got out where the sun can get at it, it'll sour on the ground afore Monday."

" 'Tain't no wonder! 'Tain't no wonder!" Grandfather called back, as he dropped his sweep and almost ran toward the trees. "Ralphie mowed under that one, and he wabbed the grass all up into hog wallows. Never seen a boy so helpless with a snath and scythe."

Unless I dragged it, I was about as helpless with a handsweep as with a scythe but, while Grandfather and Uncle Levi stood talking under the apple tree, I did the best I could. After a few minutes, they walked on to another tree or two. Then Grandfather took his scythe and hurried off to some trees that we hadn't mowed under at the far side of the orchard. He hadn't been gone two minutes before Uncle Levi called, "Ralphie." His voice was just loud enough to reach me.

I put my sweep on my shoulder and went over where he was. He wasn't hurrying at all. He sort of rolled from side to side as he stepped forward, and his arms and the big rake moved back and forth in perfect rhythm. After a little while, he noticed me watching him, and said, "Slow and steady goes far in a day, Ralphie. Thomas, he's a fast starter, but he peters out tolerable quick. With one of these cussed things, it's a waste of time to hurry. Take care Thomas don't set you too fast a pace, Ralphie. You ain't had all your growth yet."

I was three or four inches taller than Uncle Levi, and I didn't like being called Ralphie. I couldn't come right out and say so, but I thought that gave me a pretty good chance to drop a little hint, so I said, "I'm fourteen and a half now, but I guess Grandfather thinks I'm still a little boy. He always calls me Ralphie." Then I picked up my handsweep and swung it, just as near as I could, the way Uncle Levi was doing.

He stopped raking as soon as I had started, and stood, leaning on the handle of his sweep and watching me. "Hmmm, hmmm,

you're lucky," he grumbled. "Storekeeper told Father he'd give
me a suit of clothes when I growed up if they'd name me Levi.
I been wearing the cussed name for sixty-four years, but I never
did get the suit of clothes." A couple of minutes later, he said,
"Getting the hang of that sweep pretty good, ain't you, Ralph?
It's slow and easy does it."

"Well, it's still kind of awkward," I said, "but I guess I can
get it; it's the scythe that I can't learn to use."

"Don't know 'bout that," Uncle Levi told me. " 'Pears to me
you could learn most anything you had a mind to. That is, if
you didn't rare into it too hard. S'posing you let me see you
try it."

On my first swing, the blade tangled in the grass and jerked
to a stop. "I could do it better with the left-handed scythe," I
said. "I've always been left-handed."

"Got to learn, either way," Uncle Levi told me. "Might just
as well learn right-handed in the first place. There's a devilish
lot more right-handed scythes in the world than there is left-
handed ones. Devilish lot more right-handed people, too. Ain't
never a bad idea to learn to do things the way most other folks
does 'em. Leave me have hold of that cussed thing a minute."

I stood back and watched while Uncle Levi mowed a strip
ten or twelve feet long. "Take note that you don't hold the snath
so's the scythe is straight out from you like the row of teeth on
a handsweep. Keep the point of the blade close in to you all the
while. Leave your wrists go a trifle loose and it won't histe up so
much on the ends of the swing. I ain't good at this myself, but
sometime you watch Thomas—when he ain't out to set you
a pace. Father bent him a little snath and learned him to mow
afore he was belly-high to a bull. Ain't many men can best
Thomas at anything Father learnt him to do. Now you try your
hand at it a spell."

Uncle Levi never told me I was awkward, and he never
scolded. He just followed along beside me for ten or fifteen
minutes, and showed me where I was making mistakes. "Don't
reach too far neither way. Get your tail end around towards the

sun, so's you can keep an eye on that shadow and watch that your head don't swing. Don't try to hold your behind still; let it travel as much as it's a mind to. Turn that right hand down, so's you can only see the knuckles as it goes apast in front of you. That holds the point down and keeps the stubble even. Roll your right thumb up when you want to histe the blade over a rock. You're trying too hard. Ease up a dite, and fetch it across with a limber wrist. There! That's more like it! Take note how the scythe point is hugging along the ground. By hub, you got the trick of it now, Ralph."

I still couldn't mow anything like the way Grandfather and Uncle Levi could, but the scythe didn't get stuck any more, and I wasn't hitting the stones. "Cut them hogs in the barn cellar an armful of clover every night, and 'twon't be long afore you can swing a scythe as good as any man," Uncle Levi told me. "We better get back to raking now. First thing we know, we'll have Thomas over here raising ructions. Like as not, the way he started off, he's mowed under half a dozen trees by now."

Grandfather had finished mowing under his fourth tree when we went back to our rakes, but he was nowhere in sight. His handsweep was still in the corner of the orchard, where he'd dropped it, and his scythe was laid up on the stonewall by the gateway. "Never seen a man just like Thomas," Uncle Levi said, as he picked up his sweep. "Works in fits and starts. Rares into it like a gale of wind for half, maybe three quarters of an hour. Then he's off to tend the bees or look what's come in the mailbox. He'll be here and gone half a dozen times afore the day's over."

Uncle Levi was just right about Grandfather. We never saw him leave but, two or three times, we saw him coming back across the field from the barn. He'd pick up his scythe, mow under three or four more trees, and then disappear. Twice, he stopped by a tree where we were working and, both times, he told me we'd never get finished till snow flew if I didn't stop my dawdling.

Each time, as soon as Grandfather had left us, Uncle Levi

told me that slow and steady went far in a day. And by the time the sun dipped down behind the pine woods on the ridge, we'd finished raking under the last tree in the orchard.

At supper time, it was easy to see that Grandfather was pretty well tired out. We had red flannel hash: potatoes, beets, carrots, and cabbage chopped up with the corned beef that was left from dinner and fried till it was dark reddish-brown on both sides. Grandfather took just a little dab on his plate, and he only ate a mouthful or two until Uncle Levi brought his bottle and Millie made a hot toddy. He grumbled about not needing it, the same as he had the night before, but he took it, and he ate a pretty good supper afterwards.

When I came in from milking, Grandfather had his feet in the oven, and Uncle Levi was reading the Lewiston Sunday paper. He had his glasses balanced on the end of his nose, and was leaning back in his rocker, with both feet up on the hot-water tank of the stove. Grandfather was nodding, half asleep, when I took the sports page of the paper and sat down at the kitchen table to read it. Uncle Levi kept interrupting every few minutes. At first, it was something about somebody's funeral, or a baby being born, or about a horse running away. Then, as he turned the pages over, it was ads for things people wanted to sell: a live goose featherbed, a chest of drawers, or a two-row cultivator. After each of the first few items, Grandfather would say, "Too bad, ain't it?" or "Who be they; never heard tell of 'em." But, after a while, his head didn't even bob and, every now and then, he'd snore a few notes.

I'd stopped hearing the stuff myself until, suddenly, Uncle Levi asked in a good loud voice, "What kind of bees is blackbelts, Thomas?"

Grandfather's head came up with a snap. "Blackbelts? Blackbelts?" he said. "Best tarnal bee there is! What about 'em?"

"Oh, nothing," Uncle Levi told him, as he turned the page, "just seen an ad here where somebody wants to trade off a couple of colonies of 'em for a heifer calf. Don't calc'late they could amount to much if he'd trade 'em for a heifer calf."

"Where does he live at? Leave me see that paper!" Grandfather snapped, and pulled his feet out of the oven.

"Way off t'other side of Lewiston," Uncle Levi told him, and went right on looking at the paper. " 'Tain't worth looking at, Thomas. Take a man three-four hours to drive over there and like as not, he'd find the bees was traded off afore he got there."

"Pass me that paper! Pass me that paper, Levi! Where in time and tarnation did I leave my spectacles?"

I got Grandfather's glasses from the mantel. As I gave them to him Uncle Levi passed over the paper. One of his eyelids flickered just a trifle as he looked past my face.

Grandfather buried his head in the outstretched paper for a minute or two, then glanced up at the clock, and said, "Gorry sakes alive! Time flies! Come on, Levi, it's time all honest folks was abed."

10

Slow and Easy Goes Far in a Day

I'D EXPECTED that we might sleep a little later on Sunday morning than on weekdays, but Millie came in and woke me before it was hardly light enough to see across my room. She was in her stockinged feet, and didn't call me, but shook me a little by the shoulder. "Get up! Get up, Ralphie," she whispered when I opened my eyes. "Thomas wants you, but he don't want Levi woke up. Victuals is almost on the table." Then she tiptoed out through Uncle Levi's room without even making a floor board squeak.

I pulled my overalls, socks, and shirt on, took my shoes in my hand, and sneaked quietly out through Uncle Levi's room. Grandfather was already at the table. He had a pretty good-looking felt hat and a gray suit on, and was eating a bowl of oatmeal as fast as he could swing the spoon.

"Get your victuals into you just as fast as you can, Ralphie," he told me when I came into the kitchen. "I got to go right off to Lewiston this morning, and there ain't no time for dawdling over the victuals. I give Old Nell her provender a'ready, and I'll have her harnessed by the time you get to the barn." He pushed his chair back, got up, and, as he went out through the back pantry, called, "Fetch a stout piece of rope out of the carriage house whenst you go past."

Grandfather was in a dither when I got to the barn. He had the harness nearly on Old Nell and, the minute I came into the doorway, snapped, "Stir your stivvers! Stir your stivvers, Ralphie! Fetch Marthy's heifer calf out and load it on the spring wagon. Who in time and tarnation has been meddling with this tarnal harness? It's all tangled up."

Martha's calf was pretty good sized. It weighed at least a hundred and fifty pounds, and it didn't want to leave Martha. But I'd had quite a little experience with calves in Colorado. I tossed a loop of the rope around the base of the calf's tail, put an arm around her neck, and started to lead her out to the wagon. Everything would have been all right if Grandfather hadn't come to help me. He slammed the tie-up door back into my face just as I was putting a hand up to open it. I was leaning over a little to keep my arm around the calf's neck, and my head was sticking out in front—sort of like a turtle's. When the door hit me, I lost my balance, but I held onto the calf tight, and we both went down together. "What in time and tarnation you trying to do with that calf?" Grandfather shouted at me from the doorway. "Get up! Get up and leave her alone, I tell you! What you think this is; a wild West show? Turn her loose, I tell you!"

I didn't have to turn the calf loose. She jerked her head out from under me, scrambled to her feet, and raced off down the tie-up, bawling. Grandfather didn't bother with me any more, but went running after the calf. "Catch her! Catch her! Head her off!" he was shouting before I was hardly back on my feet. The more he hollered, the more he frightened the calf. She ducked in and out among the stanchioned cows like a cat having a fit. Every cow in the barn had started bellowing, the calf was bawling, and, above the hubbub, I could hear Grandfather yelling, "Tarnal fool boy! Don't stand there gawking! Help me catch her! We ain't got all day, I tell you!"

After two steeplechases around the tie-up, the calf stuck her

head between old Martha's hind legs, slipped, and fell into the
scupper. Before she could get up, I was on top of her. "Don't
hurt her. Don't hurt her, Ralphie," Grandfather was saying as
he came running over. "Handle her gentle. You got her half

scairt to death a'ready. Leave us histe her up careful and fetch
her out to the wagon."

We might as well have tried to carry a full-grown cow as that
frightened calf. And besides, she was sort of slippery from falling into the scupper. Grandfather wouldn't let me hog-tie her,
and he wouldn't even twist her tail a little, so she wouldn't hang
back when I tried to lead her. It was nearly half an hour before
we had her boosted into the wagon. We were both pretty well
messed up, and Grandfather had called me a tarnal fool boy at
least a dozen times. I was so mad when he drove out of the yard

that I wanted to throw something after him. I was still mad when I went into the house for the milk bucket. I didn't say a word to Millie; just grabbed the bucket in one hand, the swill pail in the other, and went out to do the morning chores.

Uncle Levi was downstairs when I carried the milk to the house, and he was as happy as a meadow lark. He had on one of Millie's aprons over his overalls and, as he cut oranges and bananas into a bowl at the pantry table, was singing, "Around and 'round the cobbler's bench, the monkey chased the weasel." Every time he'd come to, "POP! goes the weasel," he'd throw a banana or an orange peel at the empty swill pail. Millie seemed just about as happy as Uncle Levi. She was at the stove, frying eggs and watching a pan of biscuits in the oven. Every time Uncle Levi sang out, "POP," she'd rap the edge of the frying pan with the turner.

I was still so mad and messed up that their playing sounded silly to me. I stopped in the summer kitchen, took my shoes off, and set the pail of milk inside the pantry doorway. Then I went to the sink to wash. "By hub, Ralph, we'll get an early start on that hossrake chore," Uncle Levi called out to me between the pops. "Wa'n't it lucky running onto that bee-trade ad? I spied it out while you was gone for the cows last night. It's a God's wonder you ever got Thomas started off from here. What was you doing so long with that cussed calf?" And then he started with, "Around and 'round," again.

"Loading it," was all I said, as I pulled my shirt sleeves up and started to wash.

Uncle Levi stopped singing, I heard Millie come to the pantry doorway, then I could feel them both standing there and looking at my back. Millie was the first one to make a sound. She sort of snickered, and said, "Ain't a mite het up, be you, Ralphie?"

"My name isn't Ralphie; it's Ralph," I told her, and I wasn't a bit careful to make it sound pleasant.

"Great day of judgment," Uncle Levi chuckled. "What did you; mop down the tie-up with that calf afore you loaded her?"

"No," I said. "She fell," and went right on washing.

"Calc'late Thomas give you a little help; or was it hindrance?"

"Hindrance," I said, and scooped a double handful of soap-suds onto my face.

Uncle Levi had stopped chuckling. "By hub," he said, "I never seen a man could get a critter so het up as Thomas can! Can't lead a hoss to water without getting him atop the backhouse at least once!"

Buttons clicked on a chair seat behind me, and Millie said, "There's some clean clothes, *Ralph*. Better get into 'em afore you come to the table. Victuals is all ready."

All through breakfast, Millie and Uncle Levi kept joshing each other, but I didn't feel like joshing. And I didn't have very much to say while we were picking out the tools and carrying them down to the old hayrake. We'd just propped up the end that had the crumpled wheel when Uncle Levi said, "Thomas must have got you about as het up as he did the calf this morning. What happened?"

"Nothing," I said.

"Get it off your stomach, Ralph," he told me. "It's the things he keeps down that poisons a man; not the things he gets rid of."

"Well, I might be a fool," I said, "but I don't like to be told it forty times in five minutes."

"A tarnal fool?" Uncle Levi asked, and winked at me.

"Yes, a tarnal fool. And I don't like it."

Uncle Levi chuckled a little. "I didn't, neither, when I was a boy. Used to make me so cussed mad I 'd want to skin Thomas alive. Afore he went off to the war, I used to ache for the day I'd be big enough to lick him." Uncle Levi straightened up and patted his fat belly. "Calc'late I started this bread basket on its way afore I was ten years old; stuffing it with victuals so's I'd grow bigger than what Thomas was."

"Did you ever lick him?" I asked.

"Can't say as ever I did. Time he come back from the war, I was a trifle bigger than him, but he had malaria. Ain't been in the best of health since."

"It's a wonder somebody hasn't licked him, if he goes around calling everybody a tarnal fool."

"Licks hisself. Calc'late it's cost poor Thomas many a dollar and many a friend. Recollect hearing my half-sister, Eunice, tell of his saying it afore he was knee high to a toad. Father thought 'twas clever."

"Well, I don't think it's clever now," I said.

"No. No, 'tain't. But it's a habit. Get a habit when you're young, and it's harder to get over than blue eyes. Thomas, he don't mean no more by it than Sim Smiley means when he says he's going to kill his old woman."

"Well, I get just as mad as if he meant it," I said, "and I can't help it."

"Don't pay it no mind, I . . . Great day of judgment! This ain't doing nothing for this old hayrake, is it? First thing we know, Thomas, he's likely to come raring back here and catch us at it. By hub, I hope he makes a good trade on them cussed bees. If he don't, he'll be sorer than a cut thumb about us planing to rake hay with it."

"And if he makes a good trade?" I asked.

"Can't always tell with Thomas, but you got to watch your chances. Like as not, if he makes a powerful good trade, and if we don't wave the cussed hossrake right afore his nose, he'll never let on he knows we used it. Let's get on with it. I'd kind of like to see the orchard in windrows afore he gets home."

The horserake didn't take as long to fix as I'd thought it might. We took all the bent and broken pieces up to the forge. Uncle Levi built up the fire and, while I robbed pieces off the wrecked machine and bolted them onto the better one, he did the blacksmithing. With the early start we'd got, we were all finished by ten o'clock.

The yella colt didn't give me much trouble in harnessing, but he made up his mind that he wouldn't pull the horserake. By the time he'd settled down to do it, we'd lost more than an hour. He'd thrown himself down three or four times, squirmed and bucked out of his harness over and over, and acted exactly as if he'd been eating loco weed. I'd had to wire his ears together, tie a string around his tongue, throw dirt in his mouth, and even hog-tie him like a calf for branding. It was while I had him hog-tied that he decided to behave himself. And, once he'd decided, there was nothing more to it. He let us hitch him into the shafts without a bobble, and when I climbed up onto the seat he walked off as quietly as Old Nell would have. He didn't even jump when I tripped the gears to dump our first load.

Uncle Levi brought sandwiches and a pitcher of milk to the orchard for me, and when I'd finished raking he took one wheel and the shafts off the horserake. He said it would be sort of waving it under Grandfather's nose if we left it all together.

In Colorado, the hayracks were flat platforms on wheels, but Grandfather's was built more like a basket. The bottom was only about three feet wide, and there was a high, flaring fence all around it. Instead of having boards for the floor, it was made of half a dozen birch poles. Most of them were rotten, and nearly a third of the fence stakes were broken or missing. While I was doing the raking, Uncle Levi had made new stakes and floor poles for it. After I'd unharnessed and fed the yella colt, I helped him build them into the hayrack.

It took us till nearly sundown, and Grandfather hadn't come home when we finished, so Uncle Levi went with me to get the cows. I took him past the high stony field, told him again how well I thought it would do in strawberries and tomatoes, and then we walked along the brow of the hill above Lisbon Valley. There was a little green meadow just beyond the foot of the hill, and a girl drove four or five cows into it from behind Grandfather's beech woods. She was wearing a white dress and, against it, her long hair looked as black and shiny as polished jet. "Annie Littlehale," Uncle Levi said when she came into sight. "Clever little thing. 'Bout your age. Hear tell she can cook better than any woman roundabouts."

I wanted to ask him if Annie was pretty, but I didn't quite like to, so I just said, "I see our cows are waiting at the bars."

Grandfather was home when we got in with the cows. Old

Nell was standing in the dooryard, and Grandfather was down at the beehives. The minute we came out of the barn, he called, "Levi! Levi! Come see the powerful good trade I made. Didn't get the colonies I sot out for. Man wouldn't trade; Ralphie dirtied the heifer up too much a-loading her, but I seen most of the bee men 'roundabouts there, and I made a tarnal good trade. Come see 'em."

They were still down there when I'd unharnessed Old Nell and watered her, but by the time I'd finished the chores, supper was ready and they were at the table. Grandfather was so excited about all the trades he'd tried to make that he wouldn't eat his supper, and Millie had to make him an eggnog with a spoonful of whiskey in it. When I went upstairs to write Mother a letter, he was still telling Uncle Levi and Millie about his trading.

It was just by luck that I saw Grandfather looking over my raking job the next morning. He didn't usually get up until after I'd finished chores, and I seldom left the barn until I went to feed Clara Belle's calf, after milking. That morning Old Bess wasn't waiting to catch her squirt of milk, and when I whistled for her, she came running in, wet, from the direction of the orchard. I just happened to glance out through the tie-up window, and there was Grandfather. He had his hands linked behind his back, and was walking along slowly between the windrows. His head was turning from side to side, and he looked as if he were trying to find something he'd lost. He couldn't have stayed out there more than two minutes after I saw him. Before I had finished milking Martha, he called from the front barn doorway, "What you dawdling over them chores for, Ralphie? Time flies! We got haying to do today."

In some ways, the haying went better than I expected it to for the first few days. Grandfather worked most of the forenoon with Uncle Levi and me while we shocked the hay in the orchard. He never asked how the raking had been done, and we didn't tell him. In the afternoon, when we were ready to haul, Millie put on a pair of overalls, made a jug of switchel—Jamaica ginger and water, sweetened with molasses—and came out to help us.

I had thought I was going to show Grandfather something about pitching hay but, little as he was, he could swing up as big a forkful as I could. And he started swinging them just as fast as he could go. "Come on, Ralphie! Come on!" he sang out as Millie stopped the rack beside the first row of shocks. "I and you'll show 'em what kind of logs makes wide shingles!" Then he jabbed his fork into a shock, crouched, levered the fork handle across his bent knee, and sent the load sailing over the high rail of the hayrack. It was hardly off the fork before he was trotting toward the next.

My blisters were beginning to heal pretty well and, with my new gloves, they didn't bother me much in handling a pitchfork. I wasn't going to let Grandfather get ahead of me, so I jabbed my fork deep, pitched, and ran for the next shock. We went neck and neck for the first half dozen, and then I came to a big one. I either had to take it all at one forkful or, if I took two, let Grandfather get ahead of me. I caught the near edge of the shock with my fork tines, folded it up, and rammed the fork hard into center. Then, when I sprang back, bent my knee, and threw my full weight on the fork handle, it broke in the middle.

Out of breath as he was, Grandfather scolded me till his face was almost purple, called me a tarnal fool boy a dozen times, and went off to the barn for another fork. Uncle Levi was raking scatterings. As soon as Grandfather had gone, he pulled his rake up beside me, and said, "Cussed good thing you broke that fork handle. If you hadn't, Thomas would like as not have killed hisself afore he got to the end of the row. Always took pride that he could outpitch ary man in a hayfield. Recollect what I told you, 'Slow and easy goes far in a day'? You pitch first-rate, but take it easy and let him run off from you. He won't go more'n two-three shocks afore he cools down; just has to prove to you that he's a better man than you be. Ain't that so, Millie?"

Millie had been building load as Grandfather and I pitched to her. Her face, deep in her sunbonnet, was dripping sweat, and she was still breathing hard when she said, " 'Tain't hard for him to prove with ninety-nine men out of a hundred. Take his fork, Ralph, and let's get this load on afore he comes back." Her voice wasn't a bit mean, and it was the first time she had called me Ralph without being sarcastic.

I only had the rack loaded a little way above the rail when Grandfather came back. He passed me a heavy, long-handled fork, and as I took it, he told me to quit trying to show off before I broke everything on the place all to smithereens. I didn't say anything, and I didn't change my pace from the way I'd been going before he came. For the rest of the row, Grandfather pitched three shocks to my two. Then he stood his fork against a tree, and said, "Load's getting a little high for your old grampa, Ralphie. You throw on eight or ten or a dozen more shocks, and fetch it on to the barn. I'll go ahead and get some the culch out of the barn floor."

When we got to the barn, I found why Grandfather wanted me to build the load so high. Instead of using a horsefork, the way they always did in Colorado, we had to unload by hand. But that wasn't all. The hay had to be handled three or four times. I pitched off the rack to Uncle Levi on the low mow above the tie-up, he pitched to Grandfather on the next higher mow, and he pitched to Millie, who stowed away in the high mow above the driveway. Unloading was twice as hard as loading on in the field. With the hayrack built the way it was, the whole bottom part of the load was tangled and matted together. To tear it loose with a pitchfork was like pulling stumps.

On the second trip, we tried to get Grandfather to build load, let Millie rake scatterings, and Uncle Levi pitch with me, but he wouldn't do it. For half a dozen shocks, he'd tear into it as if he were throwing dirt on a prairie fire, then he'd either go off to see how the new bees were doing, or remember that he had to set a trap in a ground-hog hole. He was away and back two or three times to each load, and it was nearly sundown before we had the third one pulled into the barn. Both Grandfather and Uncle Levi were too tired to do the unloading, Millie had to cook supper, and I wasn't a bit sorry when Grandfather said, "Unhitch your hosses, Ralphie! We done a good job of work to-day, and we'll leave her set right where she is till morning. Can't go to hauling of mornings, anyways, till after the sun's high enough to suck up the dew."

I saw Annie when I went for the cows that evening. She had on a pink dress and, for a minute, I thought she'd spied me sitting there by the base of the big beech tree. Her face turned that way just as she went out of sight behind the woods at the foot of the hill, and I could have sworn that her hand waved a little.

11

The Horsefork Disaster

THE second day of hay hauling didn't go as well as the first. It was hot. There was a little breeze in the orchard, but the barn was stifling. It took twice as long to pitch a load off and stow it in the mows as it took to pitch it on in the field. We'd have to stop and rest three or four times during each unloading, and every one of us would be wringing wet by the time we reached the bottom of the rack.

Grandfather grew more crochety as the forenoon went on. During the first unloading, he called down to me only two or three times about pitching either too fast or too slow. By our third load, just before dinner time, he wouldn't let me alone five minutes at a stretch. If I happened to get hold of a big forkful, he'd yell at me to stop trying to show off before I broke every fork handle on the place. And if the forkful was small, he'd scold me for dawdling.

Grandfather would neither rake scatterings nor build load in the field. During each loading, he'd come to the field two or three times, stay about ten minutes and go away. Each time he came, he'd take Uncle Levi's fork, pitch hay as fast as he could swing it, and scold me for being too slow. I didn't say anything back when he scolded, and I tried not to change my pace, but before he'd leave the field, I'd be so furious that every muscle would be quivering.

Millie didn't help with the last unloading of the forenoon, but went to the house to get dinner. When we went in to eat, there was only fried salt pork, boiled potatoes, and johnnycake. Uncle Levi looked the table over when he sat down, and said to Millie, "If you'd told me this morning you was out of meat, I'd have killed a hen while Ralph was doing the chores."

"Ain't nothing the matter with salt pork," Grandfather snapped at him. "Et a-plenty of it whenst you was a boy to home, didn't you? Never heard tell of nobody starving whenst they had salt pork to eat, did you? Eggs is eighteen cents a dozen, and the hens is all laying."

Uncle Levi didn't answer, but he ate only one small potato and a couple of slices of pork. No one said another word till the meal was finished. It was the first dinner since Uncle Levi had been there that the red rooster hadn't flown up onto the window sill behind him and tucked-tucked for something to eat. As Uncle Levi pushed his chair back from the table, he grumbled, "Even a cussed rooster knows better than to come to a dinner of salt pork in haying time." Then, as we were leaving the kitchen, he turned to Grandfather and said, sharply, "How do you expect Ralph to hold the pace you're trying to set him, with nothing but salt pork in his belly?" Grandfather flared right back at him, but I didn't want to be there while they were wrangling, so I went to the barn and hitched up the horses.

The afternoon was hot and muggy. Millie and Uncle Levi tried to get Grandfather to slow down a little in his pitching, but they only made him worse. Each time he came to the field, he'd grab the fork out of Uncle Levi's hands, race into the pitching, and yell at me for being shiftless and lazy.

At the starting of the second load, Grandfather made me so mad that I didn't care if he did kill himself. I wasn't going to hold a steady pace any longer and let him keep yelling at me for dawdling. I shoved my fork deep into the shocks, and pitched as hard as I could. The faster I worked, the louder

Grandfather yelled at me, till Uncle Levi called, "Thomas, it's a God's wonder you ain't drove the boy away a'ready."

Grandfather was winded, and his voice was squeaky when he yelled back, "Mary sent him down here for me to make a man out of him, and, by thunder, I cal'late on doing it." Then he tore into the pitching again. Instead of taking each shock clean, he'd grab a forkful off the top, heave it onto the rack, and shout, "Gitap!" at the horses. I had to go just as fast as he, or be left behind. Then I jabbed my fork too deep into a big shock, sprung the handle too hard, and broke it.

Grandfather was beside the yella colt when I broke the fork handle. He jumped up and down, and shouted so loud that he set the old horse dancing and shaking his head. Then the colt braced his feet, and went into a balk. I leaned on my fork handle and waited while Grandfather yelled, "Gitap! Gitap! Gitap, you tarnal fool hoss!" He grabbed a bridle rein, tugged on it, and shouted into the yella colt's face, "Gitap! Gitap, you worthless, good-for-nothing crow bait! Gitap, I tell you!"

Then I did the most foolish thing I could have done. I stepped over and said, "If you'll let me quiet him down a bit, I think I can make him stop balking."

Grandfather yanked his hat off, threw it on the ground, and shouted, "Tarnal fool boy! Never in all my born days seen such an all-fired know-it-all boy! Stand out of the way, I tell you! What you think you could do to stop a horse a-balking?"

"Wire his ears together," I said. And I said it quietly.

"*Wire his ears together!*" Grandfather stormed. "Don't you never let me catch you wiring a critter's ears together!"

I was mad enough that I had to be careful not to shout back, but I kept my voice down, and said, "All right, I won't. What do you want me to do now?"

"*Do! Do!* Start fetching hay to the rack! What in time and tarnation you cal'lating on doing? Time flies, I tell you! Levi! Give Ralphie a hand fetching hay whilst I go to the barn for another fork! Millie, go get your victuals ready! Tarnal colt's likely as not to balk till sundown!"

When Grandfather was nearly to the barn, Uncle Levi stood his fork down, and said, "Don't let Thomas rile you no more'n you can help, Ralph. When he's tired and his nerves is jangled, he ain't accountable for what he says. Don't mean a cussed thing by it. Something I can't ravel out is tormenting him bad."

"I'm sorry I broke another fork handle," I said. "I've been trying to pitch as well as I could."

"Ain't nothing the matter with your pitching," Uncle Levi told me. "It's good, and Thomas knows it. I'd give a cookie to know what's eating him. Calc'late you could get that cussed yella colt to stop balking?"

"Not without doing something to make him forget he is balking," I said. "I think I'd have to put a wire on his ears."

"Don't calc'late Thomas could catch us at this distance from the barn," Uncle Levi said and winked at me. "Seems to me I seen a piece of wire a-hanging on the colt's harness."

Uncle Levi pitched hay just the way I liked to; steady but not rushing. Within a few minutes after I put the wire on the yella colt's ears, he forgot his balking and went back to work. I'd taken off the wire, and we had the rack piled high when Grandfather came back to the field. Neither of us saw him coming till, from right behind us, he sang out, "Now you see, Ralphie! What did your old grampa tell you? Can't nobody do nothing with the yella colt, 'cepting to leave him be till he makes up his own mind. Ruin him for all his lifetime if ever you'd go to putting wire on his ears. Levi, you climb up and build load whilst I and Ralphie pitches to you."

For the rest of the loading, Grandfather pitched without rushing. At the unloading, I heard him wrangle with Uncle Levi several times, but he only scolded me once, and that was for pitching too fast. When we were finished, and he came down from the mow, he was so tired his feet dragged.

Uncle Levi stayed at the barn to help me unharness and feed the horses. He grumbled to himself most of the time, and I could see that he was as tired as Grandfather. I told him so, and said I'd take care of the horses, but he almost snapped at me, " 'Tain't the work! 'Tain't the work! There's times Thomas wears me thinner'n a cobweb. Oughtn't to quarrel with him; he ain't well, but, by hub, there's times he riles me."

I think he was sorry as soon as he's said it. While I was hanging up Old Nell's harness, he stood with both hands crammed deep in his overalls' pockets, and said, "Man shouldn't be trying to work in the field at Thomas's age. Leastways, not a man that's got the malaria. Them of us that's never had it don't know how cussed cantankerous it can make a man feel."

Grandfather sounded plenty cantankerous when he shouted from the house, "What in thunderation you dawdling around at now? The victuals is getting cold!"

The only difference between supper and dinner was that Millie had baked a couple of apple pies. Uncle Levi didn't say a word when he looked the table over, but went up to his room. He was gone two or three minutes, and when he came down, he was sort of tasting his tongue. He passed Millie the bottle, partly full of whiskey, and said, "Here, I calc'late Thomas better have an appetizer afore he tackles this kind of victuals."

Grandfather said he wasn't sick and he wasn't tired, and that he wouldn't touch a drop of the hot toddy Millie brought him. He did, though, then he ate a pretty good supper, and went to bed.

I was just leaving the barn to get the cows when I heard a squawking at the henhouse. I thought it might be a fox or a skunk that was after the hens, so I grabbed a stick and raced back through the barnyard. As I rounded the corner of the barn, Uncle Levi was going toward the chopping block with a Rhode Island Red hen in each hand.

Uncle Levi had gone to bed by the time I'd brought the cows in from the pasture, and the kitchen was dark when I'd finished my chores. The only lighted lamp was out in the summer kitchen, where Millie was picking the hens. I turned a bushel basket over, sat on it, and began helping her pick. Neither of us said anything for several minutes. Then Millie asked, "Who learned you to pitch hay and drive hosses?"

"My father," I told her.

It was several more minutes before she said, "Proud of your pitching, ain't you?"

"Neither proud nor ashamed," I said.

I didn't look up until I noticed that Millie had stopped picking. When I did, she was looking straight into my eyes, and if her face showed any expression, I couldn't see it. "You're good, for a boy, and you know it, and Thomas knows it. Don't rub it in."

"I'm not," I told her.

"You was this afternoon," she said.

"Only for a few minutes; after he'd called me lazy."

"Know why he done it?"

"To get every ounce of work out of me that he could."

"Grow up," she said, without any change in her voice.

"I don't know what you're driving at," I said.

"You will, time you're his age and have to watch a young boy best you in the face of your own folks."

"What am I supposed to do," I asked, "let him beat me and then call me lazy and shiftless?"

"Till he cal'lates you think he's got you bested. Names don't hurt nobody. Thomas ain't going to let on to hisself nor nobody else that he's bested till he drops dead. You want to kill him, or let him row at you for a few minutes? I'll wager 'twouldn't be more than a few times."

I looked back at the hen, and picked a few feathers. After I'd had a couple of minutes to think, I asked, "Where did you learn to make such good apple pies?"

Millie began to pick feathers again. All she said was, "I got two oranges saved out from them Levi fetched. Want one afore you go to bed?"

When Millie called me the next morning, there was a pink glow in the eastern sky. By the time I'd finished milking, it looked as if the woods beyond Hall's hill were afire. Hens were oiling their feathers in the dooryard, and swallows skimmed low across the uncut hayfields. At breakfast, Grandfather snapped at me, "Eat your victuals, Ralphie! Get the hosses out quick as ever you can! There's a tarnal hard rain a-coming, and five loads of hay still in the field."

With rain coming, I expected Grandfather to be awfully hard to get along with, but he wasn't. It worked just the way Millie had told me it would. I tried to act as if I were doing my best, but took two pitches for each shock till Grandfather was well ahead of me. Now that I understood, it was sort of fun to watch him tear into the pitching, and hear him yell at me to stop dawdling and pitch hay man-fashion. Within twenty minutes, he stopped rushing, and pitched steadily a good part of the forenoon. Whenever he got tired, Millie or Uncle Levi found something for him to do away from the hayfield.

We had a light shower just before noon, but the sun came out bright and the tops of the shocks were dry by the time we'd finished eating. Millie had a good dinner. She had stewed the hens with carrots and potatoes, and the top of the bowl was covered with dumplings. We were right in the middle of eating when the old red rooster flew up onto the window sill and tuck-tuck-tucked. Uncle Levi wouldn't give him any chicken. He said it would be a sin to make a cannibal of him, but he did feed him nearly a whole dumpling.

The rain held off till the sun had dipped down behind the pines on the ridge. The last load was so high I could hardly reach the top with a long-handled fork, and there were just two shocks left in the field when the sky seemed to open and the rain came down in torrents. Before we got to the barn, we were drenched.

It was nearly dark when I'd finished my chores and took the milk to the house, and it was raining steadily, but Grandfather was doing something at the beehives. Uncle Levi had to go down and argue with him before he'd come to the house. He would neither go to bed nor put on the dry clothes Millie had laid out for him, but sat shivering in front of the kitchen stove for more than an hour. He was sure the rain was going to last for several days and was fretting about its holding up the haying. Twice, he asked Uncle Levi how many days were left before the Fourth of July.

The next morning it was still raining. The sky was like a gray bowl turned down on the saucer of the valley. Grandfather had chills and fever, so he had to stay in bed, but Uncle Levi and I hauled the old mowing machine into the carriage house and went to work on it. The wheels were the only things about it that weren't completely worn out.

We'd never had a forge on our ranch in Colorado, and I didn't know much about blacksmithing, but Uncle Levi did. He never hurried, and he didn't care how long a job took, but when he'd finished with it, every cog and bearing fitted perfectly. Besides that, he liked to show me how to do things, and I liked to have him. We spent all day, and until late in the evening, on the mower; regrinding gears, refitting bearings, sharpening knives and replacing broken ones; soda welding the pitman head, and making a new tongue of dry white oak.

While we were working, I asked Uncle Levi why Grandfather didn't have a horsefork in the barn for unloading hay. For the past two days, I'd been figuring out the different places a pulley could be hung from the rafters, so that a horsefork would drop the hay onto any mow in the barn without a bit of pitching. Uncle Levi listened till I'd told him just how a horsefork would work. Then he shook his head a little, and said, "You'd have a cussed big battle with Thomas. You're always telling about how your father done things, and always trying to do like he done, ain't you?"

I didn't know just what he was getting at, but nodded and said, "Yes, because he always knew the best way to do things."

"That's the ticket," Uncle Levi said. "That's what Thomas thinks, too. Father learned him to farm the way he done it hisself, and you'll find Thomas is pretty good at it. He ain't never changed where he could help it, and I don't calc'late he ever will."

"I was just thinking," I said. "With a platform rack and a horsefork, two men could have put that hay up in a day and a half. It took four of us two days and a half."

Uncle Levi didn't look up from his welding for at least ten minutes. Then he stopped hammering and said, "Never afore seen Thomas want to get away from the old place, but this summer he's got his heart sot on going to his regiment's reunion off to Gettysburg. Comes on the Fourth of July, but he won't go less'n the hay's all in the barn. Might happen Thomas would stand for one of them cussed machines if 'twas the only thing that would get the hay in afore the Fourth."

"Well, it's the only thing that would do it unless we have two or three more men," I said. "And, besides, it isn't really a machine. It's just a big grapple fork with ropes and pulleys."

Uncle Levi went back to the forge. In a few minutes, he said, "Calc'late we could whack one together out of heavy steel strap? There's plenty pulleys 'round here. How big a hank of rope you figure we'd need?"

The next few days the weather was fine, but Grandfather wasn't. His chills and fever were worse instead of better, and he had to stay in bed. That was when I found why Millie slept in the parlor. She'd get up four or five times during the night to take care of him, and she gave him, in teaspoonfuls, nearly a third of Uncle Levi's bottle of whiskey.

The mowing machine worked almost like new after we'd fixed it. Uncle Levi kept working around the carriage house while I was mowing the east field. He kept the forge going most of the day, and the ring of his hammer would follow me way out across the field. By night, he had most of the parts for the grapple fork shaped, and ready to be riveted together.

I finished mowing in the middle of the second afternoon. Then Uncle Levi hitched Old Nell to the spring wagon and drove down to Lisbon Falls. While he was gone, I'd figured out just where to hang the high pulley in the barn and bored a hole for it in the ridgepole. When he came home, he had steak, oranges, baker's bread, a piece of corned beef the size of the dish pan, and a big coil of heavy rope.

Before I went out to rake hay the next morning, we strung up the tackle for the horsefork in the barn. Uncle Levi stood in the center of the floor and watched me climb to the peak of the barn. When I'd hooked the pulley block to a clevis, I lifted it to the ridgepole, and pushed the clevis pin through the hole I'd bored. "You sure that's going to be stout enough, Ralph?" he called up to me. "Hole looks pretty nigh the bottom edge of the beam. There'll be a powerful strain on it."

"Sure," I told him. "It's higher into the wood than it probably looks from down there."

"Just so's you're sure," he called back. "Don't want nothing to go wrong with the cussed thing."

"It won't," I told him, then wrapped my legs tight around the new rope, and went sliding down to the barn floor.

Grandfather really wasn't well enough to be up but, when we were ready to haul hay from the east field, he wouldn't stay in bed any longer. I'd put all the low ropes and pulleys for the horsefork onto one of the side mows, so he wouldn't notice them if he went to the barn, and we hadn't even told Millie about the big fork.

Everything went fine in the loading. For half a dozen shocks, Grandfather pitched as fast as he could go. Then he ran out of breath, passed Uncle Levi his fork, and went to look at the bees. When Millie and I drove the first load into the barn, Grandfather came from the beehives and climbed to the low mow above the tie-up. He didn't notice the pulley ropes till I picked up one of the blocks, slid to the barn floor with it, and called to Millie to follow me. The pulley whanged against a wagon tire as I turned to catch it over the floor hook. The noise set Grandfather off like a charge of dynamite.

"What in time and tarnation!" he yelled. Then he saw the long rope dangling from the ridgepole, and Uncle Levi's horsefork hanging in the space between the two high mows. I heard his pitchfork slam down onto the bare boards of the low mow, and he shouted, "What kind of fiddledeedee falderal's going on here? Get that tarnal contraption out of here! Get it out, I tell you, afore it fall's on somebody's head! Levi, what in thunder you been sneaking into this barn whilst I been sick? Get it out! Get it out, I tell you!"

When Grandfather stopped for breath, it was easy to see that Uncle Levi had expected just what was happening. He squatted down on the edge of the high mow, and talked to Grandfather like a mother talking to a little boy who doesn't want to go to bed. He kept telling him over and over that the horsefork was only so he wouldn't have to break his back pitching hay all the rest of his life, and so we could get the haying done in time for him to go to the reunion.

Every minute or two, Grandfather would shout, "Lazy man's contraption!" but each time he said it, a little more of the fire went out of his voice.

In the end, he let us try it, but he wouldn't let me hitch Old Nell on the tote rope. The yella colt didn't like the whiffletree dangling around his heels, and I had to tie his blinders together before he'd stop rearing and kicking. The last thing I did before I climbed up to set the fork was to tell Millie to lead him real slow, and to stop quick if I shouted.

Except for the yella colt's jerking and jumping, everything went pretty well with the first forkful. There was about three hundreds pounds on it, and Uncle Levi yanked the trip line just at the right second to toss the hay clear to the back of the high mow.

Grandfather was still grumbling, "Lazy man's contraption!" after the first load went up. After the third one, he climbed the ladder to the high mow, and stood watching like a little boy at a circus. "By fire!" I heard him sing out when Uncle Levi jerked the trip line on the next load.

Everything would have been all right if it hadn't been for the yella colt and the way the hayrack was built. I had to bounce my whole weight on the fork to get it through the matted hay in the bottom of the load, and I bounced a little too hard. The yella colt started off as if a firecracker had exploded behind him. When he'd taken up the slack in the tote-rope, the whole rack jumped a foot into the air and crashed back onto the wheels. I knew in a second that I'd pushed the fork too far and hooked the grapples under the floor of the hayrack. But, instead of stopping when I yelled "Whoa!" the yellow colt lunged hard into the collar. There was a ripping screech from the top of the barn, and I looked up just in time to see a big piece of ridgepole come shooting down past Grandfather's head. It missed him by about six inches.

Grandfather wrapped his arms over the top of his head, and crouched on the edge of the high mow, as the strip of ridgepole shot into the barn floor and stood quivering. Ropes were still trailing behind it when he slammed his hat down onto the mow, jumped on it, and shouted at Uncle Levi, "Get out of here! Get out of here, afore you stave the whole place to smithereens! Get back to Boston afore I lose my temper! Don't you never come down here again with no more of your infernal contraptions!"

I tried to tell Grandfather it was all my fault, but he wouldn't listen to me. He wouldn't listen to a word from Uncle Levi, either, but followed him to the barn door, shouting, "Don't you durst come sneaking 'round here with your newfangled contraptions. Get out of here! Get out of here, I tell you!"

I drove Uncle Levi down to Lisbon Falls, and he wouldn't even let me tell him how sorry I was that I'd messed everything up. He only grumbled, "Say nothing! Say nothing!" when I tried to talk to him. Once he said—and I think it was to himself — "Should have knowed better . . . Ain't no sense a-trying to change him over." The rest of the time, he just sat there looking like a tired old bear.

He didn't say anything more till the train was pulling into the depot. Then he picked up his suitcase, took hold of my shoulder tight, and said, "Don't let Thomas kill hisself off a-working, just to prove we was wrong."

He had one foot up on the car step when he turned back, passed me a ring with four keys on it, and said, "Here, Ralph! You might have need of 'em. Them's to the drawers in the workbench." Then his voice dropped almost to a whisper, "The bottle's under my mattress. See Thomas gets a spoonful afore supper every night."

12

Millie Agrees to Help

GRANDFATHER hadn't even come to the house when Uncle Levi left. I had looked back as we drove out of the yard, and he was yanking the tangled horsefork tackle out of the barn doorway. When I drove back in, the ripped-off piece of ridgepole was lying on top of the woodpile, and Grandfather was mowing down in the swale.

I unhitched Old Nell, watered her, and took her to the barn. What had been left of the load was still on the hayrack, and the yella colt was in his stall, with his harness tangled around his feet. I took it off him, and went down to tell Grandfather how sorry I was for having messed things up with the horsefork.

The swale was down below the cold spring that filled the watering trough at the back corner of the barn. When I'd mowed the east field, I'd had to cut around it. The ground was so soft that the mower wheels sank deep and the grass was so rank that the cutter bar couldn't go through it. Grandfather was well out into the wettest part of the swale, swinging his scythe like fury. The cold water was above my ankles by the time I'd waded out to him. He was breathing so hard the whiskers flew around his mouth at every swing, but he didn't slow up or look up, and before I'd said three words, he shouted, "Go off! Go off! Get out of here! Go see what more you can find to stave up!"

There was no use trying to talk to him. As I walked back toward the barn, I tried to make up my mind once and for all, whether I should go straight to Colorado, or go past Medford so I could say good-bye to Mother and the other children. I was still trying to decide, when the hogs in the barn cellar started squealing as though they were killing each other. I grabbed up the nearest stick, and ran in there as fast as I could go.

At first, it looked as if they might be fighting over a sea serpent in the pond at the foot of the manure pile. As my eyes became a little more used to the dimness, I could see that it was a long heavy rope. Near the top of the heap, one prong of the horsefork stuck out, with the grapple hook curved like a beckoning finger. I don't know why I bothered to—except that Uncle Levi had put in so much work to make it—but I drove the hogs away, found a long plank, and fished both the fork and rope out of the mess. I cleaned the fork the best I could, hid it under the straw in an empty pig pen, and was stringing the rope along the top of the foundation wall, when Millie called dinner. By that time, I'd decided to stop off at Medford, and that I'd go into Boston to see Uncle Levi, so I could tell him where to find the horsefork.

There was no sense in starting off without my dinner, and I had to change clothes and get my suitcase, but I couldn't go to the house the way I was. While I was washing at the spring, I saw Grandfather clambering up over the boulder wall to the dooryard. Old Bess was standing at the foot of it, watching him and whining. I could hear Millie scolding him for getting his feet wet right after he'd been sick in bed. By the time I got to the summer kitchen, they were wrangling at each other like a pair of stray cats. Millie was mad because he'd driven Uncle Levi away, and he was calling her a tarnal fool woman for not having told him we were building the horsefork. He wouldn't take his shoes off, and tracked mud across her clean kitchen floor.

At the table, it was easy to see that they were both plenty peeved at me. They'd have paid more attention if a dog had been sitting in my chair. After a few minutes, I tried to tell Grandfather again that I was sorry about the ridgepole, and that I was going away, but he cut me off short. "Let your victuals stop your mouth! Let your victuals stop your mouth!" he scolded. Then, before I'd eaten my pie, he snapped, "Quit your dawdling! Get the hosses out! Time flies!"

I went outside, but I didn't go right to the barn. I still had Uncle Levi's bench keys in my pocket, and I thought I'd better hide them somewhere in the carriage house. I might not be able to see him when I stopped off at Medford, but I could write him a letter and tell him where I'd hidden them. It seemed to me that maybe a letter would be better than seeing him anyway. I could just write him that Grandfather had told me to go away. Then he wouldn't blame me for going, and he couldn't tell me the horsefork trouble was all my own fault; that everything would have been all right if I'd listened to him about the hole in the ridgepole being too near the edge. The more I thought of it, the more I knew that was just what he ought to tell me. It was the truth. If I hadn't been so cocksure, Uncle Levi would still be right there with us, and we'd already have three or four loads of hay hauled from the east field. All the time I'd been thinking, I'd been walking back and forth in the carriage house. I stuffed the keys back into my pocket, and went to harness the horses.

That afternoon and the next day were about the worst time I ever had in my life. Grandfather was sick enough that he should have been in bed, but he wouldn't go. He'd pitch hay till he was staggering. Then instead of going somewhere to rest, he'd rake scatterings and scold me. Once when he was about ready to drop, I said, "Uncle Levi told me not to let you . . ."

"Levi! Levi!" he hollered. "Going off to Boston and leaving me with down hay in the field and rain a-coming on! Don't you say Levi to me!" It didn't look as if it would rain for a month, and I didn't say Levi again, but I wished he were still there.

Millie was so worried about Grandfather that she was nearly sick herself, and the more she worried, the crosser she got. Beside cooking the meals and getting up to take care of Grandfather during the night, she was doing a man's work in the field. I couldn't tell whether she was still mad at me about the horse-fork, or whether she was just so tired and worried that she couldn't be decent to anybody. Twice, she yanked the yella colt around till she set him balking, then told Grandfather that if he didn't get some hired help around there, his hay could rot in the field, and slammed off to the house. He yelled after her to mind her manners, and that he didn't want any tarnal woman out in the field abusing the critters, but he did go to the road and talk to the mailman about looking for a hired man, and Millie did come back to help us.

At Grandfather's, the mailman didn't just bring the mail. He carried messages from one house to another, brought things from the stores in the village, or passed the word around if someone was looking for help.

The day after Uncle Levi went, three men came looking for jobs, but none of them stayed. One of them wanted a dollar and a half a day, and Grandfather would only pay a dollar. Another worked just long enough to be called a shiftless, lazy fool. The third man came in the middle of the afternoon and seemed to be a crackerjack. He said a dollar a day was all right with him, he could pitch hay better than most men, and he didn't pay any attention to Grandfather's or Millie's crabbiness. From the time Uncle Levi went until the new man came, we'd only hauled three small loads of hay, but before sundown we'd put two great big loads on the mows.

When the man left us, he left in an awful hurry. Right after supper, I had to go for the cows and Grandfather went down to do something around the beehives. I might have been out in the pasture a little longer than I should have, because I circled around by the high field. As soon as I had our cows in the tie-up, I went to the house for the milk bucket, and the new hired man nearly ran over me. I was right at the summer-kitchen doorway when he came tearing out with Millie right behind him. She was swinging the heavy iron frying pan like a tennis racket, and there was hot grease all over the back of his shirt. He never stopped running till he was out in the road, and he never came back for his hat and jumper. "That'll learn him a thing or two," Millie snapped, as she watched him go. "Just like all the rest of the devilish men! Ain't one of 'em you can trust as far as you can heave a skillet!"

During the night, Grandfather was pretty sick. I heard Millie up with him two or three times, and in the morning he was burning with fever. I wanted to go for a doctor, but he wouldn't let me. He said my time would be better spent hauling hay than chasing off to the village, and that Millie could take care of him better than any tarnal doctor.

I'd never thought a woman like Millie would cry, but she came awfully close to it at the breakfast table. She blamed herself for driving off the good hay pitcher, and for not catching Uncle Levi and me before we had the horsefork up in the barn. She was sure all the hay was going to spoil in the fields, but the thing that seemed to make her feel worst was that Grandfather wouldn't be able to go to the reunion. I tried to tell her that if they'd let me get a doctor, Grandfather would probably be well in a day or two, and that if we could find just one good man, he and I could take care of the haying. She'd only sniff at me, say there weren't any good men, and that a spell like this one always lasted a week with Grandfather. Then she raked me all to pieces when I admitted that the horsefork had been my idea instead of Uncle Levi's.

While I was harnessing the yella colt I got an idea. Grandfather's being sick might be the only thing that would save the hay crop. At the rate we had been going, it would take more than a month to finish the job. Long before that, the grass would have gone to seed, dried up in the fields, and be worthless for hay. By using the horsefork for unloading, I thought two men could do the whole job in two weeks. I couldn't see any chance of getting another man, but Millie was almost as good as one. If

I could get her to help me use the horsefork when Grandfather didn't know about it, we could save half the hay before he was out of bed. I was sure there was only one way I could get her to do it. I would have to make her think I was going away. I picked up the broken piece of ridgepole from the woodpile, took it to the carriage house, and called Millie. She didn't want to come and was grouchy when she got there. "Now what kind of fool notion you got in your head?" she snapped at me, as she came through the doorway.

"It won't make any difference to you what it is," I said, "because I'm going back to Colorado right now. I just wanted to let you know, so nobody could say I'd run away."

For about two seconds, Millie looked like a wildcat about to strike. Her hands drew into claws, and her eyes almost burned as she glared at me. Then, just as quickly, tears came, spilled over, and rolled down her cheeks. She swiped them away with the backs of her hands, "Fine kind of grandson for a man to have; leave him when he's needed most," she said chokingly.

"What's the sense of my staying here any longer?" I asked her. "Grandfather drove Uncle Levi away, you drove the only good man we've had away, and I've hardly heard a decent word from either of you since I've been here."

"Can't you see he's worried sick about getting the crop in afore it goes to ruin in the fields? You'd be cranky if you was worried as much as Thomas is. He's a'ready like to worried hisself to death."

"He isn't as worried as he is bullheaded," I told her. "If he had let us use the horsefork, we could have had the haying all finished in ten days."

"Thomas don't stand for no fool contraptions," she snapped at me. "If you hadn't put Levi up to making the fool thing, there wouldn't have been no trouble, and the hay would have all been in the mows afore the Fourth of July."

"It isn't a fool thing," I told her, "and the hay wouldn't have been in by the Fourth without it. As near as I can figure, there are more than sixty loads left in the fields, most of it uncut, and the way we were going, it would have taken a month to get it all in." Then I started to walk out of the carriage house, and said, "But what difference does it make now? I can't do it alone, and I've had about all the scolding I'll take from anybody."

Millie grabbed my sleeve as I went by her. When I turned, there were tears in her eyes again, and both her face and her voice were pleading. "You ain't really going, Ralphie . . . Ralph, be you? I'll help you, and we can at least save some of it."

It had worked around just the way I'd hoped it would, and gave me a chance to say, "We could save most of it if you weren't just as bullheaded as Grandfather."

"I ain't bullheaded!" she snapped. Then she looked right into my eyes, and her under lip was trembling. "I won't row at you no more, Ralph, and I'll help you any way I can."

"All right, Millie," I said, and picked up the piece of ridgepole from where I'd stood it by the doorway. "Do you see where the hole was bored at the edge of the break?" She nodded, and I went on, "That's the fool thing. That's what happened because I was cocksure and bullheaded. If I'd put a new hole higher in the ridgepole, the way Uncle Levi wanted me to, it would never have torn out. You saw how well those first three loads went up. There's nothing the matter with the horsefork. If we use it to unload with, you and I can put up half the hay before Grandfather is ever out of bed."

Millie stood for three or four minutes, looking out across the fields and twisting one forefinger. "Where's the cussed thing at now?" she asked.

"Down in the barn cellar. Grandfather threw it into the manure heap, but I fished it out."

"He'll be fit to wring your neck if he catches you using it . . . mine, too."

"I thought you said he'd be sick in bed for a week."

"He will, but you can't trust him not to get up and go poking around."

"Well," I told her, "it's just a case of whether I go now, or we get some of that hay in before he catches us. I'll take a chance on my neck if you'll take a chance on yours."

"Get the hosses out!" Millie told me. "I'll go see how Thomas is doing. Like as not he'll sleep a little after being awake most of the night." Then she hurried back to the house.

Millie

13

The Horsefork Works

For the next two weeks, Millie and I were busy from the time we could see in the morning till we couldn't keep our eyes open at night. I strung the horsefork up again, and we taught Old Nell to pull the tote-rope without being led. Millie learned to set the horsefork, and I stowed the hay away in the mows. The weather stayed good, and we alternated: mowing and raking in the forenoons, and hauling as late as we could see in the afternoons. That gave Millie the mornings to do her housework and take care of Grandfather, and it let us do the hauling when the hay was driest. By sharpening mowing machine sickles and making repairs in the evenings, I didn't have any trouble with the equipment, and always had dry hay ready for hauling in the afternoons.

Grandfather was our biggest worry. It wasn't his sickness that worried us; it was his getting better. He seemed to have been right about Millie's being able to take care of him as well as a doctor. After the first four days, we could never tell when he'd get up and come outdoors.

Almost every morning, he'd get up and have breakfast with us, then he'd often fuss around the bee shop or the hives for an hour or two. Sometimes he'd walk out as far as the pasture with Old Bess at his heels, but we never saw him go to the barn, and he'd usually be back in bed before noon. When I'd finished with the horserake, I always backed it into the chockecherry thicket at the foot of the orchard. Once we watched him walk within ten feet of it, but he didn't look that way, and the mornings that I used it were the ones when he worked in the bee shop.

One day, early in our second week, Grandfather came out to Niah's field while we were loading. He didn't offer to help, but either sat on a shock or poked around the stonewall, hunting for a ground-hog's hole. When the rack was piled so high I could hardly reach the top, he wandered toward the house. Millie stood on the load watching him as he climbed the high end of the wall, crossed the dooryard, and went into the house. "What in tunket do you cal'late's got into Thomas?" she asked me. "He ain't no sicker'n I be right this blessed minute, and there he goes, leaving us to do all his haying for him while he lays abed. I do declare! I never seen the beat of the man in all my born days. First off, he worries hisself sick abed 'cause the hay won't be in afore the Fourth, and now he stays abed so's there ain't no chance of it."

"Keep your fingers crossed," I told her. "If he'll keep on playing sick four more days, we'll just about have the haying licked, and the Fourth of July is nearly a week away. Unless it rains, or Grandfather catches us using the horsefork, the last forkful should be on the mows by sunset of the second."

On the morning of the second, I was sure our luck had run out. The sky at sunrise was as red as fire, and anyone could have told there'd be heavy rain long before the day was over. Grandfather was as fidgety as an old mare. He called me when the first streaks of pink showed above Hall's hill, and he fretted about one thing or another all through breakfast. "Get your hosses out! Get your hosses out, whilst I take the cows to pasture!" he snapped at me before I'd finished eating. "Time flies, and there's rain a-coming on! We'll have to stir our stivvers afore it gets here!"

Millie pushed her chair back, took her cup, and went to the stove. She looked frightened and, as she poured tea into the cup, she was shaping words to me with her lips. I couldn't make out what she was trying to say, but it didn't make any difference, so I just turned the palms of my hands up. The barn was stuffed nearly to the peak. Instead of leaving pitch-up landings, we'd built the mows well out over the driveway in the center of the floor. There was no way of putting more hay up, except with a horsefork. Sooner or later, Grandfather would know we'd been using it all the time. He might as well know it now. He had better sense than to think we'd been pitching hay thirty feet straight up into the air.

I went to the barn, turned the cows out, and called to Grandfather that they were ready to go to pasture. Then I harnessed the horses, called Millie, and we drove to the high field.

I'd left the high field that had all the rocks on it till the last. It had the poorest hay on the place, and was the farthest from the barn, way back by the beech woods. Millie always helped me pitch till the load was above the rails on the hayrack. That morning, the shocks were dripping wet with dew, so I set her to skinning the tops off them while I pitched the dry hay from underneath. We'd just made a good start when there was a yoo-hoo from down in the valley, and I looked over the brow of the hill to see Annie waving to us from Littlehale's pasture gate. I forgot all about Grandfather, or Millie, or haying, and just stood there, watching Annie and waving my hand, but she didn't wave again. She just put up the pasture bars, and walked back along the lane toward Littlehale's house. I felt kind of silly, because I was still standing there, watching her go and flapping my hand a little when from right behind me Grandfather said, "Come on, Ralphie! Come on! Don't stand there dawdling all day! There's rain a-coming tarnal soon."

Grandfather's sickness seemed to have done him a lot more good than harm. He didn't tire nearly as soon from pitching, and even with the rain coming, he acted a lot happier than I'd ever seen him. He pitched steadily until the load was about as high as he could reach, and he only got mad once. That was when I said the field looked to me like awfully good strawberry and tomato ground. He called me know-it-all and bigheaded, and said he didn't need me or anybody else telling him how to farm. In less than two minutes he was all right again, and sang out, "Gorry sakes alive, Ralphie, don't seem like it's took us no time at all to pitch on this load. There! That's just about as high as your old grampa can histe it. You finish it on out whilst I go look at my ground-hog trap. I'll catch up with you children at the barn."

Millie began worrying and stewing as soon as we started driving to the barn. "Thomas will skin the both of us alive soon as ever he lays eyes on that cussed horsefork," she fretted. "Like as not he'll run you off the same way he done with Levi."

I was still sore about Grandfather's calling me know-it-all and bigheaded, and I told her, "You don't need to worry about it. The horsefork was my idea in the first place, and it still is. I'll take the blame for it. How much of this hay do you think we'd have put up without it? Let him run me off if he wants to; he'll never be able to say I didn't do a good job for him. What difference does it make now? With nothing but hay on this place, he doesn't need me any longer, and I'll go where people don't think I'm bigheaded. There are only two more loads left in the field, and one wetting won't ruin it."

"Ain't there no way we can pitch what's left up by hand?" Millie asked. "If he don't have to see the cussed thing, maybe we can finish up without no trouble."

"I want him to see it," I blurted out. "I want him to know that he'd have lost most of his hay if we hadn't used it." Millie took hold of my arm, and her voice was pleading when she asked, "You ain't going to point it out to him, be you, Ralph? Don't start no row with him. Thomas, he can't abide to be crossed, and he'd run you off for certain."

I didn't want Millie to feel badly, and though I didn't believe it, I said, "Don't worry, Millie; just keep your fingers crossed. He's as sick today as he has been any day in the last week, and maybe he'll go back to bed before he catches us."

"Ain't there no way we can pitch it up by hand?" she asked again.

"Not a way in the world," I told her. "We'll have to use the horsefork, but I won't point it out to him. If there's going to be any row, he'll have to start it."

As we pulled into the dooryard, we could see Grandfather and Old Bess way off at the far side of Niah's field. They were beyond where he'd set the ground-hog trap, and were poking along the stonewall toward the woods. Millie didn't say a word, but she held her hand up in front of my face, and her fingers were crossed.

We didn't see anything more of Grandfather till we'd finished unloading, gone back to the field, and had the next load half pitched on. He came out of the beech woods, and hurried toward us so fast that Old Bess had to trot. "By thunder, Ralphie!" he called as he came. "Cal'late I and Old Bess has found the boar ground-hog's hole. All-fired great big one! Under the stonewall down nigh the twin pines. Tarnal, pesky critter! Been hunting his hole ever since the snow went off last spring. Gorry sakes alive! Didn't cal'late on running off like that and leaving you children to do all the work. Did you take note where I left my pitchfork?"

We'd finished the pitching, unloaded, and were back in the field before Grandfather found where he'd left his pitchfork in the woods. Until there were only three or four shocks left in the field, he alternated between pitching hay and telling us about all the woodchucks he and Old Bess had caught. Then he stopped, looked down at the beech woods, and said, "Gorry sakes! That's where I ought to have my trap sot, 'stead of over in Niah's field. Did ever you eat woodchuck, Ralphie? Just as good as hen, any day. Cal'late I'll go move the tarnal trap afore the rain comes. Go on to the barn whenst you're done; I'll be along in a jiffy."

It was a long jiffy. During the time Grandfather had been

sick in bed, we'd worked the tote-rope horse out through the back barn doorway, so he wouldn't see her from the house. That morning with him in the fields, we had to work the other way, into the dooryard. Old Nell was making the last pull on the last forkful from the last load of hay on the place, when I looked through the swallow hole in the peak of the barn. Grandfather and Old Bess were halfway down the orchard hill, and coming fast.

I jerked the trip cord the second the horsefork came over the edge of the mow, called Millie to unhook Old Nell and get her hitched back to the hayrack. Then I unfastened the rope from the big fork, left it lying where it fell on the top of the hay, tied the loose end around my waist, and slid down the tote-rope to the barn floor. Millie had Old Nell hitched back to the hayrack by the time I'd hauled the rope end through the block on the ridgepole. We gathered up rope, pulley blocks, and whiffletree, stuffed them into the grain bin and slammed the cover down. When Grandfather climbed up over the yard wall, we were backing the hayrack out of the barn floor. The only signs of the horsefork were the empty pulley block hanging high on the ridgepole, and the path Old Nell made in pulling the tote rope.

For the first time since Grandfather had taken sick, he walked in through the big front doorway of the barn. He didn't look up till he was standing right in the middle of the barn floor. For at least a full minute, he just stood there with his head turned back, his hat in his hand, and his mouth wide open; looking up through the narrowing cone of the mows. "Gorry sakes alive! Gorry sakes alive!" he said, half aloud. Then he swung around to Millie and me as we came back to the doorway. "Good on your heads, children! Good on your heads!" he sang out, ran and threw an arm around each of us. "How in the great thundera-tion did ever you . . . Bless my soul! Never seen the old barn stuffed so full in all my born days. Gorry! Wisht Levi was here to see it. Provender enough to winter twenty head of cattle! Ralphie, your old grampa's proud of you, boy. And you, too, Millie girl. How in the great . . ." As he talked, he had led us in to the middle of the floor, stopped, and stood looking up toward the peak of the barn.

I felt pretty good myself, but I think Millie felt even better. There was pink in her cheeks when she pushed her sunbonnet back, and her eyes were bright. "'Twa'n't nothing," she told

him, laughing, "but don't you get no ideas about me milking twenty head of cows, come winter. We done it so's you could go to the reunion off to Gettysburg."

"Foolishness! Foolishness!" Grandfather snapped out, but there wasn't much edge to his voice. "Ain't going off frittering away nigh onto a week's time whilst there's yet the dressing to be spread. Ralphie, I and you'll . . ."

I cut in on him, but I'd only got as far as "I'll take care of the . . ." when a quick blast of wind swept through the barn.

Lightning and thunder both struck together and, for a moment, I was afraid the buildings had been hit.

When we'd backed the hayrack out, I'd left the horses standing faced toward the barn doorway. With the crash of thunder, the yella colt came tearing in, dragging Old Nell and the hayrack after him. We all had to dive to keep from being run over. When Millie and I scrambled to our feet, water was pouring down as if the barn had been under Niagara Falls, the yella colt was dancing a jig, and Grandfather was lying almost under his hoofs. He rolled away, sat up, and he seemed to be looking at something far away, through the open doorway of the barn. "By fire!" he sang out. "Just like the battle of Gettysburg; guns a-blasting, fire a-spurting out, hosses a-running and stomping, and the rain a-pelting down. Gorry sakes, Ralphie, do you cal'late you and Millie could look after the farm if I was to go off to the reunion?"

It wasn't a very busy afternoon for me. The shower settled into a steady rain, and I spent most of my time mending harness and cleaning the bench in the carriage house, but Millie was as busy as a beaver. She heated water for Grandfather's bath, cleaned his Sunday suit, and packed his old valise, while he fussed around like a hen with one chick. He got soaking wet when he went out to tell the mailman to pass the word about his going to the reunion. And it was nearly nine o'clock before Millie could get him to stop telling army stories and go to bed.

14

Trouble with Bees

It WAS as black as pitch, and I could hear the rain pattering on the roof, when Grandfather called me at four o'clock the next morning. The chores were done, breakfast eaten, and the cows taken to pasture by five o'clock. Grandfather's train wasn't leaving Lisbon Falls until half-past eight, but he was all in a dither.

Anyone would have thought he was going away for a year instead of a week. He had to look at the old sow with the litter of pigs, at the hogs in the barn cellar, at the spider web and the calf in the sheep barn, and he said good-bye to the yella colt every time we went past his stall. Then I had to go to the high field with him while he showed me just how he wanted the dressing spread.

"Don't spread it stingy and don't waste none of it, Ralphie," he told me as we tramped over the field in the rain. "Didn't winter but six-seven head of stock, and dressing is tarnal scarce this year. Spread it even; no big lumps and bare spots, and dress the hilltop heavier'n the edges. Water'll leach it down whenst the snow melts, come spring. I cal'late on eight loads being a day's work, if you spread it nice and even. The dumpcart's under the barn. Might need a dite of mending afore you commence, but there ain't no call to waste time on it."

All the way to the Falls, Grandfather told me stories about Gettysburg. At the depot, four other Grand Army men were waiting for him. He only let me stop long enough for him to get out his valise, tell me he'd be home in a week's time, and pat Old Nell on the rump. Then, as I drove away, he called after me, "I'm cal'lating on you a-hauling forty-fifty loads of dressing whilst I'm gone, Ralphie. You won't have time to dawdle, and it'll keep you out of mischief. Tell Millie I'll fetch her a present whenst I come home, and you meet me here a week from this morning."

I'd seen the dumpcart backed into the corner of the barn cellar. It wasn't really a cart at all, but a wagon. There were two great big wheels in back, with the body balanced across the axle, and two little wheels in front. I was afraid it would go to pieces like the "one-hoss shay" before I got it hauled up to the carriage house. Most of the planks in the bottom were rotted or broken, nuts and bolts were missing, all the wheels creaked, and one of them was held together with rusty wire.

The rain had settled into a steady drizzle when I backed the dumpcart into the middle of the carriage-house floor, put the horses away, and went back to start working on it. I was sure it would keep right on raining for a couple of days, so I wouldn't have to hurry, and made up my mind that I'd do just as good a job on that dumpcart as Uncle Levi would have done if he'd been there. Of course, I had to take the rotten wood, rusty bolts, and old wires off before new parts could be put on. It took longer than I thought it would, and when I was nearly finished, the whole thing sort of collapsed. It acted the way an old cow does when she's been driven till she can't take another step. At first, it just groaned and settled a little in front, then the back end swayed, and thumped down on one haunch. It did look kind of wrecked when Millie came running out to see what had made all the noise.

For a minute, she just stood there in the doorway with her

mouth open and her eyes looking like white saucers with bright blue centers. "Good Lord a-living! What in tunket did you do to it?" she asked. "Thomas'll skin you alive and hang your hide on the barn door!"

"Oh, no, he won't," I told her. "By the time I get finished it will be as good as a new dumpcart."

"Hmfff! By the time Christmas comes, it'll be a-snowing, and you can haul dressing on a sled! How long you cal'late it's going to take to piece the cussed thing back together again?"

"I'll bet you I have it all done by the time it stops raining," I told her. "That wheel isn't broken; it's just fallen apart, and Uncle Levi left me the keys to his tool drawers."

"Drawers!" she sniffed. "Trouble with you is, you're getting too big for your drawers! Levi, hisself, couldn't put the devilish thing together in two days, and I'll drink all the rain that falls 'twixt now and sundown tomorrow."

I'd been so busy that I hadn't paid any attention to the weather. When I looked out through the doorway, the whole eastern sky was bright blue, hens were picking up worms in the dooryard, and the sun made drops of water on the apple trees look like diamonds. Before I said anything more, I had to think a little. "Well, tomorrow's the Fourth of July," I told her. "That's a legal holiday, and you're not supposed to have to work. By tomorrow night, I can have it looking almost new."

If it hadn't been for Millie's helping me, I'd have turned out to be a liar at that. And, though we made it strong enough, we never did get it looking nearly like new, but it took us till nearly midnight on the Fourth.

Millie called me at four o'clock the next morning. By sunrise, I was pitching my first load of dressing, while she did the chores. I didn't like the job. The dressing was smelly, as heavy as lead, and it took two hundred forkfuls to make a load. The spreading took twice as long as the loading. No matter how hard I snapped my wrists, the dressing would fall in big blobs, and I'd leave bare spaces bigger than a wash tub. After each unloading, I'd have to climb down, break up the lumps, and scatter them with the fork. It was nearly nine o'clock before I had the second load spread, and I'd run all out of breakfast. After I had the dumpcart backed in under the barn, I started for the kitchen to get a piece of johnnycake or something.

I was halfway to the house when I heard what sounded like an engine letting off steam in the east orchard. At first, I didn't see anything that could be making the noise, but when I'd poked around awhile, I found it was bees. About a bushel of them were clustered on the top branch of the tallest apple tree, and the whole mass was seething. I watched them for a few minutes, then went up to the house and told Millie about it. She couldn't have jumped quicker if one of the bees had stung her. She was peeling apples for a pie, and bounced out of the chair so fast that she spilled peelings all over the kitchen floor.

I didn't know that bees split up into families, or that they swarmed and would fly off to the woods if you didn't put them into a new hive right away. But Millie knew all about it. She went tearing down to the orchard as fast as she could run, took a quick look at the bees and shouted, "Fetch a high ladder as fast as the Lord will let you! Them's Thomas's blackbelts, and he'll skin us alive if we let 'em get away. I'll fetch the bee hats."

I ran for the tall ladder, let it down, and had carried it as far as the yard wall, when Millie called me to come to the bee shop. She already had on a straw hat with a mosquito netting veil that came down over her shoulders. She crammed another one on my head, pulled the veil down, and gave me a pair of gloves with netting sleeves at least two feet long. "Get 'em on! Get 'em on!" she snapped at me, as she threaded her own arm into a sleeve. "Never seen such a helpless, awkward boy! Make a fist! Don't go ramming your thumb through the netting. Good lands, hurry up! Bees don't wait on nobody!" Before I had one hand in a glove, she'd put both of hers on, had grabbed up an old dishpan, and was running toward the ladder. I didn't bother with my second glove, but stuffed it into my pocket and ran after her.

We had a lot of trouble getting the ladder up into the tree. The branches were thick, but where the bees were, there wasn't a branch to rest it against. Both our hats got twisted around on our heads, sweat was running down into my eyes, and Millie was yapping like a fox terrier. Before the ladder was set solidly, she grabbed the dishpan in one hand and started climbing. With the ladder sort of balanced in mid-air, I couldn't keep it from wabbling a little. Millie was up about six rungs, when she hollered down to me, "Watch what you're doing, and hold that devilish ladder still!"

I braced my feet and held my shoulder against one of the uprights but it didn't do much good. After every couple of rungs, Millie would stop and yell at me to quit mooning around like a sick calf and to hold the ladder still. Then a bee started crawling up my arm. At every step, I expected it to sting me, and when I put my head over to try brushing it off with my hat, the ladder began dancing. I just had to shut my eyes tight and let the bee crawl. It had nearly reached my elbow when Millie screamed.

When I first looked up, all I could see was Millie's pink bloomers. She'd shaken the bees off into the dishpan and started down, holding the pan in both pans, but her skirt had caught on a twig and she backed out of it. She'd yanked at the skirt a few times with her elbow, but the twig only poked through the cloth, and the bees seemed to have gone crazy. They were everywhere. The tune of their hum had changed till it sounded like forty runaway buzz saws, and Millie's howls made it sound as if all the saws were hitting nails. I didn't have time to find a solid limb for the ladder, but shoved it toward the center of the tree, and scrambled up to get Millie unhooked.

Just as I reached for the twig that was holding her skirt, the ladder lurched and one of my feet went through between two rungs. I grabbed for anything to save myself. The next thing I knew, I was hanging there with Millie's skirt hauled down over me like a tent. There were forty or fifty mad bees in there with me, and Millie was shrieking like a fire whistle. I heard the dishpan fall just as she started pounding my head with both fists and calling me a senseless idiot.

Tree branches were breaking and I could feel we were falling, but I couldn't see a thing, and clutched the skirt tighter. If it hadn't been for Millie, I wouldn't have known what to do when we hit the ground. My veil was ripped loose from my hat, Millie's skirt was split to the waist, and my legs were all tangled in

the ladder. She stopped just long enough to see that I could get free, then jumped up and ran for the watering trough at the back corner of the barn. I went right behind her, and at least half of the bees went with us. It felt as if a million wild bushmen were shooting me with poisoned arrows.

It was lucky that the old watering trough was a great big hogshead, and that all but a foot of it was set down into the ground. Millie jumped into it like a bullfrog—only she went feet first—and I jumped in right beside her. My mouth was open, and I was still catching my breath from running, when Millie ducked my head under the cold water. When she let me up, I was choking and nearly drowned, and two or three dozen bees were floating around on top of the hogshead.

I never knew before that cold water could feel so good, and would have stayed there all morning if Millie had let me. As soon as the bees had stopped buzzing around our heads, she made me climb out. She said we'd have to put mud on our welts right away to draw the poison, or we would be awfully sick, and we might even die. Millie was stung just as much as I, but mine were mostly on my face, neck, and arms. We dug into the bank below the spring and got some smooth, wet, blue clay. I plastered it on my neck and face till there were just holes for my eyes, nose and mouth. And, from the tops of her shoes to her bloomers, Millie looked like an artist's clay model.

At first, the wet clay felt about as good as the cold water, but when it began to dry out, I thought my head and arms would break into flames. All the time we were putting on the clay, Millie kept worrying and fretting about what Grandfather would say because we'd lost the swarm of bees. But as it dried, she forgot about Grandfather, and only talked about bees. The things she said about them got hotter right along with the stings.

I'd been stung so many times between the fingers of my right hand that they stuck out like red bananas on a stalk. Of course, I couldn't pitch dressing with them, and Millie had to help me unharness the horses. Mrs. Littlehale had heard Millie scream and had seen what was happening. She brought us some white pills that we had to take every hour, but they didn't seem to help the burning or the swelling. By noon, my face had swollen till I could only see a crack of light through one eye, and my lips felt as if they were big enough for a hippopotamus. I knew Millie must be feeling just as bad as I, but she did all the evening chores alone, and made me sit in the house with a cold, wet towel over my face. I couldn't eat anything, but before bedtime, she brought me a couple of eggs, beaten up with warm milk and vanilla. And she never said a word about my letting the ladder wabble so that she caught her dress in the apple tree.

In spite of the bee stings, I'd been sort of drowsy during the afternoon, but couldn't sleep when I went to bed. The night was hot, I was sweaty, and every way I turned made the stings burn more. Then I started worrying. Having lost the bees didn't bother me nearly as much as it did Millie, but I did feel worried about the dressing. With Grandfather expecting me to haul eight loads a day, that would be forty loads in a week—not counting Sunday or the Fourth of July. Three days had already passed and I'd only hauled two loads. Unless my hand got a lot better during the night, I'd lose the next day, too—and then there'd be Sunday. When Grandfather came home, he'd have every reason to say I was shiftless and lazy, and that he couldn't go away and trust me to do a job man-fashion.

Really, it wasn't Grandfather that I cared so much about; it was Uncle Levi. He might think I'd done a good job on the haying just because Grandfather was there to drive me along, and that I was no good unless I was driven. Thinking about Uncle Levi and haying, made me remember the horsefork, and I wished there was some sort of a horsefork for loading manure. Then I had an idea. Riding up on the trolley car from Bath, I'd seen a man spreading manure with a machine. I hadn't paid much attention to it, but lying there in the dark, I could almost see it working again. At the back of the wagon there had been a big cylinder that spun and threw out an even spray of dressing. I knew that, between the wagon wheels and the cylinder, there had to be some sort of a hook-up to make it spin. And I knew there had to be some way of pushing the load back against the cylinder. I lay there for a long time, trying to figure it out, then I got another idea.

There was a Sears-Roebuck catalog hanging on a string in the corner of the privy, and there were pictures of manure spreaders in it. I felt for the commode, found a sulphur match and struck it. The swelling in my eyes had gone down enough that I could see the flame clearly with either one of them. I got up, pulled on my overalls, took the card of matches, and tiptoed downstairs. I took the lantern from the summer kitchen, but didn't light it until I was around the corner of the woodshed.

Old Bess came out, licked the ends of my fingers, and begged soft in her throat to be petted. I just stopped long enough to pat her head a couple of times, and went on to the privy.

There were half a dozen pictures of manure spreaders in the catalog, all different, but from them I could see just what made the machines work. The cylinder part wouldn't be too hard to rig up, but I couldn't figure out any way to make a moving wagon bottom to push the load back. All I could do was to rig a cylinder at the back end of the dumpcart, then, by tipping it up a little, let the load slide back by itself. Since I was left-handed, my swollen right one wouldn't bother me too much in doing work with hand tools. And, with a manure spreader, I might get thirty or thirty-six loads hauled before Grandfather came home. I took the lantern and went prowling around to see what I could find for a cylinder, an axle shaft for it, and drive chains to make it spin.

The only thing I could find that was round enough and the right size for a cylinder was an old oak log. It was ten or twelve feet long, lying propped up on a couple of pieces of cord wood, and was pretty heavy. I'd only need about four feet of it, and thought the weight would help in keeping the cart body tipped back. After I'd gone down to the barn cellar and measured the dumpcart, I got the big crosscut saw from the carriage house, and cut a piece just the right length off the end of the log. The sawing took quite a while. It made my right hand hurt, but I didn't have to use my fingers, and got along all right.

The sky was getting gray in the east when I figured out a way to make the shaft and bearings. There was an old buggy with the other wrecked equipment behind the sheep barn. The wheels were all broken, but the hubs were whole, and it had a steel rear axle. By hacksawing a foot off each end of it, I could mount the hubs in the sideboards of the dumpcart and use them for bearings. Then I'd only have to bore the right-sized hole into the center of each end of the log, drive in the pieces of steel buggy axle, and I'd have as good a shaft as anyone could ask for.

I had one end sawed off the buggy axle when Millie came out and caught me. She raised more hullabaloo and called me more kinds of fool boy than Grandfather ever had. Before she'd quiet down and say she'd help me, I had to remind her that she'd thought the horsefork was a fool idea, too. I even had to make her believe that the bees' getting away was mostly her fault, that I'd have had the dressing all hauled by the end of the week if I hadn't been stung, and that I couldn't get the job done now without a machine.

We worked hard enough during the day that we didn't have much time to think about bee stings, and by late afternoon we had a manure spreader. It wasn't a fancy one, but it would work. We'd driven more than a hundred spikes into the cylinder log for teeth, had rigged a sprocket on a wheel hub to turn the spinning chain, and had fastened blocks and tackle on the front end of the cart body so we could adjust the amount of the tip-up we needed. The only real trouble came when I tried to spread the first load. As soon as all the weight had slid back behind the wagon axle, it lifted the front wheels higher than the horses' backs. We had to chain what was left of the oak log over the front axle to hold the wheels down. Aside from the yella colt's raising Cain until he got used to the spinning cylinder, we didn't have any more real trouble with the spreader, but Millie had to drive while I tended the tackle and kept the load sliding right.

Millie was so worried about all the time I'd lost that she would have helped me pitch dressing if I'd let her. She did all the chores, both morning and evening, and held the lantern for me after dark. With the spreader doing all the real work of unloading, I got a twenty-minute rest after each load I had to pitch on. In that way, I could work about as fast as I could swing a fork, and, both of the first two nights, we kept right at it till ten o'clock. On our third day—the last one we had to go— we hauled our forty-seventh load out of the barn cellar just at sunset. When we had it spread, the high stony field was covered from wall to wall with a smooth, even blanket of dressing.

15

Grandfather Sends Me Home

I'D PLANNED to back the dumpcart into the farthest corner of the barn cellar, take the spreader part off, and have it hidden out of sight before we quit work, but we didn't get it done. Both Millie and I were so tired we were ready to fall asleep, and we still had the evening chores to finish. Grandfather's train wouldn't be in until half-past eight in the morning. That would give us a couple of hours of daylight before I left to meet him, and would be all the time needed.

Millie got supper ready while I took care of the horses, and did the milking while I finished the rest of the chores. After we'd washed the dishes, we took our lamps and started to bed. I'd only gone halfway up the stairs when I heard Grandfather call, "Hi, hi, hi, children!" from the driveway. I set my lamp down on the stairs, and Millie and I went running out to meet him. He was trudging up the driveway with his valise in one hand and a big bundle in the other. "Gorry sakes alive, children," he called out, "it's tarnal good to be home again. Fred Folsom fetched me out and left me off at the roadway. Took an early train. Couldn't stay no longer."

He didn't answer when I asked if he'd had a good time, but

dropped his bundle and bag, drew a deep breath, and said, "By thunder, don't that smell good? Don't see why folks wants to live way off in them nasty-smelling cities."

I had hauled enough dressing that I didn't think I'd ever smell anything else again, but I took a long deep breath. There was hay and pine and a whiff of wood smoke mixed in with the barn smell. It did smell good, and I said, "I don't know, either. I don't like cities."

Grandfather put an arm around each of us, squeezed a little, and said, "Millie girl, I fetched you an all-fired pretty present." Then he looked up at me, and said, "Seen Mary whilst I was gone. Told her you was doing first-rate."

Mother had written me three letters, but she'd never told me what she'd written to Grandfather, so I asked, "Did she tell you why I came down here?"

"Tell me?" he snapped. "Why so's your old grampa could make a man out of you. Why else? Now you fetch my stuff along, Ralphie. That's where the presents is." Then he dropped his arm from my waist and walked on with Millie.

They'd reached the back corner of the house when Old Bess came running from the direction of the barn. She must have been out hunting when she heard Grandfather's voice. She was panting, and smelled pretty strong of skunk, but he dropped to his knees and held his arms out for her. She came into them with a rush, and it looked exactly as if she were hugging him. Both her forepaws were on his shoulders, and she nuzzled her head close against his neck. He wasn't saying any words to her, but they were both making the same sort of crooning sounds in their throats.

Millie hurried right into the kitchen to push the teapot forward on the stove and poke up the fire, and I followed her with Grandfather's things. I'd brought my lamp from the stairs, and steam was rising from the teapot before he came in. The moon had gone behind a cloud and it was dark enough outside that I hadn't noticed anything strange about Grandfather. When he stepped into the lamplight, he almost frightened me for a moment. He looked as if he'd been hung out in the hot sun until he'd shrunk nine sizes. Millie saw him the same second I did. Her hand flew to her mouth, and she just stood there by the stove and stared at him.

It took me a couple of minutes to realize what had happened. His bushy whiskers had been trimmed close to his cheeks, and into a little pointed cone at his chin. His hair was clipped so short that his Grand Army hat pushed the tops of his ears out, and his eyebrows were just rows of sandy stubble. He had on a blue suit that was big enough for a man once and a half his size. The collar stood away from his neck an inch, and only the tips of his fingers showed at the ends of his sleeves. The bottoms of the pants were under the heels of his shoes, and the extra cloth in the legs hung in folds like the loose skin on an elephant. White dog hair was plastered all over his chest and shoulders, and his knees looked as though he'd crawled up from the Falls on them.

"I've et! I've et! I've et!" he was saying, as he came into the kitchen doorway, but when he saw us staring at him, he stopped and looked up and down the front of himself. "Gorry," he said, as he shook the sleeves back from his hands and dabbed at the dog hair. "Old Bess must be a-shedding." Then he peeked up and grinned, "Bought me a new suit of clo'se. Got a real good trade on it off to Portland. Didn't want to go down to encampment not looking prosperous."

I couldn't tell him the suit looked good, and all I could think to say was, "You got a haircut, too, didn't you?"

Grandfather brushed his hands up across his cheeks so that the stubble whistled, "Neat, ain't it?" he asked. "Fred Folsom, he kept after me, and I got it in the station at Philadelphy. Barber was asking half a dollar and wouldn't make no better trade, so I dealt for a close job."

Millie had reached for the corn broom on the fireplace mantel. As Grandfather was telling about his haircut, she made a couple of brushes at the dirty knees of his pants, but he stopped her. "Leave be! Leave be!" he snapped, and went over to the sofa.

"Here, Ralphie! Fetch me my parcel! That's where the presents is."

I was pretty sure Grandfather always brought Millie a present whenever he went away. Her eyes were as bright as new pennies, and she could hardly keep her fingers from helping him as he picked the knots. I think he was teasing her a little. The knots didn't look too tight, but he kept fiddling with them till Millie put her hands out and said, "Let me do it, Thomas."

"Take care! Take care!" he snapped, but he followed it with a cackling laugh and slipped the knot apart. Inside the bundle, his old suit was folded with the pants around the coat. The lapels were short and stubby, and he must have had it long before I was born. When he'd turned the wrapping paper back, he rubbed his hand over the cloth, and seemed to be talking more to himself than to Millie and me. "Ain't scarcely wore out at all," he said. "Didn't need a new suit of clo'se . . . but I couldn't go a-wearing Rebel gray to Union encampment."

Then he peeked up again at Millie, grinned, and threw the coat open to show the doubled fold of bright red and white calico. The piece was four or five yards long. Before Grandfather gave it to Millie, he sort of measured it out with his hands and looked it all over. There was a peculiar smell about it, and a black smudge near one end. Grandfather rubbed the smudge on the front of his coat, and looked at it again. " 'Tain't nothing that won't wash right out," he said, "and I got a powerful good trade on it, Millie. There's buttons somewheres. Made him throw 'em in to close the deal." He moved the cloth along to a clean place, held it up against Millie's apron, and nodded his head in a little quick jerk, as he said, "By gorry, Millie girl, you're a-going to look awful pretty when you get that made up into a dress. Let me see. Let me see what he done with them buttons . . . pearl, they was."

Millie was as tickled with the calico as if it had been pure silk. While Grandfather was rummaging for the buttons, she draped the cloth around her shoulders, rolled the edge back like a collar, and held it in a low V on her chest. She did look pretty, and I was watching her peer into the darkened window-pane, when Grandfather shouted, "There, by thunder, Ralphie! I fetched you a present will be awful comforting come winter. Heft 'em in your hand. Them'll be powerful warm inside felt boots come zero weather." When I looked back, he was holding up a pair of white wool socks by the toes. They weren't exactly white; there were big gray blotches on them and they smelled stronger of smoke than the calico. But they were heavy and I knew they would be warm. Grandfather wrinkled up his nose a little. "Stink, don't they?" he said, "but a good airing'll fix that. Made a mighty fine trade on 'em . . . twenty-two cents . . . couldn't raise the wool for that." All the time he was holding my socks up with one hand, he was fishing in the bundle with the other. At last he pulled the card of pearl buttons out of the old coat pocket and held them up. Millie was still looking at herself in the windowpane and moving the calico into different shapes, when Grandfather sang out, "There! There! There they be, Millie girl! Mark how they catch the light. By gorry, you'll be pretty as ary queen."

In between helping me in the field, Millie had spent the whole day cooking and baking things Grandfather liked to eat. The red Astrachan apples had just begun to ripen. She'd picked wild strawberries to put in them, and made pies that were pink all the way through. She didn't pay any attention to Grand-father's having said he'd eaten, but put cups and plates on the table and brought one of her pies from the back kitchen. While she was doing it, I was trying to get Grandfather to tell me about Gettysburg. "Gettysburg?" he said, "Why 'tain't changed none to speak about. Same hills and valleys . . . same stone-walls . . . Ralphie, did ever you ride on them subway cars off to Boston?"

"Sure," I told him. "That's the only quick way to get any-where in Boston."

"Gorry!" he said, "Go like sixty, don't they? Mary took I and Fred on 'em . . . miles and miles." He sat for two or three full minutes, looking at a pine knot that stood higher than the rest of the floor. Then, more to himself than to me, he said, "What in thunder you cal'late they done with all the dirt?"

Millie had cut half a dozen shapes like strawberries in the top crust of the pie, and the pink juice showing through made them look almost real. Before she set it on the table, she tipped the pie down for Grandfather to see. "Gorry sakes alive, strawb'ry pie!" he sang out and jumped for his chair at the table.

We sat there till the clock on the fireplace mantel struck twelve. Grandfather didn't want to go to bed without telling us all about encampment. But, as it grew later, it was harder for him to keep awake, and easier for him to get the encampment mixed with the other times he had been at Gettysburg. Right in the middle of telling us about a new museum; his head nodded forward a few inches. He jerked it up quick, and said, "I seen him, Ralphie! Nigh as here to the barn . . . tall, with sparse whiskers . . . riding a big black mare . . . awkwardlike . . . A parson, name of Hale, done most the talking . . ." When we were sure he was sound asleep, his head came halfway up, and he mumbled, "Ralphie, did ever you ride them subway cars off to Boston?"

After Grandfather went to bed, Millie and I had decided to get up at the crack of dawn, take the spreader parts off the dumpcart, hide them, and not tell him anything about the bees till he'd seen what a good job we'd done spreading dressing. It didn't work that way. He got up as soon as I came downstairs in the morning, and the first place he went was to the beehives. I was slopping the hogs when he yelled, "Wa'n't the last thing I told you, to watch them bees 'cause they was nigh onto swarming?"

"No, sir," I said. "The last thing you told me was that you expected me to haul forty or fifty loads of . . ."

"Don't tell me what I said! Where's Millie at? Where's my bee hat? Where'd they go off to?"

If he hadn't been so mad, he'd have seen Millie climbing down over the yard wall, and heard her trying to tell him that we'd done all we could to save the swarm. Instead, he was storming at me, "Scatterbrain, woolgathering boy! Why don't you give heed to what I tell you? Where's Millie? Where in thunder's my bee hat?"

He didn't wait to see if I was going to answer him, and he didn't even look at Millie as he brushed past her and clambered up over the yard wall. When he reached the top, he shouted, "What in the great thunderation's been going on here whilst I been gone? Where's that oak log out of the parent tree Father clim?"

I looked at Millie, and she looked scared. There was nothing else to do, so I said, "I had to use it for the manure spreader."

"You *what?*" he shouted back.

"I had to use it for the cylinder on the man . . ."

That, and the foot of the yard wall, was as far as I got. Grandfather's face was as red as fire and the point of his beard stuck out like a quivering spearhead. "You done *what?*"

I didn't like having him yell that way, and I said—good and loud—"I had to fix a manure spreader so it would be easier to . . ."

"Easier! Easier!" he howled. "Wuthless, good-for-nothing boy! Can't think of nothing but easier!"

We'd left the dumpcart well outside the barn-cellar doors, and I think Grandfather spied it just as I hollered back at him, "If you'd just wait and see . . ."

"See! See!" he shouted. "What do you think I be? Blind?"

The yard wall was nearly as high as my head, but Grandfather jerked the axe out of the chopping block, jumped off over the edge with it and headed straight for the dumpcart.

"Can't you wait till you see how much better job it does than you can do by hand?" I called after him.

He didn't say a word till he had bent over half the spikes; knocked one bearing all to pieces, and broken the chain.

"I been farming this place for nigh onto fifty years, and I don't need no tarnal fool boy a-telling me what's better and how to do it. Get out of here! Go off! Go off home afore you stave up the whole tarnal place!"

16

I Learn to Draw a Temper

THE first Monday morning after Grandfather sent me home, I found a job, delivering bundles for a store in Boston, but I didn't work there long. Grandfather wrote both Mother and Uncle Levi that he was sick in bed and needed me. At the end of the first week, I said I'd go back to take care of the chores, but that I'd only stay till he was well again.

When I got off the trolley car in Lisbon Falls, I didn't follow the road all the way to the fourcorners. I cut across the ridge, and came out into the lane at the top of Grandfather's orchard. I hurried down the lane, through the barnyard, and rolled the back barn door open a couple of feet. There was a clattering of hoofs and shouting as I stepped in, and Grandfather's head popped out of the yella colt's stall. "Why, why, why, it's Ralphie!" he sang out, dropped the bridle, and came running toward me. "Gorry sakes alive, Ralphie! Your old grampa's powerful glad to see you, boy! How be you? How's Mary? How's the children? Gorry sakes! I was just a-fixing to hitch up the hosses and go to plowing."

I didn't know just what to say, and blurted out, "I thought you were sick in bed."

"I was! I was! Tarnal sick! Had to have the doctor, but I'm better now. Gorry sakes! Millie's going to be a'most as glad to see you as I be. Come on to the house whilst she fixes us a nice good cup of tea."

If Millie was glad to see me, she didn't show it. When we came through the summer kitchen, she was standing in the pantry doorway with both hands on her hips. "Well, I see you come back," she said. "Wa'n't there nothing you could find to do off to Boston?"

"Yes," I said. "I had a good job, but Uncle Levi asked me to come back here till Grandfather got well again. We thought he was still sick in bed."

"Ought to be abed right now," Millie snapped. "Ain't been feeling chipper since he come home from reunion. How's Levi?"

"Fine," I told her. "He sent presents for both of you. They're in this big bundle with the fruit."

"Stand aside! Stand aside!" Grandfather yapped at her. "Poor boy's all tuckered out a-fetching this stuff up from the Falls. Set the teapot for'ards!" He pushed by her, gave the bundle a swing, and landed it on the kitchen table. While they were looking at the things Uncle Levi had sent, I changed to my working clothes and went to the barn.

The yella colt was almost completely spoiled again. He snapped at me the minute I went near his stall, and I had to use the currycomb in good shape before he'd let me harness him. Grandfather was coming from the house when I led the team out into the dooryard, and the yella colt was still snapping and dancing a jig. "Take care! Take care the yella colt, Ralphie!" Grandfather called as he came. "How in thunderation did ever you get harness on him? Been so all-fired cranky of late, couldn't nobody get next nor nigh him."

"He'll be all right in a day or two," I called back. "All he needs is a few days' work. What field are you going to plow in?"

"High field," Grandfather told me. "Got to, to save the dressing. What in thunderation did ever you put so much on there for? Didn't I tell you dressing was scarce this year?"

"Yes, but you said to haul forty or fifty loads, too. And to spread it even, and heaviest on the top crown of the hill."

"Didn't tell you to spread it so tarnal fine you couldn't rake none of it off, did I? How in thunderation many loads did you waste on that wore-out old field? Looks like a quarter part of all I had saved up is gone out of the barn cellar."

"Just about," I said. "I hauled exactly forty-seven loads. But it wouldn't be wasted if that field was put into straw . . ."

"Don't tell me! Get them hosses onto the plow! Half the morning's all frittered away a'ready."

"All right," I said. "Where is the plow? I've never seen one around here."

"Where is it! Why, right in the sheep barn where it always is. Where else would it be?" He'd been almost shouting, but his voice dropped down, and he asked, "Did I put the top back on that beehive I was looking at this morning? Going to take a tarnal mess of hunting if ever I run down that swarm you and Millie drove off whilst I was gone to encampment." Grandfather had started off toward the beehives, but he stopped and called back to me, "Fetch the plow to the high field, Ralphie! Your old grampa'll be along in a jiffy."

The plow was in the sheep barn all right; three-quarters buried in the straw and manure. There was no clevis for the doubletrees, it was thick with rust, one handle was cracked, and the point on the share was as blunt as a hog's nose. I stopped to find a clevis, screw an iron plate onto the handle, and scrape a little of the rust from the moldboard. Then, when I was ready to start for the high field, the yella colt decided to put on a show. The second he heard the doubletrees dragging behind his heels, he acted as if he were trying to kick a hole in the sky. Not even a wire on his ears would stop him. He didn't balk, but at every forward step, he kicked both heels higher than my head. I was sure Grandfather would send me right back home if he caught me, but there was only one thing to do. I unhitched the colt, tied him, and went to the barn for a piece of rope.

Grandfather was still down at the beehives. When I went

back to the sheep barn, I hitched the old horse to the plow
again, passed an end of the rope around a hind leg, knotted a
loop in it, and let it slip down around his fetlock. I tied the other
end low on the cannon of his outside foreleg, picked up the
lines, and clucked. The yella colt hesitated half a second, as if
he was deciding just what to do, then took a quick step forward
and kicked. Half a second later, he was lying flat on his side.
His head popped up, like a diving duck's coming out of the
water, and he looked all around to see what had happened to
him. After the third dumping, he kept his heels down, but he
pranced all the way to the high field. Grandfather must have
seen us going up the hill by the orchard. When I looked back,
he had left the beehives, and he and Old Bess were coming
slowly across the hayfield.

I'd driven team for Father when he plowed, and we always
started a field from the center. That way, the horses didn't tread
over the already-plowed ground at the corners. Father and I
had always counted the steps across each end of a field, and
set up a marker stake where it would be the same distance from
each side and the end. By making the first furrow between the
two stakes, the plowing would come out even all around the
field. While I was waiting for Grandfather, I tied the horses,
found a couple of marker sticks, and began stepping off the high
field. I was right in the middle of it, when he shouted, "What
kind of games be you up to now? Thought Mary sent you down
here to help me plow."

I didn't like his shouting at me before I'd been back two
hours, and answered, "No, sir. Uncle Levi asked me to come
down and help out till you got well again. But now I'm here,
I'll help you plow if you want me to. I've got this end of the
field nearly stepped off."

"You've what?" Grandfather shouted, and yanked the yella
colt's hitch line off the post where I'd tied it.

"I've stepped off this end of the field."

"What kind of tarnal fool business is that? Come over here
and take these reins! Gitap! Gitap!"

When Grandfather yelled, "Gitap," the yella colt lunged forward, stopped, and went into a fit of kicking. At every kick, he was jumping about a foot backwards, and was going right toward the tipped-down plow. Instead of throwing the plow over, Grandfather ducked out of the way himself and shouted louder. "Gitap! Gitap! Whoa! Whoa, you tarnal fool hoss! Whoa, I tell you!"

I ran as fast as I could, grabbed the reins out of Grandfather's hands, and whaled the ends of them down across the yella colt's rump, just as his heels smashed the spreader bar between the plow handles. The colt looked around when I hit him, and must have remembered the kick rope. He jumped forward beside Old Nell and stood dancing.

"What in time and tarnation did you go fiddle-faddling off and leave your hosses for?" Grandfather stormed at me. "Ain't I told you time and again the colt's high-strung? Now look what you done to the plow!"

I didn't look what I'd done to the plow. I looked right at Grandfather. Then I turned and started toward the gap in the stonewall. "Gorry sakes alive, Ralphie," he said, before I'd taken more than three steps. "Your old grampa didn't cal'late on being cross to you. Never seen a critter in all my born days so contrary as that tarnal colt. There's times he riles me."

"There are times I get riled, too," I said, as I turned and looked back at him.

"'Course you do! 'Course you do, Ralphie! Tarnal fool hoss would rile a saint. Do you cal'late we could patch the old plow up with a stick and a piece of fence wire? Might get three-four-half-a-dozen turns about the field afore noontime."

We fixed the plow so that it would hold together all right, but we only plowed two furrows around the field before noon, and I nearly ground my teeth flat. There were more and larger rocks under the ground than on top. Grandfather wouldn't drive the horses and let me plow, and he was still too weak to have been plowing in any sort of ground. With the share point as dull as it was, the handles thrashed around like tree limbs in a storm.

Grandfather was thrown from one side to the other and, at every rock the size of a football, was pitched up onto the crossbar. With every pitch, he yelled at me to watch what I was doing and stop trying to stave up everything on the place. If he wasn't scolding me, he was yelling either, "Gee!" or "Haw!" or "Gitap!" or "Whoa!" at the horses.

Before we'd plowed around the field twice, Grandfather's shouting had the yella colt as riled as it had me, and set him balking. The first time was just after we'd started the second round. With Grandfather right there, I couldn't put a wire on the old horse's ears, so I did the next best thing. I scooped up a handful of loose dirt, held his nostrils closed and, when he opened his mouth, tossed it in. Then I let him stand and spit dirt till he forgot about balking.

The second balk came near the end of the second round. It was getting on toward noon, Grandfather was so tired he was staggering, and I felt as though I'd explode if he yelled at me just once more. Of course, I knew I'd be making a lot of trouble for myself later if I let the yella colt think he had won by balking. If I didn't, and we tried to make another round, I was sure it would end in my being sent home again, or having to go without being sent. And, though I didn't know just why, I didn't want to go. I clucked to the yella colt two or three times, clipped him with the end of the lines, and then looked back at Grandfather. "Unhook him! Unhook him!" he snapped. "Ain't no sense fussing with the fool hoss once he gets his head sot on balking." He waited till I'd unhitched the team, then walked away toward the house with Old Bess at his heels.

When I went to the barn, I took the blunted plowshare with me. All I knew about blacksmithing was what I'd learned from watching Uncle Levi and the smith in Littleton, but I thought I could weld a point onto the share. As soon as I'd put the horses up, I built a fire in the forge, buried the share end in the heart of it, and found a short, thick bar of steel to weld on for a point. I pumped the bellows till the pieces were both white hot, then laid the bar over the blunted plowshare point on the anvil, and whanged the heavy hammer down on it. The two pieces stuck together with the first blow, and I kept pounding till I couldn't see where they joined.

I had to heat the metal twice more before I had it hammered into the shape I wanted. Then, to harden it, I heated it to a bright red and plunged it into a tub of cold water. I hadn't seen Grandfather since I'd come in from the field, but I was so proud of the job I'd done that I wanted to show it to him. I picked up the plowshare, and had gone as far as the woodshed when I changed my mind. If I lugged the plowshare into the house, I'd only be trying to show him how smart I was. I took it back and laid it on the bench. But I put it where he'd be sure to see it if he came into the carriage house.

Millie called dinner while I was giving the horses their noon grain. Grandfather was already at the table when I went to the house, and he was so tired he could hardly hold up his head. Millie had evidently made a hot toddy when he'd first come in from the field, but he'd only taken a swallow or two and pushed it aside. "What was you hammering at the forge?" he asked, when I'd finished washing.

"I welded a new point on the plowshare," I told him.

"Temper it soft?" he asked. "Them rocks raises Ned with a brittle point."

I'd heard Father talk about tempering metal so it would be hard enough to hold an edge. And when I'd asked the blacksmith in Littleton why he dunked hot steel into cold water, he said it was to temper it. I didn't know what Grandfather meant by tempering it soft, but I answered right back, "Yes, sir, I did a good job on it. It's on the bench in the carriage house if you want to see it."

Grandfather rubbed one hand up over his head, and said, "Gorry, Ralphie, your old grampa ain't as stout as he thought he was. He's just about all tuckered out."

I drew a breath to say it would be easier if he drove the team and let me hold the plow. Then I thought what the yella colt might do with Grandfather's driving, and changed to, "Would it be all right if I tried plowing alone?"

"In them rocks? With the yella colt? Hmmff! Might as leave try to . . ."

Millie was at the stove, picking pieces of pork out of the frying pan. She hadn't said a word since I came into the house, but she broke in quickly, "I'll drive the hosses for you."

"No such of a thing! No such of a thing!" Grandfather snapped at her. "Ain't going to have no women folks working in the fields . . . less'n it's haying time. Cal'late I'll have to let the plowing go till my legs gets a trifle stouter. Wanted to get it done afore all the good of the dressing leached off the crown of the hill. Wasted enough of it on the down-land a'ready."

The more he talked about it, the more I wanted to try plowing alone, so I said, "It's my fault it was wasted. I'd like to try plowing alone, if you'll let me."

Grandfather turned toward me quickly, and his face had a sort of puzzled look. "What did you say, Ralphie?" he asked.

"I said it was my fault that the dressing was wasted, and that I'd like to try plowing alone."

"Gorry sakes! Didn't look to hear you let on to it. Well, ain't no harm in trying if you want to, but you take care the yella colt. He's powerful high-strung."

I ate my dinner as fast as I could fork it into my mouth. Then, while the horses finished their hay, I took the sharpened plowshare to the high field and put it on the plow. When I came back for the horses, Grandfather was fussing around with some pieces of board in the carriage house.

The plowing didn't go the way I'd hoped it would. The yella colt had never liked me any better than I'd liked him. But, before I went back to Boston, he'd just about stopped balking, and would do fairly near what I wanted him to. Anyone could have seen that he hated me when I came back. And I'd made a bad mistake before dinner. Just because I'd unhitched him the second time he balked, he thought he had me buffaloed. He behaved pretty well till I had him hitched to the plow, and then he raised particular Cain.

It took me nearly an hour to plow a furrow the length of the field. Before it was finished, the yella colt had balked four times, thrown himself flat twice, broken the harness in a couple of places, and every time I'd go near his head he'd strike out at me like a wild stallion. There were times when I wanted to take a club to him, but it would only have made him worse, if possible. We were both dripping wet, and I'd used every trick I ever saw or heard of before he decided to settle down and work. And then the plowshare snapped, three inches from the point.

I never hated to do anything much more than I hated to take the broken plowshare in to the forge. When we'd hit the rock, it hadn't dented the point at all, but had snapped it off like a piece of peanut brittle. I knew the fault was in the tempering, and I knew that Grandfather would know it. As I came nearer the buildings, I could hear him hammering in the carriage house, and in my mind, I could hear him call me a know-it-all, tarnal fool boy. There wouldn't be a thing I could say, either, because he'd be right.

Grandfather was at the bench, mending a beehive, when I went into the carriage house. He looked up, and asked, "Yella colt balking on you, Ralphie? Why didn't you fetch him in?"

"It isn't the yella colt," I said. "The plowshare broke."

Grandfather came over to where I was laying the broken pieces on the anvil. "Didn't I tell you to temper it soft?" he snapped. "Don't call that a soft temper, do you?"

"No, sir," I said. "It's as brittle as ice."

"Then why in time and tarnation did you tell me you tempered it soft?"

I wet my lips with my tongue, and said, "I don't know how to temper soft. I guess I was ashamed to tell you."

Grandfather looked up at me the same way he had done at the dinner table. Then he picked up the pieces, and looked at the break carefully. "Got a pretty good weld on it," he said. "Didn't bust at the joining. Think you could mend it again?"

"I'm not sure. That's the first weld I ever made, but if I have good luck I think I could do it again."

"S'posing you try it. Then your old grampa'll learn you how to draw a temper."

The first weld hadn't worried me. It had never occurred to me that it might not come out all right. By the time I had the fire blown up hot and the pieces back in it, my mouth was as dry as the cinders. I knew I'd never be able to weld the two broken edges together; there'd be no way of getting at them to hammer them tight. As I pumped the bellows, I decided I'd have to flatten the end of the big piece a little, reverse the small one, and sandwich one piece on top of the other.

Before the red faded to pink, and the pink to white, I'd picked up each piece half a dozen times with the tongs. And when I lifted the larger one to the anvil, my hands were shaking a little. I hit it seven or eight hard blows with the hammer, pushed it back into the heart of the fire, and waited for the red to fade. I was holding my breath when I lapped the two white-hot pieces together on the anvil and whanged them with the hammer. They stuck, and I found myself panting as if I'd just finished a mile race.

Grandfather was still working at the bench when I began shaping the new point on the plowshare. I didn't notice him again till I had it all finished and, from right behind me, he said, "You done it man-fashion, Ralphie. Now leave your old grampa learn you how to temper."

He did the first part the way I had: brought the steel to a cherry red, then quenched it quickly in the water. As I pumped the bellows, he banked cinders at one side of the forge, placed the hardened plowshare so that the point lay over the fire, and said, "Now mark it careful, Ralphie, whilst the hardness draws away."

After a while, he began lifting it from the fire and peering at it. "There! There she be! Straw color; that's for butcher knives." He put it back, and lifted it again, "Brown! That's for a plow in the valley ground." Next it was, "Purple, Ralphie! Sled runners! Tarnal good ones!" In another minute or two, he sang out, "There you be! Blue! That's how you want your axe head; just coming blue. We'll give her another dite for them rocks." He gave it another minute's fire, then swept it away from the forge, fanned it back and forth, and held it up for me to see. "Mark it, Ralphie! Mark the color; blue as the sky of a starry night! Tough as rawhide. You'll dull it, but you'll never bust it."

17

Grandfather Finds the Bees

I PLOWED all the rest of the week in the high field. Every morning during the early part of the week, Grandfather would come to the field with me. I'd have to drive the team while he held the plow, and we always had trouble. His legs were still weak enough that the plow handles threw him around, and he drove the yella colt nearly crazy with his shouting. After the first two days, the colt never balked with me when I was alone, but with Grandfather's shouting, he'd balk at least once on every round of the field. I found that the best thing for me to do was to bite my teeth together till we'd plowed two rounds. By that time Grandfather would be tired enough that I could get him to go hunting the lost bees.

One afternoon, late in the week, I heard Grandfather call my name from down over the hill at the east end of the field. His voice sounded as if he were in trouble and needed help in a hurry. I looped the reins over a hame knob, unhooked the yella colt's traces, and went running as fast as my legs would take me. When I got to the brow of the hill, Grandfather was standing in the green meadow in Littlehale's pasture. The minute he saw me, he waved his arm and called, "Come quick, Ralphie! Come quick! I found 'em! I found 'em!"

I hurried down across the pasture, and when I was still twenty rods away, Grandfather shouted, "Gorry sakes alive, Ralphie, they be thicker'n hops and a-loading heavy. I cal'late the bee tree ain't far distant." As I came near him, he opened the little cigar box he always carried when he was hunting bees. "Here, Ralphie," he said, as he passed me a little wire hoop with a mosquito netting bag on it. "Take some of this cotton, and line a couple from that alsike clover patch yonder, whilst I line from hereabouts. By gorry, we'll fetch 'em afore the hour's out."

I could see he was all excited, but if he had been talking Chinese, it would have meant just as much to me. I took the little net, and said, "I guess you'll have to show me how to do it. I don't know very much about bees."

"Great thunderation!" Grandfather snapped. "What kind of a farmer boy be you? Didn't your father learn you nothing?"

"Not about bees," I told him. "We never had any."

"Gorry sakes! Well, there ain't nothing to it. Mark me, whilst I show you!"

Grandfather bent over and went ranging around like a beagle hound trying to pick up a rabbit scent. He was holding the veil of his bee hat in both hands as he went. After a minute or two, he swooped it down over a clover blossom, and sang out, "There, by fire! Got her! Got her!" The bee had come off the flower, and was buzzing in a fold of the veil when I got over there. "Now mark her, Ralphie," Grandfather said. "Mark that wide black stripe ahind her wings. Them's the lost ones; don't take none other. Here! Fetch me my bee lining box whilst I show you."

Grandfather had dropped the cigar box when he dived for the clover blossom. When I took it to him, he was turning the netting back from the bee that he was holding between his thumb and finger. He had it by the sides, with its legs up. Its tail kept flipping toward his finger with the stinger out. "Gorry, Ralphie, mark them legs," Grandfather whispered. "Loaded, ain't they? 'Twon't be far to the bee tree. Now give me a smidgin of that cotton lint with a dab of glue on it." There were loose cotton, short pieces of silk thread, and a little bottle of mucilage in the box. I picked off a bit of cotton, and started to take the cork out of the bottle, when Grandfather whispered, "Time and tarnation, Ralphie, how you cal'late she's a-going to lug all that? Here, you hold her, whilst I fix the flag."

I'd had all the bee handling I wanted when Millie and I tried to get the swarm out of the apple tree. The way that stinger was flipping didn't look good to me, and it's hard to pass a bee from one person to another. Maybe I was a little too careful, but I didn't get a good hold when Grandfather passed her to me. I jumped when she buzzed in my fingers, and the next second she was gone. "Careless, heedless boy!" Grandfather snapped, as the bee darted away. "Why don't you pay heed to what you're doing? Now look sharp for another one." He snatched the bee hat and went ranging around in the clover again. It wasn't a minute before he pounced on another blossom. "There! There you be, Ralphie!" he sang out. "Now you pick a-holt of her through the veil. No, not that way! Get her by the back so she can't sting you."

I held on as tight as I could without mashing the bee, while Grandfather fixed the flag. He took a little wisp of cotton, not much thicker than a daisy petal, dabbed the end of it with the cork of the mucilage bottle, and stuck it to the bee's up-curved back. "Now, Ralphie," he whispered, "turn her loose and mark her close." As I parted my fingers, the bee zoomed away with the white flag sticking to her. In a second the bee was out of sight, but the white speck of cotton circled higher and higher till it was above the tree tops. Then, as Grandfather and I stood watching with our hands shading our eyes, the speck shot straight away across the tree tops. Grandfather's arm shot out in the exact direction the bee had taken. "Sight it, Ralphie! Sight it!" he called, as he held the arm stiff. "She'll fly home straight as a musket ball. Mark the course a-past the nigh side this beech and yonder Getchell birch. Get me a stake to mark this spot."

As soon as I'd found a stick and pounded it down to mark the spot, I wanted to follow the bee line and hunt the nest. Grandfather wouldn't let me. "How you cal'late to know when you've gone far enough?" he asked me.

"Well, if they're still making as much noise as they did in the orchard, we can hear them for a hundred yards," I told him. "And if they're on a tree in this line we should be able to see them, shouldn't we?"

Grandfather shook his head. "Poor Ralphie!" he said. "With all your big ideas, there's lots of things you don't know, ain't there? Why, you could stand right under the bee tree for a week and never know they was next nor nigh you."

"Then how can you ever hope to find them in a whole woods full of trees?" I asked him.

"That's what I cal'late to learn you," he said. "You just keep your eyes open and your mouth shut and watch your old grampa."

He gave me his bee hat to carry, picked up the bee lining box and the little net, and walked to the far end of the meadow. In a few minutes, he popped the net over a bee that was busy on an alsike clover bloom, let it rest there till he had the flag ready, then picked the bee up and stuck it onto her. When the bee had risen in circles to the tree tops, it shot away in a little different direction from the first one; a little more toward the south and west. Grandfather's arm came up stiff and straight as the speck of the cotton flashed away above the trees. "Mark it, Ralphie!" he called. "Mark it sharp a-past this silver birch and the fork of yonder maple sapling. Get your stake down. Get your stake down, Ralphie."

When the stake was down, Grandfather asked, "Think you can follow that line straight as a tight string? Keep a-sighting as you go. Don't hurry, and don't commence till I holler. I cal'late it's about forty rods." Then he picked up his little box and went back to where we'd driven the first stake. It was beyond a jut in the woods, so I couldn't see him, but when he shouted I started straight down the line the bee had taken. I sighted carefully from one tree to another, and I made sure I didn't get off the line. I couldn't see Grandfather, but every few minutes, he'd call, "Where be you, Ralphie?" and I'd call back, "Here."

After a little while, I could see Grandfather coming through the woods at my left, sighting from tree to tree as he came. The lines we were walking were at different angles, like the sides of a cut of pie. After I'd gone about the length of a city block, we came together at the point, and were under a big old beech tree that lightning had hit a long time before. Grandfather looked up into it for two or three minutes, then he said, "Good on your head, Ralphie! You laid a straight course and followed it. Mark that little hole just beneath the high crotch. There's a hollow inside there. That's where the bees is."

I found the hole all right. It wasn't any bigger than a half dollar. After I'd watched it a few minutes, I said, "I can see the hole but I don't see any bees around it. Wouldn't there be bees coming and going if the nest was in there?"

"I cal'late there is, Ralphie! I cal'late there is," Grandfather said, as he peered. "But lacking sunlight on their wings, 'twould take a powerful sharp eye to see one."

"Then what makes you so sure this is the nest?" I asked him.

"Gorry sakes, Ralphie, don't you know a bee tree whenst you see one? Mark the dull bark beneath the crotch? Hollow inside, Natural hive. Didn't ever you see bees going into a hole in a hollow tree?"

"No," I said, "but I've heard they do. Do they make honey in there?"

"Gorry sakes! 'Course they do! Have to store provender for the winter, don't they? I recollect one time I and Levi found nigh onto a hundred pounds in a tarnal great hollow-hearted oak. Mostly sugared off. Some of it must have been there from ten years back."

Grandfather stood four or five minutes looking up into the tree. At last he said, "Take an all-fired tall ladder to fetch 'em down . . . Curious things, bees . . . More sense than most people . . . Always providing ahead . . . Always laying away

for more than one hard winter . . . Putting by something for the generation to come . . . Never tire a-watching 'em." Suddenly he turned to me and said, "Lay down, Ralphie! Lay down here whilst I let you see 'em work."

Father had once told me that, looking up from the bottom of a well, you could see the stars in the daytime. I thought maybe lying on the ground would let me see bees in the shade the same way. I did want to see them work, so I lay down on my back and looked up toward the hole.

"Now stay right where you be, Ralphie," Grandfather told me, "whilst I go flag three-four for you to watch. I'll holler whenst they line out. Keep your eyes open wide, and mark how quick they come in on a bee line." Then he picked up his bee lining box, and started off toward the little meadow.

It didn't seem as if I'd been there more than two or three minutes—just looking up toward the tree and thinking of what Grandfather had said about the bees—when I heard him call, "There you be, Ralphie!" I opened my eyes as wide as I could. In three or four seconds, a tiny white streak shot like an arrow over the trees from the direction of Grandfather's voice. It dipped, and zoomed toward the trunk above me at a mile a minute. When it was close to the tree, it seemed almost to stop, then disappeared into the little hole.

Grandfather sent three more flagged bees; each from a different direction. And each one came straight from the sound of his voice as though it had been shot from a gun, dipped, zoomed in exactly the same way, braked, and disappeared into the hole. I was so busy watching and thinking about the bees that I didn't hear Grandfather till he stopped beside me. "Curious, ain't it, Ralphie, how the Almighty provided for all His critters? Did you mark how the bees come in straight as a taut line? 'Tain't from seeing, I don't cal'late, Ralphie. They'll come into a hollow stump just as straight. It's a gift of the Almighty's, so's they can hide their nest and always find it."

I had gotten up, and Grandfather and I both stood looking up at the little hole that was the doorway of the bees' nest. After a few minutes, he half whispered, " 'Tain't right, Ralphie . . . 'Tain't right, I s'pose . . . I and you a-using their gift from the Almighty agin 'em . . . sighting 'em down by the straight line of their flight." He stood for a few minutes more, then went on, "We ain't doing 'em no harm. Just fetching 'em home so's we can watch after 'em enduring the winter . . . Most prob'ly the Almighty made 'em a purpose to sweeten the victuals of His children . . . Gorry! Ain't nothing better'n new honey on a hot biscuit."

There was a deep shadow in the woods, but as we stood there, a thin shaft of golden sunlight streamed through an opening in the leaves and lighted Grandfather's face. When it touched his eyes, he jumped, almost as though it had hurt him. "Gorry sakes alive!" he sang out. "Time flies! Must be getting nigh onto evening!" He looked quickly up and down the trunk of the tree. "By fire," he said, "I cal'late that'll take the longest ladder in the barn. Come on, Ralphie! Come on! I and you'll have to stir our stivvers if we're to get 'em hived afore night falls." He hurried off toward the house, and called back to me, "Fetch the hosses! Fetch the hosses, Ralphie, whilst I go get the bee trappings ready."

When I went back to the plow, the yella colt had the harness pretty well tangled up. It might have taken me fifteen minutes to straighten it out, drive to the barn, and hitch the horses to the stone drag. By that time, Grandfather had dragged the long ladder out of the barn, and wood punk smoking in an old iron kettle; a white beehive, bellows, veils, and gloves laid out on the yard wall.

"What in time and tarnation you been dawdling around for?" Grandfather shouted, as I pulled up to the foot of the wall. "Time flies! Time flies! Can't fetch bees out of a tree in the dark! Here! Haul this tarnal ladder down, and hook it fast whilst I fetch the trappings. There she be! There she be, Ralphie! Let's get a-going, and your old grampa'll learn you how to fetch home a swarm of lost bees."

The nearer we came to the bee tree, the more I worried. The

nest was nearly thirty feet above the ground, I had no idea how to get bees out of it, and I could remember too much about what had happened when Millie tried to get them out of the apple tree. Whenever I'd try to ask Grandfather anything about it, he'd chuckle a little, and say, "You just mark your old grampa; he'll show you how to fetch 'em down in jig time."

We could only take the team as far as the lower end of the high stony field. The sun was behind the woods on the high ridge, and as I unhitched, Grandfather kept snapping, "Let be! Let be! Time flies!" All the time he was snapping at me, he kept blowing air into the smudge kettle with a little bellows. By the time I was finished, he had a smoke column that rose as high as the tree tops.

The long ladder was awkward to carry through the thick woods and stand up against the bee tree. Half a dozen times, when we got caught in the undergrowth or wedged tight between trees, Grandfather called me careless and heedless, but at the same time, he seemed excited and happy. I was worried because the top of it didn't reach up to the bee hole by three feet, but when I tried to tell Grandfather it wouldn't be safe, he only yapped, " 'Tain't nothing! 'Tain't nothing! Leave your fretting and go to fetching the stuff. First off, fetch the hive and rope, and stir your stivvers. I cal'late to get 'em hived enduring twilight."

When I came back, Grandfather had made a little foundation of rocks for the hive at the foot of the tree. He didn't let me stop to help him place it, but hurried me right back for the rest of the trappings. "Take care you don't trip with that tarnal smudge kettle," he called after me. "Leaves is dry. Be all-fired easy to burn the woods down. Stir your stivvers, Ralphie! Daylight's wasting!"

I hurried as much as I could on the way out, but I was awfully careful when I brought the smudge kettle back. From Grandfather's having blown the punk, the kettle, bail and all, was hotter than Tophet. Even through a doubled glove, it burned my hand. I didn't dare set it down among the dry leaves, and every time it touched my leg it felt as if I'd fallen on a hot stove. Between trying to juggle a couple of bee hats, the gloves, the bellows, hammer and nails, and keep the kettle away from my legs, I probably did look as if I was dancing. When I was fifty yards from the tree, Grandfather called, "Quit your playing! Quit your playing! Fetch them bellows and my bee hat. Time and tarnation! Why don't you hurry?"

He was standing at the foot of the ladder, had passed the rope around the trunk of the tree, through the back of his suspenders, and tied a running noose in the end of it. All the time I'd been bringing the stuff in, I'd been telling myself I wasn't going to let Grandfather see how scared I was to climb that ladder after the bees. But it never occurred to me that he might be going to do it himself. The minute I saw him standing there, I knew that was what he was planning, and I got the same feeling in my stomach that you have sometimes when an elevator goes down quickly. Before I even stopped to think, I hollered, "No! No! I'm going up after them." And my voice sounded just the way my stomach felt.

Instead of being mad because I hollered at him, Grandfather's voice was as mild as milk. "Why, Ralphie," he said, "you ain't scairt 'bout your old grampa falling, be you? Thunderation! Father clim ladders whenst he was ten years older'n I be. It's all in knowing how. Now fetch me my bee gloves and hat, and get your'n on. Twilight's a-falling."

I put on my gloves, pulled the netting sleeves up over my arms, and crammed the hat tight onto my head, with the bee veil hanging down around my shoulders. I'd hardly finished when Grandfather said, "Hand me the bellows, Ralphie! I'm a-going up, and you follow after with the smudge kettle." He hadn't put his bee hat on, but squeezed it under one arm, along with the bellows. With both hands, he flipped the rope a couple of feet up the far side of the tree trunk, stepped up two rungs on the ladder, and flipped the rope again. When his feet were just above my head, he looked down, and said, "Keep leaning in close agin the ladder, Ralphie. You'll have a hard chance with only one free hand for hanging on." Then he flipped the rope again, and went on.

It was hard enough to handle the hot kettle on the ground, but ten times worse on the ladder. Besides being hot, it was belching smoke like a chimney, and the chokiest smoke I ever had to breath. We got along all right till Grandfather reached the top of the ladder. When his face was just about level with the bee hole, he knotted the rope so that he could lean back against it with both hands free. I heard a bee buzz, and looked up just in time to see it light on the bottom of the little hole in front of Grandfather's face, then disappear. He took the bellows out from under his arm, but left his bee hat squeezed there tight. Without it on, I was sure he'd be stung to death but, before I could speak, he whispered, "Histe the kettle up here, so's I can get at it, Ralphie. Higher! Higher! Shin on up here and take a-holt on my leg so's you can histe it higher."

Grandfather had both feet braced on the top rung of the ladder, and was leaning back a couple of feet against the tight loop of rope. I was so afraid his feet would slip, or that the rope would come untied, that I was shaking all over. And I didn't dare grab hold of him for fear of throwing him off balance. I'd only hesitated a few seconds when he whispered, "Take a-holt! Take a-holt, Ralphie! Don't be scairt; I ain't a-going to let you fall. Histe it up high a minute."

My arm was shaking like the legs of a frightened dog, but I hooked it around Grandfather's knee and climbed up a couple more rungs. Then I held the hot kettle as high as I could while he sucked the bellows full of smoke. His leg, under my arm, was as steady as if it had been a limb of the tree. I knew from it, that he was neither afraid of falling, nor of the bees stinging his bare face. Just knowing it made me stop shaking, and I didn't even wince when the kettle burned my arm a little as I held it up to him. After the bellows were filled with smoke, he held it tight to the bee hole and squeezed slowly. Then, quick as a flash, he poked the empty bellows into the top of his trousers, and said, "Go down, Ralphie! Go down! That'll fetch 'em."

As soon as I was down a few rungs, I leaned against the ladder and looked up at Grandfather. He'd swiped the bee hat out from under his arm, and was holding the open end of the veil around the little hole as the bees streamed out. There were still more bees coming out of the hole after the veil had become a sackful. I'd been so interested that I'd forgotten to go down any farther. Grandfather closed the mouth of the veil and slacked his rope off enough to let it slip a foot or so. "Go on down, Ralphie! Go on down!" he told me. "Your old grampa's got 'em. Cal'late the queen's somewheres in the hat."

When he was far enough down to hook his free arm around the ladder rung, Grandfather untied the safety rope and let it fall. All around him, the air was thick with bees, but he seemed to pay no attention to them as he came slowly rung by rung. As his foot reached the ground, he let out a long breath, and half whispered, "There, by gorry, Ralphie! Guess we showed 'em what kind of logs makes wide shingles." He lifted the cover, and dumped part of the bees into the hive. Then he knelt, placed the throat of the veil before the stoop of the beehive, and stepped back.

"Sit you down, Ralphie," he said, as he stepped over to a big stump. "Sit you down with your old grampa and let's mark 'em for a spell. Happen I got the queen on the inside, they'll all follow her in."

The sun had gone down. The sky, through the branches of the trees, was still bright blue, but twilight was spreading through the woods. A thrush, from somewhere toward the meadow, sang her evening song. Frogs tuned their fiddles in the swale along the brook. From higher up the ridge, a crow cawed three, evenly spaced, harsh notes. They were gone for a moment. Then, when the woods across the valley echoed them back, there was music in them. Listening to the twilight sounds, I'd forgotten all about the bees till Grandfather whispered, "Curious . . . bees. Mark how they're a-piling up in front the hive?" After sitting quiet a few minutes, he went on. "Was all men as respecting of the Almighty as bees is of their queen, there'd be no call for neither jails nor courthouses."

"Why didn't they sting you when you went up there without your bee veil on?" I asked him.

"Gorry! Why would they?" he asked. "It's the cool of evening, and I wa'n't scairt of 'em. Bees won't generally sting you lest you're scairt. Cal'late they smell the scare on you, same as a dog does." Then his voice rose a little. "By fire, she's in, Ralphie! Mark how they 'pear to be flowing acrost the threshold. 'Twon't be long! 'Twon't be long now till we can nail 'em up and fetch 'em home."

Bess

18

I Meet Annie

Wɪᴛʜ no bees to hunt, Grandfather nearly drove the yella colt and me crazy. Instead of coming to the high field only for an hour in the mornings, he'd show up half a dozen times a day. I'd no more than get the colt settled down from one fit of rearing and balking, till Grandfather would come back, take the plow out of my hands, and get everything all mixed up again. I couldn't do anything to please him, and once when I happened to mention strawberries, he shouted, "Don't you never durst to let me hear you say strawb'ries again! How many times do I have to tell you this is hay land? Ain't never been nothing else since Father cleared it. Strawb'ries! Great Thunderation! Garden sass!"

Grandfather even yelled at Old Bess till she'd follow along behind him with her belly almost dragging on the ground. Millie couldn't please him any better than I could. Saturday evening, she came out to the tie-up while I was milking, and she was boiling mad. "What in tunket got into Thomas off to encampment is more'n I know," she blurted. " 'Cepting for them first few days when you come back, he ain't been fit to live with nobody. Never seen the beat of it in all my born days! Squawking about his victuals! Hiding off in his room to write letters he's scairt to let a body see! Running out to pass 'em to the mail carrier 'sted of posting 'em in the box! What does he think I be, a snooping busybody?"

"Maybe he's getting sick again," I said.

"Sick! Hmff! Ain't no more sicker than I be!" Then she grabbed up the milk bucket and hurried out of the tie-up.

Sunday didn't start off very well. Millie and Grandfather were both cross at breakfast. As I'd come in from the morning chores, I stubbed my toe on the back-pantry doorsill, and spilled nearly half the milk on the floor. Grandfather called me heedless, clumsy, and woolgathering, and Millie called me everything he didn't think of. Before I took the cows to pasture, I decided to stay away from the house till supper time. I went to my room and slipped a few sheets of writing paper, some envelopes, and a pencil into the front of my shirt. The Astrachan apples were turning red on the tree in the corner of the orchard, so I climbed the lane wall and filled my pockets. Then, when I got to the pasture, I went hunting for a good place to do a little letter writing myself.

Grandfather's hidden field was really two fields, shaped like an hourglass. It was down beyond the maple grove and the hemlock woods, and was entirely walled in by tall pines. Long ago, it had been a hayfield, but it was run-out. The bars were always down, and it was part of the pasture. The roadway that led to it was nothing but an overgrown set of wheel tracks through the woods. I decided the hidden field would be a good place for writing, and started following along the wheel ruts. I'd gone as far as the hemlock woods, just beyond the sugarhouse at the edge of the maples, when I noticed a flat table of gray stone farther up the hill. I remembered Grandfather's telling about the granite outcropping, so I climbed up to see what it was like.

It was a beautiful place for writing. A solid ledge of gray-blue granite crowned the highest point on the farm. The top of the ledge was almost as flat and smooth as though it had been planed, and was as large as the foundation of a good-sized house. On the west, it seemed to swell out of a hedge of junipers. At the north were the maples, a few white birches, and, rising above them, the great green dome of the three oaks that grew from a single stump. To the east, the ledge broke off in irregular steps to the top of the hemlock-covered hillside. And southward, the thick tops of young pines billowed away like a tossing green sea to meet their older brothers at the edge of the hidden field.

I'd promised to write Mother and Uncle Levi. When I'd slipped the paper into the front of my shirt, I'd been going to tell them that Grandfather wasn't sick any longer, that I couldn't do anything to please him, and that I thought I'd better come home right away. Sitting there on the steps, with the ledge for a table, and the smell of juniper and pine and hemlock in the air, I couldn't seem to find the words I wanted to write.

I took an apple out of my pocket, and began eating it while I thought about what I was going to say. The seeds were just turning brown and the juice was tart. It squirted every time my teeth bit through the red skin. The core was still pretty good-sized when a squirrel began scolding at me from a limb of the nearest maple tree. I asked him if he thought his name was Thomas, but he only flipped his tail and ducked away to the far side of the tree trunk. Then, from first one side of the trunk and then the other, he would stick his head out and scold some more.

I had all day, so there was no hurry about the letters. I put a stone on the paper, and took the apple core over to the maple. I laid it on the ground, three or four feet from the near side of the trunk, then went back to lie on the ledge and see how long before the squirrel would dare come down for it. I don't think it was a question of daring at all. I think it was flirting. One minute, he would pop his nose out from behind the tree trunk, not more than two feet above the ground, cock his head on one side, then the other; blink his eyes, and chatter. The next minute, he would scold at me from a branch forty feet above the ground, flip his tail and bark, as if he were daring me to come up and try to catch him.

I didn't make a sound or move a muscle, but lay there on my stomach, watching the little fellow. I don't know how long I'd lain there, but the squirrel had been up and down the tree a dozen times when the tone of his chattering changed, and he stopped paying any attention to me. He would run out a little way on the big limb that reached toward the hemlocks, scold crossly, snap his tail hard, then scurry back and flatten himself against the far side of the trunk—but in plain sight from where I was lying.

There was only the faintest breath of breeze moving. I couldn't be sure from what direction it came, so I wet a finger on my tongue, held it up in front of my face, and watched to see which side would dry first. It was the side toward the hemlocks; toward the spot the squirrel had been watching and scolding at. I was downwind from it, and no animal hiding there could scent me. I'd seen a red fox one evening when I went for the cows, and was pretty sure he was somewhere there in the hemlocks, and that the squirrel had seen him.

I bellyhooked carefully toward the hemlock edge of the out-cropping, and then my heart began pounding. Annie Littlehale was standing behind a hemlock trunk, peeking around it, and watching the squirrel tree. She wasn't more than twenty-five yards from me, her black hair rippled in a cascade over her shoulders, and her face was the prettiest I had ever seen. It wasn't white like Millie's, and it wasn't tanned dark like mine, but was light golden brown—and there was a glow of red in her lips and her cheeks. As I watched her, with my chin pressed close against the granite, she drew her lips back from her teeth, and made a ticking sound at the squirrel. They were as white and gleaming as a rift of snow caught in the folds of a brown oak leaf.

When I was a little boy, Mother used to sing snatches of an old song that I always liked. She only sang it when she was spin-ning, and never more than three verses. But she sang them over and over to the rhythm of the wheel. And always, with the first word of every alternate line, she'd take one step forward and let the newly spun length of yarn wind up on the spindle. As I lay

there watching Annie, the words and music of the old song came into my head and kept going over and over:

"Nut brown maiden, Thou hast a ruby lip to kiss,
  Nut brown maiden, Thou hast a ruby lip;
  A ruby lip is thine, love! The kissing of it's mine, love!
  Nut brown maiden, Thou hast a ruby lip."

I didn't realize that my head was bobbing in rhythm to the song till Annie turned my way quickly. Her face looked startled for half a second, then she said, "You're Ralph, aren't you?"

Maybe it was from thinking of the song about her lips. Any-

way, my heart began pounding again, and I had to swallow before I could say, "Yes. And you're Annie Littlehale. I saw you
driving the cows." As soon as I'd said it, I felt foolish. Of course,
she knew I'd seen her driving the cows; she waved to Millie and
me when we were haying.

Annie might have been startled when she first saw me there
on the ledge, but it didn't bother her long. She began picking
her way toward me over the hummocky floor of the hemlock
woods, and talking all the way. "I heard the squirrel barking
from way down by the tree where Mr. Gould's swarm of bees
nested," she said, "and was afraid our cat might be after him.
We've got one that loves to catch squirrels. Some day I'm going
to catch him in the act and teach him a good lesson."

The nearer she came, the prettier she was. Her wavy black
hair seemed to spring as she stepped, and her eyes were a bright
coppery brown. I couldn't just lie there dumb, and all I could
think to say, was, "I thought you were a fox."

"Because my hair is so red?" she asked, and laughed.

"I wouldn't want it red; it's prettier black," I told her as I
rolled over and sat up. "I've always liked black hair."

When I turned over, a couple of apples had fallen out of my
pockets and were rolling on the ledge. Annie saw them as she
began climbing the big steps of the outcropping. She held one
hand up for me to help her, as she said, "And I like red apples.
Astrachans, aren't they? Ours aren't ripe yet. Oh, you're writing
letters! I'll only stop long enough to eat an apple."

We ate all the apples while Annie and I sat there on the
ledge, and we didn't even notice when the squirrel came down
and took my first apple core. Then we went for a walk through
the pines, around the hidden field, and along the brook that ran
beyond it. Annie knew so much more about the woods, the flow-
ers, the birds, and the wild animals than I did that it made me
feel sort of stupid. She could name every bird we saw or heard,
could imitate the song or call of most of them, and knew the
signs of all the animals.

Once, where the bank was soft and bare beside the brook, she pointed to a track that looked as if a tiny baby had laid its hand there. "Raccoon," she told me. "A good big one. He was fishing last night. See where the grass is matted by that gravelly bend? He must come here often. That's where he wets his food before he eats it. Raccoons don't have saliva, as we and other animals do, so he has to wet his food before he can swallow it. A raccoon always has one place that he likes better than any other in all the world. He may go away and leave it for a long time, but he'll always come back. If anyone was mean enough, he could trap this one here where the grass is matted. You won't ever trap him, will you, Ralph?"

I told her I'd never trap him, and then, to keep from seeming too ignorant, I told Annie a few stories about Colorado; the ranches I'd worked on, and the roundups I'd ridden in. It was nearly ten o'clock when I left her at Littlehale's pasture bars, and she went running up the lane so she'd be in time to go to Sunday school with her brother.

When I went back to the outcropping, I started right in on my letters. The one to Mother came out a little too much birds and raccoons, but I kept them out of Uncle Levi's, and I didn't write either of them that I was coming home. I took another walk after I'd finished, but along toward noon I began to worry that Grandfather might forget to feed the horses, so I went to the barn. He was feeding them when I got there, and was still as cross as he had been at breakfast. "Where you been, and what have you been up to?" he asked me when I came in.

"Well, I went for a walk in the woods, and I wrote some letters," I told him.

"See anybody?"

"Yes, sir."

"Who?"

"Annie Littlehale."

"What was you doing?"

"Oh, just talking and going for a walk."

"In the woods?"

"Well, part of the time."

Grandfather glared at me, and shouted, "Don't you never *durst* let me catch you gallivanting off into the woods with no girls! When you ain't busy working, you stay where I can keep an eye on you! What was you up to?"

"Well, Annie was telling me about the different kinds of bark on different kinds of trees, and about birds, and we saw a place where a raccoon had been fishing. Did you know that . . ."

"By thunder, I know that Mary didn't send you down here to go gallivanting about the woods with no girls on the Sabbath. I'll learn you all you need to know 'bout birds and bark. Now fetch some tools and go to taking that fool contraption of your'n off the dumpcart. That'll keep you out of mischief whilst I'm busy."

"I haven't been into any mischief," I told him, "and that spreader attachment on the dumpcart would save us a lot of . . ."

"Don't you tell me! Get it off of there! Get it off, I tell you! Won't have no tarnal contraptions about this farm! Work saving! Good-for-nothing! Work never hurt nobody!" Grandfather was still grumbling when he jabbed the pitchfork into a corner and stamped off toward the house.

19

The Stone Rake

I FINISHED plowing Monday night, and expected to haul dressing Tuesday morning, but I didn't. After breakfast, I was harnessing the yella colt when, from the stall doorway, Grandfather snapped, "Let be! Let be! You go to picking rocks off the high field. There's an auction I got to attend over to Sabattus. Cal'late on keeping my eye peeled for a milk cow or two. Butter's twenty-eight cents, dressing is tarnal short, and there's plenty hay. Hitch Old Nell to the spring wagon!"

Grandfather went down to the hives, and was still there when I'd finished harnessing and had Nell hitched to the wagon. "She's all ready," I called as I led her toward the house.

Without looking up from the hive he was watching, Grandfather said crossly, "Let be! Let be! Get after them rocks!"

"How small sized ones do you want me to pick up?" I asked.

"Get 'em all! Get 'em all above the size of a hen's egg!" he half shouted. "Cal'late that'll keep you out of mischief whilst my back is turned."

"I haven't been in any mischief," I told him, "and I get a lot more work done when your back is turned."

Grandfather sprang up as if a bee had stung him. He scowled

179

up at me, and shouted, "Mind your manners! And don't go just a-picking rocks off the top neither. Fetch along a potato fork and a bushel basket, and turn up them that's under the ground. Pick 'em clean and pile 'em close agin the nigh side the orchard wall."

While I'd been plowing the high field, I'd told myself there must be ten thousand rocks on it. When I began picking them up, it seemed more like a million. A few were as big as a watermelon, but most of them were from four to seven inches through, and nearly every one was almost round. After an hour, my back felt as if it were breaking, and I'd only cleared a patch ten feet square. At that rate, it would take me six months to clear the field. Besides that, I couldn't see any sense in digging a million rocks out of that old hayfield just to plant more hay on it.

I'd never cared how hard the work was if I could see it needed to be done. But to be given an endless, useless job so it would keep me out of mischief—particularly when I hadn't been into any mischief—made me sore! The wall at the top of the orchard lay right along the brow of the hill, a quarter mile south of the buildings. Every time I'd straighten up to get the kinks out of my back, I'd look over it, and see Grandfather still fussing around the beehives. And every time I saw him, it made me a little sorer. I made up my mind that I'd be careful to stay out of mischief, but I wouldn't break my back or hurry while I was doing it.

It wasn't until about eleven o'clock that Grandfather left the beehives. I watched him go out to meet the mail carrier, go into the house for a couple of minutes, then drive away. As I dragged the potato fork through the loose dirt, I began thinking that if I were a giant, and had a big rake, I could clean off that field as easy as raking pebbles on a beach. Next I began wondering how I could make a big rake that a horse could pull. I started monkeying around with the potato-fork handle; sticking it under half-buried round stones at different angles, and pushing it along to see how they'd move. If I slanted it just right, the stones would turn and slide up the fork handle to the top of the ground.

After finding how the rocks moved, it didn't take any inventing at all to know how to make a stone rake. All I'd need would be a sort of harrow, with long teeth set at just the right angle, and close enough together that they'd rake up every stone bigger than a hen's egg. The teeth would have to be set in the shape of a V, with the point open, so it would roll the raked stones into a narrow row.

It was a little after twelve o'clock when I went to the house for dinner, and Millie was furious. My being late didn't help any, but it was Grandfather she was really mad at. The morning had been hot and muggy, the kitchen was swarming with flies, and Millie was shooing them away from the table with her apron. Every time she flapped it, she'd blurt out a few words. "Where you been? What sort of devilment you been hatching up now? Devilish wonder the flies ain't et the victuals afore you come to get 'em! Thomas tell you where he was going?"

"To an auction," I told her. "He said butter was twenty-eight cents a pound and he wanted to get another cow or two."

"He needn't think I'm going to make him no butter in this fly trap! Hmff! Come out looking like blueberry muffins! Levi promised he'd make me screens afore he went back to Boston. The wire's around here some place, and he'd have made 'em, too, if Thomas hadn't run him off. What does Thomas think I be; a sneak thief? Locking his bedroom door afore he steps foot off the place! Good Lord! I got two minds to one to go off and leave him right now!"

Millie sounded mad enough to have gone, and I didn't want her to, so I said, "I've had two minds to one to go all morning, but I'm not going, and I'll make a deal with you. I know where the screen wire is, and I'll make screens for you, the first chance I get, if you'll help me make a stone rake now."

Millie looked sort of frightened. She'd been shouting, but her voice dropped almost to a whisper, "Did Thomas tell you to make it?" she asked.

"No, he didn't," I said. "But I'm going to make it anyway. It would take me from now till next haying time to pick all the rocks off that field by hand, and I'm not going to do it. If what he wants is to get rid of the rocks, I'll do it for him, but I'm not going to do a useless job the hardest way just so I won't have time to do anything else."

"I won't help you!" Millie snapped. "Ain't Thomas mad enough at you a'ready for what you done to the dumpcart?"

"He can get just as mad as he wants to," I said. "I'll go back to Boston before I'll dig another stone out of that field."

Millie's under lip trembled, and she said, "I'll help you, Ralphie. I won't stay here alone with him another blessed day. He's so cussed contrary since he come home from his reunion that the Almighty Hisself couldn't live alone with him."

That was the first time anybody ever called me "Ralphie," when I liked it.

It took Millie and me most of the afternoon to make the stone rake. To get the right-sized spikes, I had to knock half the teeth out of a homemade harrow I found behind the sheep barn, and for the framework we used an oak four-by-six from the carriage-house attic. I didn't know just how wide we could make the rake without its being too heavy for one horse to pull, but there was just enough lumber to make it four feet, so that was the width we built it.

Grandfather had a drag for hauling heavy stones. It was just three wide oak planks bolted together, and had the front end rounded up a little, like a sleigh. I hitched the yella colt to the drag, loaded the new stone rake on it, and drove to the high field. As I drove, I had to think a little about which end of the field I'd better start on. Grandfather often came up the roadway that led through the high field. If I started there, he'd probably catch me within a day or two and make me stop using the rake. If I started on the back end of the field, he might not catch me so soon, but he'd think I wasn't getting anything done, and I'd have to show him the rake. After a few minutes, I decided I'd start right at the roadway. I wasn't going to try to hide anything, and if he got mad about it I could always go back to Boston.

I unloaded the rake at the near corner of the field, hitched the yella colt to it, and clucked to him. With the long teeth slanted well forward, the rake dug itself deep into the ground. After two or three steps, the old horse stopped and looked back, as though he were trying to tell me he couldn't pull it. When I swung the line ends up, he lunged forward a few more steps. The plowed soil inside the rake wings seemed to boil, rocks came to the surface, and rolled out through the tail of the V.

There was no question but what the rake was heavy for one horse to pull, or that it did a better job if it was pulled fast. After the first few tries, the yella colt learned to hit the collar hard, tear into it for fifteen or twenty yards, then stop and rest till he caught his wind. I never raked more than one round across the field at a time. Then I'd hitch him to the drag, load the rocks with a dungfork, and haul them to the wall. Of course, all the rocks didn't work the same way. When we'd run onto a big one that wouldn't go through the back of the V, I'd have to lift it out. And all the larger ones had to be lifted on and off the drag, too, but it was an awful lot faster and easier than doing all the work by hand—and I nearly forgot that it was a useless job.

Grandfather didn't come home till it was pitch dark and I had the chores nearly finished. I was coming up from the sheep barn with the lantern when he sang out from the dooryard, "Ralphie! Millie! Come see what I fetched you home! Come a-running!"

His voice was as pleasant as it had been cross that morning. "By gorry, I sure made me a powerful good trade over to the auction! You'll like her, Ralphie! Brindle! Clever as a kitten! Got a bag on her bigger'n a washtub! So, Bossie, so! Cal'late she'll freshen in 'bout three, four days. Powerful big in the girth. So, Boss! Ralphie ain't going to hurt you."

I held the lantern up as I went past the spring wagon. The cow tied to the back of it was in good flesh, had a nice brindle color, and looked to be awfully heavy with calf. I wouldn't have guessed her to be over five years old, and she was gentle when I led her to the spring for water and then to the tie-up.

All through supper, Grandfather talked about the auction, the new cow, what a good trade he'd made on her, and how many more cows he was going to buy. He was never cross once, and he didn't ask me how many rocks I'd picked off the high field. It was nearly ten o'clock before we went to bed.

The next morning, Grandfather came to the tie-up while I was milking. I didn't hear him till he sang out, "Gorry sakes alive, Ralphie! Ain't she a beauty?" He ran his hand along the new cow's back, pressed it against first one side of her and then the other. "Gorry sakes! Gorry sakes!" he said over and over, as he laid a palm against her, pressed it with the other hand, and seemed to be listening. "Great thunderation! Wouldn't be a mite s'prised if she was to have twin calves. Gorry sakes! Might happen they'd be steers! Ralphie, did ever you drive a yoke of steers? Powerful good critters in the woods. Steady. Ain't high-strung and flibbertigibbet like hosses. I and you might need a yoke of steers whenst we go to clearing the wilderness field."

I didn't know what Grandfather meant by the wilderness field, but it made me remember about the rocks in the high field, so I asked, "Is it all right if I use the stone drag to haul rocks off the high field? Some of them are pretty heavy to carry."

"Hosses! Hosses! Hosses!" Grandfather snapped. "Can't you do nothing without hosses? I got to use Old Nell. Got to attend every auction roundabouts. Got to keep my eye peeled for milk cows. Afore snow flies, I cal'late on having one in every stanchion in the tie-up. How many stanchions is there, Ralphie?"

Before he'd finished, the edge was all gone from his voice, so I said, "There are ten good ones and two broken. If I fix the broken ones, can I use the yella colt for hauling rocks?"

"Have to be all-fired careful of him. High-strung! Ain't fit for a boy to handle! Twelve, you say? Gorry! Afore the fire, there was twenty. Come winter, I and you'll get out the timber for building on the rest of the barn. By fire, I do believe this old heifer's going to have twin calves. 'Twould tickle me if they was steers." When I looked up from stripping Clara Belle, Grandfather was gone.

I thought there was going to be a bad wrangle at the breakfast table the next morning. The night had turned a little chilly for the end of July, and flies were thick on the kitchen ceiling. Millie was peevish about them. When Grandfather began talking about all the cows he was going to buy, she snapped, "Better get dry ones, or fetch calves along with 'em! If you're cal'lating on me making butter in this beehive of flies, you've got another cal'late a-coming."

Instead of blowing up, Grandfather chuckled, "Feisty, ain't you, Millie girl? Come fall, I'm cal'lating on fetching a hundred pounds of butter a week off to Lewiston. Ought to be thirty cents, come fall."

"Hmmff!" Millie sniffed. "What you cal'lating on selling it for, mincemeat?" She looked up at the ceiling, and sniffed again. "Time cold weather comes and them flies starts a-falling, all the extra it'll need is a peck of chopped apples."

Grandfather threw his head back and laughed right out loud. Then he stopped suddenly, with his mouth open and his eyes looking all around the ceiling. "Gorry sakes alive! Don't never recollect seeing the little critters so thick. Hmmm. Cal'late I might keep my eye peeled for a good trade on some screen cloth. Whack you up some window screens whenst I get time."

I didn't want Millie to push Grandfather any further, so I reached a foot out to tap hers under the table. Either she didn't notice it, or she didn't know what I meant. She leaned forward, and said quickly, "Levi fetched screening. Ralph knows where it's at. He'll make 'em for me. I'll help . . ."

"Eat your victuals! Eat your victuals, Ralphie!" Grandfather snapped, and pushed his chair back from the table. "Time flies, and we got to get them tarnal rocks off the high field afore snow flies. Get your hosses out! Get your hosses out! And keep an eye on that new cow whilst I'm to the auction. Like as not she'll freshen any minute now."

Even with the rake, clearing the stones from the high field was a hard job, but for the next four days I had fun doing it. I stepped off the length of the field, and found that to cover it all would take a hundred and five trips across and back with the stone rake. If Grandfather didn't catch me using it, and if I could do a row an hour, I figured the whole job could be finished in twenty days. As soon as the yella colt and I got used to it, we could clear a row and have five or ten minutes to rest in every hour. Each evening, I watched for Annie Littlehale to go for her cows, and waved to her. Friday evening, I went down to the pasture wall and talked to her for a few minutes. Before I went back, she asked me to go to Sunday school with her the next Sunday. I said I would, but I didn't.

I don't know where Grandfather found all the auctions, but he went to one every day that week. And he always did it in just the same way. He'd either be in the house or down at the bee-hives till the mailman came, then he'd drive away as fast as he could go. He brought home two heifer calves, a worn-out mowing machine, and a lot of odds and ends that he piled on the bench in the carriage house. He never came home till dark, he never came near the high field, and we never could tell what he'd be like when he got home. Two evenings, he was as proud and happy as a kitten with its first mouse. The other two, he was cross, snapped and shouted at both Millie and me, and went to bed just as soon as he'd eaten a few bites of supper. Friday night was one of the good ones, and Saturday night was terrible.

When I brought the cows into the tie-up Friday night, it was easy to see that the brindle cow was awfully near to her time. She was lying down in her stanchion, rocking her head, and sort of moaning, and she was a little feverish. After I'd stanchioned the other cows, I got her up, put her in the spare boxstall, and brought her a bucket of water. Grandfather came home just as I was going to the house for the milk pails, and he shouted to me as he turned into the driveway from the road, "By gorry, Ralphie, I fetched us home a tarnal fine trading cow. Got a calf! Heifer! Made a powerful good trade on 'em. How's the brindle a-doing?"

I didn't shout back, but waited for him at the corner of the woodshed, and told him I thought the brindle was about ready to calve. Before he'd go to look at her, he wanted me to see the new cow and calf. They were both pretty sad looking. The calf wasn't more than two or three days old, it was lying out flat on the floor of the spring wagon, and it looked like a bundle of bones done up in a spotted calfskin. The cow looked even worse. There wasn't enough meat on her to make a good meal for a coyote, she was knock-kneed in front and splay-footed in back. She had narrow horns on a narrow head that hung like a tired camel's, and her udder looked like a half peck of potatoes in an old cotton bag.

"Gorry, ain't she the best trading cow ever you seen?" Grandfather asked as he climbed down from the wagon. He didn't wait long enough that I had to answer, but ran his hand along her hummocky back, and kept right on talking. "Little dite on the thin side, but that ain't nothing some good provender won't take care of. Mark the veins along the sides of that bag. Don't put them kind of veins on there for nothing, Ralphie. Don't cal'late she's more'n eight, nine years old. Spunk right up with a little good provender in her. Cal'late she ought to be good for two, three pounds of butter a day. You fetch the calf on down to the sheep barn whilst I put the cow in the tie-up. Gorry sakes! That was a powerful good trade I made!"

When I'd taken the new calf to the sheep barn, unhitched Nell, and taken her to the barn, Grandfather was in the stall with the brindle cow. "Fetch me the lantern! Fetch me the lantern, Ralphie!" he called as I led Nell into the barn. "We got a tarnal sick cow on our hands. Tell Millie to fetch a kettle of hot water and the washbasin. It's twins a'right, and I cal'late they're tangled."

We didn't have any supper that night. Grandfather was

hardly off his knees from the time I brought the lantern. He was as gentle with the cow as a mother would be with a sick baby, but every once in a while he'd snap an order sharply at Millie or me. As he worked over her, he told us the calves would both be either heifers or steers, because they were in the same sack, and that they were going to be born backwards. It was nearly midnight before Grandfather delivered the second steer calf, moved it forward so its mother could lick it, and climbed to his feet. He was so tired that his shoulders slumped forward, but he seemed happy, and as proud as if the two star-faced red calves had been his own babies. "Gorry sakes, children, ain't they pretty ones?" he asked. Then he straightened up for a minute, and said, "By fire, Ralphie, them's going to make us a yoke of steers! Come three-year-olds, they'll fetch a log out of the woods that no team of hosses this side the Androscoggin could budge an inch. Cal'late we'll need 'em whenst we go to clearing the wilderness field." He leaned over, patted the cow's head, and whispered to her, "Your trouble's all over for this trip. You'll be fit as a fiddle, come morning."

20

The Screen Door Bangs

I'D NEVER seen a cow that milked any easier than the new one. She didn't lift a foot or even switch her tail, and the milk came in wide white ribbons until the froth stood high above the top of a twelve-quart pail. Grandfather was almost hugging himself at the good trade he'd made, and all through breakfast Saturday morning, he could only talk about how much butter we were going to have next winter and how big a log the steer calves would be able to pull when they were three years old.

Grandfather was still happy when I went to rake stones in the high field. But when I got there, I was sure he'd been there ahead of me. Along the orchard wall, there was a trail where the dew was knocked off the grass. In the soft ground at the end of the last row I'd raked, there were two marks of a man's shoes. They were the same size and shape as Grandfather's, and were within a foot of the rake. The toe marks were much deeper than the heels, so I knew the man had been squatting down and looking at it carefully. If it had been Grandfather, I couldn't understand why he hadn't scolded me, or why he'd been so happy at breakfast.

Whatever upset him must have been something that came in

the mail. I'd just hauled a load of stones to the orchard wall when Grandfather left the beehives, went to meet the mailman, and then into the house. I had the drag unloaded, and was just straightening up to get the kinks out of my back, when I heard him shouting from the direction of the buildings. At that distance, I couldn't make out a word he was saying, but I could tell that he was terribly mad. He was standing by Old Nell's head at the corner of the woodshed, and seemed to be shaking his fist at the summer-kitchen doorway as he shouted. A minute later, Millie stepped into the doorway. Her voice came sharp as she yelled back at Grandfather, but I couldn't make out one word from another. It lasted three or four minutes. Then Grandfather climbed onto the wagon and drove away at a hard trot.

When I pulled the next load to the wall, I saw Millie coming up the roadway past the side of the orchard. She had a jug in her hand and, from the way she was walking, I knew she was madder than a trapped weasel. She didn't answer when I called, "Hi, Millie," and kept her lips pressed tight together till she was right in front of me. Then she held the jug out, and snapped, "Fetched you some switchel! Ain't going to stay here another cussed day!" She kept right on spluttering while I drank. "What does Thomas think I be; a dog to get hollered at every cussed time he makes a bad trade or gets a letter he don't like? So tarnation ugly this morning Old Bess can't even abide him and has hid off under the woodshed. I ain't going to stand it another blessed day!"

"This switchel's pretty good," I told her. "It's cold, and you seem kind of hot. Let's go sit in the shade while the colt rests. I've kept him on the go all morning."

"Don't want to sit down! Don't want no switchel! I want to know what's got into Thomas! Sweet as sugar one day, and bitter as gall the next!"

"What's the matter," I asked her, "did the brindle cow die?"

"Not yet, but she will devilish quick if ever she kicks me again!"

"What were you trying to milk her for?" I asked. "Her milk won't be any good for two or three days. Why don't you let the calves suck her?"

"Can't suck her! Ain't a teat on her but it's growed up with warts till the good Lord Hisself couldn't milk her."

"Don't worry about it," I told her.

" 'Tain't the cow! It's the letters! I want to know what in tunket Thomas is up to! Sneaking mail abouts like a lovesick widow woman! Hmmff! Ain't no fool like an old fool!" Millie's eyes squinted and she pinched her mouth up tight. "Don't cal'late he's been a-writing to them matermonial papers, do you? Waiting on the mailman, and a-driving toward the Falls like as if the devil was after him! Ain't you took note he's been a-meeting the noon train? Good Lord a-living! I got two minds to one to go off and leave him right this blessed minute! I'll go off to Lewiston and get me a job in the mill."

The train whistled two long and two short blasts for the Lisbon Falls crossing. The sound came sort of faint and wailing through the woods. Millie jerked one hand up, cupped it around her ear, and said, "Hark! Do you mark that? If Thomas thinks he's going to fetch some fat old . . ."

"Oh, you're crazy, Millie," I told her.

"Ain't neither!" she almost cried. "What's he sneaking around with letters for? Why won't he eat my victuals no more? Why does he get so cussed mad when I want to get my kitchen screens up? Levi fetched . . ."

I already had the stones cleared off nearly a fifth of the high field, and had plenty of time, so I said, "You go on back to the house and get dinner ready. I like your victuals, and I'll quit for the day as soon as I get the rocks hauled from this last row. It'll take me about an hour. Then I'll make your screens for you this afternoon."

Millie was almost running as she went down the hill toward the house, and she must have worked at a run after she got there. When I'd finished and taken the yella colt to the barn, I heard her singing in the kitchen. She'd seen me coming, and had dinner all on the table. "There, by gosh!" she called when I came into the back pantry. "Let Thomas fetch home his widow woman if he wants to! I ain't going to scrinch and pinchpenny on the victuals no more for him. I killed a young fryer for dinner, and I'm going to kill another one tomorrow. Got a cake in the oven with three eggs in it, too. Let his widow woman try baking with one egg! By the Eternal, I'd like to see how long she'll live on boiled potatoes and sowbelly! Never have nothing fitting to eat 'cepting when Levi comes!"

The only way I could get the idea of a widow out of Millie's head was to talk about the screens. She kept telling me over and over that she wanted a spring strong enough to slam the door shut before half the flies in creation could follow a body inside.

With Uncle Levi's having the lumber for the frames all ripped and planed, making the screens wasn't a very big job. As I fitted the corner joints, bored holes, and drove the dowel pins, Millie tacked on the screen wire and the molding. All afternoon, she was as nervous and cranky as a setting hen. Every few minutes, she'd go to the carriage-house door and look out to see if Grandfather was coming. And every time I'd have to plane a joint over, she'd yap at me for being too particular. We had to take the hinges off the bran bin in the barn, and we used a knob from one of Uncle Levi's bench drawers but, at first, we couldn't find a spring to hold the door shut. It wasn't until we had them all hung that I thought of using a thin birch sapling.

Grandfather still hadn't come home when we were all finished, and I tended the door while Millie shooed the flies out of the kitchen. "There, by gosh!" she said, as she stood pulling the new door open and letting the bent sapling slam it to. "Bet you Thomas ain't a-going to leave that door standing half open! Time he was getting home to his victuals."

The chores took till way after dark, because the brindle cow was almost impossible to milk. She wouldn't let her twin calves suck, her teats were so overgrown with warts that I could only get a fine spray of milk from them, and she kicked like an army mule. Millie was holding a fork handle between the brindle's legs so she wouldn't kick me off the stool, and I had her about half milked when Grandfather shouted, "Whoa! Whoa, Nell!" from the dooryard. By the time we got to the front barn door, he'd climbed down from the wagon and started for the house. There was moonlight enough to see that he had his arms loaded with what looked to be crocks and tin pans he'd bought at the auction. After one glance, Millie ran toward him, calling, "Wait! Wait, Thomas! I'll open it for you!"

She was too late. Grandfather scrooched a little, stuck two fingers out from under a crock, and got hold of the knob on the new screen door. He pulled back a few inches, balanced on one foot, and poked the other one into the crack between the door and the jamb. The next second, he kicked the door halfway open, and it slammed back against his armload of crocks and pans. For a minute, it sounded as if a hurricane had struck a peddler's wagon. Then Grandfather yelled, *"Time and tarnation!"* so loud he could have been heard at Lisbon Falls. Before Millie could stop him, he'd kicked the screen out of the bottom of the door and yanked it off one hinge.

"What in time and tarnation kind of going on is this?" he hollered. "Ain't been no screen doors on this house in a hundred years, and there ain't going to be none now!"

Millie was pulling at his arm when I got there, and was yelling till I couldn't make out a word she was trying to say. Grandfather shoved her away, yanked at the doorframe again, and shouted at me, "Get it out of here! Get it out, I tell you! Don't let me see no more of your fiddle-faddle contraptions 'round this place. Won't have it! Won't have it, I tell you!"

By that time, Millie was crying like a little girl who has just broken her first doll. Her sunbonnet was pushed back off her head, and tears were rolling down her face in streams. She dashed them away with her hands, kicked the pans out of the way, and flung past Grandfather, sobbing, "I won't . . . stay here . . . another . . . cussed day."

When I heard the door of her room slam, Grandfather was still shouting after her, "Go off! Go off! Go off, and see if I care!" For a few seconds, I thought he was going to follow her but, instead, he stamped into his own room and slammed the door so hard it made the windows rattle.

I didn't know just what to do. There wasn't a thing I could say to Millie that would help. And if I tried to say anything to Grandfather, I'd only make matters worse. I got a screwdriver, and took the broken screen door down. After I'd put it away in the carriage-house attic, I unharnessed and fed Nell, and finished milking the brindle cow. When I started back to the house, Old Bess came slowly out of the woodshed. She knew something was wrong as well as I did, but she had no better idea what to do about it. She licked my hand, looked up at me, and whined questioningly.

The weatherbeaten house was dark both inside and out. In the pale moonlight, it looked as though nobody lived in it, or had for generations. I didn't want to go in, and sat down on the doorstone, with Old Bess' head in my lap. I don't know how long I sat there, just stroking her head and thinking. The shadow of the barn peak had moved nearly across the yard before I got up and went to bed. When I did, I knew what I was going to say to Grandfather if he was still cross in the morning.

Grandfather's voice was angry when he called me at five o'clock. He was stirring oatmeal into a kettle of steaming water when I came down to the kitchen. He didn't look up at me, but snapped, "Where's Millie at?"

"I don't know," I told him. "Isn't she here?"

" 'Course she ain't here, or I wouldn't be asking you," he shouted. "Where's she at?"

I'd made up my mind the night before that I wouldn't raise my voice to Grandfather. I didn't, but I said, "Probably she's on her way to Lewiston. That's where I'd be if I were in her place."

For half a minute, Grandfather stood looking at me as if he didn't believe he'd heard right. Then he blew off like an overheated boiler. After he'd told me to mind my manners, and had called me every kind of a fool boy he could think of, he began raving about Uncle Levi. He said that, between us, we'd ruined Millie till she wasn't worth a tarnal whoop, that he was glad she was gone, and that he hoped he'd never see her again. "Who in time and tarnation does Levi think he be?" he shouted. "Writing me letters how to run this place! He never run it, did he? Going off homesteading and leaving me here alone whenst I was sick abed! Come down here and stave the buildings all to smithereens with his fool contraptions! I won't have it! I won't have it, I tell you! Father fetched this place out of the wilderness with his bare hands, and, by fire, I ain't a-going to sit by and see it run back into wilderness with a bunch of newfangled fool contraptions. I won't have it! I won't have it, I tell you! Now get out there and go to digging up them rocks with a potato fork like I told you to do it in the first place."

After planning my speech so carefully the night before, I didn't intend to leave the kitchen until I'd made it. I tried to keep my voice quiet and steady, but it shook a little when I said, "I think I did you a good job in putting up the hay while you were sick. I spread more dressing while you were gone to the encampment than you thought I could. In four days I've taken all the rocks off nearly a fifth of the high field, when you thought the job would take till snow flew. I couldn't have done any one of those jobs without . . ."

"Get out of here!" Grandfather shouted, and waved the mixing spoon at me. "Get off this place afore I lose my temper! Get out! Get back to Boston where Levi can spoil you some more!"

After getting that far, I wasn't going to stop till I'd finished, so, right through Grandfather's shouting, I kept on, ". . . without contraptions, and most of the time you knew I was using them. That's why you kept out of sight till Millie and I had the haying all done. I don't mind hard work, but I won't do useless jobs the hard way just so I won't have time to do anything else. And I won't be yelled at all the time when I haven't done anything wrong."

I'd been so busy thinking about what I was going to say that, until I was all through talking, I didn't realize Grandfather had sent me home. Then I felt sort of silly. I went upstairs, changed my clothes, packed my suitcase, and left.

I heard Grandfather slamming things around in the carriage house as I went out the driveway, but I didn't look back. I did look in as I went past Littlehale's, but I didn't see Annie.

21

Grandfather's War, and Mine

AFTER I got back to Medford, I bought a Boston *Globe* and read all the "Male Help Wanted" ads. I had to try a dozen different places before I found a job, and the one I got was an easy one. That was the trouble with it. It was too easy. All I had to do was to run an elevator up and down in an apartment hotel at Mount Vernon and Joy Streets.

If the job had been in a busy office building, a department store, or a warehouse, I wouldn't have minded it, but Gray Chambers was too dignified and too quiet. I had to wear a tight green uniform, be careful never to close a door hard enough to make any noise, and to speak almost in a whisper. When there was nobody to take up or bring down, I had to stand beside the elevator doorway, and not cross my feet or lean against the wall.

Most of the people who lived at Gray Chambers were bachelors or old maids, and they were all past fifty. I went to work at three o'clock in the afternoon, and stayed till midnight, but the only time I had anything to do was when they were going out to supper or coming back afterwards. The rest of the time I just stood and looked in the mirror or at the floor or the ceiling, and thought about different things at the farm and how Annie Littlehale looked. After a week of it, I wished I was back picking up useless rocks or spreading manure, and I wouldn't have cared how much Grandfather yelled, "Tarnal fool boy," at me.

On my first Sunday night, I didn't have a single passenger after eight o'clock. Long before midnight, I was having a terrible time to keep awake and stand up straight. When I had only fifteen minutes more to wait, and was looking at my uniform in the mirror and telling myself I really was a tarnal fool boy, I heard the lobby door click. I'd just pulled my jacket down so my shirt wouldn't show around the middle, squared my shoulders, and was looking straight ahead when a familiar voice called out, "It's a God's wonder they ain't give you a bass drum. Where's the rest of the band?"

I forgot all about Gray Chambers and whispering, and shouted, "Hi, Uncle Levi! How did you get here?"

"Come in a hansom cab. Man's got to put on the style when he goes to visiting his folks on Beacon Hill. Kind of getting up in the world, ain't you?"

I'd never noticed that Uncle Levi's voice was loud till the "ain't you" came echoing down from the dome of the lobby. I think he noticed it, too, because he dropped the tone right down, and said, "Cabby's waiting outside. Ain't it 'bout time you was knocking off for the day?" As he spoke, he was slipping his watch out of its little leather pouch. He looked at it and added, "Ain't nothing but the shank of the day left noways. Just come from seeing Mary. She says you can sleep the night with me if you've a mind to."

I had never ridden in a hansom cab before, but the driver seemed to know Uncle Levi pretty well. "Fetch us to Hayes' place on Causeway Street," Uncle Levi told him. Then he slapped me on the leg and said, "Been to see Thomas. It's a God's wonder he hadn't starved afore I got there. Don't calc'late he'd et a bite 'cepting oatmeal since he run you and Millie off. Pot of the cussed stuff setting on the back of the stove when I come. Burnt on the bottom, dry on top, and sour in the middle. It's a God's wonder he ain't poisoned hisself, the kind of victuals he'll eat when there ain't nobody to watch after him. Calc'lates that what a man eats is wasted. Never seen him short a critter, but he'll pinch his own belly till there ain't enough of him left for the wind to get a-holt of."

"His own belly or anybody else's," I said.

Uncle Levi didn't seem to have heard me, and went on, "Wouldn't doubt none it come from the hard row he had to hoe the time he lost your grandma. Like to broke his heart; putting a debt agin the old place and all. Don't calc'late he et a decent meal 'twixt then and the day he paid the mortgage off. Took him thirty years. Couldn't think of another cussed thing the whole time. Scratch and dig and starve till he was wore down. Then lay abed with chills and fever, and rant 'cause the work wa'n't done."

"He rants whether the work is done or not," I broke in, but Uncle Levi didn't pay any attention. He just sat, hunched forward a little, and looking at his hands, cupped over his knees.

"Run Ralph and Frankie off afore they was older'n what you be. Lacked having patience with 'em. Lacked having the understanding that they wa'n't as het up over the mortgage as what he was."

The cab had stopped in front of a restaurant with big, bright windows. The driver had climbed down and stood by the cab step, but Uncle Levi didn't look up. "Trouble with Thomas, he can't see out nobody else's window but his own. Can't see no farther'n the walls roundabouts the land Father left him. Can't see no way of doing things 'cepting the way Father done 'em. A shame! A shame Father spoilt him afore ever he learnt him to stand alone."

"How was it he didn't spoil you?" I asked.

Uncle Levi heard me, but he didn't look up. "I come too late," he said. "Thomas come when Father was seventy-three. Father never calc'lated on getting a son at that age. Loved him more'n the Almighty loves the world. Spoilt him rotten afore ever he could walk. I come when Father was nigh onto eighty. Heard tell he clum the house chimney and sot a red flag; a-bragging to the neighbors he'd fetched another boy. Never knowed Father well. Time I was getting old enough to remember, he was getting on in years. Calc'late I was more a nuisance to him than a joy." He lifted his big-knuckled hands from his knees, rubbed one inside of the other, and said slowly, "Curious, ain't it? Me, the spittin' image of Father, and Thomas not favoring him. There's times I wonder if that ain't hurt Thomas."

Uncle Levi raised his head heavily, then turned it quickly toward the driver. "Great day! How long we been sitting here?" he asked. "Come on, Ralph! These Hayes folks whacks up a pretty good squash pie."

The restaurant had a long glass case behind the counter with all kinds of cakes and pies, fruits, puddings, cookies, and coffee cakes on it. I wasn't very hungry, but Uncle Levi kept going along the counter asking me if I didn't want some of this or some of that. It didn't make much difference whether I said I did or I didn't. He told the waiter to bring it to us anyway. When we went to the table, we had as many different desserts as they have at a church supper.

I'd just taken a couple of swallows of milk when Uncle Levi said, "Ain't like blowing back the foam and drinking it warm off the lip of the pail, is it? Never did get so's't I didn't count warm milk worth a cow hair or two."

"Old Bess likes warm milk," I told him. "I never milked but what she'd come and whine for me to squirt it at her mouth. Before I came away, she got so she'd never miss a drop."

"Curious, ain't it, the way Old Bess cleaves to Thomas? . . . Same way as Thomas clove to Father. Poor Old Bess! Dread the day of her passing. Thomas leans heavy on her for love. Children all away and wed. 'Bout all he's got left is Old Bess . . . and Millie."

I looked up so quickly that I spilled milk from my glass. "I didn't know she was back," I said. "I didn't think she'd ever come back."

Uncle Levi sat, rubbing one hand inside the other, as he said, "Always has. Prob'ly will this time. Curious, ain't it; the feeling that's growed up 'twixt Thomas and Millie? Thomas is awful fond of Millie."

"Then why did he say he never wanted to see her again?" I asked. "And why did he kick her screen door all to pieces?"

Uncle Levi didn't answer till he'd rubbed one hand over the other a dozen times. He watched them as the fingers dragged across the high knuckle bones, and said slowly, "Thomas is in the midst of the biggest war ever a man fit, and you put him into it, Ralph. He comes as nigh to loving you as ary man that walks the earth."

Something in the way Uncle Levi said it, made my throat hurt, and I blurted out, "He doesn't either; he hates me! He calls me useless and worthless, and he's always yelling and calling me a tarnal fool boy. If he cared as much about me as he does for the yella colt, he wouldn't give me senseless jobs and tell me it's to keep me out of mischief. What is he trying to make me lug rocks off that high field by hand for, if he likes me so much? He tells me to put more manure on the field than he thinks I can haul in a week. Then, when I do it, he gets mad and says I've wasted it. It wouldn't be wasted if he'd put a decent crop on that field. I've tried a dozen times to tell him it would be good for strawberries and tomatoes. They'd make him forty times what that dressing is worth. But every time I mention them, he nearly bites my head off. Millie and I put up most of the hay crop all alone, and all he does is yammer because I ripped a little piece off the ridgepole of the barn. I made a rake for the . . ."

"Having a side war all your own, ain't you, Ralph?" Uncle Levi asked me quietly.

"I don't know what you mean by this war business," I told him. "If there's a war, it's a one-sided one. Grandfather's doing all the fighting. I haven't raised my voice to him once since I went back there."

"Mmmhmmm. Ain't used no machines he didn't tell you to?"

"Well, the stone rake isn't really a machine. It's more like a harrow with the teeth set so they'll bring the rocks to the top."

"Mmmhmmm. Thomas, he's mighty proud about it. Took me out to the field to see it."

"Then why did he call it a contraption and tell me to pick up the rocks by hand? And why did he tell me to haul more dressing than he thought I could, and get mad because I did it?"

" 'Tain't 'cause you done it; it's how you done it. For more'n fifty years, Thomas has farmed the old place the way Father learnt him to do it. He run his own boys off 'cause he made 'em do things the way Father done 'em, 'stead of keeping up with the times. He dug his heart out on them stony hills till the years and the malaria dried most of the sap out of him. It's a God's wonder it didn't kill him. 'Twould a-killed ary other man I know, but Thomas, he wouldn't change jot nor tittle. Like to broke his heart to start a-using that cussed old mowing machine. Come the time he couldn't hand-hoe the crops, he turned the whole place into hay, and sot back to ride out what further years the Almighty give him."

When I looked up, Uncle Levi's eyes were blurry, but he smiled and laid one hand over on mine. "Then you come along and the war commenced. He seen you was a farmer. He seen the mark of the land on you, Ralph, and that you knowed the worth of a field. Why do you calc'late he fit you on the high field? Why do you make him so cussed mad when you say strawberries and tomatoes? 'Tain't 'cause he thinks you're wrong; it's 'cause he knows you're right. It's 'cause he knows it can't be done without hired help and without the things he calls contraptions. He's fit agin 'em so long, it's come to be his nature to hate 'em."

For two or three minutes Uncle Levi was quiet. Slowly his fingers stopped rubbing across his knuckles. He held his loosely closed fists side by side, with the knuckles up. Then the two forefingers lifted above them till they stood together like the spire of a church. "Curious," he said. "Never come to think of it this way afore, but Father and the Almighty stands shoulder to shoulder in Thomas's belief, and the land they give him is holy ground. I calc'late, when he sees strangers and contraptions a-working that ground, his feelings is a sight like them the Lord had when he seen the money changers in the temple."

Uncle Levi looked up from his fingers, and the ends of his mustache lifted with his smile. "Leastways, Thomas piles into 'em in about the same fashion as the Lord done."

Ever since I'd had the elevator job, I'd known I wanted to go back to Grandfather's. The want had been growing stronger and stronger as Uncle Levi talked. When he'd said Grandfather knew I was right about the strawberries, I'd wanted to break right in and tell him I was going back and that Grandfather could yell at me all he wanted to. Then, when he talked about the money changers, I felt as if I'd gone all empty inside. I swallowed hard and said, "Then I'm not going back. It's better to let the whole place stay in hay. I don't want to be a money changer. I don't want to be a stranger on the place. And I don't want to be the cause of Grandfather's having a war with himself." I tried to keep my voice steady, but it was quivering a little at the end.

Uncle Levi reached over and took hold of my wrist, hard. He looked right into my eyes, and said, "God love you, boy, you ain't a stranger to Thomas. You're his own blood and his father's blood. He's lacking in the grace to show it to you, but he loves you and he's proud of you, Ralph. If he wa'n't, there wouldn't be no war. One day he looks at your young hands and sees 'em as his own when he was young; a-turning the soil, a-making it bloom, and a-fetching them wore-out, rocky hills again into mellow plowing fields. He sees the run-out hidden field a-bloom with clover, and the wilderness field took up again. Then, up pops the devil. Thomas, he ain't nobody's fool. He knows there ain't no hope to hold you 'less'n you have the tools you'll need to do the job. Don't nobody have to tell him the job's too big for a young boy and an old man to do with their bare hands."

Uncle Levi reached into his inside coat pocket and took out a bundle of letters tied with a white thread. "Curious, ain't it, the way this thing's a-working on Thomas?" he said. "Writ me more letters this last month than in all the days of his life put together. If 'twa'n't for the handwriting, you'd swear to God they was from two separate men. One of 'em's full of what he's about to do: clearing the wilderness field anew, building a piece onto the barn, twenty head of milk cows, and asking me this and that. Even asking me what I know about strawberries. . . . Didn't know that he'd wrote the gover'ment and half the seed comp'nies 'bout strawberries, did you? Never guessed why you was clearing that high field of stone? The next, he's a-ranting and raving at me for trying to tell him how to farm. Poor Thomas! It's an awful war he's got hisself into! 'Tain't easy for a man of seventy-two to cast the idols out of his temple. Don't calc'late he's been too easy to live with."

"I thought I knew all the fields on the place," I said, "but I don't know the wilderness field. Which one is it?"

"West end of the pasture now; 'twixt the orchard wall and the hidden field," Uncle Levi told me. "Might happen that could be the field where Thomas could win his war. Father and my half brothers, Niah and Stephan and Jacob, cleared all the fields, 'cepting only that one. That's how come Thomas left that field to be the one to slip back to wilderness. Couldn't find it in him to let a field go that Father'd cleared."

"How could he win his war on a field?" I asked. "I thought you said his war was all inside of him."

" 'Tis! 'Tis! If 'twa'n't, there wouldn't be no war. Thomas, he's like ary other man in lots of ways. Wants to leave his mark on the face of the earth when he's gone. Father left the wilderness field for Thomas to clear. We done it once; him and I. Took us nigh onto three years. Thomas ain't sure there's three years left to him."

"I still don't know what field you mean," I said. "It couldn't be the far west end of the pasture. That land is still covered as thick as a spatter with rocks the size of a rain barrel."

Uncle Levi looked up at me across the top of his glasses. "Don't you know where rocks comes from?" he asked.

"Well," I told him, "I read in my geography book that they were left by the glaciers when they melted."

"By hub, must a-been one of them cussed glaciers melt atop the whole state of Maine. Hmmmm, hmmmm. Could be that's where they come from, but it ain't what makes 'em such a pesky nuisance. Frost! Frost heaves 'em up every winter. Pick a field clean as a whistle in the fall and, come spring, it'll be peppered thick again. 'Cepting for a few great boulders, there wa'n't a stone the size of your fist left on that field forty years agone. Mostly, Maine land's a struggle 'twixt man and the wilderness. Clear it and turn your back on it, and in a few years the wilderness will crowd in and claim it again."

Uncle Levi sat looking at his hands for a minute or two, then said, "By hub, I'm glad this meeting 'twixt you and me come about. Curious, ain't it? You recollect, when first I come down to the old farm in haying, Thomas and you and me a-setting in the kitchen after supper?"

"The night I was soaking my blisters and we all went to sleep?"

"Mmmhmm. Thomas a-setting with his feet in the oven."

"Yes, I remember it."

"Recollect what he said to you?"

I had to stop and think for a minute. "Well, I remember that he said the bull bellowed something awful when the barn burned."

"Mmmhmm. What else did he say to you? Didn't catch it all myself. Must have been dozing."

"Why, if I remember right, he said something about the new barn being twenty-some feet shorter than the old one, and that we were going to build the piece back on."

"That's the ticket! Now we're getting someplace."

"Maybe so," I said, "but I don't see how that has anything to do with Grandfather's battle."

"You don't, don't you? I didn't neither till two minutes agone. I ought to had sense enough to seen through this afore ever Frankie went off to learn a trade."

"I guess I'm dumb," I told him, "but I don't have any idea what you're talking about."

"Why do you calc'late Thomas has been so cussed ugly?" he asked me. "Why do you calc'late he's come to be a man that can't get along with hisself nor nobody else? Why do you s'pose he don't want nobody to come to the old place? What makes him so tarnation stingy the devil hisself wouldn't want him? Great day of judgment!"

"Maybe it's the malaria," I said.

"Some. Some. But that ain't the half of it. How would you feel if your father'd left you a job of work to do, like putting the wilderness field under the plow, and the day was fast coming when you'd be a-going to meet your father, and you'd have to look him in the eye and tell him the job wa'n't done? How'd you feel if you'd made your mark on the earth; built the biggest barn in all the country roundabouts, and fire had burnt it down, and you knowed you couldn't build it back alone, and through your own cantankerousness, you'd run off them that could help you do it?"

"Well, I don't think I'd feel very good about it."

"Thomas neither! I calc'late it's been a-gnawing at him like a canker all these twenty years agone; poisoning his in'ards till he heaves it off in spite and meanness. Thomas, he's like a little kettle with no spout and too tight a lid. Never learnt to talk with other folks and leave off his steam wisp by wisp; holds it back till the lid blows off and the nearest one gets scalded. Scrouge and scrimp, squeeze and hoard up a few pennies so's't he'll have something to pass on to his children 'cepting a wore-out old farm in the place of the fertile one Father left him."

"Yes, I know," I said. "I've been scalded. But what can I do to help it?"

"I ain't certain. Ain't certain of a blessed thing, but there's a pill I'd for certain like to try on him. S'posing we was to get him all het up on you and him a-clearing the wilderness field again, and building back onto the barn. Ain't nothing in the Almighty's world he'd sooner have to look back on, come his time to go. That is, if I been calc'lating right, here. There's lots of foolish things Thomas does, but he ain't foolish. He'll know there ain't a living ghost of a chance of you a-doing it the way we done it afore. He'll know . . . give him time to study it out by hisself . . . you got to have the tools to do the job.

"'Pears to me a man will generally always—given his chance —take the thing he wants the most. If we can make Thomas want the clearing of the wilderness field and the building of the barn more'n he hates contraptions, it might haply be we could help to swing the tide of the war. Great day! We better get out of here afore they mop us up for leftovers. Here it is nigh onto two o'clock in the morning, and it don't seem like we been here no time at all. It's a God's wonder you ain't fell asleep long ago. Ain't you going to finish your victuals?"

The next morning I found a boy to take my elevator job, and that evening, the whole family came in to the wharf with me when I took the boat for Bath. Uncle Levi was there with as many bundles as he could carry, and he bought me a ticket for a stateroom up on the deck of the ship. After the man had called, "*All Ashore That's Going Ashore,*" and Mother and the other children had started for the gangplank, Uncle Levi popped his head back into my room and whispered, "Don't say nothing to Thomas 'bout the pill business till I get down there. 'Twon't be no longer'n I can help. Might try a-getting him to wisp off steam a trifle as he goes, 'stead of building up too big a head. Keep your nose clean."

I'd planned to go out on the deck and watch the lights of Boston fade away as the ship sailed out of the harbor, but I didn't do it. As soon as everyone was gone, I realized I was awfully tired, and thought I'd lie down for just a few minutes while we pulled away from the pier. The next thing I knew, the ship was quiet, there was only the gentle pulsing of the engines, and pale gray light showed at the window. I still had all my clothes on, so I slid off the bunk, and went out on the deck.

It was gray dawn, and not a breath of air was stirring. The water lay like a great table top with a blue-gray silk scarf spread over it. A light mist rose from the water, and through it I could see dozens of islands, like big handfuls of dark green leaves dropped here and there on the scarf. The only living thing seemed to be the wide wake, like a great, white-flecked sea serpent following us through the water.

There was only one man on the deck, and from his blue uniform and white cap, I knew he must be an officer of the ship. He

was leaning his elbows at the side rail, and looking off toward the islands. I wanted to be all alone, so I walked up the passageway on the other side of the ship, past the rows of cabins, and almost to the very peak of the bow. Then I leaned on the rail, too.

From there, I could feel, more than hear, the engines. It was almost as though the ship were alive, but sleeping, and its heart was beating slow and steady in its breast. The only real sound was the whisper of water, as the prow slid forward. For me, it was like that moment just before church service . . . when you're waiting for the organ to sing out, "Praise God from whom . . ."

So slowly that I didn't know it was happening, the daylight grew stronger and the mist drew back into the water. The islands became clearer. I could see shoulders of rock at their water lines, and dark green pines covering their domes. Off to the left, the hills of the mainland seemed to be gliding toward us across the surface of the water. They rolled down in great curving folds to the shore. And as they came nearer, birches stood clear and white against the black-green background of the pines.

I had always thought that nothing could be as beautiful as the Rocky Mountains, west of Denver, when the first rays of sunlight caught their peaks. For me, there had always been excitement and glory in their strength and roughness. They always made me want to shout and clench my fists and sing. Here on the ship, leaning against the rail, with the wooded hills and islands gliding toward me across the still water, the feeling was entirely different. I wanted to be quiet and alone. It must have come gradually like the daylight, because I only came to realize slowly that the Lord's Prayer was going over and over in my mind.

Off to the right, about half a mile away, the islands grew larger and higher. Then the sun touched the tops of pines along the ridge. I knew it must be mainland, and that we were moving into the mouth of a great river. When I looked back from watching the sunlight grow along the ridge, the blue-uniformed officer was leaning on the rail beside me. He was an old man. His face was lean and leathery, with deep lines, and it was as calm as I felt inside. He must have known the way I was feeling, because his voice was just above a whisper when he said, "Kennebec. Pretty, ain't it?"

I couldn't have spoken out loud right then, and whispered back, "Yes. Beautiful."

He didn't say anything more till we'd stood there five or six minutes, and there was only the pulse of the engines as we came into the river itself. Then he laid his hand on my shoulder for a moment, and said, "Maine blood in ye, ain't there, lad? Man can always tell it." I just nodded, and he walked away as quietly as he had come.

22

Homecoming

THE trolley ride from Bath to Lisbon Falls seemed longer than ever before. I didn't go to Grandfather's by either the ridge road or the county road. At the edge of town, I turned into a path that led toward the wooded hills to the northwest. The path turned west after I'd followed it into the woods, so I left it and picked my way through the underbrush in the direction I thought would bring me out at the farm. Twice, I had to make a wide circle when I came to swampy ground, and once I had to fight through heavy junipers and brush to get across a brook. By the time I got across, there was mud up to the tops of my shoes, and my suitcase and bundles felt as if they weighed a ton. I had scratched my face and hands on twigs and bushes, and was sure I'd got twisted somewhere in my directions. The only sensible thing to do seemed to be to turn east, get to the county road, and follow it to the fourcorners.

I changed my direction, and had gone about a hundred yards through a thick stand of hemlocks when I came out into an open space. The ground was sandy, and there was sparse hay on it. Across the open space, there was a brook with alders growing along the banks, and the grass was trampled at the edge of a gravelly bend. It was the place Annie Littlehale had shown me, where the raccoon washed his food, at the far end of Grandfather's hidden field. When I'd gone to walk with Annie, I'd only known that I liked to be with her, and had noticed only the things she had pointed out to me. Now, coming onto the spot so suddenly, just when I'd decided I was lost, made it look beautiful. After I'd drunk from the brook, I crossed it on the stones, and hurried through the pines to the edge of the lower hidden field. I had never noticed before how much it looked like the inside of a great cathedral. Tall pines walled it at the back and on both sides, and the morning sunshine streaming through their upper branches looked like the tinted light that comes through high church windows.

Through the hemlock woods and the maple grove, tree after tree that I didn't know I'd ever noticed before stood like old friends waiting to welcome me home. There was the hemlock Annie had been standing behind when I'd seen her watching the squirrel, the maple he'd been playing in, and the three great oaks that grew from the single stump. At the high field, the row of stones I'd piled against the orchard wall was just as I'd left it, but the stone rake had been used. From the footprints, Old Nell had been hitched to it, and had pulled it about thirty feet. A line of stones trailed out on the ground behind it.

Going down the orchard hill, I saw no sign of life at the buildings. When I opened the back barn door, the yella colt snaked his head out of his stall and jerked it back again. A calf bawled from the tie-up, and the hogs in the cellar set up a chorus of squealing. Old Nell's stall was empty, the spring wagon was gone from the carriage house, and Old Bess didn't answer when I whistled. Ashes and grease had been spilled on the front of the kitchen stove and the floor around it. Grandfather had tracked through the mess, and left a trail of footprints leading into his bedroom. Dirty dishes were piled on the kitchen table, the stove, and in the old iron sink. The bottom of it was yellow with rust. After I'd changed my clothes, I built a fire, heated water, and put the dried-on dishes to soak, then I swept the kitchen floor and scrubbed it with lye. I didn't go into Grandfather's room, but scrubbed up the pathway of ashes as far as his door. It took me till noon to get the place cleaned up, the dishes washed, and the sink scoured.

The barn wasn't much better than the house. From the condition of his stall, I was sure the yella colt hadn't been used, but Nell's showed that she had been out the greater part of every day. I cleaned the tie-up, carried water to the hogs in the barn cellar, cleaned the horse stalls, and harnessed the yella colt. He was as mean as I had ever seen him, and I had to use the currycomb in good shape before he'd let me put the bridle on him.

In Colorado, I thought I had handled all kinds of horses, but there was never one like the yella colt. Old as he was, he reared and fought me all the way to the high field. I knew it was either a case of his forgetting me while I was gone, or that he hated me so much he'd only do what I wanted him to after he'd learned again to be afraid of me. I decided that I'd fussed with him enough, and that, this time, I was going to teach him to be afraid in a hurry. On each of the three balks he went into before he settled down to work, I wired his ears together tight enough to pull wads of hair, and each time I forced big handfuls of dirt into his mouth. After that, he fought the rake; lunged into each pull as if he were trying to tear his collar off, and stood blowing and watching me whenever I stopped him for a rest.

Now that Grandfather knew about the stone rake, there was no need of hauling the rocks away after raking each row, and I thought that a hard afternoon's work would be good for the colt's disposition. I kept him going steadily till it was time for Annie Littlehale to come for her cows. By then, he was glad to stand quietly while I went down to the valley.

When I'd come back to the farm, I'd wanted to bring Annie a present; something that would be sort of special. The prettiest things I had, and the ones I liked best, were the silver spurs the cowboys in Colorado had given me for my first roundup. I'd put one of them into my suitcase, and had brought it to the high field with me. I carried it in my hand when I went down over the hill to meet Annie. It wasn't until we'd called "Hello" to each other, and Annie was standing right across the stonewall from me, that I realized what a silly thing a spur was to give a girl. My face felt as if it were afire, and I sounded just as silly as the spur looked, when I held it out and said, "I brought you something. I don't know if you'll have any use for it."

Annie took the spur in her hands, and turned it over and over. Then she looked up and said, "It's beautiful. Where did you get it? It's a riding spur, isn't it?"

The spur did look shiny and nice. I'd been polishing it every time I stopped the yella colt for a rest, and the light of the setting sun made fire seem to sparkle on the points of the rowel. "Mmmhmm," I said. "It's a riding spur, but I'm not going to be riding any more. I wanted you to have it." Then I turned quickly and started climbing the hill.

"Don't run away," Annie called after me. "I'm glad you've come back. We were all worried about Mr. Gould. Is he all right?"

I only stopped long enough to say, "I don't know. I haven't seen him yet. I guess he's gone to an auction. I'll have to get back to the yella colt before he's all tangled up in the harness."

"Thanks for the present. It's lovely," Annie called when I was part way up to the high field. "If there's anything I can do to help, cleaning or cooking or anything, I'll be glad to come over."

"I guess my grandfather can cook," I called from the top of the hill, "and I can wash the dishes and take care of the cleaning, but thank you anyway." Then I hurried back to the yella colt. I could have turned him loose and let him go to the barn alone, but I led him to the pasture when I went for the cows. The more I kept him with me when I didn't have to fight him, the sooner he'd get used to me again, and the sooner he'd settle down to behaving.

Instead of standing quietly at the pasture bars, as they had always done, the cows were restless, and hooking at three strange calves that were with them. The brindle kicked wickedly at one that was trying to nurse her. At the barnyard, I separated them; put the calves into the sheep barn, and the cows into the tie-up. After I had unharnessed and fed the yella colt, I went to the house, built a fire, and put potatoes on to boil for supper. Then I lit the lantern and went back to the barn. The brindle cow wouldn't let her twin calves nurse, and it took me nearly an hour to milk her. Her bag was caked, and the warts on her teats were worse than before I went to Boston. She kicked wildly, the milk squirted in every direction, and I couldn't catch more than half of it in the pail.

I'd just finished milking the brindle and started on Clara Belle when I heard Grandfather drive into the dooryard. I didn't stop to take the lantern, but hurried to meet him. He had stopped Old Nell by the doorstone, and was just going into the summer kitchen when I came out of the barn. I ran the length of the dooryard, and followed him into the house. When I got there, he had struck a match, and was lighting a lamp on the pantry table. "I've got potatoes on to boil for supper, and the chores are nearly done," I said, as I came into the doorway.

For as much as a full minute, Grandfather just stood looking at me with his mouth a little way open. Then he said, "You did come home, Ralphie! You did come home!" He took a quick step, threw his arms around me, and pushed his cheek against my chest so hard his hat fell off. "You did come home, boy," he said as gently as he might have said it to Old Bess. "Gorry sakes alive, your old grampa's glad to see you, Ralphie. How be the folks to ho . . . to Medford?"

I couldn't keep tears from coming into my eyes, and my voice was a little choky when I said, "They're all right."

I think there were tears in Grandfather's eyes too. He didn't look up at me, but turned toward his room, and said, "Your old grampa's all tuckered out, Ralphie. Don't want no supper. Cal'-late I'll go to bed. Been off to Lewiston all day a-fetching the eggs to market." I'd started back out through the summer kitchen when he shouted angrily, "What in time and tarnation you been in my room for?"

"I haven't been in your room," I told him. "I only mopped as far as the doorway." Then I went to take care of Nell and the rest of the chores. Old Bess had followed Grandfather into the house, and she followed me out. I might not have noticed her at all if she hadn't touched her nose against my hand and whined softly in her throat. As I knelt to pat her, she looked up and whined again, as if she were trying to ask me what the trouble was. She never left my heels till all the chores were done and I'd gone to the house for the night.

I got up with the first streaks of daylight, but Grandfather was already in the kitchen when I went downstairs. Smoke was pouring from the stove, and he was stirring Banner Oats into a kettle of water that wasn't steaming. "Gorry sakes! Gorry sakes alive, Ralphie," he sang out as I came through the doorway, "Tarnal nice having you to home again. I and you has got a heap of work to do afore the snow flies. I be fixing us a nice mess of victuals so's to put a leg under us for the day. Ain't nothing like a good mess of oatmeal porridge to hold a man's ribs out. Thunderation! Guess I wa'n't heeding what I was about."

Grandfather had looked up at me as he spoke, but was still holding the tilted oatmeal package over the pot, and the premium saucer had slipped out. It hit the edge of the iron kettle, broke into a hundred pieces, and scattered over the stove, on the floor, and into the pot. "Ain't that a tarnal shame," he muttered as he picked pieces of china out of the oatmeal with his thumb and finger. "Nice pretty saucer like that all broke to smithereens. Well, what's the odds? Likely as not there'll be as pretty a one in the next box and I don't cal'late it's hurt the porridge none. What I don't skim out will sink to the bottom. Did ever you eat porridge with maple syrup on it, Ralphie? Awful good. Fetched a pail of it down from the open chamber whilst Levi was here. It's right there in the cellarway. Pass it here, and fetch up a piece of pork out the barrel. Pick a good fat piece. Fat pork goes good with oatmeal. I'll set it a-frying whilst you do the chores. Leave the milking to the calves."

"I don't think they're doing a very good job of it," I said. "Don't you think it would be better if I'd milk by hand and feed the calves? That pair of little twin steers is awfully skinny, and the brindle won't let them touch her."

Grandfather's head jerked up. He looked at me crossly for half a minute, and I thought he was going to shout, "Don't tell me!" but he didn't. He looked back at the pot, stirred it a couple of minutes, and said, "Cal'late you might just as leave. Veal calves is fetching a good price off to Lewiston, and butter's twenty-eight cents. Cal'late Millie'll be a-coming home most any day now, and she makes awful nice butter."

Before I'd much more than started on the chores, Grandfather called me to breakfast, and he was all in a dither when I went to the house. The kitchen was blue with the smoke of burned pork, and the smell of scorched oatmeal was so strong it made the air bitter. "Come eat your victuals, Ralphie! Come eat your victuals!" Grandfather snapped at me while I was washing my face and hands. "By fire, I got to get an early start! First calves in the market always fetches the high dollar! Ain't no time for dawdling. Afore you went off to Boston, didn't you tell me Millie was prob'ly 'twixt here and Lewiston, somewheres?"

I had to think a minute, and then I said, "I'm not sure, but maybe I did."

"Why'd you tell me that?"

"Well, because she said that was where she was going."

"*What?*" Grandfather shouted at me. "When did she tell you?"

"The day she left."

"Why didn't you tell me? You was hatching it up betwixt you to go off and leave me."

"No, sir," I told him. "We didn't hatch anything up. I don't think she really had any idea at all of going when she said it. She was mad about the flies, and came out to the field right after you drove away that morning. That's why I made her the screens. I didn't see or say a word to her after . . . after the door got broken."

Grandfather's voice dropped right down, and he asked. "What did she say to you, Ralphie? What was her words?"

"Well, I don't think I remember them all, but she said she wasn't going to live with the cussed flies for another blessed day, and that she had two minds to one to go off to Lewiston and get a job in the mill."

Grandfather was watching me like a fox watching a chipmunk. "What mill?" he asked.

"She didn't say. Is there more than one?"

"Tarnal lot of 'em! Eat your victuals! Eat your victuals! Time flies! Hitch Old Nell to the spring wagon and fetch them three new calves."

I didn't bother about breakfast. Besides burning the oatmeal, Grandfather had forgotten to salt it, and there were at least forty flies drowned in the maple syrup. I harnessed Nell, tied the legs of each calf, and loaded it into the wagon. When I drove up from the sheep barn, Grandfather had on his best suit and was waiting for me. "Sot some pans out for you on the butt'ry table," he told me. "Put the milk to rising in the cellar. I'm cal'lating on fetching Millie home with me whenst I come." Then he climbed up onto the wagon seat and spanked Old Nell with the reins.

23

The Colt and I Become Friends

THERE had been a big piece of corned beef in one of the packages Uncle Levi gave me to bring down to the farm. The first thing I did after Grandfather drove away was to fry myself four eggs, and put the corned beef on to boil. While I was finishing the chores and taking the cows to pasture, it boiled dry and burned black on the bottom. Before I left for the high field, I scraped some of the black off the meat and filled the kettle with water. Then I crammed the stove full of hard wood and closed the dampers, so it would keep cooking most of the forenoon.

The yella colt fought me again that morning when I harnessed him, and he raised Cain during the first hour in the field. He got a leg outside one of the traces after I thought he was all settled down. Without thinking, I stepped forward to make him put his foot back in, and he kicked quicker than a flash of lightning. His hoof spanked sharply on my thigh, just above my knee. If I'd been a few inches closer, it might have broken my leg. I grabbed up the line ends to beat him with them, but stopped myself. It wouldn't have done any good, and would only have made him hate me worse. Instead, I kept him working hard all the rest of the morning, with only rest enough to keep from hurting his wind.

I'd thought I would have some corned beef for my dinner, but I didn't. The fire had burned out when I went to the house at noon, and the beef was as tough as whang leather. The water around it looked like strong black coffee, and was as bitter as walnut husks. I drained it off, put on fresh water, then built up the fire and fried myself four more eggs.

The colt worked pretty well during the afternoon. I didn't have to wire his ears together once, but he was sulky, and kept his head turned just enough that he could keep an eye on me all the time. Except for the couple of times I ran to the house to put more wood on the fire, I kept him working hard. By the time Annie came for her cows, he was plodding as steadily as Old Nell would have, and I let him stand in his traces when I went to the brow of the hill to wave to her.

I didn't go down to the valley, but Annie called up to me, "Are you sure there isn't anything I could do to help you around the house? Couldn't I make the beds and help out with the cooking?"

I wanted to say yes, but I remembered how crabby Grandfather had been when he thought I'd gone into his room, so I called back, "I've got a big piece of corned beef on cooking for supper, and the beds only take a few minutes, so I guess we'll be all right, but thank you anyway."

I went back to the yella colt, started him for the barn, and went for our cows. Without the calves to bother them, they were waiting at the pasture bars, and lowed for their milking when they saw me coming. Grandfather hadn't come home when I had the barn chores finished, the milk put away in the cellar, and the potatoes on to boil. The corned beef was fairly tender by then, so I pushed the pot onto the back of the stove and went out to wait for him. He hadn't taken Old Bess with him that morning, and it was a bright starlight evening, so I blew out the lamp, and Bess and I sat on the doorstone, waiting.

I must have been more tired than I realized. I didn't wake up till Old Bess raised her head quickly from my lap. There was the slow clump of a horse's feet coming up the driveway, and the squeak, now and then, of wagon wheels. When I got up, Nell was coming slowly past the side of the house. Her head was hanging low and, against the light of the sky, I could see Grandfather's outline on the wagon seat. His head was low, too, and he was hunched over enough that I thought he was asleep. I called, "Hi, Grandfather!" to wake him, but he didn't answer. As I ran to the wagon, he raised his head slowly, and said, "Couldn't find a trace of her no place. Ralphie, your old grampa's all tuckered out."

"I've got some good supper cooked," I told him. "You'll feel better after you've eaten. I'll take care of Old Nell while you get washed up. There's hot water on the stove."

"Gorry, I be a little weary," was all he said as he climbed down over the wheel and sort of stumbled toward the doorway.

I had just pulled the harness off Nell when Grandfather called me angrily from the house. "What in time and tarnation you been up to whilst I been gone?" he shouted, as I came out of the barn. "What's all them eggshells a-doing in the swill pail? What did you ruin the meat for?"

"I didn't ruin the meat," I said, as I went toward the house, "and those are just shells from the eggs I had for breakfast and dinner. There wasn't anything else to eat."

"Plenty pork in the barrel, wa'n't there? Plenty potatoes in the bin. Don't be so choosy 'bout your victuals; eggs is eighteen cents a dozen!" Then, without waiting for me to get to the house, he stamped off to his room and slammed the door.

While I'd been sleeping on the doorstone, the corned beef had burned and the burnt taste had cooked all the way through the piece. Hungry as I was, I couldn't swallow any of it without gagging. The potatoes had boiled to a porridge of mush and skins. I strained out some of the best of it, ate it, drank some milk, and went to bed.

I expected Grandfather to be cross the next morning, but he wasn't. When he called me, his voice seemed cheerful, and when I went down to the kitchen he had flour scattered all over the back pantry. "Whacking us up a nice mess of biscuits, Ralphie," he called to me. "Ain't nothing better of a morning than nice good hot biscuits and new honey. Got a busted comb out to the bee shop. I'll pop these biscuits into the oven and fetch it whilst you're at your chores. Come a-running whenst they're hot."

I came running when Grandfather hollered, but the biscuits weren't the best. They were dead brown all over, as hard as rocks, and not over an inch high. "Curious, ain't it?" Grandfather said, as he pulled them out of the oven. "Must be the tarnal saleratus was damp, or the milk wa'n't sour enough. Curious! Oh, well, what's the odds? I got to attend an auction over t'other side of Lisbon Village, but I'll whack you up a nice mess of biscuits for your dinner afore I go. Now you run on and finish your chores whilst I cook us a kettle of porridge."

The oatmeal wasn't burned that morning, but it wasn't half cooked either, and there were hard lumps in it. I ate a few mouthfuls, drank some milk, and took the cows to pasture. Grandfather was down at the beehives when I came back to harness the horses. I didn't go down, but slipped into the kitchen through the woodshed. I couldn't pick stones all forenoon without something more to eat. I boiled four eggs good and hard, put them into my pocket, and took the yella colt to the high field.

The colt balked only once all morning, but most of the time he kept watching me, and he laid his ears back whenever I went near him. I carried a stout stick on the stone rake, and I never went past his heels that I didn't have it ready to swing at them. I almost hoped he would kick at me, so I'd be able to teach him a lesson he'd remember, but he didn't lift a foot. After each trip across the field and back, I'd let the old horse rest a few minutes by the orchard wall. From there, I could see Grandfather at the beehives. He hadn't changed a bit from the way he was doing things before he'd sent me home. As soon as the mailman came, he went to the box, into the house for a couple of minutes, and then drove away.

When the yella colt and I left the high field at noon, we had half of it raked. On the part we'd done since I'd come back, the stones lay in even rows across the ground, like gray stripes on a big piece of brown cloth. The raking hadn't been very hard work for me, but it had been awfully hard for one horse. For the last hour of the morning, the colt plodded along with his head as low as the check rein would let it hang. At the barn, I took his harness off, wiped the sweat from his belly and legs, and gave him an extra quart of bran. I knew I had him worked down enough that he wouldn't give me any more trouble, and I was a little ashamed of myself for fear I'd worked so old a horse too hard.

When I went into the kitchen, I found the second batch of biscuits Grandfather had baked on the back of the stove. They were still in the pan, were cold, and no higher than the first ones. The only difference was that these were white where the others had been brown, and the only reason they weren't as hard was because they were half raw. I tried to eat one, but couldn't, and there was nothing else in the house except oatmeal, raw potatoes, and salt pork. Grandfather had taken every last egg with him when he drove away. After I'd put potatoes on to boil, I went hunting hens' nests. Altogether I found nine eggs, boiled them while the potatoes cooked, and hid them in the barn for a time when I'd need them. Then I fried pork, and sat down at the table. While I was eating, I got an idea how to save myself a lot of work in unloading the stones.

When I went back to the high field, I took along a heavy piece of chain with a hook on it, and the ropes and pulleys from the horsefork. After I'd hauled the first drag load of stones close to the orchard wall, I climbed over and fastened one of the pulleys to the trunk of an apple tree. It happened to be an August Sweet tree. The apples were just beginning to turn yellow, and I was still hungry, so I ate one. It was sweet and good. Before I went back to the field, I filled my pockets with apples. The yella colt either smelled them or saw me chewing. He turned his head toward me and nickered softly.

In all my life I'd never been around any horse long without loving him, but I'd almost hated the yella colt right from the

first day. If I hadn't been ashamed of myself for working him too hard, I would probably have remembered his kicking me, and would still have been peeved at him when he nickered. Instead, I thumped one of the apples on a stone to crack it, then held the pieces up on my palm for the old horse to eat. He picked them off carefully with his lips, and stood rubbing his nose against me as he ate them. Then I cracked another apple and fed it to him. As he chewed, I scratched his forehead, and said, "You haven't had any barns burn, or fields go back to the wilderness, have you? What makes you so crabby? Did your mother spoil you when you were little, or have you got horse malaria? They say people grow alike from living together. Is that what ails you? I'll bet, if you'd been my colt from the day you were born, you'd never have grown up to be so onery."

I fed the colt four apples, and ate two myself, before I went back to the tackle. All the time I was fussing with him, he kept rubbing his nose against me and nickering quietly. Of course, I knew he was only asking for more apple, but it almost sounded as if he were trying to answer me. With the last piece of the fourth apple, I told him, "I'll be friends if you will, and I won't tie your ears together again until I know for sure that you don't want to be friends any more."

I wasn't too positive the tackle idea would work. With one pulley fastened to a tree trunk in the orchard, I brought the doubled ropes across the top of the stonewall, hitched the chain to the pulley on the opposite end, and slipped the hook under the far edge of the stone drag. If a horse could pull hard enough, I thought the drag would skid sideways till it was against the wall, then turn up on its side and dump the load. If everything went right, it would save nearly half my work. I'd planned to give the yella colt a little slack on the tote rope, then rush him hard into the pull. For some reason, I didn't want to do it that way after I'd fed him the apples. I wanted to see if he'd do it for me on a pull that he wasn't sure he could make. Not very many balky horses will stay with a pull if they think it's too much for them.

When everything was ready, I hooked the old horse's single-tree to the tote rope, led him forward till the rope lifted off the ground, and stopped him. Then I looped the reins over his hame knob, went back, and leaned against the wall. I didn't make a sound until he'd turned his head to see where I was and what I was doing. I wanted him to know I wasn't near enough to hit him, and that I didn't have hold of the reins. As his head turned toward me, I clucked—just twice, about two seconds apart. The yella colt stepped forward, leaned a little into the collar, and felt the load with his shoulders. He didn't slack off, but turned his head again, as if he were trying to tell me it was too heavy. I didn't move, but clucked twice more. On the second cluck, the knots of muscle began raising along his haunches and thighs. He crouched a little, and his hind hoofs sank deeper into the soft ground. Inch by inch, the heavily loaded stone drag began to skid sideways. The edge met the wall, and slowly, slowly, the far side began to lift from the ground. When I looked back at the yella colt, his neck was bowed, every sinew in his legs was taut as a harp string, and his ears were pointed straight forward. I could hardly wait for the drag to tip clear up and spill its load. My fists were clenched, and my own muscles pulled till they ached. Before the rumble of stones faded, I called, "Whoa," to him, and ran to his head. I wasn't even ashamed that tears were running down my face as I told him I'd never fight him again, and that he was always going to be my horse.

24

A Thousand Things to Show Me

UNTIL Saturday evening, I didn't see much of Grandfather. Every morning, he was up before daylight, drove away by sunup, and didn't come home until after dark. He never told me where he was going, but, from what he took with him and what he brought home, I knew he was going to Lewiston every day, and to whatever auctions he could find. Before the end of the week, he had taken away every egg the hens laid, all the frying chickens, Clara Belle's calf, and the new spotted one; and had brought home a big, ugly, Holstein bull and two more cows. He brought the last cow just after I'd finished milking Friday night, but was so tired that he didn't go to the barn when I put her in the tie-up.

Twice, while I was frying the pork for supper, Grandfather told me to hurry up and get the victuals on the table, but when it was ready he ate only a few bites. For several minutes, he sat staring at Millie's pink apron that still hung on a nail by the pantry door. Then he said, wearily, "Gorry, there's a tarnal lot of mills off to Lewiston. Cal'late I'll go to bed. Got to make an early start, come morning. Cal'late I'll fetch them twin steer calves off to market. Wouldn't make pulling critters no ways for two, three years, and eat as much provender as a pair of milk cows. I and you is going into the butter business, Ralphie. No sense a-keeping steer critters 'round."

I was sure that Grandfather didn't want to get rid of the little steers, and that they were just an excuse for his going to Lewiston to hunt Millie. I wished I could have thought of something else for him to take instead, or that I could have told him something that would help him find her, but I couldn't.

Even with the tackle, stone hauling was hard work, but it had become sort of fun since the yella colt and I found we were friends. My biggest troubles were meals and milk. Neither Grandfather nor I could cook anything but boiled potatoes and fried salt pork. He always burned the oatmeal, and his biscuits never raised. By the end of the week, he was hardly eating anything, and I was getting awfully tired of pork and potatoes. Apples and milk helped, but they didn't put much of a leg under me for hauling stones.

With all the calves gone and seven cows in the barn, I was swamped with milk. When I finished the chores Saturday morning, I had every pan, crock, and pail in the house full to the brim, but didn't know how to make it into butter. I hurried our cows to pasture, and went down to meet Annie Littlehale when she came with hers. I thought that if I could get her to come up to the house for an hour or two, she could show me about the butter and teach me to make johnnycake and biscuits. Annie said she'd come, but that there wasn't any need for me to stay out of the field; that she'd show me how to make them when I came in for dinner. Then she asked me which I liked best, pie or cake.

"My grandfather likes pie best," I told her. "Millie made one with apples and wild strawberries, and he ate nearly half of it."

"Well, I'll see what I can do," she said, as she started back to the pasture gate. "I'll come up as soon as the breakfast dishes are finished, and I'll call you when I'm ready for you to come in for dinner."

It was a long forenoon for me. I never drove the yella colt to the wall with a load of stones that I didn't stop to look toward the house. Once Annie came to the orchard for apples, once I saw her in Millie's little garden, and another time she was walking up the road from her house with some packages in her arms. I didn't want her to see that I was excited when she called me to dinner, so I led the yella colt slowly down the hill. But when we reached the barn, I rattled his harness off as fast as I could, fed him, and then walked to the house as if I wasn't in any hurry.

Annie had all sorts of things laid out on the pantry table. There was a bowl of eggs she'd gathered from the henhouse, cream she'd skimmed from milk in the cellar, and butter, chocolate, and white lard she'd brought from home. After I'd washed my face and hands, she tied Millie's pink apron on me, and said, "There's no sense in making both johnnycake and biscuits for dinner; which one do you want to try?"

"Both of them," I told her.

"Don't be silly," she said. "They're only good when they're hot. There'll be lots of other days. Which one shall we make today?"

"Well, I'd still like to make them both," I told her. "Tomorrow is Sunday. I won't be working in the field, and you'll be gone to Sunday school. If I knew how, I'd make hot biscuits for breakfast and hot johnnycake for dinner." It wasn't so much that I was in a hurry to learn to make them, but I liked to be with Annie. It seemed to me the more things she taught me, the longer the lesson might last.

She still said it was silly, but I made both biscuits and johnnycake, and she told me just what to do and when to do it. Before I started the biscuits, she explained to me about having to judge the amount of soda to use by the sourness of the milk, and about sifting the flour twice to get plenty of air into it. Then, as soon as I'd poured the sour milk in with the flour, she made me hurry to beat the band. She said it was hard to make bad biscuits if you had them in the oven within two minutes of the time the sour milk touched the soda.

The johnnycake was easier than the biscuits. The batter was looser, it didn't have to be rolled or cut out, and Annie didn't make me hurry with it. After I had a cup of sour cream stirred into the meal, flour, and molasses, she had me beat in three eggs. "You can use as many eggs as you want to," she told me. "If you and Mr. Gould are going to try to live on salt pork and potatoes, I'd put plenty of eggs in the johnnycake. They'll do you just as much good that way as any other, and it makes a nicer johnnycake. You can use sour milk instead of cream, but if you do that, you'll have to put in shortening. You should always use cream instead of milk when you're doing hard work like hauling those stones. It will be good for Mr. Gould, too. He's apt to be sick if he doesn't eat good rich food. Goodness! You're going to beat that into a froth. Let's get it into the pan; the biscuits should be ready by now."

The biscuits were ready, and they were pretty. The last second before they'd gone into the oven, Annie had frosted the tops of them with cream and marked them with fork pricks. When they came out, they looked like little white castles with brown roofs.

I'd had lots of good dinners at home, and at some of the ranches where I'd worked, but never one that I liked much better than that one. Annie had made a boiled dinner of vegetables she found in the garden and, beside the biscuits and johnnycake, there was a warm apple pie and cupcakes with maple sugar frosting on them. As she cut the pie, Annie said, "This one hasn't any strawberries in it, but this afternoon I'll make one that does have. I didn't have a chance to go for them this morning. My! You had lots of milk set. I couldn't find a bowl to cook with till I skimmed some of it. I'll take care of the rest of it this afternoon, and the first of the week we'll have to churn. You shouldn't let it set so long. Every evening, you should skim the milk from the day before."

Annie let me tell her a little about Colorado while we were eating, and she told me a little about the high school she went to at Lisbon Falls, but she wouldn't let me stop to help her with the dishes after we'd finished. She said that Grandfather was too old to do hard work and that she'd only come to help me if it wouldn't interfere with my work in the fields. Just before I went back to the barn, she said she'd leave a pot of beans in the oven, and told me to keep them filled with water, and to keep a slow fire going till bedtime. Then she said she'd leave everything for supper on the back of the stove when she went.

The sun was low enough that the shadows of the pines on the ridge stretched across the orchard before I left the high field. When I went to the pasture for the cows it was twilight. I had them halfway to the barn when I saw Grandfather and Old Nell coming down the road. Nell was walking with her head bobbing low, and from the way Grandfather was sitting hunched on the wagon seat I knew he hadn't found any trace of Millie. I hated to have him feeling so bad about it, but I didn't know what I could say or do. Instead of leaving the cows in the barnyard and going to meet him, I put them in the tie-up, and closed the stanchion yokes on their necks.

There was no sound from the dooryard, so I went to see what Grandfather was doing. Old Nell was standing in the driveway, but Grandfather was nowhere in sight. Then a light showed in the windows of the open chamber above the kitchen. I saw the lamp move past one window, then the other, and then the light faded away. I was sure Grandfather wouldn't have gone up there, and went running to the house. I'd just come into the kitchen when the door from the front stairway opened, and Grandfather stood in the doorway with a lamp in his hand. His face looked like a little boy's when he first spies the Christmas tree, and he sang out, "You fooled me, Ralphie! You fooled me! Why didn't you tell me Millie was a-coming home? Where you cal'late the little minx is a-hiding at? Gorry! Gorry sakes alive!"

For half a minute, I thought Grandfather was right, and that Millie had come back. Then the lamplight spread across the set table, the pots and pans on the back of the stove, and Grandfather's slippers, set neatly beside his rocker. I knew in a moment that he was wrong, but I hated to tell him so. While I was hunting for the right words, Grandfather looked at me questioningly, and asked, "What's the matter, Ralphie? Be she gone off again? Why didn't she stay till I come home? I'd a . . . Was it account of the . . ." And then he just stood there looking at me blankly.

"No, she hasn't gone," I said. "She didn't come home. Annie Littlehale came up to show me how to cook. She stayed to do the dishes after I went back to the field at noon. It looks as if she did some scrubbing too, and left supper ready for us."

As I spoke, I noticed that Grandfather's hand was trembling so that the lamplight flickered. The flickering grew sharper for a minute as he peered around the kitchen. Then he snapped, "Don't want no supper! Don't want no tarnal neighbor womenfolks a-snooping 'round this house a-cooking the victuals! I won't have it! I won't have it, I tell you!" With every word, his voice grew louder until, at the end, he was shouting.

"Annie wasn't snooping," I told him quietly. "I'm sure she didn't go into any part of the house except the kitchen, the pantry, and the cellar."

"Keep her out of here! Keep away from that girl, I tell you!" Grandfather shouted, shoved past me, and started toward his room. At the pantry doorway he stopped and shouted again. "What in thunderation you been up to anyway? Four pies! Layer cake! Cup cakes! Wastin'! Wastin'!"

Four swill pails were lined up under the sink, filled nearly to the tops with sour skimmed milk. Grandfather snatched the long handled mixing spoon from its nail by the table, and scooped deep into the nearest pail. When the spoon came up, there were two broken eggshells on it. He dipped again and again. Each time there was a shell on the spoon. "Wastin'! Wastin'!" he snapped out as he scooped. "Wastin' as her mother! Throws out more in a teaspoon than what Fred Littlehale can fetch home in a wheelbarrow. Best tarnal bottom-land farm in the country roundabouts, and what'll he have to pass on to his children? Nothing! Nothing! Mortgaged to the handle! Work like a fool and watch his womenfolks heave his worth away in fancy victuals! Them womenfolks better go to watching the bees! Bees don't eat theirselves out of house and home! Saving! Saving for the generations to come! Great thunderation! Eggs is eighteen cents a dozen! Stay away from that girl, Ralphie! Stay away from her! First thing you know, she'll learn you to be a spendthrift." Then he stamped off to his room and slammed the door.

I hardly slept at all that night. It was nearly midnight before I went to bed, and then I couldn't get Annie out of my mind. I thought of dozens of ways I might be able to get Grandfather to let her come back again, and then I'd think of the reasons he'd say she couldn't come. When the first gray of morning showed at the window, I got up, dressed, and took my shoes in my hand. I didn't put them on till I'd tiptoed through the kitchen and out to the doorstone. As I sat tying the laces, Old Bess came from the woodshed and tucked her head into my lap.

When I'd got up, I hadn't any idea what I was going to do, but as I stroked Old Bess' head, I whispered, "Let's go for a walk, Bess. Let's go down to the brook in the hidden field, and see if the raccoon still comes back there to wash his food."

It was a beautiful morning. Dew had settled thickly on the grass. As the light spread across the eastern sky, mist lay in the valley like milk in a great green bowl. The smell of pine was sweet and heavy in the air. From the ridge above the house, a crow cawed as though he were calling someone. There were three separate, throaty notes, and, from somewhere in the valley, a rooster answered.

The light grew and spread as Old Bess and I climbed the hill through the orchard. A pink glow touched a cloud above the dark pines along Hall's hill. Slowly, it changed to red. The red widened and deepened along the hill, till it looked as if the whole world beyond were in flames. Meadow larks sang from the stonewalls and, as Bess and I walked along the brow of the hill above Littlehale's pasture, a partridge strummed in the

beech woods. We stopped, and standing there on the hill, looking down at the little meadow where I had first seen Annie,
Mother's "Nut Brown Maiden" song began going through my
mind.

All the way, down through the maple grove, the hemlock
woods, and the hidden fields, the rhythm kept swaying back
and forth in my head. It was still there when we had walked
over every inch of ground where Annie and I had walked before. When Bess and I had gone back and were sitting on the
granite outcropping in the pasture, words began to fit themselves along the path of the rhythm. They were beautiful, rhym-
ing words. I wished Annie had been there beside me, so I could
have said them to her, and I was afraid I might forget them before I ever saw her again. While Old Bess slept, I found a sliver
of flint, and scratched the verse into the gray table of the outcropping. I sort of hoped that, someday, Annie might come
there again and see it.

When it was finished, I read it to Old Bess. The words
sounded better aloud than they had when they were just in my
mind. I read it again; but, that time, to the hemlock woods. I
made each word as round and full as I could—the way Mother's
voice always sounded when she recited the last verse of *Thana-
topsis*.

The last sounds were just echoing back from the hemlocks
when, from right behind me, Grandfather said, "Gorry sakes,
Ralphie, what you doing way off out here in the woods a-spout-
ing poetry at this hour of the morning?"

When he spoke, I slid over and tried to cover the verse, but
Grandfather had already seen it. "Gorry," he said, "rit it yourself, did you? Hmmmm! Hmmmm! Poetizing is for poets and
farming is for farmers. Every man can't be a poet, no more'n
a sheep can be a goet. The cows is bellering to be milked."
Grandfather pulled at the end of his whiskers a minute, then
asked, "Wa'n't writing that for Annie Littlehale, was you?"

"No," I said, "I wasn't. It just came into my head while I was
sitting here, and I wrote it down so I wouldn't forget it."

"Ought to fetch out a chisel one day and cut it deeper. Rain and time will wear it away afore you know it."

I had stood up, and Grandfather slipped one of his arms in under mine. For a minute or two, he stood looking down at the verse, but I don't think he saw it. Then, he said, "Time wears lots of things out of a man's mem'ry, too, Ralphie. Ones he hates to lose, and ones he yearns to. Father stood here on this selfsame outcropping with me the day afore I went off to war. Ninety-four, he was, and commencing to feeble a mite. He passed away whilst I was gone. Ain't come to mind for years, but now I recollect us a-standing here as if 't was only yesterday. Father a-telling me how he come to this outcropping whenst first he blazed his way up through the woods from Bath in the year of 1793."

"1793!" I broke in. "Why, there wasn't any State of Maine in 1793."

"Wa'n't no United States whenst Father was born. He was in his twenty-first year whenst George Washington was swore in to be the first president. No, there wa'n't no State of Maine, Ralphie, but the land was here; been here ever since the Almighty smote on the waters and raised the land above 'em.

"Father, he come onto this outcropping whenst him and his first wife was seeking out a place to rear up a family. Where yonder hummock stands was a tarnal great white oak. Father clim to the top of it and could see all the country roundabouts. 'Twas solid woods and wilderness then, Ralphie. Not a tarnal tree left of them that was standing, save the two virgin pines in the beech woods.

" 'Twas a cloudy day in early spring. Whilst Father was atop the tree, a rift come in the clouds, and the sunshine lit on this whole side the ridge and out onto the valley beneath. Ralphie, 'twas the hand of the Almighty parted them clouds and marked the land for Father. He come down the oak and blazed his mark on the trees roundabouts the land the Almighty marked to him. There'll come a day, Ralphie, you'll love it the same as Father and me. The feel of the land is in your hands. There'll come a day you'll clear the wilderness field yonder. I and Levi, we cleared it once—hauled the stone off with three-spanned yoke of oxen, laid up the foundation of the big barn out of 'em; cut off the timber, hewed the beams, and framed the biggest barn in all the country hereabouts."

I felt Grandfather's arm weighing down on mine. His head was bowed, and his shoulders slumped forward a little. It was a minute or two before he went on. When he did, his voice was low and thick. "Then the clouds closed in, Ralphie. Levi, he went off a-homesteading, the malaria come on me heavy, and the children. I lost your grandma and the fire come and the woods and wilderness commenced a-pushing back into the fields Father had cleared. 'Tain't been easy to watch it a-slipping back. Ain't been able to keep enough stock to dress the fields. Hated awful to see 'em petering out, but now we'll save 'em, Ralphie. I'm cal'lating on filling what barn there is with cows. With you to help me, we'll fetch back what fields is left, and whenst I'm gone, you'll claim back them I ain't been able to save."

My throat hurt. I forgot what Uncle Levi had said about not giving Grandfather the pill, and blurted out, "I won't either! We'll claim them back while we can do it together. I like hard work. This is my home now, and you're no older than your father was when you were born. If he could clear the land he did, I guess we can clear the wilderness field again and build the piece back on the barn."

While I was speaking, the weight of Grandfather's arm eased on mine. He drew the sag out of his shoulders, and his head lifted till his whiskers stood away from his chest. When I'd finished he was facing me. His hands reached out for the muscles in my arms. As his fingers closed tighter and tighter, he looked up into my face, and said, "I *ain't* too old, Ralphie! I *ain't* too old! There's still power left in them old hands! The way you've skun the stones off'n the high field, I don't cal'late there's nothing we couldn't do betwixt us. Come on! Let's get at them chores! We're a-going to walk the field today; there's a thousand things I got to show you, boy."

25

Grandfather Sets His Cap for 'Bijah

GRANDFATHER had never helped me with the chores, but Monday morning he was at the barn when I came downstairs at sunrise. He must have been up since four o'clock. A skillet of baked beans was simmering on the back of the stove, the oven door was open, and a plate of johnnycake and one of Annie's pies were warming on the top shelf.

He was pitching hay down from the mow when I went to the barn, and he peeked over the edge like a squirrel looking down from a tree. "Got the hogs all slopped," he called out to me. "By gorry, Ralphie, we'll get an early start at it this morning. We ain't going to stop for nothing till the rocks is all off the high field. By fire, 'twixt the two of us, we'll make 'em fly! We'll show 'em what kind of logs makes wide shingles! Provender the hosses, and we'll eat our victuals afore you do the milking."

As I fed the horses, Grandfather came down the ladder, and hurried away to the house. He still had his hat on, had set the table, and was dishing out beans when I got there. "By gorry, them ain't bad looking beans," he called to me as I was washing.

"Pie looks uncommon good, too. Strawb'ries in it, ain't there, Ralphie?"

"Yes, sir," I told him. "I think Annie is a pretty good cook, don't you? She taught me how to make biscuits and johnny-cake."

"Wastin'! Wastin'!" Grandfather snapped. Then, as he drew his chair up to the table, he said, "Well, what's done is done. No sense a-wastin' the victuals now they're cooked. Fetch a couple of them little cupcakes, Ralphie. Goes awful nice with hot tea."

Grandfather ate more for breakfast than he had for any meal since Millie left. He seemed to enjoy every mouthful, but when I tried to swing the talk around to Annie's coming again, he snapped, "Eat your victuals, Ralphie! Time flies, and we got a tarnal heap of work to do afore the snow flies."

All during milking, Grandfather kept coming into the tie-up and telling me that time flew. I always saved the brindle cow till the last. She still kicked as much as ever and, if anything, the milk sprayed worse. Grandfather watched me fight the milk from her for a few minutes, and said, "Leave be! Leave be, Ralphie! There ain't no time for fiddle-faddling."

"If I do, her bag will cake, and it will ruin her," I told him.

"Ruin her! Cal'late she's tarnal nigh ruined for a milker a'ready. Let me see . . . Who be there I might trade her off to?" Grandfather walked up and down the length of the tie-up three or four times, just pulling the end of his whiskers and looking at the floor. Suddenly, he sang out, "By fire, I got him! I got him, Ralphie! 'Bijah Swale! Don't know a man I'd sooner trade her off to."

"I know him," I said. "I rode up from Lisbon Falls with him the first day I came here."

Grandfather stopped walking, and looked at me closely, "Don't cal'late he said nothing good of me," he said.

"Well, I don't remember just what he did say."

"Wager you 'twa'n't good. 'Bijah, he ain't told the truth yet if a lie would do. Meanest man this side the Androscoggin River.

"Cheat a widow woman out of her last hen! Skun me out of four cords of wood. By fire, Ralphie, I cal'late to set my cap for 'Bijah. Hmmm, hmmm. There's an auction over Pajepscot way this afternoon. 'Bijah, he don't buy nothing, but he don't never miss an auction. Goes for the free victuals. Gorry sakes! If we wa'n't so all-fired busy, I'd go set the wheels a-rolling to get him het up for a trade."

"I don't see any reason for your not going to the auction," I told him. "By eleven o'clock, you and Old Nell could rake all the stones the yella colt and I could haul in a day. I'd be awfully glad if we could get rid of the brindle."

"Gorry sakes! Cal'late maybe I best! Cal'late maybe I best!" Grandfather sang out. "I'll drive the cows to pasture whilst you set the milk and fetch the hosses to the high field."

If stone hauling had been fun when I was working alone, it was ten times as much fun with Grandfather along. He handled Old Nell as if she'd been a team of oxen, and anyone could have heard him a mile away. She couldn't take six steps without his hollering, "Gee off! Haw to! Gitap! Whoa back! Whoa, you tarnal fool hoss!"

The yella colt knew every move of stone hauling as well as I, so I had no use for the reins, and kept them tied on the hame knobs. When I was forking or lifting stones onto the drag, he'd move forward a step or two at my cluck, or stop at a hiss. Because I always gave him a piece of apple after every pull on the dumping tackle, there was nothing for me to do but to switch his singletree over to the tote-rope hook and let him go. He'd swing around for a straight pull, throw his weight into the collar, then, when he heard the stones roll, come back to the drag for his apple.

I'd noticed that Grandfather stopped shouting at Old Nell each time the yella colt and I took a load of stones to the wall. On about the sixth trip, I looked up and saw him watching us. "Gorry sakes alive, Ralphie!" he called out. "You got the old hoss to reading your mind. How in thunderation does he know what to do without neither voice nor line? By fire! Never thought to tell you! The colt, he won't work single! Never would! Never do nothing but balk and rare!"

If Grandfather had told me that a month before, it would have made me awfully mad. The first thing that came into my head was his making me use the colt on the tote rope that day in haying when I'd broken the ridgepole in the barn. Even though I wasn't mad, I wanted Grandfather to know that I knew, so I called back, "He does all right now. I'll bet we could even use him on the tote rope for the horsefork."

"Like as not! Like as not!" Grandfather snapped quickly; then, "Gitap! Gitap, Nell!"

By the time he'd made another trip across the field and back, Grandfather's voice was pleasant again. "By gorry, Ralphie," he called, "mark how the rocks is coming a-tumbling out back of this little harrow! Come the Sabbath, I cal'late we'll have this field skun clean as a whistle. Gorry sakes! Won't have nothing left to do but the dressing afore we tackle the wilderness field."

The mailman had come and gone before Grandfather would stop raking stones and go to the auction. I didn't expect him home until after dark and, all afternoon, kept planning the things I'd say to Annie when she came for her cows. I couldn't tell her what Grandfather had said about not letting her come to the house again, and I wouldn't tell her he'd said I couldn't see her any more. When the sun was dropping behind the pines on the ridge, I went down to the valley and waited for her. I just told her that Grandfather expected Millie home in a few days and wanted to save the butter making for her. Then I said we had enough pie and cake to last that long, that it was the best I'd ever tasted, and that I'd come down to see her again the first chance I had.

Grandfather came home that night while I was milking. I didn't know he was there until he'd unharnessed Old Nell, and came into the tie-up shouting, "I got him, Ralphie! I got him! Old 'Bijah riz up for the bait like a horned pout for a night crawler."

All the while I was milking, he gloated over the trade he was planning to make with Mr. Swale, and followed me from cow to cow, telling me stories of dozens of different trades he'd made. "Ain't no two ways about it, Ralphie," he told me as I stripped the brindle, "a farmer ain't a farmer less'n he's a good trader. There's traders and traders, but there's tarnal few good ones. Father, he was one of the best. Wouldn't no more lie to you in a trade than he'd steal off'n you, but you could put what meaning you might on what he said, and you was lucky if you come away with your boots on. What I know of trading, I learnt from Father. Don't cheat ary man in a trade, Ralphie. If it comes about that he wants to cheat hisself, I don't cal'late that's none of your affairs. Don't never be anxious, and don't never hurry a trade. Good trades has to be sot up afore the dickering commences. Take 'Bijah Swale now. The hook's in old 'Bijah so deep there ain't no chance of his spitting it out. Cal'late we'll be seeing something of 'Bijah afore sundown tomorrow. If chance should happen I and you ain't together, you come a-running whenst he heaves in sight. Your old grampa'll learn you how to make a powerful good trade, Ralphie."

Along in the middle of the next afternoon, Grandfather and I had stopped to rest the horses. The stones had been cleared from more than three-quarters of the field, and Grandfather called to me, "Gorry sakes alive, Ralphie! Getting tarnal nigh the end of it, ain't we? S'posing I and you cast about a bit and cal'late what best we might do with this old field." I was sure he was going to say something about strawberries, and wanted to throw my arms up and shout, but I didn't. I lifted one more stone onto the drag, and then walked over to him slowly as if I was just going for a drink of water.

We'd walked a little way, quartering across the top of the hill, when Grandfather knelt and scooped up a handful of dirt. "Just about petered out, ain't it?" he said, as it sifted through his fingers. "Your old grampa ain't kept stock enough these last ten years to feed the soil proper. Mark how yella and spindling the nigh side the crown is? Needs a power more of dressing to fetch it back. T'other slope's browner; you take note? Don't need quite so much. Yonder, 'twixt the orchard wall and the pasture bars, you mark that black streak? 'Twon't need next to none."

I nodded my head, because I couldn't trust my voice not to sound too happy if I spoke.

"Cal'late you could ration out thirty loads more dressing, nice and even, 'cording to the color of the soil?"

I was so excited that I started to speak before I'd thought what I was going to say. "I could if . . ."

Grandfather looked up at me with a half smile, and said, "Could you if you had a . . . Mark! Mark, Ralphie!"

There was a ring of metal against stone, then the chuckle of a loose wagon hub on a spindle, and I looked around to see a gray horse's head come above the hill at the top of the orchard.

"It's somebody with a gray horse," I told Grandfather.

"Cal'lated 'twould be," he said, and went on sifting dirt.

He didn't look up or move from his knees, and I didn't want to be staring, so I kept watching the sifting dirt. In a minute or two, a man called, "Howdy, Tom. How be you?"

Grandfather looked around, but didn't get up. "Tol'able, 'Bijah. Tol'able," he said, and reached for another handful of dirt.

I glanced over my shoulder to be sure it was the man who had given me a ride the day I came. It was, and he was driving the same horse, hitched to the same blue dumpcart. Tied by her horns to the back of it, was a long-legged, slab-sided, red cow. Her head was twisted sideways, and she was pulling back on the rope.

"Just a-driving by, and stopped in to pass the time o'day with you." Mr. Swale shouted.

"Nice one, ain't it?" Grandfather said, and let the dirt trickle through his fingers.

Mr. Swale waited a minute or two, and then called back, "Mite early for fall plowing, ain't it, Tom?"

Grandfather nodded his head.

"See you got a boy to help you. Your daughter Mary's boy, ain't it?"

Grandfather nodded again.

Mr. Swale waited two or three minutes that time, and shouted, "One boy can be a big help to a man; two ain't worth shucks. Learning him to pick rock? Cal'lating on sowing back to timothy?"

That time, Grandfather said, "Mmmhmm," as he nodded.

My heart jumped quickly. And then I felt empty inside. When I looked up from the ground, the red cow was twisting her neck and pulling back on the rope. "So, boss, so." Mr. Swale said, just loud enough I could barely hear him, then shouted, "Hear you got a new bull, Tom."

"All-fired good one," Grandfather said that time, and stood up. "Gorry, 'Bijah! See you fetched a cow."

"Heifer," Mr. Swale shouted back. "Milking Shorthorn. Close to purebred."

"Bull's Holstein. All-fired big one," Grandfather told him, as he started toward the dumpcart.

I felt so bad about his planning to plant timothy hay again that I wanted to be alone, so I turned toward the wall where I'd left the yella colt. I'd only taken two steps when Grandfather said, in a real low voice, "Let be, Ralphie! Come watch the fun."

"What you a-standing him at, Tom?" Mr. Swale shouted before Grandfather was through speaking to me.

"Fifty cents," Grandfather called, and reached down for another handful of dirt. As I bent with him, he said into his whiskers, "Cow ain't in. He's here for trading."

"Trifle steep, ain't you, Tom? Eb Kennedy hain't asking but thutty-five for his Jersey."

"Ain't far up to Eben's," Grandfather said, as he walked on toward the dumpcart.

I'd seen plenty of Shorthorn cattle in Colorado, but I'd never seen one that looked like Mr. Swale's cow. Her horns turned in like a Jersey's, and her head was nearly as wide at the muzzle as it was at her eyes. Her neck was scrawny, and she kept twisting it as she pulled at the rope. Mr. Swale noticed Grandfather looking at the cow, and said, "Heifer's a leetle timid. Hain't used to being drug on a rope. Mighty gentle spirited critter."

Grandfather walked around the cow with his hands folded behind his back. "Breechy, ain't she?" he asked, as she slatted around to keep an eye on him.

"Lord sakes, no! Hain't a breechy bone in her hide. Timid, Tom! Timid! 'N awful good milking heifer. Wouldn't swap her off for the world if my pasture wa'n't so nigh the county road. Them automobiles a-passing worries the jeeslin' out'n her. Throws her off her feed."

"Dite ganted, ain't she?" Grandfather asked, as he looked at the deep hollows under her hip bones.

Mr. Swale climbed down off the dumpcart and started to walk around the cow, too. "Yes, siree, Tom. Ganted out. Pore critter; them automo. . . . Heavens to B . . . !"

It happened so fast that I hardly saw it. Mr. Swale was right beside the cow's hip when he said, "Pore critter," and she kicked as he reached a hand out toward her. Her hoof flashed through the air like a stone from a slingshot, and there was a click as it hit his leg just below the knee. He caught himself quickly, but there was a hurt sound in his voice when he went on: ". . . etsy wouldn't have a pore critter scairt so. Needs a big quiet pasture, the like of yourn, Tom."

As Mr. Swale limped back and climbed onto the dumpcart, Grandfather winked at me across the old cow's back. "Trifling little bag," he said. "Cal'late she's tarnal nigh dried up, Ralphie."

"No, siree, Tom!" Mr. Swale said, as he sat rubbing his leg. "No, siree! My missus, she's been a-feeling porely; rheumatiz in her hands. Didn't get her milking done this morning till nigh onto noon. You can count on a steady ten, 'leven quarts to a milking. 'N awful good butter cow."

"Got a good butter cow," was all Grandfather said.

"Pasture like your'n, Tom, you'd have this here heifer up to fifteen, sixteen quarts to a milking inside a fortnight."

"Ain't cal'lating to overcrowd the pasture. Ralphie, I and you'd better get back to them rocks."

Mr. Swale started to turn his cart, and he let Grandfather and me go fifty or sixty feet before he stopped and called, "Might give a dollar to boot on a swap, Tom. Shorely do hate to put this timid heifer back in that county road pasture. It's again my conscience."

"I don't think she's a heifer," I whispered to Grandfather.

"Older'n I be," he mumbled into his whiskers. Then he turned and called out, "Always willing to talk a fair trade. What kind of a critter you looking for, 'Bijah?"

"Hain't partial to getting 'nother heifer, Tom," Mr. Swale said. "Something easy milking, account of the old woman's stiff hands."

"By Gorry, 'Bijah," Grandfather said, as he walked back to the cart, "cal'late I got just what you're looking for, but she'd cost you more to boot than you can afford."

"Who told you what I can afford?" Mr. Swale asked angrily.

"Gorry sakes alive, 'Bijah," Grandfather said, "all I was a-getting at . . . This cow of your'n's farrow, you say. I'd have to feed her through the winter afore she freshened, and I was a-cal'lating on swaping you a spanking fresh one. Couldn't make no dicker less'n eight, ten dollars boot."

"Easy milking?" Mr. Swale asked.

Grandfather looked over at me, and asked, "What would you say, Ralphie; could a stiff-handed woman milk that spotted cow?"

I didn't want to see the spotted cow traded off. She was the best milker in the herd, but I had to say, "Sure. Anybody could milk her."

"Kick?" Mr. Swale asked me.

"No, sir," I said. "She's never raised a foot when I've been around her."

"Might be we could deal, Tom," he said. "It's agin my conscience a-putting this timid heifer back in that cussed pasture of mine. Where's your cow at?"

"Fetch 'em in to the barn, Ralphie," Grandfather told me; "I'll look after the hosses. No need a-fetching Clara Belle and the brindle." And then his eyelid flickered just a trifle.

It was early, and the cows were way down at the back end

of the pasture. I didn't hurry much going down there, and the more I thought about it, the less I could be sure that Grandfather's eyelid had flickered on purpose. Myra and the spotted cow were the first ones I found, but I didn't take them right in. I still hoped there might be a chance of getting rid of the brindle, and Grandfather hadn't said I couldn't bring her. I decided to start them all into the lane, then get in front of the brindle and Clara Belle, and let them follow along by themselves.

Bijah

26

'Bijah Out-trades Himself

GRANDFATHER and Mr. Swale were waiting in the barn-yard when I brought the cows in. Old Myra was out in front, as usual, the spotted cow next, and the brindle and Clara Belle were only a few steps behind me. "There you be, 'Bijah! There you be!" Garndfather sang out when the spotted cow came up past the sheep barn. "There's a nice good cow for you. Easy milking, and clever as a kitten. Freshened less'n a month agone. Cal'late I could let you have her for about ten dollars boot. Fetch her right up here, Ralphie, where 'Bijah can get a good look at her!"

The old spotted cow weaved a little as I drove her up toward the barn. Her box-shaped bag with its uneven teats flopped from side to side, and her hip bones stuck out like sawed-off tree limbs. Halfway up, she stopped, turned her head back toward the sheep barn where we used to keep her calf, and lowed. It was almost a wail. "Gorry sakes," Grandfather said, " 'Tain't half-past four yet, and her a-bellering to be milked a'ready. Fetch a milk pail, Ralphie, so's 'Bijah can try her out his own self."

Just as he said it, the brindle cow bellowed from the door of the sheep barn. Even though her twin calves were gone, she always stopped there and bawled when she came in from the pasture. "Time and tarnation!" Grandfather shouted at me. "Didn't I tell you not to fetch Clara Belle and the brindle in?"

"I didn't." I told him. "They just followed us."

"Whyn't you put the bars up so's to keep 'em back? Get 'em out where they can get some grass in their bellies." He sounded awfully mad, so I drove them back into the lane and put up the bars at the end of the barnyard. When I came back, he was stroking the spotted cow on the forehead, and Mr. Swale was standing away and looking at her. His mouth was pulled down at the corners, and he grumbled, "Never mind! Never mind the milk pail!"

Grandfather's face looked worried, and he said, " 'N awful good cow, 'Bijah. 'N awful good cow. If you don't trade for her you'll always regret it. I'll guarantee her and stand right behind my word."

Mr. Swale walked around to the other side, bent over, and looked at the cow's bag. "Don't cal'late she's just the cow I'm a-looking for, Tom," he said.

" 'N awful nice good cow." Grandfather said. "Might shave the boot fifty cents—seeing's she ain't fleshed up much since the calf come. All-fired nice easy cow for Miz Swale to milk."

Mr. Swale stood back with his arms folded and teetered up onto his toes two or three times. "Hain't worth it. Nope! Nope! Don't cal'late my missus would cotton to this here one, Tom. How 'bout that brindle critter?"

Grandfather's face looked almost frightened. "Gorry sakes, no! Couldn't let you . . . 'Bijah, I don't cal'late that brindle'd be the right one for Miz Swale. You being an old neighbor, I be a-going to let you have this spotted one for nine dollars boot. You'll always be sorry if you don't take her."

I was so mad I wanted to yell at Grandfather, but there wasn't a thing I could do or say. Mr. Swale wagged his head back and forth as he walked over in front of the cow. He stood a foot or two behind Grandfather, just above me on the little hill that ran up to the barn foundation. Then, as he teetered, he looked over my head toward the lane.

The brindle was reaching for clover through the fence. The afternoon sun struck along her back and side so that her color looked like weathered bronze. And, in the long grass, her round, bulging bag almost seemed to reach the ground. "Nope, Tom, nope," Mr. Swale said as he teetered. "Can't make you no trade on this here one, but I'll give you nine dollars and take the brindle."

"Great thunderation, no!" Grandfather shouted. "Butter's twenty-eight cents, and Ralphie can't get all she gives at a milking into a sixteen quart pail. Gorry sakes, no!"

A hot flash went all over me, and I thought I knew what Grandfather was doing. I could hardly help grinning when I said, "Not by at least three quarts."

It didn't take more than fifteen minutes to make the trade after that. Mr. Swale just walked around the brindle once, looked at her bag from both sides and the back, and talked Grandfather down from twenty to fifteen dollars boot.

We turned the red cow loose in the barnyard, and tied the brindle to Mr. Swale's dumpcart. After he'd driven away, Grandfather folded the bills and stuffed them into his wallet. "There you be, Ralphie!" he said. "Wan'n't that all right? Never told him a tarnal word 'twa'n't gospel truth. Just sort of cal'lated 'Bijah'd do his own trading; wouldn't trust t'other man not to lie about a critter. Let me see. Let me see. Not a-counting what the twin calves fetched, I cal'late this breechy red cow stands me eighteen dollars and a quarter."

The red cow was standing at the far side of the barnyard. Her tail was turned our way, but she had her head twisted just enough so she could watch us. Grandfather picked up a stick and flung it toward her. Before it was hardly in the air, she dashed for the lane bars and sailed over them like a frightened deer. "Just so! Just so!" Grandfather said. "Did you mark how she jumped with her head up like a hoss? Two, three days, we'll cure her of that, and with a little provender morning and night,

I wouldn't doubt she'll make a pretty good cow. Mostly scairt; that's all. 'Bijah, he don't treat his critters gentle."

I was glad Grandfather had traded off the brindle, but I worried quite a little about it while I was doing the chores. The new red cow surprised me. I gave her a quart of meal just before I

started to milk her, and was careful not to do anything to frighten her. But I still remembered how quick she was when she kicked Mr. Swale and I kept one knee between her hocks. When I'd seen her tied to the dumpcart, I hadn't thought she'd give two quarts at a milking, but she gave more than six, and she was easy to milk.

Grandfather had built a fire and put potatoes on to boil, but he was in his room when I took the milk to the house. Instead of scalding the pans and setting it right away, I scrubbed my hands and made a pan of biscuits. They didn't come out as well as the ones I made when Annie was there to tell me just what to do, but they were a lot better than Grandfather's. And then I mashed the potatoes with cream in them, while the pork was frying.

When I called Grandfather to supper, he was still excited about his good trade. "By fire, Ralphie," he told me, "soon's ever we get this breechy one cured of jumping fences and get a little meat under her hide, I cal'late she'll make awful good trading stock. I been a-turning over in my mind just who I ought to swap her off to."

"Maybe you won't want to trade her off," I said. "She gave at least six quarts of milk tonight, and she didn't kick once."

"Six quarts! Gorry sakes! Didn't cal'late she'd give six cupfuls. Great thunderation! I certainly did even up with 'Bijah for beating me out of them four cords of wood."

"Being sick, and with rheumatism in her hands, I'm kind of worried about Mrs. Swale," I said.

"Gossiping old battle-axe!" Grandfather exploded. "Meaner'n 'Bijah with critters! Seen her bust a milking stool acrost a fresh heifer's back. Ain't nothing more the matter with her hands than there be with your'n. Seen her a-picking blueb'ries side the road t'other day, nimble fingered as a fiddler."

As he talked, Grandfather had been sitting with a piece of fried pork balanced on his knife. All at once, he began laughing, bumped the heel of the knife down on the table, and sent the pork flying. "By fire!" he laughed, "Did you mark the kick the breechy one fetched 'Bijah? Quicker'n scat, wa'n't she? Heap up her measures of provender, Ralphie. I cal'late that one kick was worth five dollars in meal."

"Whew!" I said, "I was afraid for a little while you were going to trade the spotted cow off to him. I'd have hated to see people like that get her."

"You needn't to have worried none, Ralphie. I know 'Bijah, and I knowed his father, and my father knowed his grandfather. Crooked as a rail fence, all three of 'em and alike as crows a-setting on it. Wa'n't one of 'em would tell the truth if a lie would do, and always cal'lated everybody else done the same. Gorry sakes! Them three men has lawed and been lawed more than ary three men this side of Kingdom-come. Did ever I tell you 'bout the white oaks?"

"The one great-grandfather climbed?" I asked him.

"No. No. No." he said, as his knife chased a scrap of pork around his plate. "You recollect a stump field east'ard of the county road as you come up toward Cowen's Tavern?"

"The one that's in even rows?"

"Did you mark how the brook runs 'twixt it and the road?"

"Yes," I said.

"Well, 'twa'n't always there. In the year 1800, Sam Starboard bought the land joining Father on the east. His deed run from Father's wall to the brook, and follering south'ard to a tarnal great beaver dam. Four, five years later, 'Bednego Swale—he was 'Bijah's grandfather—come in and bought up a piece of land t'other side the brook.

"Well, Sam Starboard—next to Father—he was the best farmer hereabouts. Crack of dawn till twilight he'd be a-chopping and a-burning till he'd cleared him a ten-acre potato field in the valley. Virgin soil 't was then, Ralphie. Black, and didn't need no dressing. Wa'n't no roads in them days, but Sam, he had an all-fired great wide-horned ox. Come fall, he'd histe two hundredweight of potatoes onto the back of the ox, and lead him off down to Bath two, three times a week. Shipmasters was a-paying high for potatoes, and Sam, he commenced to prosper.

"Winter of 1812–13 was an all-fired hard one. Come spring thaw, water riz in the valley till 'twas higher'n a tall man's head. When it run off, the brook had changed its course, followed the nigh edge of Sam's potato field 'stead of the far one, and ripped out the beaver dam. Didn't bother Sam none. Just throwed a log bridge acrost, come planting time, and went on about his business of growing potatoes.

"All enduring the spring and summer, he'd hear 'Bednego a-swearing at his oxen and a-working in the woods along the old stream bed. 'Twa'n't none of Sam's business, and him and 'Bed-nego wa'n't on the best of terms noways, so he didn't pay it no heed.

"Come the spring of 1814, and Sam finds his log bridge chopped out and hauled off. When he sot about building him a new one, old 'Bednego come a-running down through the woods a-hollering, 'Get off my prop'ty! My deed reads to the east side of the brook.'

"Well, sir, Ralphie, there wa'n't nothing for Sam to do but law him. And he lost. 'Bednego had sot out seven- and eight-year-old trees in the old water course and sowed grass 'twixt 'em. To look at it, ary man would have swore on a Bible the brook hadn't a-run there in half a score of years."

"Didn't Mr. Starboard ever get it back?" I asked.

"No. No. But there's more to it. You might fetch the pie, Ralphie. There's a couple pieces left, ain't there?

"Well, as I was a-saying, Sam, he lost out in the lawing, even after he'd showed the squire where 'Bednego had rolled three, four tarnal great boulders into the stream bed to turn its course.

"Wa'n't many folks 'roundabout these parts in them days. Father, he was off with the militia—the British had fetched in soldiers—and there wa'n't nobody else to swear 'bout when the water course had changed over. 'Course, 'Bednego swore 'twas afore ever he bought the land.

"Well, sir, when the lawing was all over, Sam, he went to 'Bednego, and he says, ' 'Bednego, when a man's beat, he's beat, and there ain't no sense a-squabbling over that little parcel of land. I come to you to let you know I still want to be neighborly. I been a-farming that bottom land so long I know the quirks of it, and I cal'late I can raise more on it than ary other man. It'll take me a year to clear another potato field, and I'm a-hankering to raise one more crop on that bottom land. 'Bednego, I come here to make you a cash offer of twenty-five dollars rent in advance if you'll let me raise just one more crop on that ground. 'Course, I'll expect you to pay the taxes and keep the fences good, and not get rid of the land till my crop is harvested. And

I'll want a writing on it sot down in the squire's book. After I've paid you, I don't cal'late to have no more water courses changed on me, and I want everything shipshape and legal.'

"You know what he done, don't you, Ralphie?"

"Did it have something to do with the stumps?" I asked.

"That was it, Ralphie. Twenty-five dollars was a lot of money in them days—still is a lot of money. Well, soon's ever the writing was all writ, and the money was all paid, Sam, he planted him one crop of white oak on that ten acres. You know how long it takes a crop of white to grow?"

I shook my head.

"Hundred years. Sam Starboard's grandchildren took them oak off the land less'n five years agone. Made 'em wealthy. The taxes and fences has kept 'Bednego's offspring poor all their lives, and there ain't been nothing they could do about it. Sometimes, Ralphie, 'tain't the part of wisdom to think you're smarter'n your fellow man. Gorry, I'm a-getting sleepy. Cal'late your old grampa'll crawl off to bed."

27

Butter Making

TAKING care of the milk after I got it to the house was about as much work as milking. After supper every night, I had to scald crocks and pans, strain the milk, and set it in the cellar to rise. Then I had to bring up the batch from the day before, skim it, wash the pans and bowls, and put the cream in covered crocks.

The night Grandfather made the trade with 'Bijah Swale, I noticed that mold was growing on the cream in one of the crocks. At first, I was going to skim it off, and then I got an idea. If I showed it to Grandfather, he'd see that the cream would spoil unless it was churned into butter right away, and he might let Annie come up to help me.

It was nearly ten o'clock when I found the cream, but there was still a light under Grandfather's door, so I knocked, and told him about it. "Gorry sakes! Gorry sakes alive!" he said in a wide-awake voice. "By fire, I and you'll have to do a churning afore we go to the field in the morning. Did ever you make butter, Ralphie?"

I told him I'd worked the dasher for Mother, but that was all I knew about churning. "Ain't nothing to it! Ain't nothing to it,

at all, Ralphie!" he called back through the door. "Come morning, and your old grampa'll learn you all you'll need to know.
By gorry, I'm a-getting a far piece ahead of you on raking up
them rocks. Cal'late I might fetch the butter off to Lewiston
soon's ever we're done with the churning."

At supper, we'd eaten the last scrap of food Annie had cooked
for us. In the morning, Grandfather was so anxious to get
started on the butter that he wouldn't let me stop to make biscuits. He cooked the breakfast and got the churning ready while
I did the chores, but he didn't have very good luck. He usually
forgot to salt the oatmeal, but that morning he must have salted
it at least three times, and he spilled cream all over the floor
when he filled the churn.

"Gorry sakes alive! Salter'n Lot's wife!" Grandfather spluttered when he tasted the oatmeal. "What in time and tarnation
did you go and put extra salt into it for? I salted the water afore
ever I stirred in the oats!"

I had to remind him that the kettle wasn't even on the stove
when I went to the barn, and that he had the oatmeal all dished
up before I came back into the kitchen. "What's the odds?
What's the odds? Salt never hurt no man," he snapped. "Put
plenty sugar on and you won't never taste the salt."

A pound of sugar wouldn't have covered up the salt in a bowl
of that oatmeal. Grandfather tried two or three more spoonfuls,
but it nearly gagged him, and there wasn't another thing in the
house to eat, except salt pork and raw potatoes. "Gorry! Gorry
sakes!" he sort of gasped, and looked out toward the pantry.
"Ain't a stray piece of pie or one of them little cupcakes a-laying
roundabouts, is there, Ralphie? Gorry! This stuff would turn
a man's in'ards into tripe."

"No, there isn't a bite of anything left," I told him, "but I
think I could get Annie to . . ."

"Nothing of the kind! Nothing of the kind!" Grandfather half
shouted. "Don't need no neighbor women folks a-snooping
'round here. Ain't nothing a man can't do for hisself if he's
a-mind to. You go to fetching that churn of cream to butter.

whilst I cook up another mess of porridge. There ain't no time for dawdling. I cal'late there's two more churnfuls of cream in the cellar."

The churn was a tall wooden cylinder, a little wider at the bottom than at the top. It had a loose lid, with a round hole in the middle. A dasher handle, with crossed paddles at the bottom, stuck through the hole, and the churning was done by thumping the dasher up and down. Grandfather had filled the churn so full that cream pumped out of the hole and around the lid when I started thumping. "Take care! Take care!" he snapped at me from the stove. "Butter's twenty-eight cents! Don't go to heaving it all over Kingdom-come!"

I cut down the length of the stroke and the speed of the dasher, but kept it going up and down, up and down. When one arm ached, I changed to the other, but there was no change in the feel of the cream. Every time I shifted the dasher from one hand to the other, Grandfather would ask, "Ain't it come? Ain't it come yet, Ralphie?" Then he'd leave the oatmeal, come over, and peek under the lid of the churn.

After the fourth or fifth peek, he snapped, "Stand back! Stand back! Leave your old grampa have a-holt of that stick. He'll fetch it 'round in a jiffy!"

Grandfather fetched it all right. He grabbed the dasher out of my hand, and started it going like a triphammer. Cream spurted from the top of the churn, spread like an open umbrella, and went all over us and the floor. "Wastin'! Wastin'!" Grandfather shouted. "Why in thunderation didn't you tell me 'twas brimming full? Oh, well, what's done is done. Scoop it up, Ralphie! 'Twill all make good hog's victuals."

It wasn't a pleasant morning. Grandfather blamed me for letting the second kettle of oatmeal burn. I was so empty I was shaking, and, by ten o'clock, the cream looked just as it did when we first started churning. Grandfather had tried putting cold water and warm water and soda and vinegar into it, but nothing would make the butter come. After he'd raised Cain with me for not doing the skimming right, he let me go down to

Littlehales and get Annie. Before I went, he told me, "Understand me now! This ain't for nothing but butter making. Don't
you let me catch that girl a-messing 'round the victuals. Wastin'!
Wastin'! Eggs is eighteen cents!"

I hadn't had a chance to take the cows to pasture before we
started the churning that morning. As Annie and I came up the
road from her house, we saw Grandfather driving them up the
lane by the orchard. He had his hands folded behind his back,
was walking slowly, and Old Bess was following right behind
his heels.

"Good heavens!" Annie said, when she first looked into the
churn. "No wonder the butter wouldn't make! Didn't you know
any better than to fill a churn brim full? Cream has to have
room to slop and splash if the butter's ever going to make."

"Then we should have had butter by six o'clock this morning,"
I told her. "We've had cream slopped and splashed all over the
kitchen. Grandfather even got it in his whiskers."

It's strange the way cream will turn to butter for a woman
when it won't for a man. All Annie did was to dip out a little
cream, give the dasher a few beats, and say, "There! It's beginning to come. Now you put some elbow grease into the churning, and we'll have butter."

She was as right as we'd been wrong. I could feel the difference when I first took hold of the dasher and, within a few minutes, there was a big lump of butter sloshing around in the
churn. I had never thought I liked buttermilk, but I drank more
than a quart of it while Annie was kneading the lump on the
butter board. Bright yellow flakes floated thick on the top of
the glass, and it left my mouth feeling clean and tart.

Annie had started me churning on the second batch of butter
when Grandfather came in through the summer kitchen. "Gorry
sakes alive!" he sang out, when he saw Annie working the big
yellow lump on the board. "Gorry sakes, Annie girl, how'd you
fetch it so quick?"

I was afraid she'd say the same thing to Grandfather that
she'd said to me, and caught my breath to try to head her off,

but I didn't have to. "Oh, you had it just about all done before I got here," she laughed. "My! You had a lot of cream saved up, Mr. Gould. It will take us half the afternoon to get it all churned and printed."

"Gorry sakes! Gorry sakes!" Grandfather mumbled. "Was cal'-lating on fetching it off to the city this afternoon. Hmmmmm. Hmmmm. Where's my spectacles at, Ralphie? Didn't I see something in the paper 'bout an auction over to Topsham to-day? Still four empty stanchions in the tie-up, ain't there? Cal'-late I'll have to put off taking the butter till morning."

"Are you going bright and early?" I asked, as I passed him his glasses.

"Crack o'dawn! Cal'late to be on the road afore sunup!"

"Then do you want me to pick some of the sweet apples for you to take along?"

"By fire! Like to skipped my mind! Pick all you can of 'em, Ralphie. There's bushel baskets in the carriage-house attic. Gorry sakes! Ought to fetch fifty, sixty cents a bushel this season of the year."

Grandfather stood peering at the paper for a few minutes, then muttered, "Hmmm, hmmm, hmmm. Ain't going to be no milk cows to this auction. Oh, well, what's the odds? Cal'late I might as well attend it anyways. Might happen I could stir up a good trade for another day." A few minutes later, he drove Old Nell out of the dooryard.

The sound of the wheels had hardly died away before Annie called from the pantry. "I'll have this batch all printed out in a few minutes, and then I'll get some dinner started. I wonder why Mr. Gould went away without waiting for his dinner."

The first thing that came into my head was what Grand-father had said about 'Bijah Swale going to auctions for the free victuals. The next, was what he'd said about my not letting Annie cook. I was trying to find some nice way to tell her, when I happened to remember that he hadn't said she couldn't cook; he'd only said not to let him catch her messing with the victuals. So I just called back, "Grandfather often goes to auctions without waiting for his dinner." I didn't even say anything about saving eggs when she made an omelette with six of them. But as soon as we'd eaten, I did take the swill out to the hogs.

Annie and I finished the butter by two o'clock. There was fifty-four pounds of it. When we had it all set away in the cellar to cool, she helped me pick the apples. The afternoon was about as nice as the first part of the morning had been bad. We talked about Colorado, and the high school at Lisbon Falls; and about strawberries and tomatoes and butter.

It was while we were talking about butter that I told Annie I thought Millie was working in a mill up at Lewiston. I told her that Grandfather had watched all the people coming out of the mill gates two or three times, but he'd never been able to find Millie.

"Why does he watch the gates?" Annie asked me. "Why doesn't he go to the different mill offices? They keep payrolls in the offices, and have the names of everybody who works there written down in alphabetical order. My Aunt Susan used to keep the payroll in one of the mills. It only takes a minute or two for looking up a name, and in one afternoon, Mr. Gould could go to every office in Lewiston."

When the sun was dipping down toward the top of the pines, Annie wanted to take some of the Gravenstein apples to the house and make a couple of pies, but of course I couldn't let her. I had to tell her that too much green apple pie always gave me a stomach-ache, and that maybe we'd better wait until the Gravensteins were riper. Then I said that Grandfather wanted to take all the August Sweets he could while the season was still early, so we kept right on picking till it was time to go for the cows. We both went together, and we stopped by the granite outcropping to see if our squirrel was still around the big maple. We didn't see him, and Annie didn't notice the verse I had scratched in the stone. Once I thought I'd show it to her, but I didn't. It seemed a little too much like bragging.

It was nearly twilight before we stopped watching for the squirrel, and Grandfather was outside the tie-up door of the barn when I drove our cows over the top of the orchard hill. When I first saw him he was waving his arms, and shouting, "Come quick, Ralphie! Come quick!"

The only thing that I could think of was that the bull had broken loose. I jumped the orchard wall, and raced toward the barn as fast as I could run. Grandfather kept shouting till I was halfway down the hill, then went to the big barn door, pushed it open a foot or so, and went in. I was so out of breath and my legs were so tired that I couldn't jump the bars at the end of the barnyard. I crawled through them, and ran up the slope to the big door. As I pushed through the opening Grandfather had left, I saw him going out of the front doorway. "Come quick, Ralphie! Come quick!" he called. "See what I fetched you home!"

I slowed down, and my knees were rattling together as I walked the length of the barn floor. "There you be! There you be, Ralphie!" Grandfather sang out when I reached the dooryard. "Ain't that a beauty!"

Old Nell was standing, hitched to the spring wagon, just beyond the barn doorway. Her head was hanging low, her shoulders and neck were dripping sweat, and her sides were heaving. At first, I didn't notice the old manure spreader that was tied to the back of the wagon. Grandfather didn't pay any attention to Nell, but grabbed my arm and led me back past her. "There! There! There you be, Ralphie!" he said as he stood back and looked at the spreader. "Ain't scarcely nothing wrong with it— 'cepting a couple of busted slats—and I made a powerful good trade on it. All-fired nigh enough scrap iron in it to fetch what I had to give for it. Cal'late it'll save us a powerful lot of hard work. Going to have a tarnal lot of dressing to spread with a big barn full of cows."

The spreader must have been one of the first ones ever made, and it was easy to see that it hadn't been used for years. The iron was rusted brown and scaly, the wood was weatherbeaten, and there were only a few patches of faded red paint, but I couldn't have been happier if it had been brand new. I stepped closer, rubbed my hand along the top rail, and said, "It sure is a beauty, and I think I can fix it all right, but I wish Uncle Levi was here."

"Cal'late he will be! Cal'late he will be, Ralphie!" Grandfather told me. "Stopped off to the depot at the Falls and writ him a telegraph. Most generally, I don't waste money on a telegraph less'n I be in bad trouble, and Levi knows it."

28

A Holy Place

IT WASN'T until after I'd finished milking that I told Grandfather what Annie had said about the mill payrolls. He was slicing pork for supper, but he dropped the knife, and said, "Tell me that again! Tell me that again, Ralphie!"

I was starting to strain the milk when I told him the second time, but he stopped me. "Let be! Let be!" he snapped. "Why in time and tarnation didn't you tell me first off when I come home? Leave that tarnal milk be, and get the harness back on Old Nell. Time flies!"

"Won't the mill offices be closed this late at night?" I asked.

"Didn't say they wouldn't, did I? Don't cal'late on frittering away half the morning a-getting the wagon loaded. The butter wrapped and ready? How many apples did you pick?"

"Nine bushels," I told him, "and there were fifty-four pounds of butter. It's . . ."

"Good on your head, Ralphie! Good on your head!" Grandfather sang out as he reached for his hat. "How in thunderation did ever you do so much? Gorry sakes! Ought to fetch nigh onto a twenty dollar bill! By fire, Ralphie, I and you is going into the butter business. Gorry! Won't Millie's eyes pop out whenst she sees the way we're a-going? Get your hoss! Get your hoss! Cal'-late on having the wagon all loaded and ready afore we set down to our victuals."

All the way up through the orchard, while we were loading the apples, and on the way back to the barn, Grandfather kept talking about Millie and butter.

After I'd put Old Nell in her stall, I expected that we'd go to the house, but he didn't seem to want to. For a minute or two, he stood by the spring wagon, holding the lantern up to the baskets of apples, and looking at them. Then he set the lantern down, took an apple in his hand and, as he rubbed it slowly, said, "Don't cal'late you knowed it, Ralphie, but Millie's been on my mind a heap of late. Being as she ain't wed a'ready, don't cal'late ever she will. Was I to live as long as what Father lived, she'd have a home here for a long spell to come. But the work-ings of the Almighty is mysterious. Ain't no prophesying what the years will fetch. Might come about she'd need a dollar put by for a rainy day. I been cal'lating that, after the provender money was took out, I and you would share and share alike on the butter business, Ralphie, but . . ."

As soon as Grandfather hesitated, I said, "I think Millie ought to have a share. Taking care of the milk and making the butter is about as much work as taking care of the cows and milking."

Grandfather didn't look up, but kept on rubbing the apple, and said, "S'posing we'd say there was ten parts to it; five for the provender, two for me, two for you, and one for Millie. How'd that strike you, Ralphie? 'Course I'd still pay Millie her two dollars a week wages, and I'd cal'late on you a-sharing in the crops that come from the dressing."

"That would strike me fine," I told him. "And I think you'd better have some supper and get to bed, if you're going to make an early start in the morning."

"Gorry sakes! Gorry sakes! Victuals like to slipped my mind," Grandfather said quickly, and started to the house. "By fire, ain't it going to be nice a-having Millie home again and no victuals to fret about?" He walked along with his head down and his hands behind him till we reached the summer-kitchen doorway. Then he lifted his head quickly, and said, "Don't cal'-late I'm hungry. Cal'late I'll go off to bed, so's to make a power-ful early start, come morning."

It took me till nearly midnight to take care of the milk, fix myself some supper, and wrap the butter. In the morning, Grandfather had to come to my room and shake me before I woke up. It was still dark, and the chimney of the lamp he carried was so smoked that I could only see his outline against its dim light. "Victuals is on the fire, Ralphie," Grandfather said, as he rocked my shoulder back and forth. "Daylight is fast a-coming, and I cal'late to be on the road afore sunup. Give Old Nell an extra quart of provender, and put the nose bag in the wagon."

Grandfather was dishing up the oatmeal when I came down to the kitchen. He had his new suit on, and had trimmed his beard. There were steps in it, so that his chin looked as if it had been newly shingled. "Stir your stivvers! Stir your stivvers, Ralphie!" he said while I was lighting the lantern. "Victuals is on the table, and time flies. Did you say the butter was wrapped and ready?"

Grandfather could get along with less to eat than anyone I ever knew. He'd gone to bed without a bite of supper, and he only ate a few mouthfuls of oatmeal for breakfast. I wasn't sur-prised that he wanted me to eat as fast as he did, but I was sur-prised at his snapping, "Let be! Let be!" when I started to go down cellar for the butter. "Get to your chores! Get to your chores afore half the morning's wasted away!" he told me. Then he went into his room and shut the door.

Whenever Grandfather had made an early start before, he had always wanted me to get everything ready. And I'd always stood by the doorstone and, as he drove out to the road, called after him to have a good trip. I couldn't imagine why he was so anxious for me to get at my chores that morning. It wasn't day-light yet, and before, I'd always left the chores until after he was gone.

I was still wondering about it when I went back to the barn, harnessed Old Nell, hitched her to the wagon, and led her up to the doorstone. There wasn't a sound from Grandfather's room when I went to the sink for the swill pails, and Nell was still standing by the summer-kitchen door when I went into the tie-up to milk. I'd milked one cow and started on another when I heard the sound of hammering. I thought one of the butter-boxes had pulled apart, or that there might be something broken about the wagon, so I went to see if Grandfather needed any help. It was nearly daylight, but there was a yellow glow from the carriage-house doorway, and the hammering sound came from that direction. I went across the yard to the doorway and looked in. At the far end of the room beyond the forge, Grand-father was kneeling in the circle of light from a lantern. His back was toward me, and I started to go toward him, but stopped and tiptoed out when I saw what he was doing. He had the broken screen door laid out, and was nailing boards across the bottom of it.

After I'd gone back to the tie-up, I heard hammering again that seemed to come from the direction of the house. I didn't go out, but listened closely. A few minutes after the hammering stopped, I heard Grandfather shout, "Gitap! Gitap, Nell!" and there was a rattle of wheels on the stones in the driveway. When I took the milk to the house, the screen door was back on the summer kitchen. It sagged crookedly from the hinges and, instead of the sapling, there was a turn-button to hold it closed.

There wasn't much fun in hauling rocks off the high field, now that I'd heard Grandfather tell Mr. Swale he was going to plant it back to timothy hay. I didn't loaf, and I kept at it all day, but I didn't hurry as much as I had before.

It was late when Grandfather came home. I had the evening chores finished, had taken care of the milk, and was sitting on the doorstone with Old Bess when he drove into the dooryard. He didn't really drive. He just sat, hunched down on the seat. Nell was walking slowly. Her head was down, the reins were hanging loosely, and Grandfather's hands were folded in his lap. He looked as if he were asleep, and he hardly roused when I went to meet him. All I could think of to say was, "Well, I got quite a few stones hauled today."

Grandfather's head came up a little, but I don't think he heard. He just looked down at me, and said in a tired voice, "She ain't nowheres to be found, Ralphie." Then he climbed down over the wheel and walked slowly toward the house. There was nothing I could think of to say. As I unhitched Nell from the wagon, I watched him go, as though he didn't care whether or not he ever got there. When he reached the screen door, he opened it carefully, went in, and closed it gently behind him.

I watered Nell, put her in her stall, and fed her. Grandfather hadn't lighted a lamp, and when I went into the house he was sitting at the kitchen table. His hat was still on, and his face was resting in his hands. He heard me, but he didn't move. And his voice was hardly more than a whisper when he said, "Ralphie, she ain't to be found nowheres. I been to every mill in both Lewiston and Auburn. She ain't there, and she ain't been there."

Grandfather often put his hand on my shoulder, but I had never put mine on his. That night I couldn't help it. I stood beside his chair and, though I didn't more than half believe it, I said, "Don't you worry, Millie will come back bye and bye. This is her home, and she loves it the same way you and I do."

Grandfather didn't move his head, but one hand came up and rested over mine. His voice was quavery, but there was warmth —almost joy—in it. "You do love it, don't you, Ralphie? I seen it, Ralphie! I seen it soon's ever you come home from Boston the last time. Your roots was a-reaching down into the soil you sprung from. I and you be a-going to fetch it back to fertile fields again."

"Sure we are. Sure we are," I told him, as his rough old hand patted up and down on mine.

The moon had risen, and as a cloud moved from its face, moonlight poured through the east kitchen windows in a soft, warm flood. The curtain was half drawn, so that I stood in the shadow, but the full richness of the light reached into the darkness of the room and spread around Grandfather. His head raised slowly, and he turned his face toward the window. For several minutes we were quiet. His hand stopped moving and lay still on mine. Then, in a voice that was almost as soft as the moonlight, he asked, "Ralphie, did Millie ever mention to you liking ary man?"

"No," I said. "She certainly didn't like the one that helped us that day in haying."

"Curious, curious," Grandfather said, after another minute or so, "she be nigh onto twenty-nine." He didn't move his hand from mine, but spread the other and drew it slowly down across his face—almost as though he were trying to wipe something away. "I ain't been square with her," he said, at last. "I been selfish, Ralphie. I been scairt someday there'd be one of 'em toll her away from home. I ain't let no young ones stay hereabouts."

"Oh, I don't think Millie cares anything about men," I said.

" 'Tain't in nature. 'Tain't in nature, Ralphie," he whispered. "You wouldn't know yet; you ain't old enough. There's a day comes when a man hankers for a woman to hold in his arms . . . and a woman hankers to be held . . . ary woman . . . It's in nature . . . The Almighty planned it so, Ralphie . . . and Millie's come to be a full-blown woman."

I don't know how long I stood there with my hand on Grandfather's shoulder. I forgot all about being there. Instead, I was remembering the day Annie had first sat with me on the stone outcropping. "I think I know," I said.

"There'll come a day you will," Grandfather whispered, and still looked away toward the low rising moon.

After a while, I said, "You're awfully tired, aren't you? What would you like me to fix you for supper? I think I could make an omelet."

"Ain't hungry for victuals," Grandfather said slowly. "Cal'-late I better go to bed." Still he didn't make any move to go.

I slipped my hand out from under his, went to the pantry, and took a glass and the bottle from the cupboard. When I came back, Grandfather hadn't moved from the table. By the moonlight, I measured out a spoonful of whiskey, stirred in sugar, and filled the glass with water from the teakettle. It was barely warm, little of the fragrance rose from the liquor, and I wasn't sure Grandfather would take it. I set it down in front of him, and his hand reached out for it almost eagerly.

A cloud drifted across the face of the moon and, as if a door were closed, the kitchen became dark. Grandfather's chair slid back, and I felt rather than heard him get up from the table. I was afraid he might stumble, and reached an arm out toward him as I stepped forward. As it touched him, he was turning toward the south window. The sofa was only a foot or two in front of him, and I caught his arm so he wouldn't bump against it. "You needn't to mind, Ralphie," he said. "There ain't a sofy or a rock or a tree on the old place I couldn't find was I stone blind. Just let me set a minute and drink the medicine. I do be a little weary."

On the high field, at the top of the orchard hill, a patch of moonlight lay golden in the blackness. We both must have seen it at the same moment. "Mark!" Grandfather said. "Glory be! The finger of the Almighty, Ralphie!"

Slowly, as the clouds moved, the bright spot on the hilltop widened and grew. Stonewalls traced their lines across it; deep shadows of the orchard trees dotted it here and there, and, as it spread, the whole picture was framed in the dark fringe of the pine woods. As slowly as the moonlight swelled, I realized Grandfather was whispering. The sound was hardly more than a light breeze makes in a field of ripened grain. I bent my head closer to him, and could just make out the familiar words: "Hallowed be Thy name."

I felt almost as though I had broken into a holy place, and moved far enough away that the sound was only the breathing of air through his beard, but in my mind I followed the words of the prayer. When it was ended, Grandfather said aloud, "Here, Ralphie, here! Dump it in the swill pail. Don't need no medicine tonight. Cal'late I'll go to bed."

29

Annie Is Woman of the House

SUNDAY morning I slept until after sunrise, and there was no sound from Grandfather's room when I went out to do the chores. I'd fed and watered the horses and the bull, slopped the hogs, and was nearly done milking when I heard a familiar voice outside the big barn doors. "Thomas, it's a God's wonder the both of you ain't starved to death! No wonder you're sick! If you can't find Millie, why in tunket ain't you got another housekeeper?"

I wanted to run right out there, but I didn't. The bull picked just that time to bellow, so I couldn't hear what Grandfather said, and a couple of minutes later, he and Uncle Levi came into the tie-up.

"Hi, Uncle Levi," I called when I heard the tie-up door bang. "I was hoping you'd come today."

"Cussed good thing I did come," he called back. "Where be you, Ralph? Stand up so's I can see if there's anything left of you but skin and bones. It's a God's wonder . . . Thomas, how long since this boy's had a square meal of victuals?"

Grandfather didn't answer right away, so I said, "Oh, we're getting along all right. Annie Littlehale came up and showed me how to bake biscuit and johnnycake. She made us pies and a layer cake, and baked a pot of beans."

"Them two cold biscuits I seen in the pantry a sample?"

"Well, not a very good one," I told him. "They came out better when Annie was right here to tell me what to do."

"What you having for breakfast? Didn't see nothing but a pot of burnt oatmeal."

Before I could answer, Grandfather shouted, "I and Ralphie's a-getting on all right. You don't need to be coming down here a-telling us what we'll eat. If you don't like . . ."

I didn't want Grandfather to get all excited and say something to make Uncle Levi go right back to Boston, so I hollered, "How did you get here so early, Uncle Levi? I thought there wasn't any train before quarter of twelve."

"Come down to Brunswick on the Bangor sleeper, and got fetched over in an automobile. Sound of Thomas telegraph, I calc'lated he was on his deathbed. About all ails him, he ain't et. It's a God's wonder you ain't in your graves, the both of you."

"We had a tarnal great pot of beans," Grandfather shouted. "Don't nobody starve whenst they got pork and potatoes and beans."

I tried to stop the row by shouting to Uncle Levi, "Did you see the new manure spreader, Uncle Levi?"

"No, I didn't!" Uncle Levi said. "I seen a cussed old wore-out one. Thomas, it's a . . ."

"I'll bet you can fix it," I hurried to say.

"Calc'late 'twould take a month of Sundays, and I got to be back in Boston come Friday morning. Here, give me one them pails of milk. I'll fetch it to the house and change my clothes. Went to see your mother and the children last night. They're making out all right. She sent you down a batch of doughnuts."

With Grandfather and Uncle Levi both being a little edgy, I wanted to be where I could break in if they started to quarrel, so I finished the chores as fast as I could go. Uncle Levi was still upstairs when I went to the house. There were two big paper bags and a cardboard box on the kitchen table, and

Grandfather was slicing salt pork. He still had his hat on and was grumbling more to himself than to me, "Don't know what in tarnation there is 'bout living off to Boston that makes Levi so finicky 'bout his victuals. Pork and potatoes and beans was good enough for him whenst he was a boy to home . . . and pie. Ralphie, you cal'late you could whack us up a nice good johnnycake? I got a good roaring fire a-going and the tea's on to boil. I'll run down cellar and fetch you up some sour milk."

I fussed around as long as I could while I was washing my face and hands, and hoped Grandfather would go into his room or outdoors. I'd made two johnnycakes since Annie had showed me how, but both times I'd used four eggs and the heaviest sour cream I could find. I was sure I could make another good one the same way, but I was worried about what it would be like without either cream or eggs.

Grandfather brought me a pan of clabber with every bit of the cream skimmed off, and then he stood and watched me. I'd just put the salt and soda into the corn meal and flour, and was sifting them when Uncle Levi came downstairs. "Gorry sakes, Levi," Grandfather sang out, "you ought to see the nice good victuals Ralphie can make. By fire, he whacked up the nicest johnnycake t'other day ever I et. He's a-making one of 'em right now."

With both Grandfather and Uncle Levi watching me, I forgot what Annie had said about putting pork fat into the johnnycake if I didn't use cream, so I just poured in some sour milk and began to stir. The batter didn't act right. It stuck till the spoon was bigger than my fist, and it plastered thick around the sides of the bowl. Instead of being reddish, it was whitish-yellow. That made me remember the molasses. I poured a little in, but it only made the mess stickier. While I was putting in a little more sour milk, Uncle Levi said, "Ain't you forgot the eggs?"

"Don't need no eggs in johnnycake!" Grandfather snapped.

"With all the hens 'round here, Thomas, it's a G . . ."

I didn't let him get any further. I dropped the spoon, and

said, "I guess I've forgotten how Annie showed me to do it. This dough doesn't feel right."

Uncle Levi looked over Grandfather's shoulder and winked at me. Then he said, "Fetched you down a little fruit, but the meat market at Brunswick wa'n't open. Calc'late we'll have to sacrifice a hen after breakfast."

Grandfather swung his head around, and grumbled, "Hens is all a-laying good, and eggs is fetching eighteen cents. Plenty pork in the barrel."

"Fetched you some blood oranges, Thomas. Want one afore breakfast?" was all Uncle Levi said.

"Gorry sakes! Gorry sakes! Believe I would! Believe I would," Grandfather said, and reached for one of the big bags on the table. "Great thunderation, Levi! Where in tarnation did ever you find oranges the likes of them? Must weigh tarnal nigh onto a pound apiece."

Grandfather still had his hand down inside the bag, and was peeking over the edge of it. "Them ain't oranges," Uncle Levi told him. "Them's grapefruits. Comes from Florida."

"Grapefruits!" Grandfather said, as he took one out. "What in tarnation kind of grapes is they that grows so big? Must take a tarnal stout vine to hold 'em up. More like punkin fruits than grapefruits! Gorry sakes! Cal'late a vine like that must need a powerful lot of dressing. Great thunderation! Cluster of 'em's prob'ly bigger'n a weanling calf."

"Don't grow on vines; grow on trees, like apples," Uncle Levi told him. "Hear tell a man out in California invented 'em. Calc'late it's a cross 'twixt a lemon and an orange."

Grandfather was turning the grapefruit in his hands. He smelled it, and asked, "Why don't they call 'em lemonges 'stead of grapefruits if they be crossbred?"

"Same reason they don't call mules donkosses," Uncle Levi said. "Some folks thinks they tastes like grapes. Why don't you try one? Here, Ralph! Fetched some red bananas, too. Like 'em?"

When Uncle Levi emptied the bags onto the table, it looked as though he'd bought out a whole fruit store. There were red and yellow bananas, grapefruit, tangerines, two or three different kinds of oranges; a big bar of pressed figs, a lump of dates nearly as big as my head, and a bag of light green grapes with ground cork around them. I'd never seen so much or so many kinds of fruit in one house in my life. "There!" Uncle Levi told me, as he folded the paper bags. "Ought to be bellyaches enough there to last you a week. Dip right in! Red bananas goes a cussed sight better for breakfast than burnt oatmeal."

Grandfather looked the table over, and grumbled, "Wastin'! Wastin'! Cal'late it cost the worth of a barrel of flour." But, as I peeled my first red banana, he opened his jackknife, wiped the blade on the leg of his pants, and began peeling the grapefruit as if it were a potato. The knife was dull, and white pith hung on the blade. Grandfather scraped it off with his thumbnail, and popped it into his mouth. His eyebrows raised as he pinched it a few times between his gums. Then he blew it out, shut his eyes tight, and howled, "Gorry sakes a-body! Levi, them ain't fitting to eat! Grapefruits! Gorry sakes! Bitterer'n puckerberry! 'Tain't fit victuals for hogs!"

Uncle Levi showed Grandfather how to skin all the white pulp off the grapefruit before he ate it. He was still skinning when Uncle Levi started for the back door, and motioned to me. "Bet you ain't had a square meal of victuals since you come back," was the first thing he said when we were outside. "Had to get Thomas a-going on that grapefruit so's we could knock over a hen. Did ever I show you how to pick out the ones that ain't laying?"

I just shook my head, and he said, "Fetch me a handful of cracked corn, if you've a mind to."

When I came back with the corn, Uncle Levi was standing in the middle of the dooryard with a long beanpole in one hand. "There, stand right behind me," he said when I poured the corn into his hand. Then, he called, "Biddy-biddy-biddy-biddy," and tossed the corn in a half circle in front of him. Inside of two minutes, nearly every hen on the place was picking up corn as fast as she could bob her head. Uncle Levi crouched, watching them like a fox, and holding the pole like a baseball bat. When the whole flock was pecking away with their tails pointed up, he let out a quick, "Yipe," and swung the pole. It broke the necks of the first three hens that poked their heads up. "Go get 'em, Ralph!" he told me. "Chop their heads off afore the blood sets! I'll fetch the teakettle."

I was a little puzzled, and before I went to pick up the hens, I asked, "How do you know those are the ones that aren't laying?"

"Well, if they ain't they ought to be, elseways they'd keep on pecking corn to make eggs out of," he said. Then he stood the pole back against the woodshed and went for the teakettle.

"There!" Uncle Levi said, when he came back and poured the hot water into the scalding pail. "Douse 'em good, so's they'll pick easy. Calc'late I got Thomas took care of for a spell. Fetched him down the funny pictures out of the Boston paper. Spare his feelings not to see these hens till they're ready for the pot."

I'd only picked the back and one wing of my first hen, when Uncle Levi asked, "What happened to the johnnycake?"

"I must have forgotten to put something in it," I said.

"Calc'lated so. Eggs, wa'n't it? And maybe butter?"

"Maybe I didn't put in enough molasses," I told him.

"That ain't no good, Ralph. You know it well's I do. What did you put in when it come out so good?"

I'd always felt sneaky when I was using eggs and cream in the johnnycakes, and I didn't want to tell Uncle Levi about it, so I said, "Annie Littlehale helped me with the one that came out best."

"Mmmhmmm. What did Annie put in?"

"She didn't put in anything; she just told me how to do things as I went along."

"How many eggs did she tell you to put in?"

I picked the other wing, but I couldn't think of any way to get around Uncle Levi's question, so I said, "Three or four."

"Good girl! Got some sense in her head," Uncle Levi said. "How much butter?"

"None. We didn't have any."

"What did you use for shortening; salt-pork fat?"

"No, sir," I said. "We didn't use any fat."

"Must have, if 'twas any good. What else did you put in?"

Uncle Levi seemed to know a lot more about johnnycake than I did, and I was sure I couldn't fool him, so I said, "A cup of sour cream."

"That's more like it. Calc'late you could get Annie to come cook us some victuals if I was to get Thomas out of the way?"

"Grandfather won't let her," I said.

"Catch her using a couple of eggs?"

"He found some shells in the swill pail."

"Careless, wa'n't you? What did he have to say?"

"He said she was wasting, and never to let him catch her messing around with the cooking any more."

"Don't calc'late on him a-catching her. Calc'late to keep him off somewheres till sundown. You fetch her and I'll look after Thomas. Don't aim to go on a ration of salt pork and last year's potatoes."

While I finished picking the last hen, Uncle Levi brought a piece of board and began cleaning the first two we'd picked. Both of them were full of unlaid eggs. "Foolish virgins," he mumbled, as he cut the little eggs out carefully and put them aside, "Should a-kept their minds on their victuals and they'd a-kept their necks out of trouble. Here, let's see if there's eggs in that one."

There were. When Uncle Levi had them all taken out and put with the others, he passed me the piece of board, and said, "Go throw 'em in the hogs' trough, Ralph. I'll put the rest of these insides in a pail so's Thomas can look 'em over when I ain't around. Got to keep him thinking my system of picking out hens is good. 'Tain't what he loses hurts Thomas; it's what he knows about. Eggs and cream in the victuals is good for him; he needs 'em. You, too. Did ever you notice how quick a flock of hens will gobble up eggshells if you crumble 'em and heave 'em out a window?"

I nodded.

"Calc'late Annie might come up if you was to ask her? Might be she'd like red bananas."

I nodded again, and Uncle Levi winked at me.

Things worked out just right for me to ask Annie to come up and help me cook. Right after we'd finished dressing the hens, Uncle Levi began asking Grandfather about this or that neighbor. "By hub," he said, after a while, "ain't seen some of them folks since the spring of the late freeze. Don't calc'late old Aunt Lucy Stevens ever et a blood orange or a red banana. How 'bout us doing a little visiting today, Thomas? Why don't you take Aunt Lucy two, three of them grapefruits? Ralph could mind the place and maybe whack up some victuals while we're gone. Ever you make dumplings, Ralph?"

"No," I said, "but aren't they about like biscuits?"

"They be! They be!" Grandfather chirped. "Just spoon 'em in atop the soup whenst the hen's done. Levi, did ever you see the suit of clo'se I bought me whenst I went off to encampment? Made a powerful good trade on it."

"Seen it when you was up to Boston," Uncle Levi said. "Don't pinch you no place, does it?"

"Powerful good fitting suit of clo'se; plenty of room for shrinking, case I get catched in the rain." Grandfather stood for at least two minutes just looking at a knot in the kitchen floor. Then, without looking up, he asked, "Levi, what in thunder you cal'late they done with all the dirt?"

"What dirt?"

"They dug out of them subways off to Boston."

"Dumped it out on the marshes, I calc'late."

"Gorry!" Grandfather said. "Must have took a power of men and hosses . . . and a power of victuals and provender to a-fed 'em. Fetch Old Nell, Ralphie! Hitch her to the top buggy whilst I get my new suit on."

Uncle Levi came out to the carriage a minute before Grandfather did. He made a fuss over helping me spread the duster on the dashboard and mumbled, "Tell Annie to fetch whatever stuff she needs from home. I'll stop by and settle with Miz Littlehale tomorrow. Don't be sparing with the cream and eggs, and don't leave no shells about. You can calc'late on us being home sharp on sundown. See how much of that fruit you can get outside of afore we get back." Then he talked good and loud about Aunt Lucy Stevens as he climbed up to the carriage seat.

It was an awfully nice Sunday for me, and I think Annie sort of liked it, too. She'd never eaten red bananas or blood oranges or grapefruit before. She liked them just as well as I did, but she would only eat one of each, and said people were gluttons if they didn't make the things they liked best last the longest.

Annie didn't let me do much of the real cooking. After she'd looked all through the pantry to see what we had, she sent me down to her house for a whole basket of things; like powdered sugar, cream of tartar, a bar of chocolate, and good white lard. Then she kept me busy bringing in wood, picking and peeling apples, getting vegetables from Millie's garden, and bringing up cream and eggs from the cellar.

I think Annie liked being the woman of the house, and I liked being the man. She kept bustling around from one thing to another; lifting the covers off pots and trying the hens with a fork long before they were done, opening the oven door a crack to peek in at the pies, and poking the fire when it didn't really need it. Right from the first, it was easy to see that Annie wanted to show Uncle Levi what a good cook she was. Instead of putting all three hens on to boil in one pot, she had me cut them up, and fixed each one a different way: one stewed with carrots, onions, and lots of soup, one fricasseed, and one taken off the bones and set to jell in a breadpan.

She made two cakes—one chocolate, and one vanilla with maple-sugar frosting—molasses cookies, two pies, and a creamy yellow pudding with sliced bananas in it. I don't know how many eggs Annie used, but it was a lot of them. As soon as she'd lay the shells down, I'd crumble them and take them out to the hens.

Annie told me she would never marry a man who didn't like good food, or one who wouldn't bring her home the things she'd need to cook with. And I told her that, when I had a home of my own, I was going to keep the pantry full of red bananas and blood oranges and powdered sugar and chocolate. I told her quite a little about Colorado, too; about my trick-riding in the roundups, and some of the horse races I'd won. I told her about a couple of them I'd lost, too, so she wouldn't think I was bragging.

Everything came out right at sunset. The johnnycake was almost ready to come out of the oven, I was beating butter and hot milk into the mashed potatoes, and Annie was dropping dumplings into the kettle when Grandfather and Uncle Levi turned the corner at the ridge road. She would only take one tangerine for her mother, a blood orange for her father, and a red banana for her brother. Then she ran down across the field where Grandfather and Uncle Levi wouldn't see her from the road. I think it was so that, if I wanted to, I could make it look as if I'd done the cooking.

Annie had set the table in the dining room just before we did the last-minute things. And Uncle Levi unhitched Old Nell while I was getting everything dished up. When we were pulling our chairs up to the table, Grandfather sang out, "There, Levi! There you be! Didn't I tell you Ralphie could cook better'n ary woman? Didn't I tell you we don't need no tarnal womenfolks 'round here till Millie comes home?"

"Fiddlesticks! Every house needs a woman," Uncle Levi said.

Grandfather jerked his head around toward Uncle Levi, and snapped, "Then why in tarnation didn't you wed one?"

I couldn't let them wrangle, and didn't want to try to take credit for the cooking, so said quickly, "I didn't make . . ."

Just as quickly, Uncle Levi's toe caught my shin under the

table, and he said, "By hub, Ralph, you're a better cook than I'd ever have guessed you was. Don't know when I've set down to a better looking mess of victuals."

The supper was good, and we all ate as if it had been Thanksgiving. All through the meal, Grandfather and Uncle Levi talked about the people they'd been to see, and what this one said, or that one said. Grandfather dropped off to sleep at the table while Uncle Levi was eating his third piece of custard pie. While I was clearing the table, he woke up just enough to go to bed.

Uncle Levi came out to the tie-up while I was milking. After he'd told me the supper was the best one he'd had since he was a boy, he said, "Thomas knows you didn't cook it just as well as we do. And he's got a pretty good notion how many eggs went into it."

"Then I wonder why he didn't scold me about it," I said.

"Couldn't! I had him over a barrel. Been a-telling him he's got to get another housekeeper 'round here. The both of you'll be sick abed if you go on eating the kind of victuals you've been getting. Only way out for Thomas was to make me think you done the cooking. By hub, that Annie's a right pert little cook. What color hair ribbons does she wear?"

"Well, she had on a blue one today," I said.

"Black-headed, ain't she?"

"Coal black," I said.

"Red, bright red!" Uncle Levi said, as he turned a pail over and sat down on it. "Red's awful pretty on black hair. I'll fetch you a piece to give her. Kissed her yet?"

I shook my head.

"Wanted to?"

I started to shake my head again, but stopped. "I haven't thought very much about it," I said.

"You will," Uncle Levi told me. "Kisses and red hair ribbons kind of goes together. How old be you now, Ralph?"

I didn't feel comfortable with him talking about kissing Annie, so I said, "Fifteen in December. Do you think we'll be able to fix that manure spreader all right?"

"Fix anything if you got a mind to—and the time. Looks of it, I calc'late 'twould be a standoff 'twixt building a new one and fixing this one. How in tunket did ever you talk Thomas into getting it?"

"I didn't," I said. "He bought it all by himself at an auction." Then I told him about the talk Grandfather and I had up on the granite outcropping the Sunday before; how I'd thought for a while that he was going to plant strawberries and tomatoes on the high field, and what he'd said about the partnership on the butter. At the end, I said, "I think he'd be happy if Millie was home, but I don't think he'd be happy with any other house-keeper. I wonder where Millie could have gone. She said she was going to work in a mill at Lewiston, but Grandfather has been to every mill office. She isn't working at any mill in either Lewiston or Auburn, and she hasn't been there."

Uncle Levi looked up quickly. "You dead certain she ain't?"

"Almost," I said. "Grandfather has had them look on all the payrolls for two months back in all the mills."

For two or three minutes, Uncle Levi sat looking at Clara Belle's hocks, and rubbing his mustache out across his cheeks. "Had any hired hands this summer that she cottoned to?"

I shook my head. "There was only one here that stayed more than an hour, and Millie ran him off with a skillet."

"Hmmm. Hmmm. Curious! You dead certain she went to Lewiston?"

"No, sir, but that's where she said she was going."

"Recollect her a-speaking of any place else?"

I had to think for a minute, then said, "No, sir."

Uncle Levi got up from the pail, pushed it against the wall with his toe, and began walking slowly up and down the tie-up. After the third or fourth trip, he stopped behind Clara Belle, and asked, "Fetch away all her knickknacks and clothes with her?"

"Grandfather's awfully touchy about her room," I told him. "I haven't looked in there, but I don't think she did. Her pink apron is still hanging on the nail by the pantry door."

"Hmmm. Hmmm. Curious," he mumbled, and began walking again. His head was down, his hands were shoved deep in his pockets, and he seemed to be watching his feet as they moved slowly forward. He stopped suddenly and said, "I'll fetch these two pails of milk to the house for you, Ralph. Calc'late I'll turn in."

Uncle Levi always snored loud enough to be heard way out to the barn. During the hour I was in the kitchen taking care of the milk that night, I didn't hear a sound from his room. There still wasn't a sound when I'd finished and was tiptoeing through his room to mine. I was sure he was awake, and whispered, "Good night, Uncle Levi." Instead of answering me, he began to snore steadily.

30

Grandfather's War Is Almost Over

I'D FINISHED my chores Monday morning, and was starting
for the house with the first two pails of milk when I saw Uncle
Levi out by the old manure spreader. He had a piece of clean
board in his hand and, as he looked the spreader over, was writing on the board. At breakfast, he was quiet. He only ate a few
mouthfuls of oatmeal and a couple of oranges, and he answered
all Grandfather's questions with a "Yes," or "No." As he peeled
the second orange, he said, "Might hitch Old Nell to the top
buggy if you've a mind to, Ralph. No sense of us trying to mend
that cussed old spreader till we've got the hardware we'll need
for it."

"I'll go fetch the stuff, Levi, whilst you and Ralphie is a-getting her apart," Grandfather told him.

"Fetch it myself," Uncle Levi grumbled. "Like as not you'd
come home with a mess of wore-out, secondhanded junk."

"No such of a thing! No such of a thing!" Grandfather
snapped. Then he dropped the tone of his voice, and asked,
"Where be you cal'lating on getting it, Levi; the Falls?"

"Lewiston," was all Uncle Levi said.

Grandfather chased the last piece of pork around the platter with his knife, and said, "Cal'late I'll go 'long with you, Levi, for comp'ny."

"Don't want no comp'ny," Uncle Levi said, without looking up from the orange. "Going alone." Then he pushed his chair back and left the table.

Grandfather was grumpy after Uncle Levi went out. He grumbled into his whiskers, slatted his chair around as he got up from the table, then went into his room and slammed the door. He was still there when Uncle Levi climbed into the top buggy. He leaned out toward me, and said quietly, "Don't calc'-late Thomas'll be too good comp'ny for you today, but I couldn't fetch him along. Got a bee in my bonnet, and it might sting 'stead of make honey. What time is it?"

I sighted the sun past the corner of the barn, and said, "Just about a quarter of seven, I'd say. Not past five minutes of."

Uncle Levi spread the duster over his knees, and said, "If you've a mind to, you might go to taking the old bolts out of that spreader. No need trying to save 'em. Chop 'em off with a cold chisel if they're rusted tight and it comes handiest." Then he spanked Old Nell's rump with the reins, said, "Keep your nose clean," and drove out of the yard.

Grandfather wasn't good company. He spent the day between jawing at me and fussing with the bees. At first, he scolded me for being too slow. Then he said it was wasting to break good bolts instead of saving them to use again. He could never remember which way to turn a nut to take it off, and he always blamed me when he tried to turn one the wrong way. Long before Uncle Levi came home, late in the afternoon, Grandfather had rowed at me till I wanted to throw a wrench at him.

He was grouchy when Uncle Levi drove into the dooryard but he got over it quickly. I'd just reached for Nell's rein when Uncle Levi called out, "There, Thomas! There's a bee lining box you won't leave about in the woods! Don't know if it's big enough to hold all your stuff or not." As he spoke, he held a brown leather box out toward Grandfather. It was the shape of a good-sized book, and had a long loop of strap on it. "Goes over your shoulder," Uncle Levi told him. "Makes it hard to go off and leave some place."

"Gorry! Gorry sakes, Levi!" Grandfather chirped, as he turned the box over and over in his hands. "Gorry! Shouldn't a-done it, Levi! Must a-cost a power of money. By fire, I cal'late I'll go see how my stuff fits into it."

After Grandfather had gone, I cramped the wheel of the buggy around, and Uncle Levi got out. "Fetched a little something for you, too," he said, as he put his hand into his pocket. When he brought it out, there was an Ingersoll watch in it, and a bright chain hung down from his fingers. "There you be," he said. " 'Tain't good for your eyes to keep a-looking at the sun."

I'd only had one watch in my life. It was a gold one. I'd won it in a trick-riding contest in Colorado, and never carried it except when I was dressed up on Sundays. My throat got tight when I took the new watch in my hand and tried to say thank you. "No! No!" Uncle Levi said, and reached under the seat of the buggy. "Ingersolls ain't thank-you watches, but they keep pretty good time; nigh enough to let you know to come in for your victuals. Speaking of victuals, there's a few parcels here under the seat." Then he fished out a package that looked like a fancily wrapped can of salmon. "There's a little something you might like to give Annie," he said. "Bright red."

As soon as Uncle Levi had changed his clothes, he helped me on the spreader, and Grandfather went off hunting for a bee to line. It was at just five minutes past six when Uncle Levi noticed me looking at my new watch. He laid his wrench down, and said, "There, by hub! Let's us knock off for supper. Why don't you fetch your present down to Annie afore we have our victuals?"

"Well," I said, "maybe I'd better go and bring the cows in first. We've got a new one that's breechy, and I might have trouble finding her if I wait till after dark."

"Go 'long, fetch your present to Annie; I'll get the cows," Uncle Levi said, as he was putting his glasses into the case.

I didn't want to take the ribbon down to Littlehale's house, and maybe have to give it to Annie with her mother and father and brother there. "If that red cow has jumped the fence," I told Uncle Levi, "you might have to chase her all over the woods. I'll go get them. It will only take me a few minutes."

As I spoke, I'd reached over to the bench for Annie's package. Uncle Levi caught me when I was slipping it into the front of my shirt. Wrinkles came around the corners of his eyes, one lid dropped just a trifle, and he said, "Maybe you best. Calc'late I'm getting a mite old for chasing heifers about the woods. I'll go kindle a fire for supper."

I walked sort of slowly till I got out behind the barn, then I ran up the lane as fast as I could go. It was ten minutes after six, and I was afraid Annie might already have her cows started for home. I didn't go by our pasture gate, but cut across behind the orchard hill to the maple grove. Just as I got to the edge of it, I heard Annie calling her cows from down in the meadow beyond.

All afternoon I'd been thinking of things I'd say when I gave Annie the ribbon. When I heard her voice, I went running down between the trees to find her. As I came out of the maple grove, I jumped over the stonewall, and almost on top of Annie. She was kneeling down, picking checkerberries at the edge of the meadow, and she sprang up quickly when I landed behind her. I was all out of breath, my heart was pounding like a runaway horse's hoofs, and I forgot everything I'd planned to say. Before I stopped to think, I blurted out, "Have you seen our red cow?"

"No, I haven't," Annie said. "Is she lost?"

And then I didn't have any better sense than to say, "I don't know; I didn't look."

Annie did look. She looked at me as if she thought I'd been in the loco weed. "What's the matter, Ralph?" she asked. "What have you been running for?"

"I just wanted to get here before you went in with the cows,"

I told her. "I brought a present for you." Then I took the package out of the front of my shirt and passed it to her. "It's red," I said. "It will look nice with your black hair."

Annie sat down on the grass to open the package, and I sat down beside her. "Oh, taffeta ribbon!" she squealed, as she unrolled the paper. "Why, it must be six inches wide and how much did you get? There's enough here for seven or eight bows."

"I didn't get it," I said. "Uncle Levi did. It's from all of us."

Annie took the ribbon out of the paper and sat smoothing the end of it between her palms. Then she put her face down and rubbed her cheek against it. "It's lovely," she whispered, "I never had ribbon like this."

"I think it would look awfully pretty on your hair," I said. "I wish you didn't have it braided."

Annie usually wore her hair loose; falling like rippling black silk from a bow at the nape of her neck. That night it was braided into a thick rope, with a white bow just below her shoulders. She looked up at me, smiled, and said, "Why?"

"I just like it better that way," I told her. "It always looks like ripply black silk."

Annie flipped the braid across her shoulder and untied the white ribbon. Her fingers moved quickly as they began taking out the lower strands of the braid. My own fingers felt itchy, and I said, "Could I unbraid it for you while you fix the ribbon?"

"Don't tangle it," was all Annie said, and then she began shaping one end of the ribbon like a bow.

I was careful not to pull or to make any tangles, and as I untwisted each strand, I let it slip, clear to the end, through my fingers. And I wished that Uncle Levi hadn't said anything about kisses and red hair ribbon going together. Each time my hand went up to loosen another strand, it brushed against Annie's neck, and I wanted to put my cheek against it, the way she'd done with the ribbon.

"I really should have a brush and a glass," Annie said when I'd separated the last strands of the braid. "With one long end, it will be a little hard to tie a good bow behind me." Then she threw her head way back, put ʋoth hands under her hair, and tossed it till every trace of a braid strand was gone. She gathered the wavy mass at the nape of her neck; running both thumbs close above her ears, and drawing the sides and top in with her fingers. "Can you hold it right there," she asked, "while I tie the bow?"

I could and I did. There was just enough breeze that the silky ends moved against my forearm. And once, when I was a little too close, a wisp brushed across my cheek and mouth. "Isn't it lovely?" Annie whispered as her fingers shaped the bow.

And as the glistening flood of her hair brushed my arm, I whispered back, "Mmmhmm, lovely."

From the far side of the meadow, a cow lowed for her evening milking. "Goodness!" Annie said, "I'd forgotten all about the cows. I must run; Father'll be waiting to milk." Then she told me to thank Grandfather and Uncle Levi for the ribbon, folded the long red streamer that ran across her shoulder and chest, and sprang to her feet.

I looked back quite a few times as I climbed the hill through the maple grove. Once Annie looked back and waved. The late sunlight glistened on her hair and the bright red bow. Then she was gone behind the clump of white birches by the pasture gate, and I hurried on after our cows.

Supper was over, Grandfather had gone to bed, and I was just finishing the milking when Uncle Levi came into the tie-up. He turned the old pail over, and sat behind Clara Belle, just as he had the night before. I expected him to ask me how Annie liked the ribbon, but he didn't. When I looked over at him, he just said, "Found Millie."

I caught a quick breath, and said, "Why didn't you bring her home? Wouldn't she come?"

"Wants to come just as bad as Thomas wants her to," he said. "Too cussed stubborn to come by herself."

"Then why didn't you bring her?" I asked.

"Calc'late Thomas might like to do his own fetching," he said. "Don't aim to let him know I found her."

"Then how will he know where to look for her?"

"Don't have to tell a hound where to look for a rabbit, do you? Calc'late if I put Thomas on the trail, he'll do his own finding."

"Well, how did you ever find the trail yourself?" I asked.

"Wa'n't nothing to it. All I done was to make out like I was Millie. If I was to go off to some place a-looking for a job of work, I wouldn't go to no mill. I'd go casting about for a place there was bricks to lay. Was I Millie, I'd go looking for a place where there was victuals to cook and butter to make. Calc'lated if I was her, I'd go to a job agency. And, by hub, that's just what she done. Come across her trail in the second agency I went into. She's a-working on a farm, t'other side of Auburn. Told her Thomas would be along to fetch her home 'bout noontime tomorrow. She ain't going to let on she seen me. Here, let me fetch one of them pails of milk to the house for you. By hub, I'm going off to bed early. Got to cast about for a way of putting Thomas on the trail without him smelling a mouse."

Then, on the way to the house, he put his free arm around my shoulder, and asked, "Did you kiss Annie when you give her the ribbon?"

"No, sir," I said. Then, after a few steps, I added, "But I wanted to."

Uncle Levi's fingers tightened just a trifle on my shoulder, and when we were near the kitchen door, he sort of mumbled, "Don't hurry, boy. Wanted kisses is sometimes sweeter than had ones."

At breakfast Uncle Levi was all full of talk. He never mentioned Millie at all, but told us about a book he had read where a detective found a criminal by going to every employment office in Boston. He was still telling the story when Grandfather snapped, "Eat your victuals! Eat your victuals, Ralphie! Time flies, and there ain't no time now for dawdling. Rattle the harness onto Old Nell whilst I get my clo'se changed. Time and tarnation! Slipped my mind to have Levi take the eggs off to market yesterday." While Grandfather bounced out of his chair and started for his room, Uncle Levi kept right on with the story, but his eyelid on my side dipped just a trifle.

I had a nice day with Uncle Levi. As we worked on the old spreader, he told me stories about the time he was homesteading, and he listened when I told him about the ranches where I had worked in Colorado. It was the middle of the afternoon when we heard the pound of a horse's feet on the road coming down from the ridge. We both knew who it would be, and peeked out of the little windows at the side of the forge. Grandfather was sitting as straight as a coachman, and holding the reins as if he were driving Dan Patch. Millie was beside him. She had on a sailor hat and a new dress, and was sitting as straight as Grandfather.

When we lost sight of them, past the front of the house, Uncle Levi laid one finger across his lips. Then we listened as Nell's hoofs pounded on the gravel of the driveway. Grandfather kept her trotting till they were right up to the doorstone, then shouted, "Levi! Ralphie! Come a-running! See what I fetched home! By fire, I cal'late I ought to a-been a detective! Run her down over t'other side of Auburn!"

Anyone would have thought Millie was an only daughter who had been away for years. Grandfather wouldn't let her get her hat off till he'd taken her to the cellar to see all the milk and cream we had, to the barn to see the new bull, and to the carriage house to see the spreader. "There! There you be, Millie girl!" he crowed. "Look what I fetched home for Ralphie! I and him has tarnal nigh took all the rocks off'n the high field. Cal'late on growing strawb'ries and tomatoes up there, come spring. Going to give it a thundering heavy top-dressing afore the frost sets in. Can't hand-spread dressing for them kind of crops. Got to have tools that'll do the job right.

"Gorry sakes, Millie, can't you see the womenfolks a-picking berries up there; you a-canning 'em for winter, and me a-fetching 'em off to early market. Didn't I tell you things was a-pop-ping 'round the old place? By thunder, 'twon't be long afore the wildernes field is under the plow again, and an all-fired big new piece built onto the barn. Didn't think to tell you 'bout us a-going into the butter business, did I? Partners! I and you and Ralphie . . . and Levi, if he'll stay to home. By gorry, we'll be a-fetching butter off to market by the firkin. Cal'late it'll be up to thirty cents afore spring."

I wanted to run and throw my arms around him and hug him, but I didn't. I just stood there with a lump in my throat and a hot feeling behind my eyes. I think Uncle Levi felt the same way. As Grandfather led Millie off toward the house, he watched them out of sight, and said almost reverently, "It's a God's wonder! Could be the war's all over for Thomas; could be it's only an armistice. Calc'late we done about all we can, and the rest is in the hands of the Almighty."

It was late on Thursday afternoon when Uncle Levi tight-ened the last new bolt on the manure spreader, stood back, and said, "There you be, Thomas! Wisht there'd been time enough to give it a good coat of paint, but there wa'n't. Still-and-all, 'twouldn't help the spreading none, and I'll be a-coming back down afore long. Ralph, how 'bout hitching the hosses on? Calc'late we got time to try one load afore I have to go?"

With three of us pitching, the load went on in a hurry. When he threw the last forkful up, Uncle Levi said, "You and Thomas climb up on the seat, Ralph, so's you can show him how the le-vers works. It's time I was getting washed up and my clothes changed."

I looked at my new watch. It was quarter of six, the man with the automobile wasn't coming for Uncle Levi till seven, and there was something in his voice that made me know he'd like to show Grandfather himself. "You know a lot more about it than I do," I said, "and besides, it's nearly six o'clock and I'll have to get the cows in."

"Well, we'll have to hurry," Uncle Levi sort of grumbled.

Grandfather climbed to the high seat like a squirrel. He

snatched up the reins, and before Uncle Levi was hardly beside him, started shouting, "Gitap! Gitap! Gitap!"

I watched them as I went up the lane for the cows. The yella colt was dancing and jumping, the way he always did when Grandfather drove. The shadows stretched long across the stubble of the hayfield, and Uncle Levi and Grandfather sat so close together that they made just one shadow.

31

Dynamite

UNTIL we had the talk on the granite outcropping, Grandfather hadn't put in a full day's work in the fields. After Millie came home, we had trouble in keeping him from working himself to death. All through the rest of the stone hauling from the high field and the manure spreading, I had to hunt ways to keep him from trying to do too much. He was so proud of the new spreader that he'd rush the loading, then ride to the fields with me and work the levers. The wilderness field was always on his mind, and when I'd try to slow him down, he'd tell me, "Can't dig stumps after the ground's froze, Ralphie, and there's a tarnal heap of 'em to dig."

The evenings changed as much as the days. Where Grandfather had usually gone off to his room as soon as supper was over, he began sitting in the kitchen till nine or ten o'clock. He brought out a stack, nearly a foot high, of catalogs, seed books, government pamphlets, and magazines about strawberries and tomatoes that he'd read until the corners were dog-eared. As soon as I'd come in with the last pail of milk, Grandfather would call, "Let be! Let be, Ralphie! What in time and tarnation took you so long? Millie'll look after the milk! By gorry, there's an awful good piece in the *Country Gentleman* 'bout mulching strawb'ries with marsh hay. Come read it to me; these spectacles of mine is getting wore out so bad I can't see next to nothing with 'em." Then, as I read, he'd keep breaking in to have me go back and read something over, or snap, "Set that down! Set it down on paper, Ralphie, afore we forget it! By thunder, I cal'late on us a-knowing how to do the job afore we tackle it. Man shouldn't ought to tackle a job less'n he knows what he's about and the best way of doing it."

As soon as we'd finished hauling dressing, we began the clearing of the wilderness field. It was a little more than eight acres. None of it was heavily wooded. On the northern part, nearest the orchard, there were thirty or forty pines, none of them more than fifteen or sixteen inches at the butt. On the east side, south of the granite outcropping, as many hemlocks were scattered and, here and there, a spruce, a hackmatack, or a fir. The rest of the field was covered with rocks, junipers, hazel bushes, and birch, beech, or maple saplings. Before we started the clearing, Grandfather blazed a cut on three pines that marked off the north quarter of the field. "There, Ralphie!" he told me. "That marks our stint for the year ahead. I cal'late we'll do tarnal well if we lay the north end under the plow come planting time. Let's heave an axe into this one; we'll lay her yonder, 'twixt that white birch and the hazel bush." By noon, we had six pines felled and trimmed out.

In the afternoon, we brought shovels, picks, and crowbars; and Grandfather started me on taking out the first stump. It wasn't the kind of a job I liked. The roots snaked in and out between hidden rocks. Around and 'round the stump, each root had to be dug free and chopped away, at least a foot below the ground. And every time I cut one out, there was another one under it. Long before the afternoon was over, my axe was so nicked and dull that it would bounce off the tough roots as though it were made of rubber.

All afternoon, I kept hearing Grandfather's axe ring, and half a dozen times there was a crash as another pine went down. By sunset, my first stump would wiggle, but there were still some uncut roots under it, and I'd dug a hole big enough to bury a bull in. I was sure Grandfather would scold me for dawdling, and for dulling the axe, but he didn't. When he came over, he said, "Gorry sakes alive, Ralphie! Been digging like a wood-chuck, ain't you? Leave be! We'll hitch the hosses on and twist it roundabouts till it gives up. By thunder, the way we're a-start-ing off, I cal'late we'll be ready to go to hewing stone inside a fortnight."

It rained all our third day in the wilderness field, and Grand-father caught a cold. Then the malaria flared up, and he had to stay in bed with chills and fever. He was irritable, and kept fret-ting about the freeze-up coming before we'd get the stumps all dug.

Road work started the Monday after Grandfather was taken sick. Most farmers worked out part of their taxes on the roads, and Grandfather sent me to work out part of his. A new piece of road was being built through the field where Sam Starboard had planted the white oaks that Grandfather told me about. The old stumps had to be taken out, and they were doing it with dynamite.

Bill Hubbard was the blast man, and I made friends with him the first day I worked on the road. Most of the time, I was haul-ing rocks and gravel, but whenever I had a spare minute, I spent it with Bill. He wasn't more than thirty, and was big and slow-talking, but he was always joking, and he knew a lot about dy-namite. The thing that surprised me most was that he wasn't afraid of it. He'd let me watch him while he made his primer cartridges, put in the firing caps, and crimped on the fuses. I watched him often when he looked over a stump, dug a hole under the heaviest root, set the charge, tamped it, and packed the hole, but he'd never let me get close enough to watch him fire it. He'd blow a whistle when he was going to shoot, and we all had to get out of the way.

They had a steam engine for moving heavy rocks and stumps. One day when Bill and I were eating our dinner together, the engine got stuck in a sandy spot. The big drive wheels dug themselves nearly three feet deep, and the boiler was right down to the ground. I'd seen a steam engine stuck that way in Colorado, and had seen it pulled out with a team of horses. The men had pushed fence posts down in front of the drive wheels, then pulled the horses just hard enough to hold the wheel lugs against the posts, and the engine had come out of the hole on its own power.

Ever since I'd been on the road job, I'd been wishing we had some dynamite for blowing out stumps in the wilderness field, so I said to Bill, "If four sticks of dynamite would lift that engine out without hurting it, would you use them?"

"Or six, if need be," he answered.

"Then would you give five sticks to get it done?" I asked.

Bill nodded, and said, "Or six."

The engine came out of the hole just the way the one in Colorado did, but I had a hard time getting Bill Hubbard to give me the dynamite. I didn't tell him that Grandfather had used lots of it before, or that he was the one who was going to blow a stump, but when he thought that was what I meant, I didn't correct him.

Bill cut the fuse for me, and crimped on the firing cap before I took the dynamite home Saturday night. I didn't want to leave it around the buildings, so, when I went for the cows, I put it in a box and hid it in the pasture. Sunday morning, I took a crowbar and a fork handle with me when I drove the cows to pasture. I planned that I'd get everything ready, and set the charge before I went to Sunday school. Some day when Grandfather was well and had gone to Lewiston, I'd fire it. Then, when he saw what the dynamite would do, I might be able to get him to buy some.

I picked out the meanest stump I could find. It stood right in the middle of a nest of rocks the size of washtubs. Some of the roots were as thick as my legs, and they writhed around and between the rocks like the arms of an octopus. I looked the stump over carefully, and tried to guess just where Bill would have set the charge. When I'd picked what looked to be the right spot, I punched the crowbar hard under the root, but it hit solid rock. I had to try a dozen different places before I found one where I could work the bar between the rocks and under the stump. Then, as I loosened the dirt, I had to lie on my stomach and dig

it out with my fingers. There was just room for my hand between the roots and the top of a boulder.

I'd been sure I wasn't going to be any more afraid of the dynamite than Bill was. But by the time I'd made the primer, tamped the charge in under the stump, and packed the hole, I was shaking, and soaking wet with sweat. Then, as I started to the house, I began to worry. I had two more days' work on the road, and Grandfather was up and around the house. He might come to the field while I was away, do something to set off the dynamite, and be killed. I ran back, struck a match, and held it against the end of the fuse. At the first splutter, I dropped the fuse and ran for the nearest good-sized tree.

Nothing happened. It seemed as if I'd been behind that tree for ten minutes, but there wasn't a sound. I was sure I'd set the charge wrong, or had put the fuse out when I dropped it. I let my breath out and was sort of glad it had been a failure. Then, just as I stepped from behind the tree, the whole wilderness field seemed to be flying in the air. Before the crash of sound came, I went heels over head. Sticks and stones were falling all around me, and I was sure I was killed. When I picked myself up, I wasn't hurt at all. I was only dizzy, had a nosebleed, and my ears felt as if someone were beating on tin pans inside them. Where the stump had been, there was nothing but a big hole, with broken rock edging it, so that it looked like pictures I'd seen of a volcano crater.

I sat down on a big rock to let my head clear, and time must have passed faster than I realized. I was still shaking my head when I heard Grandfather shout. It sounded miles away, but when I looked around, he and Millie were running toward me from the pasture bars. "What in time and tarnation you been up to now?" Grandfather shouted, as he came panting up. "Be you hurt? Be you hurt, Ralphie?"

"No, sir," I said. "I'm not hurt at all. I just fell down and got a nosebleed."

"Tarnal hard fall, by the sound of it! What you been up to?"

"I blew a stump," I said. "I guess I blew it a little too hard."

"Gorry!" Grandfather said, when he looked around. "Gorry sakes alive!" Then he walked over to the hole.

Millie was just starting to give me the dickens for scaring Grandfather half to death, when he shouted, "How in thunderation did ever you do it, Ralphie? Looks like somebody's smashed the ground with a tarnal great hammer!"

Instead of scolding me, as I expected he would, Grandfather was all excited about the dynamiting. "Gorry sakes! Gorry sakes alive, Ralphie! You cal'late you could do some more of 'em?" he asked. "By fire, four men couldn't a-done that much in a day. How long you been a-working on it?"

"It didn't take more than an hour," I told him, "and I guess I could do it again, but I don't know much about it, and it might be dangerous for both of us. Bill Hubbard knows all about dynamite. He's only got two more days' work on the road, and I think we could get him to come and do it for us."

"No sense hiring somebody to do for you what you can do for yourself," Grandfather said.

"Well, I don't know what dynamite costs," I said, "but the men on the road say Bill can get more out of it than anybody else. I'm afraid I'd waste too much."

I thought the wasting part would be the most interesting to Grandfather, but he turned on me sharply, and snapped, "Don't know what it costs! Where did you get what you used; steal it?"

"No, sir, I didn't steal it. I earned it," I said. "Any of the men on the road job will tell you."

"Hmmm, hmmm," Grandfather said, as he stood looking at the hole. "If you're cal'lating on going to Sabbath school with Annie Littlehale, ain't it 'bout time you was getting cleaned up and ready?"

Bill Hubbard wouldn't come to do the dynamiting for us for less than two dollars a day, and, at first, Grandfather said he wouldn't pay any man over a dollar. But on the last day of road work, he said it would be all right if I asked Bill to stop by and talk to him. Bill came home with me that night, and Grandfather told him to get all the things he'd need for the job, and to bring them with him the next morning.

I never saw a little boy have more fun on the Fourth of July than Grandfather had on the first day of dynamiting the wilderness field. Bill showed us where to dig the blasting holes under the stumps, and he was shooting a charge nearly every half hour. Every time he'd blow his whistle, Grandfather would dive behind a tree or boulder. Then, when the explosion came, he'd wave his arms and shout, "There! There, by thunder! 'Twon't be long afore we have her flatter'n a thrashing floor. Gorry sakes alive! 'Minds me of the battle of Bull Run! Did ever I tell you, Ralphie . . ." Sometimes he'd tell about some battle for a few minutes, but it would never last long. He was too anxious to get the holes dug, and be ready for another blast.

Along toward the end of the afternoon, Bill blew the last stump from the trees Grandfather had cut. I liked to work with Bill, and was afraid Grandfather would say we didn't need him any more, so I asked, "How many potatoes did you raise on this whole field after you cleared it the first time?"

"Thousand bushel," Grandfather said quickly. "How come you to ask that?"

"I was just thinking," I said. "The way Bill is knocking the stumps out, we might be able to clear more than a quarter of the field this year."

"Clear it all!" Grandfather said sharply. "What's to hinder? Take a tarnal hard freeze to stop that damanite a-blasting out a stump. Fast as ever I and you gets 'em ready, I cal'late on having the Hubbard boy come and histe 'em out for us. Gorry sakes! Don't cal'late there'll be a tarnal stump left, come Thanksgiving time."

"How about the boulders?" I asked. "Do you think the dynamite would break the big ones?"

"Don't know why not! Thundering powerful stuff! Cal'late to find out, come morning."

We didn't find out about the big boulders in the morning. Bill said they'd take more dynamite than he had with him. But we did find out about Bill. He could swing an axe fully as well as Grandfather, and could make a treetop fall within a foot or two of where he wanted it. He was strong as an ox, and he never tired. It didn't make him mad when Grandfather got irritable, and he knew how to get him over it. Once they started chopping side by side, on two trees that looked as if they might have been twins. Bill wasn't hurrying, but every time his axe bit, a big chip would fly, and the scarf would widen. Grandfather wasn't going to be beaten. He was making three swings to Bill's two, and his breath rasped through his throat at every swing.

I'd been limbing a felled tree, but I stopped to watch them. Bill was halfway through the trunk of his tree before Grandfather was more than a third of the way through his. And then Bill did a nice thing. When his axe came down, it bit into the tree five or six inches above his first scarf. He didn't change the timing of his swing, and the chips were just as big, but he still had several inches of solid wood left when Grandfather's tree groaned, swayed, and fell. Bill stood his axe down, leaned on the helve of it, and panted, "By gosh, Mr. Gould, for an old duffer, you can surely make the chips fly. Danged if you ain't got me winded!" From there on, I didn't have to worry about our losing Bill, or Grandfather's letting him go.

We took the horses and the stone drag to the wilderness field in the afternoon, and hauled the first big rocks for the stonewall that would separate it from the pasture. Grandfather took his axe, cut stakes, and marked the line. It ran from the corner of the high field south, past the edge of the granite outcropping, and on to meet the old wall at the corner of the hidden field. No rock that we hauled weighed less than three or four hundred pounds, but they handled easily. Bill had sprung them above the ground with dynamite, Grandfather fastened the heavy chains with what he called a rolling hitch, and as I eased the horses into their collars, the big rocks would turn, slide, and roll up onto the drag. If one hung or caught, a heave of Bill's crowbar would move it along. By the end of the first week, the row of base rocks for the new wall stretched the whole length of the field.

Bill didn't work with us every day, but if there was any heavy hauling to do, or blasting, Grandfather would tell the mailman, and Bill would be there the next morning. By Thanksgiving time, all the blasting had been finished, the stonewall nearly laid up, all the felled timber was yarded, and the boulders for the barn foundation had been hauled to the barnyard.

Bill Hubbard came over from Lisbon Village and ate Thanksgiving dinner with us. It was a fine one, and when we were all in our places at the table, Grandfather bowed his head and mumbled a blessing. The words were lost in his beard, but I think we all felt as though we had heard them. I took some beechnuts down to Annie after dinner, and when I came back, Bill was helping Millie with the dishes.

The air was sharp all the next day, and the stones rang against each other as Grandfather and I lifted them onto the wall. At sunset there seemed to be a hard, cold pressure that bore down from the clear sky. The horses stood close together and shivered as we unloaded the drag. "There! There she be, Ralphie!" Grandfather said, when the last stone had settled into its place. "Cal'late we done all we can for the fall. Come the heavy snow, we'll burn out the junipers and cut the brush. And come the spring thaw, I cal'late we'll be ready to set the plow to it. By thunder, wa'n't it a lucky day you sot off that first charge of damanite?"

Grandfather stood for a minute or two, looking off across the torn and pockmarked surface of the wilderness field. "Gorry sakes alive, Ralphie, who'd a-believed it three months agone?" he asked. "Took I and Levi tarnal nigh three years to do this much whenst we cleared it afore. Took Father and Niah and Stephen and Jacob—them was my half-brothers, Ralphie—took 'em tarnal nigh all the days of their lives to clear ten, eleven times this much. Gorry sakes! Gorry sakes! Wisht Father could a-been here to have saw the stumps a-flying and the boulders splitting asunder." Grandfather's hands dropped to his sides, and he stood, staring at a blasted stump that lay with its roots twisting into the air. "Prob'ly he was. Prob'ly he was, Ralphie," he said quietly. Then he snapped, "Fetch the cows! Fetch the cows, Ralphie, whilst I take the hosses in. Cal'late this is the last day of pasture for 'em till spring; there's tarnal heavy snow in the offing."

32

The Story Pole

DURING the fall, Grandfather had traded for several more cows. By the time we finished working in the wilderness field, there was a good milker in every stanchion in the tie-up, and Hannibal, the bull, had been moved into the spare box stall. The milking took me a couple of hours morning and night, and Millie's part of the butter business took nearly as much time as mine. From one end of the cellar to the other, there were pans and bowls of milk set to rise, and it seemed as if she spent half her time washing and scalding pans. Two or three times each week, she'd have to churn, and there was seldom less than a hundred pounds of butter for Grandfather to take to market on Saturday. He never liked to sell it to the creamery, but went from store to store to see where he could make the best deal. Usually, he had to take part of the pay in trade, and the pantry shelves began to fill with groceries. There was an extra barrel of flour in the summer kitchen, and two or three hundred-pound bags of sugar were stored in the bee shop. Before he came home, he'd always send Mother a money order for my share of the butter money, and put Millie's in her savings account.

We'd started fatting three pigs right after Millie came home, and had butchered early in November. The Saturday after Thanksgiving, I helped Grandfather when he carried the hams, shoulders, and sides of bacon from the smokehouse and hung them in the summer kitchen. "There you be! There you be, Millie girl!" he shouted as he hung up the last ham. "Don't cal'late there's ary house this side the Androscoggin River better provisioned with victuals for the winter! By gorry, I wisht Levi was here to cast a look at it! Never seen a man that sot so much store by his victuals as what Levi does."

Sunday, it snowed all day, and Monday morning the fields, stretching away toward the maple grove on the hill, lay glistening pink in the first glow of sunrise. Grandfather came to the tie-up, and stood looking out through the back window as I milked. "Stir your stivvers! Stir your stivvers, Ralphie," he called to me after a few minutes. "Don't cal'late ever we'll find a better day for laying out the barn frame. Time flies, and there's snow enough in the woods for logging."

Grandfather was waiting when I took the milk to the house. As I set the pails down, he pulled on his mittens, and said, "Fetch the twine spool out of the carriage house, Ralphie. Your old grampa's going to learn you how to frame a barn that will weather the years and bear up thundering great mows of hay. Ain't but tarnal few men left that knows how to frame a barn so's it can be built laying flat and histed up in a single day. Cal'-late we'll build the new piece four poles long. Millie, keep Old Bess in the house, so's she don't track up the snow on us."

When I'd brought the spool of builder's twine, we took a ladder from the barn, and made a wide circuit to the back of the barnyard. From there, Grandfather sighted along one side of the barn, told me to follow right in his footprints, and walked in a straight line to the corner by the tie-up door. "There, Ralphie!" he said, as he looked back along our tracks. "I cal'late that's where the sill will lay. Histe the ladder up, and don't step off the sill line. We got to find the length of the story pole."

I had no idea what Grandfather was talking about but, as I raised the ladder against the corner of the barn, I was careful to keep my feet in his tracks in the snow. He took the spool from me, gave me the end of the twine, and told me to go up and hold it exactly where the sidewall met the rafter. Then he drew the twine snug to the top of the foundation stone, and held the mark tightly with this thumbnail. "Now we got her, Ralphie!" he called up to me. "Fetch the end down, and we'll go cut us a pole. Can't frame a barn without a story pole."

I still had no idea what he was planning to do. We followed our tracks back to the carriage house, with Grandfather holding his thumbnail tight on the twine. After I'd found him a good straight beanpole, about two inches thick, he had me saw one end of it square, then he divided the twine carefully into thirds, measured, and marked the place for me to saw the other end. "There!" he said when I'd cut it. "Let's go see if we done a good job on the pole. Barn's six poles wide, three high at the eaves, and five at the peak. Cal'late to build the new piece four poles long."

Before we went back to the barnyard, Grandfather took the pole and measured the front of the barn. He laid one end of it carefully at the corner, pressed it lightly into the snow, then laid it again at the end of the mark. When he had laid it down the sixth time, its end was within a quarter of an inch of the opposite corner. "There we be, Ralphie! There we be, true as a trivet! Less'n the story pole's right, the barn wouldn't fit together whenst 'twas made."

Grandfather and I spent all day laying out, and tramping into the snow, the framing plan for the addition to the barn. Lines were snapped with a tight twine, and no measurement was made except with the story pole. When twilight came, the full-sized pattern of every sill, joist, upright, beam, and stringer was tramped into the snow of the barnyard.

When we had finished, the barnyard looked as if the barn addition had once been built, and that some giant had tipped each wall back, pressed it into the snow, and taken it away again. As he'd planned the size of each upright, sill, girder, or cross-brace, Grandfather had cut a V-shaped circle around the story pole to match the width laid out in the snow. The space between joists, studs, and rafters was notched there too. And long before twilight, I knew why he called the pole a "story pole." The sun was nearly down to the tops of the pines when Grandfather counted the number of timbers of each kind we would need, and I carved the figures beside the rings on the pole.

"There! There she be, Ralphie!" Grandfather sang out as I cut the last figure into the pole. "Now we got her where she can't get away. Fetch it to the carriage house, and paint the ends afore some tarnal fool whacks off an inch or two. By thunder, I cal'late to keep that story pole right under my bed till the last treenail is drove in place. Come morning, I and you'll go over to the Bowdoin wood lot. Bark canker killed off more'n half the trees in the chestnut grove a year agone. Don't cal'late a man could find better timber for barn framing nowhere's this side the Androscoggin River."

Before I painted the ends of the story pole, I measured it carefully with Uncle Levi's rule. It was eight feet, two and three-eighths inches long. None of the rings that marked the sizes measured to even inches, but were set according to Grandfather's estimate of the needed strength. The uprights and sills were to be about sixteen inches square, the girders twelve; the cross-braces and joists, ten; and the rafters, three by twelve.

The Bowdoin wood lot was five miles east of the farm. Before sunup Tuesday morning, Grandfather and I had the chores done and were on the road. There was a sharp bite in the wind. As they pulled the bobsled through the fresh snow, the horses' breath rose in white clouds around their heads. Hoar frost covered their shoulders, and the hair on their rumps lifted till it stood out like cats' fur. The dinner pail, peavies, cant hooks, and heavy chains hung from the back sled. The double-bitted axes were stoned razor-sharp, wrapped in gunny sacks, and lashed along with the crosscut saw to the front bolster. Above them, Grandfather and I sat on bags of hay, with the horse blankets wrapped around us, and pulled well up on our chests. We both wore arctics over heavy felt boots and woolen stockings, thick horsehide mittens, reefers, and caps with ear muffs. After we'd passed the fourcorners at the county road, and were on the two-mile pull up Hall's hill, we took turns walking and flailing our arms. Whichever one of us rode held the story pole.

The wood lot had been lumbered for pine twenty years before, but hemlock, spruce, and hardwood had been left uncut. Maple, beech, and oak, three feet at the butt, stood bare-armed against the dark green of the hemlocks. Here and there, yellow or silver birch glistened in the frosty air. And gaunt and lifeless, at the far end of a clearing, the tall chestnut trees stood bleakly in the wind that rattled their dead branches together. "Gorry sakes," Grandfather said sadly, as we drove into the clearing, "looks like the tarnal blight has took ever last one of 'em. Pity, ain't it, Ralphie? Always cal'lated the chestnut was the prettiest tree in the woods. Wouldn't be s'prised if the cussed blight should wipe 'em off the face of the earth. Tarnal shame! Tarnal shame!"

As we left the bobsled, and walked among the trees, Grandfather pointed his arm and showed me the wart-covered, reddish-brown blotches on the bark. "Mark the canker, Ralphie," he told me. "Take heed how it girdles the trunks and branches roundabouts and chokes 'em. Wood's alive below the girdle; dead as stone above. Ain't heard tell of a blessed thing to stop it, once it's in a grove. Cal'late the bugs and birds fetches it from tree to tree or, like as not, it rides the wind the same as pollen. Leave 'em stand here another year, the worms would riddle 'em; make 'em worthless for aught but firewood. Hew 'em and build 'em into a barn, they'll stand sound and solid more'n a hundred years. Unhitch your hosses whilst I kindle a fire. This cold a morning, the axe heads needs to be het, so's they won't bounce off hardwood."

While I blanketed the horses, tied them out of the wind in the hemlocks, and fed them, Grandfather put the axe heads to warm by a little fire of cones. Then he took the story pole, and we went to pick out the trees we'd use for framing the barn. "First off," he told me, "we'll spy out the gable uprights. Keep your eye peeled for ary big trunk that's straight and tall, and where the branches is high. Don't cal'late to have no knots in the up-rights, and the hewing logs need be five poles long and two foot thick at the little end. We'll find 'em nigh the middle of the grove, where they had to reach high to get their tops out to sunlight."

Grandfather was right about our finding the straight, tall trees at the center of the grove. Standing almost in a circle, were five great trunks that looked like the pillars in pictures I had seen of the old Greek temples. "There they be, Ralphie! There they be!" he said, as he looked each tree over carefully from root to top. "Four to fall whole, and one to bust. Have to be tarnal careful of 'em with the wood dead and brittle. Cal'late we'll do well if we lose but one."

As he spoke, Grandfather turned slowly, and seemed to be studying every tree, rock, and stump around us. "Gorry sakes," he said, when he'd made the full turn, "ain't a living tree nigh enough to fetch 'em down on. Cal'late we'll have to cradle 'em with spring-poles."

I didn't know what he meant, and asked, "What is a spring-pole?"

"Spring-pole! Spring-pole to fell 'em onto! Gorry sakes, Ralphie, you didn't cal'late we'd drop 'em flat on the ground? Stave 'em all to smithereens! Them trunks weighs close onto a ton apiece. With no live branches to break the fall, we got to ease 'em down gentle. Let me see. Let me see. Where's best to lay this nighest one?"

Grandfather picked an alley through the trees, where there was room for the first great trunk to fall. After he'd walked the length of it, and looked at every hummock and stump, we built the cradle. It was made of four white-birch trunks, seven or eight inches thick, for spring-poles. After we had their ends lifted to stumps on opposite sides of the alley, it looked like a steeplechase course. When everything was ready, Grandfather sighted the line of fall, and marked it in the snow with his axe handle. At the base of the tree, he drew a right-angle mark across the line, and said, "Fetch the story pole, Ralphie! We got to be tarnal sure the cross-mark's true and square. Can't run no risk a-felling so tall a tree off line."

Careless as Grandfather was in most things he did, he was as careful in the woods as Uncle Levi was at his workbench.

"Never fell a big tree in a tight place till you line it true, Ralphie," he told me. "Always square your angle with the story pole: three lengths one way, four t'other, and five acrost the angle. Fetch the crosscut saw. I cal'late we're all sot to lay the first one down."

I'd been shivering while Grandfather laid out the felling marks, but pulling the big crosscut saw warmed me all over, and made my heart pound. For Grandfather, it didn't seem hard work. He swayed back and forth with the sweep of the long saw.

When it was his turn to pull the blade ran smoothly, but on mine it caught and jerked. "Hold it steady! Hold it steady!" he snapped at me as the saw bound in its kerf. "How in thunderation do you cal'late to fall a tree straight with a crooked scarf?" The saw was still binding and catching a little when we'd cut nine or ten inches into the three-foot trunk, and Grandfather sang out, "Leave be, Ralphie! Leave your old grampa learn you how to lay a tree on a line."

I stood and watched as Grandfather drew the saw back and forth carefully; sighting it with the cross-mark in the snow. When the saw and the mark were exactly in line, he stopped and looked up at the treetops that were rattling in the wind. "Hmmm, hmmm," he hummed as he watched them. "Cal'late the wind force will heave it five, six feet afore it's down." Then he sawed the kerf a half inch deeper on the upwind side, took his axe, and chopped away the wood above the kerf. When the notch was cut to a half V that met the back of the saw mark exactly, Grandfather straightened up, and crowed, "There she be, Ralphie! True as a trivet! Cal'late she'll fall dead center acrost the cradle. Fetch the saw, and we'll tarnal soon find out."

Watching Grandfather, and remembering the things Uncle Levi had told me about swinging a scythe, helped me with the long saw. I took a lighter hold on the hand grips, let my wrists loosen, and swayed on the balls of my feet. Within ten or fifteen minutes, we'd sawed in from the back of the tree till only a few inches of solid wood stood between the two kerfs. Grandfather stopped the saw, came to my side of the tree, and said, "By gorry, you done all right, Ralphie. Didn't cal'late you'd be that far along, nor keep your cut so straight." He scratched a line on the bark, and told me, "Hold off a trifle, and don't let the teeth pass that mark. I cal'late she'll go in a minute or two."

We'd only taken a few more strokes with the saw, when there was a sharp crack, and Grandfather shouted, "*Timber!* There she goes, Ralphie! Stand back afore the butt hits you!"

For a moment or two, the great tree stood balanced, then slowly, slowly, the top began to move. The trunk leaned a little, but not in line with the cradle. Then there was a loud crack, as if a gun had been shot close to my ear. The speed of the fall grew faster, the wind caught the top branches, and the trunk fell in a swerving crash. The butt kicked free from the stump, and through the thunder of the crashing trunk and snapping branches came four sharp explosion sounds. Snow flew high, broken branches and twigs shot through the air, and then the woods were still. When the snow settled, the great chestnut trunk lay squarely in the center of the alley. There wasn't a crack in it anywhere, but the four birch spring-poles were bent beneath it like sprung bows.

On the second tree, I knew more about what we were doing, and Grandfather let me guess what alley we should use, where to set the spring-poles, and how much to allow for windage. He said I was about right on the wind allowance and the spring-poles, but I'd picked the wrong alley. If we'd used the one I thought we should, there would have been no way of turning so long a log to get it out of the woods. We had as good luck with the second tree as with the first. It fell squarely across the spring-poles of the cradle, and didn't break. Grandfather had picked an alley just opposite to the first one, so that the two great trunks lay almost end to end in the snow. Before we built a fire and ate our dinner, we measured each trunk with the story pole, and sawed the logs five poles long. Neither of them had a knot in the whole forty feet of their length, and neither was less than two feet through at the small end.

Before the logs could be loaded onto the bobsled, the tops of the fallen trees had to be cleared away. Then half a dozen smaller trees had to be felled, saplings cut, and turns in the logging road widened, so that the forty-foot logs could be sledded out of the wood lot. The last thing before we started the loading, the spring-poles were chopped away, skids laid, and the logs rolled with cant hooks to one side of their alleys. To start the big logs and roll them on the level skids took every ounce of strength Grandfather and I had. I was sure we'd never be able to load them on the bobsled alone. "There! There they be,

Ralphie!" Grandfather puffed. "Fetch your hosses, and your old grampa'll learn you how to load a log man-fashion. By fire, I wisht we had a good yoke of oxen."

When I'd harnessed the horses, Grandfather had me drive the bobsled up beside the log that was farthest from the clearing. He had me move it until the back runners were the length of one story pole from the side and end of the log. Then he unhooked the coupling chains, and had me pull the front runners to the butt end. "Keep off! Keep off!" Grandfather called to me as I drove. "Butt end's bigger'n the top. Leave a pole and a half length 'twixt the runner and the log." He was as particular about setting the sled runners as he had been about felling the trees. He measured the big end of the log carefully with the story pole, then the small end, and had me set the runners even with the butt and a pole and three quarters away from the log.

Next we cut maple poles, ten inches through, flattened them at the ends, and placed them for ramps between the bottom of the log and the top of the sled bolsters. After we'd rolled the log back, so that its weight was resting on the ends of the ramps, Grandfather wrapped the loading chains. They were long and heavy. At both the front and back sled, he hooked one end of a chain to the center of the bolster, passed the loose end under the log, wrapped it once around, and I carried it to the far side of the sleds. Then we hitched Old Nell to one chain, and the yella colt to the other.

Grandfather was nervous. "Hosses! Hosses!" he spluttered as I hooked the yella colt's singletree to the end of the chain. "Ain't worth a tinker for loading logs! Like as not the tarnal critter'll go to jerking and upset the sled or bust a chain. Let that infernal log get to slipping back whenst it's halfway up, and 'twould take the Almighty Hisself to stop it. Aptly as not, 'twould throw both hosses and kill 'em."

I was as nervous as Grandfather but I tried not to let him know it. "You lead Old Nell," I told him, "and I'll take the yella colt, but don't shout if we get stuck. He's high-strung, and I might not be able to handle him. Just raise one hand when you're ready for us to pull."

While Grandfather was walking over to where Nell was hitched to the other chain, I eased the yella colt up into his collar till the chain was tight. Then I stepped a couple of feet away from his head and watched Grandfather. When he raised his hand and called, "Gitap! Gitap!" to Nell, I clucked quietly to the colt. He pushed his weight into the collar, looked toward me, and I clucked again. The muscles in his thighs and legs swelled into knobs, the tendons in his flank stretched taut, the chain links crackled with the strain, and the maple ramps groaned as they took the full weight of the log. Step by straining step, the old horse put every pound of his strength behind the collar. I looked back and saw the great chestnut log rolling slow and steadily up the ramps. Then there was a thump, as it settled onto the sled bolsters. Grandfather shouted, "Whoa!" and the yella colt stood trembling. I was patting his neck and telling him he was a good horse when Grandfather came running toward us. "Good on your head, Ralphie! Good on your head!" he called out as he came. "By fire, we'll show 'em what kind of logs makes wide shingles! Never in all my born days seen a yoke of oxen fetch a log aboard no steadier'n that. By thunder, I knowed all the time the old critter would do it. Never yipped a yipe once, did I, Ralphie?"

The butt had rolled enough farther than the small end that the log lay straight on the sleds. When it was chained fast to the bolsters, it made a bobsled forty feet long, with thirty feet between the front and back runners. The second log loaded just as the first one had. Half an hour before sunset, we had the two great logs bound side by side, and were leaving the woods for home.

The wind went down with the sun, and the still cold pressed in from all sides. Until our faces stiffened, Grandfather told me stories of logs and logging. Then, one or the other of us walked most of the time; thrashing arms to keep warm, throwing blankets over the horses when they stopped to rest at the top of a hill, or binding chains onto the runners to act as brakes on the way down. From the top of Hall's hill, we could see Millie's lamp in the kitchen window, and when we drove into the yard, she came to the door and called, "Victuals is hot and on the table."

As the week went on I got more used to the crosscut saw and the long-handled double-bladed axe. I didn't have to think to turn the axe at the top of the swing. I could make it hit fairly close to the spot I aimed at, and had learned to hold the snap of my wrists back till the last moment, so the blade would bite deep. With the logging road packed and widened to the chestnut grove, and my being more help to Grandfather, we were able to haul two loads of logs a day. We'd get to the wood lot by sunrise, set up our cradles, and fell all the trees for the day. Then, while Grandfather was taking the first load home, I'd cut the tops and larger branches to cordwood length, clear away the brush, and chop spring-poles for the next day's cradles. By Friday night, we had all the logs for the barn sills and uprights piled in the dooryard.

Saturday morning Grandfather took the butter and eggs to Lewiston, and he seemed as excited as he had been on those mornings when he was going to hunt for Millie. While he was gone, I burned junipers in the wilderness field, and he came home while I was milking. I didn't hear him till he pushed the big barn doors open and drove the pung into the runway. I couldn't guess why he had driven it into the barn, so I left stripping Clara Belle and went to see. Instead of shouting, as he usually did when he'd brought something home, Grandfather met me at the tie-up door, and whispered, "Come see what I fetched home for Millie! Don't cal'late on letting her lay eyes on it till Christmas Eve. Come help me histe it out and hide it away."

When Grandfather turned the horse blanket back, I saw a big box lying in the back of the pung. *Sears Roebuck* was printed in red letters at one end of it, and under the name, *This end up. Handle with care.* "Cream Separator," Grandfather whispered. "Tarnal good one, and I got a powerful good trade on it. Writ

off to the mail-order comp'ny in Chicago. Cal'late 'twill save
Millie a power of work on her skimming. Saving on the cream
too. Catalog says that nary a drop can get a-past it. Let's fetch it
into the stall with Old Hannibal. Don't cal'late ever Millie'll go
in there, do you?"

Before I went to Medford for Christmas, we had all the logs
for the barn timbers piled in the dooryard, and had hauled the
rafter logs to the mill for sawing. We butchered a suckling pig
for me to take with me, and my suitcase was crammed with butter, honey, and apples. It was a fine Christmas. Mother's cooking tasted better than ever, the tree was loaded with presents,
and it snowed all three of the days I was home. We hardly went
out of the house, but played games, remembered stories about
Colorado and the Christmases we'd had there, and in the evenings Mother read aloud to us. I was both sorry and glad when
the time came for me to go back to the farm.

Uncle Levi went back with me, and stayed through most of
February. He didn't often go to the woods with Grandfather and
me, but spent most of his time doing the fine carpentry for the
barn. He made the big rolling door for the new addition, all the
smaller doors, the window frames and sash, the stanchion yokes,
and the feedbins. Uncle Levi didn't like to work out in the
weather, so I dragged logs into the barn runway for him to hew
square, mortise, and tenon. He made himself patterns, and every mortise and tenon was cut to a perfect fit. By the middle of
February, all the girders and cross-braces were hewn and ten-
oned; the straight mortises—and the tricky angled ones for the
cross-braces—cut into the uprights, and the framing made for
the window in the gable peak.

Soon after Christmas, Grandfather had sent away for the tomato seed. Most of them were Earliana, but there were a few
later varieties. As soon as Uncle Levi had finished all the window sashes for the barn, he used them to build one of the hen-
coops over into a hothouse. After he'd set up an old pot-bellied
stove, he and Millie planted the tomato seed, and she adopted
the hothouse for her own. Half a dozen times a day, she'd go to

see if the temperature was right, and to watch for the first shoots to come through the ground, but she wouldn't let Grandfather or me go any nearer than the windows.

Between dark and chore time, I often had an hour or two to work with Uncle Levi. I worked with him the whole last Saturday before he went back to Boston. When we were putting away the tools, we heard the sleigh bells on Old Nell's harness, and Grandfather turned into the driveway from taking the butter to Lewiston. Uncle Levi laid a hand on my shoulder, and said, "By hub, I calc'late the war's all over for Thomas. Wa'n't you tickled 'bout him sending off for that cream separator? Wouldn't hardly guess 'twas the same Thomas that raised all the ruction over the horsefork, would you? Ain't seen him so chipper since he come home from the war."

While Uncle Levi had been working on the barn and the hothouse, Grandfather and I had been busy in the woods. We'd cut and sledded to the mill all the chestnut logs that would be cut into floor planks, sheathing, and clapboards. There were eighteen or twenty cords of firewood stacked by the logging road in the Bowdoin wood lot, and we'd felled the cedars that would be sawed into shingles—wide ones.

All through February and most of March we worked on the blighted chestnut grove. Grandfather had only one light touch of malaria all winter, and by the first day of spring there wasn't a stick of chestnut left in the woods. Long rows of cordwood stood along the top of the dooryard wall, floor planks, rafters, sheathing boards, and bundles of shingles were piled high beside the hewn barn timbers in the barnyard, and in the hothouse the tomato plants were two inches tall. The deep frost was leaving the ground, and the first green grass was showing in the hayfields.

33

New Crops

Bill Hubbard came to work for us steady on the first day of spring. The ground was still too muddy for working in the fields, so the first job we did was to dig the cellar for the barn addition. Then, while Bill and I laid the base boulders for the foundation, Grandfather hauled gravel and brought cement from Lewiston for the concrete floor. We didn't build the new cellar like the old one, but laid a smooth floor for wagons and farm machinery at the front.

The fields were dry enough that we could haul dressing as soon as the new cellar floor was laid. Grandfather liked to do the spreading with the machine Uncle Levi had rebuilt, and it kept him from working too hard on the barn foundation. All three of us would pitch on the loads, then, while Grandfather was spreading them in the fields, Bill and I would hoist boulders to the walls, chink them in place with broken stone, and fill the spaces around them with cement.

Bill helped me with the milking, so we could get an early start on the day's work, and we never quit till it was too dark to see.

By April tenth the foundation was finished, and we plowed

the first furrow in the wilderness field. Grandfather let me hold the plow, and he drove the horses. During the winter in the woods, he'd learned not to shout at the yella colt, but as he drove he couldn't help chirping, "Gitap! Gitap! Gee off! Gee off, Nell!" or "Haw to, you tarnal fool colt." Often when we'd stop the horses for a rest, Grandfather would look back along the furrows, and gloat, "Gorry sakes alive, Ralphie! Never cal'lated I'd be laying a plow to this field again in all the days of my life."

Once, when we'd stopped to rest he said, "Let your old grampa have a-holt of them handles for a spell. Gorry sakes! Gorry sakes alive! Ain't it pretty to see the black earth a-turning up again. Mellow! Mellow and fertile, Ralphie! Cal'late 'twill fill the cellar to overflowing with potatoes, come fall. Been a-reading 'bout putting phosphate beneath the rows. There's a power more money in the provender bank account than what we'll be needing for grain. Don't you cal'late 'twould be a good notion to put some of it into phosphate?" It was the first time Grandfather had ever asked me what I thought about the farming. A lump came into my throat. I didn't trust myself to speak, so just nodded my head and grinned.

During our first few days of plowing in the wilderness field, Bill blasted rocks, cut brush, and burned junipers in the hidden fields. Then he came and blasted or pried out buried rocks that were too big for the plow to move. The smaller stones were left in the furrows and, after the plowing was finished, Grandfather raked them with my old stone rake, while Bill and I hauled them to the wall.

The harder Grandfather worked, the happier he seemed to be, and he didn't have an attack of malaria all through the spring. He even disliked to leave the fields to take the butter to Lewiston on Saturdays, and instead of being gone all day, he'd leave before daylight and be home by noon. The Saturday after we'd finished clearing the wilderness field, he drove the dump-cart to Lewiston, and when he came home, he brought a brand new, two-section, spike-tooth harrow.

Grandfather didn't do any whispering when he drove into

the dooryard with the new harrow, but shouted, "Ralphie! Millie! Come a-running! Come see what I fetched us home. Brand, spanking new! Ain't never been drug a foot! By fire, I cal'late on having them fields as soft as goose feathers!" Then, while Bill and I lifted the harrow out of the cart, Grandfather dropped his voice, and told Millie, "Strawb'ry plants is tender little critters. Costs a heap of money to buy 'em, and I don't cal'late to scrimp on the tools and lose a half of 'em 'cause the soil ain't tended right. I and Ralphie is a-going to write off for 'em tomorrow. Going to get 'em from them Breck folks off to Boston—best tarnal seed and plant folks in the country. Got all the newfangled kinds: Everbearers, that fruits from early spring till frost; Excelsiors, that ripens the first warm days of June; and Commonwealths, that comes on just afore the early frosts—after the fetched-in berries is all gone—half the size of your fist and dark red. By gorry, Millie girl, my mouth's a-watering a'ready."

Grandfather and I spent most of Sunday afternoon on the order for the strawberry plants. He'd read Breck's catalog until all the pages about strawberries were worn dog-eared at the corners, and he could almost recite every word it said about each variety. The thing that worried us most was the number of plants we'd need to the acre. When we first sat down, Grandfather said, "Nigh as I can cal'late, Ralphie, there's just a little shy of eight acres in the high field. I'm cal'lating on tomatoes for five of 'em, and strawb'ries for three. Counting on the rows being three feet apart, and a plant to every foot, how many plants are we a-going to need? Most of 'em comes to seven dollars a thousand, but the best everbearers is Pan-Americans, and they're asking fifteen cents apiece for 'em. I don't cal'late on getting over a hundred of them kind."

Sometime in school I'd learned the number of square feet in an acre, but had forgotten it. I could only remember: "three feet, one yard; five and a half yards, one rod; forty rods, one furlong; eight furlongs, one mile." And I did know that a section of land was a mile square and had six hundred and forty acres in it. After I'd figured all over three or four sheets of paper, I got an answer of 43,560 strawberry plants for three acres. I knew I must have made a mistake somewhere, so I threw the papers in the stove and started all over again. That time Grandfather kept fussing at me to stop my dawdling and do the job man-fashion. He made me lose my place two or three times, but when I came to the answer, it was the same one I'd had before. "Fiddlesticks! Fiddlesticks!" Grandfather snapped when I told him what the figure was, "Any tarnal fool would know better'n that. An acre ain't but seventy paces each side."

"Well, let's see what that does," I told him. "I know my answer can't be right, but I got the same one twice. If an acre is seventy paces long, then three acres would be two hundred and ten paces; and with three plants to every pace, that would be six hundred and thirty plants in a row. And with the rows a pace apart, there would be seventy rows, so . . ."

Grandfather snatched the paper, and figured for half a minute. "Gorry sakes alive! Great thunderation!" he said as he sat looking at the figures. "By fire, it comes out to six of one and half a dozen of the other. Gorry sakes, Ralphie, that's a tarnal lot of strawb'ry plants. He figured again, and said, "Hmmm! Hmmm! Comes to over three hundred dollars. Didn't cal'late it would run into no such sort of money."

I was sure the chance of having a strawberry field was gone. My mouth went dry, and my voice sounded thin when I said, "We wouldn't have to put in three acres. Strawberries grow new plants on runners. Sometimes an old plant will make a dozen or so new ones in a year. If we just had a few, we could root all the runners, and in a few years we could build up the three acres."

Grandfather just said, "Hmmm . . . hmmm," some more, and walked up and down the kitchen floor with his thumbs locked together behind his back. It was two or three minutes before he stopped, and asked, "Will they bear fruit and put out new plants at the same time?"

"Yes, sir," I said. "If we just had a couple of hundred plants, I think we could spread them into three acres in three years."

Grandfather walked and hmmmed for another two or three

minutes. Then he stopped suddenly, pounded his fist on the table, and said, "By fire, Ralphie, we're a-going to do it! Once these folks roundabouts sees us fetching strawb'ries off to market, they'll tarnal nigh all of 'em want a field of their own. By gorry, I and you is going to raise the plants to sell 'em. Cal'late we'll start off with about two acres of them Excelsiors, one acre of Commonwealths, and five hundred of them Pan-American Everbearers. If it costs fifteen cents apiece to buy 'em, the new plants ought to fetch a pretty penny whenst we got 'em to sell. Fetch a clean paper and the ink bottle. By gorry, if we're a-going into the strawb'ry business, we're a-going in whole hog."

The next three weeks were busy ones, and there were days when we had as many as a dozen men and boys working in the high field. As soon as it was harrowed smooth, we set out the tomato plants Millie had been taking care of in Uncle Levi's hothouse. I made a marker with the teeth three feet apart, then drove it carefully, both ways across the field. When all the tomato plants were set out, the rows ran straight in every direction. The strawberry plants came right after we had finished setting out the tomatoes. Though the strawberry field was only a little more than half as big as the tomato field, it took twice as long to set the plants.

While Grandfather and I were working with the men at strawberry and tomato planting, Bill plowed the hidden fields, raked the stones, and harrowed and trenched the wilderness field for potatoes. In that field, Bill and I put the dressing into the trenches, and Grandfather followed us, strewing a line of phosphate on top of the manure. We sent to Aroostook County for the best cobbler seed potatoes, cut them—two eyes to the piece—and Millie and I laid the pieces in the trenches, while Grandfather and Bill covered them with a few inches of fine soil.

After we finished the potato planting, we began getting the hidden fields ready for corn. Bill Hubbard and I were laying blasted rock onto the stonewall when Grandfather stopped the harrow beside us, and said, "Gorry sakes, Ralphie, did ever you see prettier plowing fields in all your born days?" He reached down, picked up a handful of the sandy loam, and rubbed it between his fingers. "Hmmm! Hmmm!" he hummed, as it sifted back to the ground. "This upper field is a dite more petered out than the lower one. Hmmm . . . cal'late I was a trifle over-generous whenst I spread the dressing on the lower field, and I scanted this one according. Needs a tarnal good mess of phosphate throwed in the hills with the seed. By thunder, that phosphate stuff runs into money. Hmmm . . . hmmm . . . By gorry, I got it! I got it, Ralphie! Them folks at the cannery over to Lisbon! I hear tell they'll provide a man with phosphate and seed, if he'll plant and pick and cultivate whenst and how they tell him . . . and contract to sell 'em the whole crop. No, by thunder! No! Ain't a-going to have nobody a-telling me how to farm this place! Gitap! Gitap, Nell!"

For two more rounds of the field, Grandfather walked along behind the harrow with his head down and Old Bess trailing at his heels. Then he stopped beside us again, and asked, "How much you cal'late them cannery folks would stick their noses into our affairs if we was to deal with 'em, Ralphie?"

"I don't know," I told him. "But, if we take good care of the field, I wouldn't care how often they came around to see it. Is there as much money in raising sweet corn as there is in field corn?"

"Tarnal lot more, but, by thunderation, they ain't a-going to . . . Gitap! Gitap, colty!"

That time, Grandfather made three rounds of the field before he stopped again. He walked slowly over to us, stooped, and picked up another handful of soil. From the harrowing, the loam had dried a little on the top, and it sifted away between Grandfather's fingers. He looked up at me, almost sheepishly, and said, "Cal'late I'll drive over and talk to them folks at the cannery, Ralphie. Might happen, come fall and the market goes down, we could sell 'em some tomatoes to can."

Before noon, Grandfather came back from the cannery, and brought a man with him. They walked all over the upper hidden field, then the man took samples of soil away with him. In the afternoon, Grandfather drove the dumpcart over to Lisbon, and brought home the phosphate and the seed corn. It was Country Gentleman corn, still on the cobs, with the husks braided together in bundles.

Uncle Levi came right after we'd planted the sweet corn. We didn't know he was coming, and Grandfather was just leaving for Lewiston with the butter when the taxicab from Brunswick came into the dooryard. Uncle Levi was riding with the driver, and the back seat was loaded with bags of fruit, presents, and big packages of fresh meat.

"Gorry sakes! Gorry sakes alive, Levi! You don't know how glad I be to see you," Grandfather called out, as he climbed down off the democrat wagon and hurried toward the taxicab. "Ralphie, take care of Old Nell whilst I fetch Levi out and show him what we been a-doing in the fields. By gorry, Levi, you won't scarcely know the old place. Come on, Levi, whilst I show you."

I'd started to open the back door of the taxicab to take the bags and packages out, but Uncle Levi bumped against me and mumbled, "Let be! Let be!" Then he said to Grandfather, "By hub, Thomas, ain't you getting a late start for Lewiston this morning? Calc'lated you'd a-been on the road afore sunup. This man's waiting to fetch me over to see Aunt Lucy Stevens. She writ me she's been ailing this spring, and I fetched her down a little drop of medicine. You go on to Lewiston afore the sun gets high enough to melt the butter on you. I'll stay out of the fields till you get home to show 'em to me. Hi, Millie! Set the teapot on, and I'll be back soon's ever I fetch this bottle of spirits over to Aunt Lucy." Then he climbed back into the taxicab and drove out of the yard.

If Uncle Levi went to see Aunt Lucy Stevens, he couldn't have stopped longer than a minute. Grandfather was hardly out of sight when the taxicab drove back into the yard. "Great day of judgment!" Uncle Levi laughed as he got out. "It's a God's wonder Thomas didn't stave my playhouse all to pieces! By hub,

I had to do some tall thinking there for a minute. Here, Ralph, give me a hand with these cussed boxes."

Bill had been turning the separator for Millie, and they both came running when they heard Uncle Levi. Bill stepped in front of Uncle Levi and helped me lift out two heavy, flat boxes from the floor of the taxicab. "Been in talking to them Breck folks," Uncle Levi told us, as we set the boxes by the doorstone. "The way Thomas has been a-writing me, he's calc'lating on having some strawb'ries to pick this summer, but them Breck folks say there won't be none afore next spring. Didn't want Thomas to be disappointed, so I had 'em to find me a parcel of Everbearers that's old enough to set fruit this year. Got 'em in pots. That's what makes the boxes so cussed heavy. Calc'late you boys could scatter 'em about the field real careful so's Thomas won't smell a mouse?"

Bill and I set the new strawberry plants as carefully as we could. There were a hundred of them, and we scattered them pretty well over the whole field. They were bigger than the other plants, so we picked off a few of the outside leaves, set the plants in little hollows, and raked out the footprints around them. When we'd finished we couldn't look across the field and pick out any one of them. Then, before we went to hoe hills for the yellow corn in the lower hidden field, we stacked the pots together, laid them by the orchard wall, and covered them with stones.

Grandfather got home from Lewiston at noon. He brought Old Nell in dripping sweat, and blowing like a steam engine. We had steak for dinner, but Grandfather would eat only a few mouthfuls before we took Uncle Levi out to see the tomato, strawberry, and potato fields. They came to the hidden field while Bill and I were dropping the yellow seeds into the corn hills. After they'd walked all around the field, dropping pumpkin seed here and there in the hills, Uncle Levi stopped beside us, and said to Bill, "I'll drop corn with Ralph a while, if you're of a mind to hoe in the cover dirt." Then he took Bill's seed basket and we worked side by side.

Uncle Levi and I were about in the middle of the field, when he stopped and reached his hand deep into his overalls pocket. When he took it out, he had a few red kernels of corn in it. "There, by hub!" he said as he looked around. "Calc'late this is as good a place as any for the red ears." Then he knelt and dropped five kernels, carefully spaced in a circle, as he said, "One for the blackbird, one for the crow; one for the cutworm, and two to grow. There! There by hub! Know what them's for, Ralph?"

"Well, so as to raise some red ears, I guess."

"Know what red ears is for?" he asked.

I just shook my head, and said, "No, sir."

"Great day!" Uncle Levi chuckled. "Well, you will. Come the husking, first boy to find a red ear gets to kiss his girl." Uncle Levi was still kneeling. He peeked up at me, and asked, "Kissed Annie Littlehale yet?"

I didn't want to tell him I had, and I didn't want to lie to him, either. I was trying to think of some way to change the subject when Uncle Levi sprang up, put his arm around my shoulder, and said, "Shouldn't ought to have asked you, but, by hub, I'm glad you done it. Awful nice girl, Annie. Clever as a kitten. I fetched down a box of candy in my valise. Calc'lated you might like to take it along when you went for the cows." After we'd gone on dropping seed for a dozen or so hills, Uncle Levi laid a hand over on my shoulder. When I raised my head, there was almost a sad look on his face. "A picked flower soon fades, and there ain't nothing to do but heave it out," he said. "The Almighty meant 'em to be left on the bush till seed time." Then he went back to dropping corn.

34

A God's Wonder

UNCLE LEVI didn't care much about working in the fields. He did come out and ride the new two-row cultivator for a few minutes, when Grandfather first brought it home. But, until haying, he spent most of his time on the barn addition. The big timbers were too heavy for one man to lift and move into place, so Uncle Levi built himself a derrick, and rigged it with ropes and pulleys from the horsefork. The first Saturday after he came, he went to Lewiston with Grandfather. They were gone nearly the whole day, and when they came home, there was a new horse tied to the back of the democrat wagon. She was a bay, about the same size and type of horse as Old Nell. When I looked at her teeth, the pits showed that she was seven years old, just as Nell was. "Yella colt's a-getting on in years," Uncle Levi told me when I was putting the new mare into the spare box stall. "You boys been working him pretty cussed hard this spring, and a little rest wouldn't hurt him none. Do you calc'late he'd work for me on that derrick the way Thomas says he done for you in the woods?"

"I think he would," I said, "but there's something Grandfather doesn't know. I always bribe the colt with a piece of apple after he's made a good steady pull."

"A bribe ain't a bad piece of business in the right place," Uncle Levi said, and winked at me. "You'll find a box of choclates under the wagon seat when you go to fetch your cows."

The yella colt did work for Uncle Levi just as well as he had for me, but for a while his teeth got edgy from eating too many apples. With the derrick and a hand tackle, they could move the heaviest timbers into any position Uncle Levi wanted. First, he laid the sills on the new foundation, set supporting posts in the cellar, and placed the two sixteen-inch-square center struts to carry the weight of the barn floor. Next, he mortised the floor joists into the struts and sills. They weren't hewn square, as the other timbers were, but, after they were all mortised solidly in place, he adzed the rounded tops, so that anyone could sight across the whole floor frame without finding a single hump or hollow.

All through the winter, and during my first summer on the farm, no one but Uncle Levi had come to visit. After we set out the strawberry plants, there was never a Sunday that several carriages weren't driven into the dooryard. Grandfather began wearing his best suit all day Sunday, and he loved to take people from field to field and show them the growing crops, the stonewalls we had built, and the big pile of blasted tree stumps in the pasture. Berries on the potted plants Uncle Levi had brought began to ripen in early June. Grandfather would watch them all through the week, but he'd seldom pick one. On Sundays, he'd take the visitors all around the field, let them pick berries to eat, and boast about the plants that were bearing in their first year.

Late one Sunday afternoon, when we thought all the visitors had gone, Annie and I walked through the strawberry field on our way to the pastures for the cows. The sun was just slipping down behind the pines on Lisbon Ridge, I was holding Annie's hand in mine, and we were watching how the long shadow ran up and down the row as we swung our arms. I heard the rattle of wheels, and looked up to see a buggy coming through the gap in the stonewall at the end of the orchard. Grandfather was sitting between a man and woman I had never seen, and we heard him tell them, "That's my grandson; Ralphie. Mary's boy. Him and Annie Littlehale is awful sweet on one another." For just a fraction of a second, Annie's hand loosened on mine. Then it squeezed tighter, and we kept on toward the pasture gate.

Of all the visitors who came during the summer, the one Grandfather liked to see best was the one he'd dreaded most in the spring. Every time the man from the cannery came, Grandfather would drop whatever he was doing and go to meet him. They didn't only go to the sweet-corn field, but to every field on the place. By haying time, samples of the soil from every field had been tested, and Grandfather knew just what kind of fertilizer would be best for each one, and what crop would probably do the best on it. He kept himself, Bill, and me going from daylight till dark, cultivating, hoeing, weeding, spraying potato vines with Paris green, and dusting the corn with powder to keep worms out of the ears. Each time he'd come back from taking the cannery man around, he'd pick up his hoe and sing out, "By fire, we'll show 'em what kind of logs makes wide shingles! Wager you there ain't a cleaner field of sweet corn nowheres this side the Androscoggin River."

Where haying had been a big, hard job the year before, it was almost like a holiday that summer. Uncle Levi did most of the mowing and raking while the rest of us worked in the row crop fields. Grandfather hardly pitched a forkful of hay, and he never scolded or tried to hurry me once. In the field, Bill and I pitched, Uncle Levi built load, and Grandfather raked scatterings or showed visitors the strawberry field and the tomatoes that were beginning to set on the vines. The yella colt had become an expert on the tote rope. Uncle Levi would set the big horsefork deep in the load, cluck quietly, and the old horse would ease three or four hundred pounds of hay smoothly to the mows. As soon as I'd jerk the trip line, he'd come back to the rack for a bit of sugar, a piece of biscuit, or whatever Uncle Levi held out for him. Bill and I stowed away in the mows, and Grandfather tended the bees during the unloading.

We left Jacob's field till the last. When all but one load of hay was in the barn, I slid down from the mow to find Millie with her sunbonnet on and a pitchfork in her hands. "You don't cal'late I'm a-going to let this haying go by without so much as a hand in it?" she asked Uncle Levi. "Ralph and I done it all alone last summer, and, by gorry, we're a-going to do a piece of it alone this time. You and Bill find something else to do while we finish the haying." Then she laughed and climbed up onto the hayrack with me.

Right after haying, we sprinkled nitrate of soda around each tomato plant, and were lucky enough to get a rain that dissolved it and soaked it down to the roots. It worked wonders. During the next three weeks, the vines spread out till it was hard to find a path between them, new tomatoes set by the thousands, and the early fruit swelled like fatting pigs. Grandfather found the first one turning pink on the twentieth of July. He shouted so loud that Bill and I heard him way down in the hidden fields, and Millie and Uncle Levi heard him at the buildings. "Come a-running! Come a-running, children!" he called, as we hurried toward the high field. "Come see what I got to show you! By fire, we'll show 'em what kind of logs makes wide shingles!" As we all picked our way carefully through the field, Grandfather pointed out one tomato after another that was turning whitish-pink. "Gorry sakes! Gorry sakes alive!" he gloated as he turned the thick leaves back and peeked under them. "Did ever you see such a tarnal crop of early tomatoes in all the days of your life? Gorry! Gorry sakes alive! And I didn't cal'late this old field was good for nothing but timothy hay!" He stopped suddenly, looked up into my face, and smiled. "Cal'late we're a-going to have to call this Ralphie's field," he said.

I wanted to laugh and cry at the same time, and my voice was husky when I said, "You scared me that time when you told Mr. Swale you were going to plant it back to timothy."

"Didn't tell him no such a thing," Grandfather chuckled. "I recollect it well. 'Bijah, he asked me two questions to once. Wa'n't no call to answer but one of 'em, was there?"

On Grandfather's next trip with the butter, he took two market baskets of tomatoes to Lewiston. They brought twelve cents a pound, and he had the money tied up in the corner of his bandanna handkerchief when he came home. He called for us to come running as he turned Old Nell into the driveway, and was climbing out over the wheel before she'd hardly stopped at the doorstone. "Take it, Ralphie! Take it!" he said, as he untied the handkerchief and showed us the money. "Four dollars and eighty-four cents for them two little baskets of tomatoes. Take it, Ralphie! The first idea of 'em was your'n, and the first money from 'em is your'n, too. Gorry sakes! Gorry sakes alive! The crop off that old stony field's a-going to fetch a tarnal heap of money. Don't cal'late Mary'll have to worry now 'bout how she's a-going to fetch up the children."

The tomato crop did make a good profit. We'd taken a good many spring wagon loads off the field before the price dropped below ten cents a pound. After the first ton, Grandfather came home with a new Studebaker wagon. From then till the height of the season had passed, Uncle Levi took a load to Lisbon Falls every day to go on the Portland train, and Grandfather took a democrat wagon load to Lewiston. Bill and I did most of the picking, while Millie and Annie packed the fruit in bright, new boxes.

With our being so busy in the tomato field, we had to hire two men and a team of horses for cultivating and hoeing the corn and potatoes. The man from the cannery watched the sweet corn carefully. When it was ready, he brought pickers and wagons, and cleaned the whole field in a single day.

Every minute that Uncle Levi wasn't working in the hayfield or hauling tomatoes, he and the yella colt worked on the new addition for the barn. Uncle Levi had built a cradle that reached forty feet back into the barnyard from the new foundation. On it, he'd put together the whole gable end for the addition. Each upright, girder, and cross-brace was exactly over the paths Grandfather and I had tramped in the November snow, and the story pole was polished from handling till it shone like new bronze. There wasn't a nail or a spike anywhere, but all the joints were driven tight, bored through with a pair of two-inch auger holes, and pinned solid with wooden treenails. Overlapping the gable, with its lower ends resting at the mortise holes where it would stand on the sills, was the center-frame. Except for the cross-braces, it was built exactly like the gable. The walls lay spread back on either side of the foundation, like the open pages of a great book. Each beam, upright, and cross-brace was in place, but the treenails were driven only part way home, so they could be pulled and the raising done piece by piece.

When the price of tomatoes dropped to fifty cents a bushel, we stopped packing them for the Portland and Lewiston markets. From then till apple-picking time, we picked twice a week for the cannery, and people from miles around came with bushel baskets to buy them for canning. Most of the apples were in the cellar when, one morning, the whole floor of the valley was sparkling with white frost. Grandfather and I went to the high field right after breakfast, to see how badly it had hit the tomatoes. It hadn't touched them at all. The millions of small rocks had held enough of the sun's heat to keep the frost away from the ground.

Grandfather worked with the bees that forenoon, waited for the mailman, and told him to pass the word for all who wanted to, to come and help themselves to pickling tomatoes. Before evening, there were a couple of dozen buggies lined up by the wall at the top of Niah's field. And the high field looked as if a Sunday school picnic were being held there. Every woman that had any children had brought them, and they were carrying ripe and green tomatoes away in pails, baskets, tubs, and wash boilers. Grandfather spent most of the afternoon lugging the smaller children around the strawberry field and hunting them the last ripe berries.

Bill and I mulched the strawberry field deep with marsh grass as soon as the apples were picked. Then we cut and shocked the yellow corn in the hidden field, and started the potato digging. All fall, Grandfather had been digging his hands in under the potato vines. Whenever he'd find a big one, he'd shout, "Gorry sakes! Gorry sakes alive! Didn't I tell you? Didn't I tell you, Ralphie? Best potato soil this side the Androscoggin River. Wouldn't be s'prised a tarnal mite if it would fetch a crop of 'leven, twelve hundred bushels." Then he'd straighten up, look around the field, and say, "Gorry sakes! Gorry sakes! And to think, scarcely a year agone we sot axe to the first tree for the clearing. By fire, I wisht Father could see it."

The potato crop on the wilderness field did a lot better than even Grandfather had expected. We had four men to help us dig, and as the forks opened the hills and raked through the black loam, wide rows of smooth russet-brown potatoes stretched the length of the field. Before we began hauling them to the cellar, as many men had come to see them as there had been women and children come for pickling tomatoes. Hundreds of bushels were sold right from the field, and Grandfather would give each neighbor who came a bushel basket, and say, "Walk abouts the field and pick yourself out a basketful for seed. Don't cal'late there's better seed potatoes this side the Androscoggin River." He had a little brown book that he carried in his pocket, and he marked down every bushel that was sold or hauled to the cellar. When the last load was in, we added up the book, and the total was sixteen hundred and twenty-nine bushels.

Uncle Levi had been as busy on the barn as Grandfather, Bill, and I had been in the fields. After every rafter was cut, and every joint in the new frame fitted and pegged, he'd taken the clapboards and sheathing off the end of the main barn. Then he had cut the mortises in the old frame to hold the tenons of the new side and roof girders. "There, by hub!" he told me when he showed me the end mortises in the gables for the four-by-sixteen-inch ridgepole. "There's going to be a ridgepole that cussed yella colt can't jerk out with a horsefork!" Then he chuckled, and said, "Great day of judgment! Him and Thomas has trod the same path this year agone, ain't they? Recollect the first day we hitched the old critter to the hayrake?" He looked down to the foot of the derrick, where the yella colt was standing, resting with one hip dropped low. Uncle Levi laid his hand on my shoulder, and his voice was sort of hushed when he said, "It's a God's wonder."

The first week after the potato harvest was as exciting as roundup week used to be in Colorado. The mailman had passed the word that Grandfather was going to have his barn-raising on Saturday, and there wasn't a day all week that three or four men didn't come to see the solid chestnut frame, and to say they'd be on hand for the raising. One woman after another drove into the dooryard, offered to help Millie with the cooking, asked what kind of pies she should bring, and said to count her husband in on the raising. We butchered Clara Belle's big spring calf and the fattest hog for the dinner, and apples were taken to the press for cider.

Saturday morning was frosty and clear. Grandfather came to the tie-up while Bill and I were milking, paced up and down the runway, and snapped, "Stir your stivvers! Stir your stivvers, Ralphie! It's nigh onto sunup a'ready and time flies! Gorry sakes! Gorry sakes alive! Ain't been an old-time barn-raising hereabouts in I-don't-know-when. Ain't many men left that knows how to frame a barn solid a-laying down, and fetch it up all-standing. By thunder, I wisht Father could be here to see it." Then he locked his thumbs behind his back, walked up and down a few more times with his head bowed, and left the tie-up. We'd hardly finished the chores when the first neighbors drove into the dooryard. By eight o'clock, a dozen wagons were lined up by the long rows of cordwood along the yard wall, the horses unhitched, and toolboxes unloaded.

Three of the strongest teams were picked to do the pulling on the tote rope. The heaviest pulley block was anchored to the peak of the main barn, ropes were run to the gable point of the new center-frame, and pointed irons were driven into the ends of long pike poles. Twenty men were standing ready with pikes and mauls when Grandfather called, "Histe!" and the horses leaned into their collars. With a squeal of turning pulley wheels, the tackle ropes came taut, and the peak of the forty-foot frame lifted from its cradle. Slowly, slowly, like the turning hand of a clock, the great uprights rose, hinged on the wide tenons at their bases. Men with heavy wooden mauls hammered the timbers to bring the tenons exactly in line with the sill mortises, and those with poles jabbed their pikes into the uprights to steady them. As the frame came straight up, there was a screech of tight-binding dry wood, the great tenons wedged down into their mortises, and the frame stood alone.

Grandfather and Uncle Levi each had a crew of men ready at the side walls; telling them which timber to put in place first, and giving each man his own part of the job. The foot-square side beams were lifted into place, their tenons set into the mortises in the main barn frame, and cross-braces and center uprights fitted into place. Then the pike men rocked the center-frame back just enough to let the tenons of the side beams and rafter joists slip into their mortises. The two-inch-round tree-nails were driven, and the sixteen-foot section of the ridgepole pegged into position. By noon, the framing was all finished, the plank floor laid, and men were putting up scaffolds for the sheathing and roofing.

As soon as the floor was laid, Bill and I set up plank tables and benches, and the women brought pots of beans, brown bread, big roasts of veal and pork, a dozen pies, and pitchers of cider. When Millie called, "Victuals is ready," there were thirty-eight hungry men washed up and ready to eat. Everyone was laughing and joking, and Millie and Annie ran back and forth between the table and the kitchen, bringing more pitchers of cider, tea, milk, hot johnycake, and more pie.

The first spikes were driven when the three-by-six wall studs were fitted into place between the cross-braces. As fast as a section was studded, other men put on the sheathing, and still others followed with the clapboards. While the last shingles and clapboards were being nailed on in the afternoon, Uncle Levi, and some of the men who were the cleverest with tools, put up the door track, hung the big rolling door, and fitted the window sash. When the last nail was hammered and the last screw driven, Grandfather climbed to the peak of the new addition, and set the story pole for a flagstaff.

The sun stood just above the tops of the pines on Lisbon ridge when the last neighbor drove out of the dooryard, and I started for the pasture to get our cows. I'd only reached the barnyard gate when Grandfather called, "Wait up, Ralphie! Wait a minute, and your old grampa'll walk along with you, boy." He slipped his arm under mine as I stood holding the gate open for him, and said, "Leave us go for a walk about the fields afore night comes on. Cal'late I'd like to look down on the buildings from atop the orchard hill. Gorry sakes! Gorry sakes alive, Ralphie! Never thought I'd live to see the day."

We did walk the fields and the woods, and there was hardly a rock, a stump, or a tree that didn't have a story connected with it. At sunset, we stood together on the granite outcropping that crowned the pasture hill. "Hark, Ralphie," Grandfather whispered, "the woods is about to talk; they always do, come sunset, and I never tire of hearing 'em." As we stood there listening, the liquid, throaty song of a wood thrush came from the hemlocks, a fox barked from somewhere deep in the woods, and a crow taunted back at him from high on the ridge. In a moment or two, a whippoorwill's lonely call rose from the hackmatack thicket near the brook, and Grandfather whispered, "Pretty, ain't it, Ralphie?"